PARADISE

A.L. Kennedy has published four ~~novels~~, two books of non-fiction, and three collections of short stories, most recently *Indelible Acts*. She has twice been selected as one of *Granta's* twenty Best of Young British Novelists and has won a number of prizes including the Somerset Maugham Award, the Encore Award and the Saltire Scottish Book of the Year Award. She lives in Glasgow and is a part-time lecturer in creative writing at St. Andrews.

ALSO BY A.L. KENNEDY

Fiction

Night Geometry and the Garscadden Trains
Looking for the Possible Dance
Now That You're Back
So I am Glad
Original Bliss
Everything You Need
Indelible Acts
Day

Non-Fiction

The Life and Death of Colonel Blimp
On Bullfighting

A.L. Kennedy

PARADISE

VINTAGE BOOKS
London

Published by Vintage 2005

4 6 8 10 9 7 5

First published in Great Britain in 2004 by
Jonathan Cape

Vintage Books
Random House, 20 Vauxhall Bridge Road,
London SW1V 2SA

www.vintage-books.co.uk

Addresses for companies within The Random House Group Limited
can be found at: www.randomhouse.co.uk/offices.htm

The Random House Group Limited Reg. No. 954009

A CIP catalogue record for this book
is available from the British Library

ISBN 9780099433491

The Random House Group Limited supports The Forest Stewardship
Council (FSC), the leading international forest certification organisation.
All our titles that are printed on Greenpeace approved FSC certified paper
carry the FSC logo. Our paper procurement policy can be found at:
www.rbooks.co.uk/environment

Printed and bound in Great Britain by
Cox & Wyman Limited, Reading, Berkshire

For Mother

Mo rùn geal òg

I

How it happens is a long story, always.

And I apparently begin with being here: a boxy room that's too wide to be cosy, its dirty ceiling hung just low enough to press down a broad, unmistakable haze of claustrophobia. To my right is an over-large clock of the kind favoured by playschools and homes for the elderly, the kind with bold, black numbers and cartoon-thick hands that effectively shout what time it is whether you're curious or not. It shows 8.42 and counting. Above, is a generalised sting of yellow light.

8.42.

But I don't know which one – night or morning. Either way, from what I can already see, I would rather not be involved in all this too far beyond 8.43.

In one fist, I notice, I'm holding a key. Its fob is made of viciously green plastic, translucent and moulded to a shape which illustrates what would happen if a long-dead ear were inflated until morbidly obese. I only know that it's actually meant to be a leaf, because it is marked with an effort towards the stem, the ribs and veins that a leaf might have. I presume I'm supposed to like this key and give it the benefit of the doubt because people are fond of trees and, by extension, leaves. But I don't like leaves, not even real ones.

I'll tell you what I do like, though: what I adore – I'm looking right at it, right now and it is gorgeous, quite the prettiest thing I've seen since 8.41. It concerns my other hand – the one that is leaf-free.

It is a liquid.

I do love liquids.

Rising from the beaker to the jug in that continually renewing, barley sugared twist: falling from the jug into the beaker like a muscle perpetually flexed and reflexed, the honey-coloured heart of some irreversibly specialised animal. It's glimmering and, of course, *pouring* — a drink *pouring*, hurrying in to ease a thirst, just as it should. I put down the jug and I lift up the glass, just as *I* should.

I presume it's filled with some kind of apple juice and, on closer acquaintance, I find this to be so — not very pleasant, but certainly wet and necessary. The air, and therefore my mouth, currently tastes of cheap cleaning products, unhappy people, a hundred years of stubborn cigarette smoke and the urine of young children, left to lie. Which means I need my drink. Besides, I really do have, now I think about it, a terrible thirst.

'Terrible weather?'

I'm swallowing ersatz fruit, not even from concentrate, so I can't have said a word — it wasn't me who spoke.

Terrible thirst: terrible weather — but the echo is accidental, I would have to be feeling quite paranoid to think it was anything else. Nevertheless, the remark feels intrusive — as if it had access to my skull — and so I turn without even preparing a smile and discover the party responsible tucked behind me: a straggly, gingery man, loitering. He has longish, yellowish, curly hair, which was, perhaps, cute at some time in his youth, but has thinned now into a wispy embarrassment. I can almost picture him, each evening, praying to be struck bald overnight. God has not, so far, been merciful.

Mr Wispy's expression attempts to remain enquiring although he says nothing more and I do not meet his eyes or in any way encourage him. He is the type to have hobbies: sad ones that he'll want to talk about.

Checking swiftly, I can see there are no windows, which may explain his lack of meteorological certainty. There's no way that either of us can know what the weather is doing outside. Then again, Straggly has the look of a person habitually unsure of things: it may be he's stolen a peek beyond the room and already *has* prior knowledge of whatever conditions prevail – monsoon, dust storm, sleet – he may simply hope I'll confirm his observations.

Of course, I have no prior knowledge, not a trace.

There is a fake cart rigged up, beyond us both – it's clearly made of stainless steel, but is burdened with a feminine canopy and fat, little flounces of chintz. Inside, I can make out a seethe of heat lamps and trays of orange, brown or grey things which ought to be food, I suppose. The whole assembly smells of nothing beyond boredom and possibly old grease.

'Really dreadful . . . Yes?' He tries again: maybe harping on about the weather, maybe just depressive, I can't say I care.

'Appalling.' I nod and angle myself away.

But Straggly has to chip in again. 'Tchsss . . . .' He seems to be taking the whole thing very personally, whatever it is. And I notice there's something slightly expectant in the scampery little glances he keeps launching across at me. It could be that he will give me a headache soon.

'Ffffmmm . . . ' He nods, as if his repertoire of noises has any meaning beyond his own mind.

But I can't deny that he is also speaking English, just about – which is a clue. It means that I can probably assume I'm in a hotel somewhere English-speaking. Either that, or I've been ambushed by Mr Wispy who is himself English-speaking and has guessed that I am, too, and I could, in fact, be anywhere at all.

Meanwhile, he's continuing to linger inconclusively and I do hope this won't blossom into some weird expression of long-term, national solidarity. To help him move on, I try to sound forbidding, although I will never discover what I'm trying to forbid: 'Ghastly. Almost *frightening*.'

That seemed to go well, though. He edges back a step, and another, then bolts into a crestfallen retreat. I feel I am safe to believe our exchange is exhausted.

Around me, various groups and solitaries are hunched over bowls of cereal, plates of glistening stuff, collapsing rolls. The carpet is liberally scattered with a sort of bread-related dandruff: each table has its dusting, too, along with a thread or so of unconvincing foliage in a throttled vase. At uneasy intervals the walls display reproductions of old European advertisements: a British hotel, then. This particular level of grisliness could only be fully achieved in the British Isles. And this surely must be breakfast. So: 8.44, no 8.45, in the morning and breakfast in a cheap, British hotel.

I'm home. Perhaps.

Their backs to a wall, a shouting wife and inaudible husband are picking at mushrooms and sausages. 'We have to get a gas grill. That was the loveliest meal I had when we were there, the loveliest. That was the loveliest meal.' Her partner chews and chews while I try not to imagine the finer and finer paste he is producing. 'And that Continental . . . Continental . . . Continental . . .'

Continental **what**? *Quilt? Breakfast? Lover? Self-improving language course?*

She is never going to finish and I'm never going to know and he is never going to swallow – I can tell. I do not wish to think of them travelling freely across the globe, dementing people, everywhere they go – driving them into gas grills for relief. I refill my glass and concentrate.

Then I remember, with aching clarity, an air steward blocking the ragged perspective of an aisle and dancing his arms through the usual safety drill: the oxygen mask for yourself before your gasping children, the floor-level guides to coax you through darkness and smoke. He was enjoying himself, sweating only a little with all of those swooping indications in time to the comforting script. Then he tried to put on his For Demonstration Only life jacket and failed comprehensively.

I watched, couldn't stop myself watching, while his previously smooth hands stuttered and the rubberised yellow crumpled and began to look unhelpful – like a grubby bib. By the time he was meant to be tying a firm double bow at his waist (and then moving on to display his inflation tubes, his convenient whistle and nice light) his drawstrings were only tangling perversely and the more he jerked them and smiled to reassure, the more everything twisted and snagged. His head dropped then and he fought at the jacket outright, a neck blush rising to his hair. Full-blown knots had developed now, his fingers scrabbling round them, wetly impotent. He blinked up for a breath and I grinned at him – what other expression was possible, but a firmly encouraging grin? – and something about the moment made it plain that we both knew he was now demonstrating a true emergency. This was precisely the way that we really would panic and fluster and take too long as the plane went down. This was how we'd be trapped in the dark, inanely struggling. This was how we would stare, while horrors struck against our wills. This was how we'd be plunged into water and feel every trace of protection ripped easily adrift. He was showing us how we would die.

The demonstration ended, but he stayed where he was, puzzled by himself, almost tearful, the jacket still round him, lopsided, improperly tied.

This is a recent memory, it tastes close at hand.

And I am, once again, grinning firmly and thinking that I must have been somewhere and must now be coming back, which is new and important information and a cause for joy.

One of the many pleasures of forgetting is, as we all of us know, remembering. You trot from room to room and can't imagine where you left your keys the night before: without them, you're locked in your house. Under the bed, in the knife drawer, behind the Scotch, behind your shoes, in the pockets of every garment that has pockets, the pedal bin, the compost bin, the bread bin: you have panicked into every likely nook. You sit on your bed, despairing, unsure of who has your spares and if they still like you and then – your hand gently brushes that lovely clump of metal, that heavy, little spider of keys to everything. They've been lounging on the duvet the whole morning, just winking whenever you've passed. But you have them at last and you are happy, much happier than you would have been if you'd picked them up without confusion from their customary place.

This morning it's very clear that I've misplaced at least a day, so you can imagine that I'm pretty much delighted.

But still thirsty.

Now, I already have a substantial glass, filled and in my possession – probably 300 millilitres, or even a drop in excess. I've left a decent interval between the meniscus and the brim – anything else is antisocial and draws attention – but even if the juice were slopping right up to the top, it wouldn't be enough. A litre might begin to be enough, might start to feel refreshing, a litre and nothing less. So I need to down this while I stand, refill, down, refill again and then sit somewhere secluded, rehydrate. You have to be undisturbed to rehydrate. I presume I am safe in believing that this is the usual snatch–all-you-can rolling buffet sort of situation and no one will intervene when confronted with naked appetite.

As it turns out, I'm not wrong.

Clutching glass number four, I wander through the wreckage and mumbling, keeping an eye out for somewhere bearable to sit. The place seems clotted suddenly, nothing unoccupied.

I may have a little toast later, if there is toast. I can only assume I have money to buy some, it's unlikely I'd have come here otherwise.

'Ah . . .?' *Again.* Mr Wispy is flapping one hand annoyingly above an empty seat. The only visible empty seat. 'A-ah . . .?' He keeps repeating that one sorry, wheedling vowel.

I could just stand.

On either side of him lurk what can only be his children: a surly-looking blonde girl of maybe eight and a smaller, darker boy. Happily, neither of them has inherited his hair. They are both intent on squeezing the contents from several tiny plastic containers of jam and then spreading the resultant mess across random objects.

I could dodge back to the fruit-juice counter.

I could run.

'You won't disturb us. Really. It's all right.'

'I will.'

'No you won't.'

'I think I will.'

'No-o.'

The children lose interest in smearing the milk jug and the girl sucks at her palm, eyes me appraisingly.

'Perhaps for a moment.' I edge past the worst of it. 'Like pustules, aren't they?'

Father Straggle swallows less than happily.

'The jam packets – when you squeeze them out, they're just like . . . well, they're a little like . . .' I give up, sit and sip my apple juice in the silence. Five or six swallows and breakfast will be done. Except I still feel below my volume, somehow, a glass or three owing, nagging me.

'Whee-HA. Whee-HA.' Of course he has an abnormal laugh, why would he have a normal one? How often would he get the chance to use it with his life? '*Pustules.* Whee-HA.'

In any case, it's ugly and should be stopped. 'So . . . You're leaving?'

He is sombre again, flushed, and softly offers, 'Coming back.'

'Uh-huh.'

The little boy nudges me under the table, his hand unmistakably adhering as it leaves my leg. I'm wearing jeans – they look new – new jeans and a T-shirt. My forearms have a vague tan. The boy tries again. I engage him with my best patient-andopenfunloving expression. Sooner or later, this always works. I am a person other people warm to – without exception, they all warm. My lack of memory, if I were in a film, would mean that I am a killing machine, patiently trained by

9

some dreadful governmental agency and soon my amnesia will evaporate in a bloodbath of conscienceless combat and burning cars. But I know I'm not any variety of machine. I am a human being, a proper one. And I am likeable – almost unnaturally easy to like. The boy turns shy under my attention, but is not truly uncomfortable. The girl glowers with some vehemence. She would take me more time.

'Amelia. That's not how we behave.'

'She's fine. Don't fret. Tired perhaps. Not used to strangers.' I gulp down the last of the juice, preparatory to moving off – somewhere I may have a room with other resources and no jam. Father Straggle's ears are almost scarlet – he is obviously a man who prefers that his children should be polite, which is admirable, but such hopes can be taken too far. He is patently furious now, insisting on being annoyed, so I become placating. 'Amelia. That's a lovely name.'

At this, the girl gives me a slightly wounded flick of her eyes and stares at the tablecloth. She expected me to know her name, then. She expected me to remember. So we've met before.

On a flight? Inside an airport? Hotel foyer? At 8.35?

I do recall an airport and scuffling about in the usual way as I waited to be off to somewhere else – wasting time in the record shop, thumbing through the DVDs.

'Tell me, *Lesbian Tarts Having Sex* – what's that about?'

The counter man sleepy, or drugged-up, or clinically bored, 'Hm?'

'*Lesbian Tarts Having Sex* – seems a bit vague. I mean, I wouldn't want to end up buying something I wasn't sure of. Does it have harpsichords? Or skating? Folding chairs? Do any characters feign amnesia as a ruse?' I was in that running-off-at-the-mouth mood, chirpy, in need of a chum to banter with.

The counter man was not my chum. 'Do you want to buy it.'

Even as I opened my mouth again, I realised he might be

misinterpreting my chatter as a come-on of some kind, which it wasn't, not in any way.

'Of course I don't want to buy it – where's the mystery in it, the imaginative flair?'

Actually, he wasn't responding as if he was being seduced – he was barely responding as if he was still alive. 'You don't want to buy it.' He was, in all respects, monotone.

'No. I have no desire to make a purchase.' And I removed myself before I could say something else.

Or.

I really said, 'I wouldn't buy that DVD if it was the last one on earth.'

And then he said, 'You know what you can do.'

And then I said, 'Fuck myself and make a video of it called *Fucking Myself.*'

I can remember both endings, which is tricky. But I think I'm more convinced by the first. I think I told him I had no desire to make a purchase and then left. However it played out, there were no children anywhere near me at that stage – I would never have used offensive language and referred to sexual acts had there been any young folk present. I have standards.

'Amelia?' I try not to look like someone who is thinking of bad words and begin to make amends with the daughter, which is good of me because I will have done her no genuine wrong. She had thought of me as a friend, perhaps, and I've seemed to be slightly non-friendly, forgetful, nothing more. That's the sort of behaviour my brother detested when he was her age. Me, too. It's nothing serious, but even so, 'Amelia, I hope you have a pleasant journey home. Are you looking forward to it?'

'Mummy likes it better at home.'

'Oh.' Thank God, they have a mother: they're not wholly dependent on Wispy Dad. 'Well, that's good then.'

At this, Wispy Dad can't resist butting in to slow the conversation. 'Their mother is still in our room. Tired.'

Well, that's understandable, I'd be eternally bloody exhausted if I was married to you. 'Travelling is a strain.'

At the food cart, a woman is shovelling out what could be eggs. Even from here, I can see them shudder and slide. They unnerve me in a way they should not – because eggs ought to have no particular power over me – and I realise that I'm about to have a feeling, something unpleasant, an episode. What I can only imagine as a huge, grey lid is threatening to close on top of me. This means that, far too soon, I may cry, or become unsteady, or find myself vomiting. Without doubt my head is, once again, about to let me down. There will be pain involved: there always is: and it will be bad unpredictable pain: it always is. After so many years, I can recognise the signs.

I softly stand and the boy glances at me, definitely glum to see me up and off. 'Goodbye, you.' *No idea what his name is.* 'Goodbye, Amelia.' Amelia kicks at nothing and ignores me. 'Goodbye . . .' I move forward and brush against a restraining hand – who else but Dad, standing, wriggling from foot to foot. He ought to know he shouldn't do this, not now. I am becoming urgent and so is my head. Wispy adjusts his gesture into one half of a handshake, faintly pleading, and, courteous to the last, I clasp his soggy fingers and soggier palm. 'Goodbye.'

'Goodbye, Hannah.'

'Yes.' *We exchanged names across the board, then, how extremely chummy and civilised.* 'That's me away then, bye.'

'Great to have met you. Sorry about the ah . . . children.' He licks his lips with an odd, little grating sound, as if he is made of something peculiar.

'Yes.'

'The way they are, ha?' He seems not to grasp the essential intention of saying goodbye. 'Well. Hmm. Goodness . . . Blow me.'

Not in a million years. 'Yes.'

'Safe home.'

'Yes,' I nod – which sparks up a layering sensation, the

impression of being loosely, poorly stacked – the head is growing delicate and I don't move it again, but pause – wring out a grin – and finally he does first loosen his grip, and then abandon it.

'Good-uh . . . bye.'

Although I fear he may snatch it again.

I withdraw as smoothly as I can. 'Goodbye . . . all of you. Really.' Trying to balance myself at the top of my neck, not picturing my personality starting to slop out over my sides, running down to my chin.

Which carries me past a last view of Wispy's vaguely stricken offspring and off on a wavery march for the doorway, then out, a passageway (passageways lead to staircases and lifts, they are my friends), through a fire door and into a foyer complicated with several queues – not helpful – but, yes, here is a lift.

When I stop, the momentum of my thoughts sends them rushing forward, pressing and wetting the backs of my eyes. I raise my key to aid steadier inspection – it is attached by a chain to leaf number 536: fifth floor, then.

And, thankfully, no one else is with me when the doors whump shut and seal me in the queasily rising box. The surrounding walls are mirrored from waist height up which suggests an illusion of space and must be a comfort to claustrophobics, but which also – due to the laws of physics – does have one truly horrible consequence: I can see myself. Not only one's self, naturally: from a few especially disastrous angles my right selves and my left selves reflect each other unrelentingly. On both sides, I can watch my head diminish along an undulating corridor of shrinking repetitions until I finally coalesce into one last, pinkish drop of light. This aches.

It isn't fair. All I wanted to do was find 536 and take care of my head, but instead I'm trapped inside this 3-D memento mori – staring at eternity while it howls graphically away, before and after (as if I were an extra in some truly sadistic, educational short), and all that I'm fond of as me is cupped up in this single, staring instant – which isn't enough. Look at me – this is the only point where I'm recognisable, where I make sense – beyond it, I'm nothing but distortion and then I completely disappear. What is this – *a Jesuit lift*? I am not at an appropriate moment to be metaphysical. For Christ's sake, I was only trying to cut out the stairs. I didn't ask to be forcibly reminded that I don't want to die, not ever, no thank you very much. I am not well and terrified and I don't have the room to be either properly.

So I am not in quite perfect condition when the lift shunts open and gives a gloating little *ding*. Meanwhile, my sweat gets a chance to chill in the passageway where small metal plaques with arrows are waiting for me, all set to suggest hypothetical directions.

543–589, this way: 502–527, that way; 518 over there.

I'm taking little runs to blind ends, finding corridors that loop round on themselves, cupboards, fire escapes, while the floor starts to pitch down quietly beneath my feet, as if I were aboard some ghastly submarine.

The world cannot be as this is, I refuse to accept it.

*543–589 this way. But they were **that** way before.*

I deny the existence of this hotel in its current form. I deny the existence of this hotel in its current form.

528, 529, 530 . . . which is encouraging, fairly, I should be okay, it can't be far –

500.

Bastards.

I deny the existence –

I'm not going to be sick.

I deny the existence of this hotel –

533, 534 –

in its current form.

I deny –

535 . . . 536.

Well, well.

Slowly. Approach it slowly, it may move. Don't let the key chain rattle, make no sudden cries, but, as soon as I'm ready . . . hold the bloody handle, grab it, key in the lock, key in the lock, right in, in, okay. And. Turn. Turn everything.

The room agrees to be opened and it is, indeed, my room – here is my holdall on its floor, lolling open, and this is my own, my personal alarm clock, ticking primly by the raddled bed: the soft, the horizontal, the wanted bed. There is nothing better than being bewildered and unhappy and very tired and then discovering you have a bed.

'Could I, uh . . . I'm in Room Five Three Six, I wonder could you tell me if I'm checking out today . . . five . . . thirty . . . six . . . That's right, three six. *Five three six.*'

I will admit that I had expected someone who worked in a hotel might be able to keep a grip of perhaps one room number, now and then, but I won't be snappy, that would be unconstructive and would not reflect my mood. I have slept for two blank hours – nearly two and a half – slept through, I can only assume, the whole of my head-related distress and every threatened intimation of death and doom. I am quite fine now, and had I been calmer, I would have known – the whole source of my earlier trouble was tiredness.

As I let myself be comforted, there comes a dull clunking on the line – perhaps the receptionist playing with loose teeth. She mutters a name.

'I'm sorry, *who*? . . . Oh. And I'd have to check out at twelve? . . . *Eleven?*'

*Why do they do that? – Twelve is bad enough, but now everybody wants you outside in the snow by eleven. Try **checking in** before five and see what it gets you: a bloody lecture: your bags in a cupboard somewhere until it's dark: that's what.* 'In that case, could you be very kind and give me the room for another day? . . . Well, no, not *give*. Just . . . the usual arrangement. You have my credit card? . . . You *do*?'

Good. That's a good sign. Cash is a bad sign – credit is good. 'Then that's all very fine then, isn't it? That's all extremely fine.'

Above the window comes a laboured thunder, like a broad stone being rolled in overhead. I get up gently, examine my view.

Dove-blue clouds, a gold edge to them and spindles of light behind. Nearer, there is a fat concrete tower, topped with the scoop of a radar dish, revolving, and a runway and the slanting rise of a plane, charcoal-coloured. Another stone grinds by.

Which is disturbing. I could swear that I'm on my way home, so why am I still at the airport? Reproachful on the felty, dun carpet, my holdall is waiting – it can usually explain.

Dishevelled contents, the clothes have been worn. Still, they seem to be nobody's clothes but my own and

I need to be sick, immediately.

Thank God the room is tiny – it means the en suite facilities are close.

Shock will do that, unbalance the system, and it always unsettles to be less than clear about where you are. Or, in this case, where *I* am. Or, more precisely, *why*.

A dash of cold water on the face, though, and I'm approaching some level of definition, feeling good.

No. Not good. I was mistaken. That was a mistake.

Because my forehead has started torquing – it's a reaction to the cold, or the water, the force of the dash. I can see in the mirror that my bones are not actually moving, not visibly, not as such, but I can – even so – feel them buckle against my brain, suck in and down and squeeze above my tongue. Inside, there's twisting, pulsing where I can't reach, and once that's started, it only gets worse. So I haven't escaped my head: it was just waiting until I'd woken to make itself felt.

All right, then – do what you like up there, run amok. It's not as if we haven't been introduced. But don't think we're friends or that you're welcome. I still know exactly how to cut you short.

So it's back to the holdall and feel for those delicate items, the ones you wrap up in sweaters, the special things you need to take with you and have for company. It isn't great to lean forward while I search, it doesn't aid my equanimity, but this is a necessary evil and will be rewarding in the end.

Yes. First out is something called Affentaler, tucked up snug in a tiny bottle, shaped like a flat, heavy tear – a map on its back to say where it comes from: the meander of a river, Strasbourg marked, the suggestion of fertile plains and peacefulness. It's full, which is never a bad thing, but only 250 millilitres and only 11.5 per cent. What on earth was I thinking? It's practically bloody fruit juice: what good did that ever do?

But then, but then, God bless me – I love it when I leave myself prepared.

ORIGINAL
GRANT TO DISTIL
1608

And God bless metrication, because 700 millilitres is so much more roomy and cheerier than a pint.

Bushmill's, County Antrim, 700 millilitres, 40 per cent. I mean, what else do you need to know? Not that, as an additional courtesy, you don't turn it in your hands and love the rounded corners and the dapper weight and the elegant cut of the label: the black with the white and the gold, all shaped around each other to mark out an arch: a long, slim doorway to somewhere else.

And God bless the rectangular bottle, for it will not roll and harm itself.

I pop the seal on the Affentaler and put it out of its misery. Then I move back to the Black Bush, open it and let it speak to me. It says that I have, until quite recently, owned more than a pint of *delicate grain whiskey* and I now have a shake under half of it left, smelling clever and hot and masculine and jolting to the glass from the bottle with the sound of a little dog coughing: that wonderful bottle cough.

matured in oloroso sherry casks – that's nothing if not melodious: inside and out.

And you'll notice I go to the trouble of serving the whiskey, although I don't have to, there is no one here to see. The point is that I stay civilised, no matter what. The most reliable measure of a person lies in what they do when they're alone, when they have no need to pretend – are they firm when solitary, or do they slide? I take the trouble to search about, check the bathroom and hunt down a single, cellophane-sealed plastic glass (more of a cup, really) and I tear it free and use it, as any human being with dignity surely would. I do not slide.

After 100 millilitres I get the good sweat, the fine one that follows nourishing exercise, and my headache lifts off like a velvet hat and leaves without me. My stomach feels a trifle naked, unlined, and does give the odd twitch or two before it begins to mellow and buzz with that neat, medicinal sting. But I know I'll be fine, nonetheless. In the absence of any further pain, the next 200 millilitres are all mine.

I drift back to the bed, trapping warm little teases of whiskey against my gums: quarters of quarters of gills making my facial bones static again and smoothing my hair. Here I am, fixed and certain, lying on the mangled taupe and duck-egg coverlet with the day relaxed and clean ahead of me, beckoning. I need no more, or less, than this, I am balanced in my skin and whatever has gone before is unimportant and whatever has yet to come will make me smile.

Because once you've begun to have blackouts, you'll never stop and so before and after don't exist – you've mastered the art of escaping from linear time. The jumps and jolts take a bit of getting used to – driving is particularly tricky, guessing what gear you're in, or if you're trying to overtake – but this

keeps you bright and springy, alert. And there is nothing unnatural about it, nothing dreadful: some level of blacking out is
what lets most people survive. If you asked them about their
way to work, the colour of the bus seats, or the pattern of the
office carpet, the name of the trainee who brings in the tea,
the post, the wage slips, the number of strangers ahead of them
in the evening supermarket queue: they couldn't tell you a
thing. They can't make their minds remember and no one who
wasn't a monster would want them to try. Any person truly
pausing to examine the miserable details of their life would at
once choose a merciful dash to the nearest unattended well.
You have to dissolve your bleak points and blur your edges:
if you didn't they would hurt. So continuous minor blackouts
are fair enough.

But not enough. Not once you realise that one minute
unremittingly following another, and then taking sixty seconds
to drag by in the customary order, is a totally unsupportable
waste of time. Why not get the highlights, the hot spots, and
skip the rest? Why not hugely enjoy a fine afternoon with
quality people, while simultaneously recalling a splendid
evening you've been keeping in reserve and now unveil to
yourself in a bouncing rush that, in its turn, freshens your taste
for the matters you have in hand? Why not surf between time
and time, content in yourself as yourself and the only constant
point?

Not that it doesn't take a lot of work to be this way, to free
your personality from events. Most people exist through what
they do, they have lost the clarity that once permitted them
to *be*. Me? – I'm completely simplified, I am distilled. Washed
down to nothing, I remain exactly who I am, no matter where
or when. I understand my fundamental sources, my provenance.

For instance, I lived in the same house from the time I was
born until I was seventeen – that's the sort of stability you
can't buy. Such things build reinforcement into your whole
identity. My parents both stay in that same home, even now.

Or rather, if this is a weekday, my mother is out and working in the offices of Busby, MacDonald & Hume – a company of solicitors which, within living memory, has never been able to boast a Busby, or a MacDonald, or a Hume. But their premises are wholly unfanciful – I have visited my mother there often, heard her answer their telephone with her best, unquestionable voice – the one which anticipates no disagreement, but which is softened with a definite sympathy, an unlooked-for gentleness. Straight from school, I have sat and waited for six o'clock and our time to go home, reading old copies of *Scottish Field* and *National Geographic* until she relaxed into her typing and I could watch the marvellous economy of her hands, the assurance in her swing and rise as she stood and took some document she'd made and moved to file it in its proper place. There can't be many years left until she will have to retire, but I won't believe in the office once she leaves it. I will picture the walls turning porous and the furniture fading away and everything turning as fictional as Busby, MacDonald & Hume. My mother's job exists through her.

Still, I usually imagine her in the garden, working out the weekends or the few hours at the end of summer days. Where we come from it rains a good deal, but often our Augusts are fine, blaring with a sudden rush of flowers and other expansive preparations for vegetable breeding. In August my mother wears sandals, a loose skirt and a blouse, something quiet and light, the style has always been the same: a tiny hint behind it of the fifties and the girl she used to be: waved hair, thick-framed glasses, bobby socks. Sometimes, she'll incline slightly by a shrub, as if it were whispering to her, confiding its state, and after that she'll inhale above it and close her eyes, considering. She doesn't just stroll in the garden, she is constantly intent. And pruning, digging, lopping, planting, edging the borders of beds: every act of cultivation becomes mysterious, because she can perform any task without apparent effort, or disorder, everything executed with this – well, the only word is *grace*. She has grace. When I was younger I'd try to help her: annoying the weeds on her behalf, but I never could manage much beyond a batter and mash about, ungainly, all scratches and mud. In time, I've developed degrees of assurance, naturally. I am a woman and not unwomanly, I suppose; but I realised years ago, before I was seven, that I won't be a woman the way that my mother is, I'll never do it right. She is a heartbreaker, really.

I think my father would agree. Also a gardener, but a greenhouse man, my father. She has her perennials, her bedding plants and shrubs and he breeds up his succulents, cacti, bromeliads, listens to Radio Four and sits inside his little glass walls, smoking at his house leeks and staring. Although he very rarely drives, my father has a motorist's attitude to glass — behind it, though perfectly visible, he will act as if unseen: sighing, yawning, scratching and pestering at his thermos far more easily than he ever does indoors. My brother and I fell into the habit of seeing him without seeing, rather than take offence at the obvious implication — that he couldn't relax at home with us.

Father will be in his greenhouse now, undoubtedly. It's no more than one yard across by three, crowded with defensive greenery and gravel-lined benches, but he dashes away towards it as if he were escaping some savage confinement by a lucky fluke. When his headaches are particularly bad, I've known him sleep there.

'You're sure about this?'

'Mm-hmm.'

My father padding one foot up and down on the tiny pump that's nudging air into a wrinkled inflatable mattress. A type of Lilo, I've never seen it before and it looks fun: unsuitable for adults.

'Absolutely sure.'

It's obvious that my mother is asking him about more than the mattress and equally plain that he is already decided and no longer minds this discussion, either way. What they are really talking about, I haven't a clue. Father has that placid look he takes on when he's about to make a run for it outside: he seems peaceful as — uffha, uffha, uffha, uffha — he pumps in air and Mother is trying to look at his face but, fighting shy of personal engagement, he's ducked his head and is firmly aiming his concentration at his foot, as if the pumping were some strange phenomenon and therefore fascinating. A tuft of his fringe has fallen forward towards his eyes and is making him look younger and more like my brother who is upstairs and already asleep, because he is younger than me — but I'll tell him about this later, I will wake him up.

uffha, uffha

'Well, Peter.'

'Yes, I know.'

uffha, uffha, uffha, uffha

Occasionally, it seems that my parents have been together for so long they have run out of words for each other, or have found something else they can use between themselves that I can't hear.

uffha, uffha, uffha, uffha

They don't speak again, but she keeps frowning and he pumps and they are definitely having an entire, silent conversation.

My father kneels and disconnects the air tube from the valve — it wheezes — and allows himself a glance up to my mother's eyes. And this rushes in a tenderness between them, quick and complete, with a wash of some type of pain across them both which even I can feel and which they seem to welcome, even like. It makes the kitchen feel slightly pinched around me. Then she touches his head, very lightly and he turns to me — I didn't make a noise, but probably he has remembered I am there — and he makes this kind of shrug, looking very breakable for a moment and happily perplexed.

It takes him quite a while to work the mattress out and

clear of the kitchen door – he really should have set the pump up in the greenhouse, I don't know why he didn't. By the time I've finished seeing him struggle it outside and then go up the lawn into the dark where his hideaway is hiding, my mother has already slipped off into the rest of the house and I am by myself. I decide that I won't tell my brother about any of this, after all. The parts of the story that are most important would be impossible to say.

And my brother? He does the things that brothers do – he makes me a part of a family and not an only child, which is important. Early solitude does great harm. Whereas, he's a point in my favour and, born four years after me, he was my very first exercise in responsibility. For most of my childhood, I assumed we would be together for a very long time and eventually we'd buy a house to share and we'd look after ourselves and have great times. This isn't the way things have turned out – which is hardly a surprise – but it does seem odd that we see each other so little now.

He comes to mind quite often, though: he did this morning, when I saw those children, that quiet son. The time before that, I'm almost sure, I was in a tunnel: sitting in the dark leather passenger seat of a stranger's car and suddenly thinking of Simon. Somebody must have explained my position to me because I was quite aware that my journey would start soon and would not involve taking a drive, not right then. Because the car was waiting on a narrow train (just a flat bed and some girders holding up a metal roof) and in a moment the whole thing would take off into a twenty-, thirty-minute tunnel, screaming clear under a mountain range while I focused on relaxation and fighting for breath. After that it was permissible to leave, go on my way.

And none of this was fun. I'd popped out into awareness beside a cheery driver who was talking in a German kind of English about having met his wife on the Internet – although he wasn't especially ugly or mad so this seemed barely credible.

The wife was sitting behind me, I think, with someone else, a shorter woman, brown-haired. As the train lurched off, I was reflecting on the unpleasantness of my position and cubic capacity when the German – or maybe Swiss, or maybe Austrian – guy yelled above the surrounding batter and drum that he could open the window if we'd like. Before any of us could ponder this, he'd stretched out his arm in the gloom and punched up the skylight, laughing away.

Horror blasted in immediately: a whirling shove of violent air, the stink of risky machinery, violent filth, long-dead construction workers, frightened blood: beyond that was a noise so loud it immediately ceased to be a sound – was only a sweat and a writhing variety of fear. I was sitting in a stationary car (albeit inside a moving vehicle) but I was also drowning in a sensory crush that anyone sane would associate with a massive accident. I couldn't avoid believing this was a sign, a premonition of something appalling and close at hand.

The Austrian/German/Swiss guy kept laughing, his face tinged with green and shadow from the dashboard glow. I could see that he was speaking, now and then, but I couldn't hear him and I wished that my brother was with me, that Simon could be there, too. Not Simon as he is – I wanted Simon the smaller person in a knee-length overcoat that made him look like a miniature businessman, Simon whose hair was cut by my mother for years, very neat, Simon who would have loved the tunnel and made it easy for me to do that, too, or Simon who would have been scared of it and allowed me to be courageous, to forget myself. Simon with the blue eyes, like mine.

As he wasn't there, I solved the problem by the one logical method available. I precipitated a blackout with what I think was apricot schnapps: very successfully, as it happens, because I cannot recall the far end of the tunnel, or another moment of the laughing Swiss/Austrian/German and his two companions. I do not know why I was with them, where we went, or how they came to abandon me, or why I abandoned them

– there isn't a scratch or a stain left to prove they weren't my invention, a florid lie.

My whiskey is down to the final glass, that always adds a weight to the moment, a solemnity in my wrist when I pour out the last. And this is the lesson of life: all that was full will be emptied.

But there's always the chance of resurrection, a bar at hand to sort things out. In this case, it's back downstairs and beyond reception on the right – I took note. I'm getting incredibly tired again, so what I have here should ease me into a nap. Then I'll wander to the lift, go down and reconnoitre the place, and, as long as last night involved no embarrassments, I should be able to start the day up merrily. No one's day really begins much before teatime. You may be out of bed and moving before then, but that will only be for the convenience of some employer or invalid relation. Left to your own nature, you'll discover that mornings are not indispensable: plenty of daylight left to you in the summer, after four or five, and no more than wet dark to greet you the rest of the year.

I'm nibbling the final mouthfuls, letting them sting my lips, winking my goodbye to the trustworthy bottle, the black label and white script, the tasteful sort of evening dress they put against the naked glass. And was this a present that someone else gave me, or was it a gift I intended to give? Or did I just buy this for me? Sometimes I am generous with me.

But sometimes I am other things, which I should probably find out about – how me and myself have been getting along lately. Draped over my only chair, I've left a hooded sweatshirt – one that is familiar and which I like. It has the marsupial brand of large, front pocket which – yes, indeed – contains my wallet, which contains – yes, indeed – fifty pounds in stickily new English notes (so I went to a cash machine, then) and a grey, metallic credit card in the name of M. H. Virginas.

If that rings any bells they are very quiet and far away – M. H. Virginas.

Still, all is well, because Virginas may have money and I will not. All is less well, because – examining the back of the card – Virginas has a signature which is complicated and strange and I have no recollection of what I may have signed when I arrived here and may well be unable to reproduce said signature on request. I do not have forgery in my nature. Even less great, Virginas may have cancelled the card.

I should try it in a cash machine later.

No. Can't remember the number, or how I got it, or if I did.

But I have fresh money and how else would I have managed that?

Foreign exchange – new notes from a bureau de change. I have been abroad, that would make some sense . . .

Another aeroplane threatens across the horizon and the noise of it pushes me into a forceful recollection of myself sitting, extremely recently, in a khaki-coloured booth, a khaki-coloured wicker lampshade very close to my head and khaki walls behind – in fact, the whole sodding place is fawnish/beigey/khaki, now that my memory bothers to take a look. I'm squashed in with too many people and one of them is – fancy me knowing this - Kussbachek, or a friend of Kussbachek, or a man who says he is one or both of these things – he can be his own friend if he wants. I am mine.

I came here to meet a friend of Kussbachek, who is himself a friend of Doheny, who is another friend's friend, or something equally repetitious along those lines – I'm not taking a great deal of interest at this time.

Instead, I am being nervous for various reasons – mainly because this is Hungary and Hungary's currency is absurd. I have a huge roll of valueless notes covered in Vlad the Impaler hats and moustaches in my pocket and this is sending telegraphic messages to anyone who wishes to assault me and otherwise steal it away – thugs and muggers are closing in on the bar from miles around. I can hear them.

Don't get me wrong, Budapest is a beautiful place and I do try to concentrate on this. *Beauty is truth and truth is sometimes beauty and beauty is often good company – although it does also lead to deaths – but not so much to petty theft and I feel that I am most at risk of that.*

And things with me are, in other ways, not right. As I walked here it was raining too much and a dog in a steel-mesh muzzle was giving me looks and then over the road (Szekely Utca: I had to memorise that), over the road there was this man – I could see him clearly through a basement window, chopping lazily at pale meat. No butcher's shop, no restaurant, no explanation for his actions on hand: only the man in his dirty white apron, hacking his cleaver through the meat, a lot of meat, eyes on a level with my knees and the window stretched wide open in the drenched heat.

There is no one else in the bar, only Kussbachek and me, four men who know Kussbachek and a mouse-brown woman with wilting clothes who asks me loud questions about ethnic matters that I do not understand. She, for instance, has ethnic misgivings about the waiter. I have no reservations about him, myself, as he is swift and wise and smiles every time I announce to him one of the two useful things I have learned to say in phonetic Hungarian.

'Kerem adjon erzeshteluh neetort kersunum.'

I pronounce this very badly, gluing it together as I go, but it will make any waiter in Hungary laugh and then bring me a glass of white spirits, or fruit-flavoured turpentine, or other local delicacies. Hungary boasts many local delicacies.

'Please give me an anaesthetic, thank you.'

I can also say *sorry* which is the most important word in any country you may visit. *Forgive me, excuse me, oh dear* – every language seems to have a pleasant, shortish word that will imply all three, that will save you in uncomfortable circumstances and help others to forgive. It is therapeutic to forgive.

But I think I leave the bar without inspiring any therapy.

Afterwards, when the rain has stopped, there is loud dancing somewhere horrible – an uneasy queue and then dancing, or watching dancing while developing a thirst, it isn't clear.

I am certain, though, of my ears roaring with silence and our party being larger – ten or twelve – when we start to cross the bridge. All of the bridges here are famous for jumpers, but this is the newest and the favourite. People drop from this one daily, maybe more often than that. If they don't die the first time, they scramble ashore and try again – somebody tells me this, or a story not unlike this. There were Imperial jumpers and then Communist jumpers and now there are Capitalist jumpers: people remaining dissatisfied, no matter what their government claims to be.

A fox-eyed man is explaining this to me but I am distracted because the bridge is becoming unlikely. Its dim cables are fraying and chattering, up in the dark, and the pale bow of its surface is beginning to be scoured by a current, a drag that leads everyone's feet off to the side until we are single file, close beside the barrier, bouncing playfully against it, as if we may hope it will snap. Below us there are patches of random light that make the water visible, uneven as raw glass and racing. I watch it and I find that I understand the Danube to be a long and highly determined river and undoubtedly the force of it surging through the bridge could tug at the liquids in any human body (we are all mostly liquids) and draw them in its own direction, sideways: it could even haul at us until we tumble over the guard rails tonight and are wrapped up in the cold of its eddies and rushed away. Politics and despair may not be killing anybody – it may be their essential mois-ture that's at fault.

I want to set this suggestion in front of the group for their approval and am only interrupted by two of them who yank at my shoulders and lead me away from the parapet and tell me to stop leaning over so far and laughing. I would protest, because I haven't laughed at anything – have been mute – but I do not because, retracing our steps, everyone in our group simultaneously sees the lights of the fine, high hotel where one of us is staying and can order drinks for unlimited periods, or where one of us is keeping drinks in bottles that we can take advantage of very soon, or where we can be warm and friendly together with the bottles we already have in our pockets and hands and with those same bottles' local and delicate insides.

Beyond that, there's nothing until 8.42 this morning − only a soft, neutral space within which I would like to suggest that a meeting occurred between myself and Kussbachek with a passing-on of thanks, or greetings, or messages from family and friends, or some other communications of importance. Also M. H. Virginas must, at some point, have responded to my conviviality by placing his or her credit card in my wallet, or by lending the card to me, but neglecting to give me a note of the necessary return address. I don't know. This is how my stories stop, they peter out into more and more lists and I find myself saying *or* far too often and thinking that a life rich in possibilities is not, in other ways, perpetually delightful.

Kussbachek − if my mother had been meeting a Kussbachek, or an M. H. Virginas, for that matter, she would have brought a little present with her. She would have paid her visit properly. In Hungary, I didn't do what she taught me. This is the way with me − I was brought up well, but the details of that don't always show.

Whereas my mother gets it right. If she knows someone, her gifts to them will be precisely the next thing they would have thought to like: if they're strangers, she'll give them something which appears to be less specific, but is still very pleasant and useful. Lithe wooden boxes, unusual cufflinks, a silk hand-kerchief: what she offers doesn't really matter, the key lies in the way she can guess exactly what each recipient happens to lack. Whatever small need you have − too minor to bother yourself about, an indulgence you won't admit, a kind of tiny shame − she will know it and let you know it and then fulfil it and make it go away.

The wrapping, that's important as well: special paper, origami folds, ribbon, on at least two occasions real ribbon you could use again. Only what if a wasteful person didn't, what if they just ripped and cut at everything until it was turned into rubbish and nothing more? When I was small I would worry about that – the carelessness of others, their lack of appreciation. Here was my mother, offering nice things to people who might not deserve them and she was spending money on them that she ought to maybe keep by for herself and that was unsettling. And the niceness of the things was a problem, too. When she sent me off to other children's birthdays, to Christmas events, I would be given a present to pass on and I would know that it was too much, too pretty, an embarrassment for everyone which made people think of her oddly when they shouldn't dare. My own Christmases and my brother's – they were overshadowed by perfect wrapping and presents we could only get at by spoiling something. We tried to be so excited that we didn't mind hurting all the work she must have done, we tried to focus solely on how happy she seemed to let us burrow through her packaging and find wooden ducks, or a kaleidoscope, or whatever. But we didn't always manage to be as glad as she was – or I didn't, anyway.

I wrap badly, as a preference, and avoid presents when I can. They are sad.

Me too, at the moment – which is ridiculous. All I've done is spend some time in Hungary and come back again, no harm done. I and whoever was with me will have parted as good friends. I won't take more of Virginas's money than I need and I'll cut up the card to stop anyone else from using it after me. I have my health, basically, much of the time. There is no current cause for gloom, or maudlin recollections of the family home and how handy my mother might have been with fancy paper and adhesive tape. She enjoyed giving stuff to people, still does, and that's fine – I have to let others like what they like, I really do, it's a character flaw of mine, this urge to disapprove of pleasures I can't share.

The best move I can make is to have a shower: nothing like external liquid to calm and soothe. There might even be a change of clothing in my bag, although it doesn't appear too promising in that direction.

No, I'm in luck – a fresh T-shirt that's tightly folded in an unused way and, three, four pairs of knickers left in my little clean underwear sack. Which is odd – I usually only take what I'm going to need. Maybe I left Budapest four pairs early. I'm sure I had my reasons.

The bathroom here does not invite nudity. The blue textured floor feels impossible to clean effectively and the available fixtures and fittings are all formed out of beige-coloured plastic in an effort to pre-empt yellowing and staining by choosing a shade which makes everything look both stained and yellow from the start. The sink's edge is marked with round, tarry burns and the signs of a tumbling slide made by at least one lighted cigarette as it dropped into the basin. The shower – there is no bath – seeks to suggest the possibilities of bathing by building a dangerous, high lip up around its stall. Small or desperate people could crouch in the square box this forms, avoiding the discomfort of the central drain, and pretend they were curled in a tiny jacuzzi – small or desperate mad people, anyway.

But the water is fine, pretty much the heat I like and stroking over the forehead gently, I have no complaints. Other than a sting in one shoulder – I must have scraped myself there, fallen against something. My knees are bruised, too, but not badly. Soft skin runs in our family, we are easy to damage, on the surface at least, but also quick to heal. On the surface at least. No, we're resilient, honestly. I'm healing right now, if I think about it, rebuilding whatever is amiss.

I don't even mind that the soap smells of dog, or that the drain is looking nastily clogged. That's really – it's not what you'd want near your feet – a grubby, perforated plate that's matted with hairs which are clearly not mine, clearly moving in the flow of water, reddish yellow, some of them definitely pubic, others more wispy: wispy would be the only word to describe them.

The only word to make the shower curtain crawl along my side and cling, the only word to make the water blind me, the only word to show me elbowing open my bedroom door in the grey stumble of last night, last early morning and Wispy trying open-mouthed kisses and missing, thumping like a wet, cupped hand against my chin, my cheek – I am already ducking him, but I am also still letting him in and seeing his damp struggle out of his jacket and his shirt and he can't take off the ginger hair across his stomach, that's part of him – we're down to him now, down all the way. Although he's shy next, turning his back for the shoes and socks, trousers, the coy slip down of the underpants, bending over fast but not fast enough to deny me that glimpse of his scrotum, strangled red, the sad hang of it like a perineal suicide between the stringy thighs. And into bed he scrambles, only facing me once he's under the covers – sparing me any view of him from the front – staring now, all married fright and want and disbelief that he's in luck.

I join him and disbelieve it also. I am not myself. I am watching from above as if I were in a pleasant coma, or improperly anaesthetised, just drifting off safely somewhere near to death, not here.

And then *Well. Hmm. Goodness . . . Blow me.* And, being someone else and absent, I do.

I did.

I really did.

If I go through and inspect the sheet now, I'll find more of him, more hair, and the other usual indications. I don't think I'll bother, though. I'll stay under the shower a while longer and scrub the way he must have done, meticulously removing what his wife shouldn't find and working out the story to tell her if she's still awake when he reaches her room – that he stayed late in the bar, that she was asleep when he came in, dead to the world, and he's newly back from the bathroom, that's all, nowhere else, she only dreamed he was undressing, sorry to disturb her, night-night.

I told you I didn't like presents and this is why. When I have a need that isn't thirsty, I never know the way to make it stop. I give myself unsuitable remedies, bad distractions, and that's how I end up remembering, time after time, that I do very much disapprove of pleasures I can't share.

Funny, this is the kind of thing traditionally thought to make one abstemious. Sober, it could be argued, I would not have had sex with a man who had the IQ of a table and a body that would be funny if I couldn't remember it, hadn't touched it, hadn't known it touching me, my privacy. Sober, nothing unamusing need have happened.

It's a persuasive hypothesis – it just doesn't persuade me. I feel grisly because I have done something grisly, not because of drink. But if I now go down to the bar I can have another drink and that will make me feel not grisly at all, I can guarantee. People who do not drink correctly cannot understand. They can only whine on about *what a torment – having to drink, really needing to drink, how awful.* I am much more clear-headed, because I have studied the matter long and hard and have realised – *my condition does indeed mean that I'm ruined without drink and yet, equally, drink will save me from all of my ruinations: those it inspires and every single other trouble, large and small. It keeps me free.* That isn't a torment, it's a gift. It is my one and perfect gift.

It assures me this morning that once I've scraped myself thoroughly clean I can go downstairs and melt my unease down to a whisper within half a gill. And it's not even Mr Wispy that's upsetting me, in any case. I'm mildly troubled because, for some reason, I keep hearing my younger voice ask my mother why she couldn't give flowers: they would be cheap out of the garden, and – although I don't say this – they would be normal, a present that people would expect.

But she never did like to give her flowers away, they were far too important. Only my father, on his birthday, would find a bouquet of freshly slaughtered blooms at the dinner table, killed for him: my mother's eyes soft as she looked from the vase to his mouth, *his* eyes. They didn't talk much on those evenings and they would seem, I believed, both proud of themselves and secretive, their hands brushing whenever they thought that Simon and I couldn't see. I'm sure they are much the same now, but without us to watch them and stunt their tenderness.

And I would like to cry as I think of this, although I won't – not because of my parents, or last night, or even drink – it's because I want somebody I can give flowers to, someone here with me, for me.

I am in a photograph. I'm aware both of the camera and of the new friends that I have to either side and I am keeping myself in check. But I am also smiling. We are all smiling: all together at a table which runs level with the bottom of the frame, carries a mess of glasses, spills and ashtrays to clutter in between it and the lens. The state of the table suggests that we've been here for a while, because we have, and now we're staying, permanent. Our hands are stilled by the shutter, held as smirs of light, fixed where they rest against jacket sleeves, cheeks, thin air, or caught illustrating words that have escaped us. In the background, a friend that I don't know has started to walk across. I keep smiling.

Actually, I'm in quite a lot of photographs, but this is the only one I carry with me. It shows the end of a pre-wedding dinner for somebody's brother, the brother of a distant friend, more an acquaintance. Already, there have been tiny cousins, running about until shouted at, and a range of slightly tearful older ladies, to whom I have not spoken despite ingenious opening gambits on their part. The food has been vaguely harassed – an effort at Jewish traditional: chopped up eggs and bland chicken livers, clear soup, that kind of thing – but the restaurant was improvising, I think: intense conversations with management taking place before each course, and most people not even caring, being either not traditional, or not Jewish.

Throughout the dinner I have drunk water, having been warned that a semi-serious, putatively kosher, dinner would only offer drinking matter in amounts that would act as an unfulfilling tease. But then comes the final set-menu choice

35

between ice cream and cake and I choose the latter, my first mouthful unleashing a rabbit punch of spirit and the smell of a cheap, hard brandy, impatient after impregnating raisins for so long. I can tell it's been expecting me – which is the kind of thing to make anyone want to play.

So, having the taste of a better evening kissed in tight behind our teeth, a number of us, cake-eaters to a man, move through to the bar and the table – the gloss of its surface lying beneath our elbows like a tidy pond, busy with our reflections, our liquid selves. And here we are forever, being happy about our good company, or its immanent relaxation, or even the thought of someone else's marriage, hopeful and far off.

I am pictured beside a man who has recently told me that hypnotising dogs is very easy: you stare at them calmly and close your eyes for longer and longer periods until they start to echo you, believe in you, and then gradually fall asleep. Cats are much more wary and tend to call your bluff. I already know this and am slightly bored, but the man is smiling and I am smiling, too and we give every appearance of having reached some happy agreement just as the iris opens and bares the film.

The smiles are why I keep the picture. They are evidence. You see, there are many types of smile. Everyone is familiar with the insincere *screwyoureally* sort, the *I'mdyingbutkeepingitin*, the *thinkingofsomethingelseentirely*, the *JesusI'mscaredandIhaven't acluewhatmyfaceisupto* – any expression can imply any emotion, that's something everybody understands. But there is a special smile also, one that can be neither prepared, nor simulated, and which convinces me completely of God's essential bene-volence: it has the effect of unquestioning, undiluted love and is entirely beautiful.

Let me put this another way: people will tell you that angels watch over idiots and children, so that no one does them any harm. Well, how many people *want* to do them harm? They are at least unthreatening, if not attractive, they are obviously

36

large-eyed and weak and soaking with confidence in strangers: only a maniac would think of abusing their faith. But the drinkers: who'll watch over them? When they are late beyond imagining on the one night which is inexcusable, when they have stolen from you and then blamed you for the theft, when they have broken and dirtied and laughed at whatever especially personal treasures you care about, when they have lied and bullied and tricked and then wept before you can start to, when they have taken even that, when they have relied on the irreversible stupidity of your love, when they have just forgotten you exist — what is it that prevents you killing them? Only this, their smile.

Occasionally, I'll admit, a drinker will meet an unpleasant end, but if logic and justice had their way, this would happen constantly. Murder shouldn't be the exception, it should be the rule. We do terrible things — I don't personally — but some of us are unthinkable, grotesque and punishment is the least that we deserve. Still, when we drink and act as the structure of our characters leads us to, we go almost universally unscathed. We study to move like wirewalkers, all mesmerising tensions and hot sweat, we cut away our languages, our names, and in return for this tiny effort we are given our wonderful smile and it protects us, because God is on our side. He left word to that effect in the Bible. Surprising this, I realise, but I have known my Bible well for many years and it's all there: we are His favourites.

How did I come to discover this? The Gideon man paid a visit to my school when I was fifteen, maybe sixteen, a fraction less than half a life ago. The whole school was summoned into assembly — my brother towards the front among the younger classes — where the Gideon man held up a cheap, red-bound edition of the New Testament, held it as if it were liable to sting, and said that he would give a copy to each of us. He hinted we might not read it and expressed brisk doubts that any of us would manage a whole Bible, even if he had one to hand: not chewing it down and digesting it, wearing it out, in the way that the Gideon's founder had when he was much younger than us. The Gideon's founder had done nothing but read the Bible from the age when he first began to puzzle letters out, hundreds and hundreds of times he'd read it – or a tale to that effect, I wasn't listening, I was already deciding that I would read the red New Testament and then the full, fat Bible after that. I was going to read it more than once, because no one should ever be able to say there were things I couldn't do.

Which is how I learned that Isaac chose Rebecca to be his wife because she offered him a drink and Gideon – the warrior, not the book-pusher – was ordered by God to pick his troops according to the way they drank: no ducking in the head and guzzling blindly: watchful drinkers, those are the ones the Lord prefers. Who better than God to know that any wise drinker should always be on guard? These were matters concerning water, of course, but you know what water ends up turning into – like father, like son.

Obviously, for almost the whole of my senior school life I wasn't exactly legal for wine: as it happens, I didn't much like it, anyway – still don't. My inclinations then leaned towards sweet cider and the kind of sticky sherry you might buy for an elderly aunt – which made it quite easy to purchase as an innocent, young lass – *now what's the brand that Auntie said she favoured?* – limpid-eyed and dressed in my uniform – *do you have a larger bottle?* – *she likes it a lot* – I could have requested mescaline and got it, because I knew how to ask. Never disguise what you are when you can be open, when you can be disarming, when you can smile.

Smile in the way that you might as a precaution while you're leaving a hotel, sliding along beside the cover of the checkout queue and then lolloping softly off with your friendly holdall towards the plain door that looks like a fire exit, but has no alarm and opens without complaint on to naked concrete stairs, descending. This is a guess, an inspiration, brought on by a reflective afternoon spent watching a poker championship on the lounge bar's cable TV and considering M. H. Virginas's credit card. You could become apprehensive thinking of items like that and apprehension is well on the way to fear and fear is bad for you, shortens your life, any normal individual would avoid it.

This means that you are justified in leaving now, a day early, without troubling yourself, or anyone else, over paperwork and payment. It is reasonable for you never to consider going back, pausing only briefly at the foot of the stairs, then leaning through another door and walking down what you find to be an underground passage between cupboards and boilers, ventilators, tanks, and a small room with a dartboard and a fridge and a thickening of old cigarette smoke around a woman in a pink overall. She looks at you, at your friendly holdall and at your eyes, and it is simply and beautifully clear that you are leaving, are running away, and it is equally plain that she knows this.

Internally, several areas of your body have clenched or shivered defensively, but outside you can feel yourself start smiling. She has wonderful hair, this woman, a marvellous tumble of coppery grey, and a face of some significance – a face you'd want to vote for, or see on a postage stamp – and you concentrate on this and on her other impressive qualities and, although they are not clear, you do still love them: you care for them and empathise and you are deeply aware of your shared humanity: and this wealth of fellow feeling and every other subtle elaboration of your heart – it all finds its ideal expression in your smile. The smile allows her to both understand and absolve you simultaneously, which is a special, spiritual pleasure for anyone. So next she leans her head a degree or two to the side, breathes out audibly and then glances back down at her paper, as if you had never been. She turns her page.

You make it to a corner, round it, and then a real fire exit is waiting for you, propped open by a plastic chair that stands empty, half in sunlight. There is no difficulty to leaving, no tricks or last-minute shouts. It is simple to cross the car park, kicking between a grey hedge of low shrubs and on into another car park and then to a pavement and traffic and everyday life.

In the photograph, I can see I have that fire-exit smile: it is there and ready for the camera, as if it wants to be on the record, for once. And I can see that the man beside me shares precisely my expression, equally absolving and untouchable and tenderly alight. We are the only ones: any observer would quickly pick us out and say we are alike.

I saved the picture because of this and because it reminds me that even a person who has the drinker's smile is not immune from someone else who has it, too.

II

He's called Robert.

But I am terrible with names, constantly losing my grip on them when I shouldn't, so I'm shoving a handy sentence round and round, behind my thoughts – *His name is Robert, Robert Gardener, as if he digs things up: his name is Robert, that's his name* – I am concentrating on this hard enough to find conversation tricky.

Not that anyone is talking to me, right now. I am leaning my chin against the top of a whitewashed wall and looking across at a sand track, looping and glowing up under lights. The electric hare whines past me, sounding like every anxiety I've ever had, and triggering the flip of the dog traps, the start of their gangly, pelting run. Greyhound paws on sand: they make a remarkable noise, very soothing and quietly festive. Astride the wall to my left, a fat boy in a shellsuit giddy-ups the bricks with his heels, but seems to have no interest in any particular dog.

This was Robert's idea. After the pre-wedding dinner, we were escorted out by a weary barman, the last to leave, and nothing much happened between us, I do clearly recall all the nothing that went on between Robert and me: but I did give him my number and he did ring me the following week.

'Who?'

'Robert . . . Gardener. From the . . .'

'That meal, yes . . . Yes?'

I was still in bed, which makes for a nice unease in these situations: there is always something horizontal in your tone that gives you away and you may occasionally wonder whether

43

this is, in fact, what you want. Then again, he was given away before me – his own voice losing a note when I didn't recognise his name at once, then settling, opening, as we calmed and warmed. I could hear we were calming and warming: people forget that the telephone lets you hear *everything* – all the information around the words, their external music, and every noise that works beneath each voice – as devices, they are merciless.

'You didn't lose my number, then.'

'No, I wouldn't do that.'

Which was being very frank for this early in a chat – so he was doing the frank thing, the disarming thing, the one which suggests *you are safe with me* and is therefore dangerous.

'You could lose it if you wanted.' Not that I don't like danger – it puts that spike of brandy in the blood.

'But I didn't – want.'

A slight breathlessness now on both our parts, because this was turning into exercise: from a standing start, we were having to perform, be convincingly witty, flirtatious and carefree and demonstrably likely to be a good date, trying to catch each other's rhythm and pass it back. Not that we weren't also liking the good strain of something which did tend to suggest there was pleasantly harder work to come. With any luck.

'What are you doing this afternoon?'

'Oh, I don't know . . .' In my experience, I have quite a small allowance of luck, relatively. 'Saturday things.'

He murmured a laugh at that, although it wasn't funny. Apparently he was one for the nervous laugh.

'What? What's the matter?' Not that there's anything wrong with being given a nervous laugh – it arrives with a sense of its owner's breath and the heat of their throat. I myself don't laugh nervously half enough, which is a shame, because it's useful.

'Nothing's the matter. What Saturday things have you got on?'

I, of course, had nothing on – in any sense. And I, of course, wondered if he'd guessed, would have preferred it if he'd guessed. And this, in its turn, coloured my reply, licked around its tone without further effort on my part. 'Well, there's a charity gravel collection at two o'clock. And then I have to finish plaiting my wicker man.' It didn't matter what I said.

'Chippings for Needy Nippers? – it's a great cause.' Or what he answered.

The two of us doubling meanings where there were none, making them shine. 'Everyone makes an effort when they know it's for waifs and strays.'

'And which do you favour? Waifs?'

'No, I always go for strays.'

'That's very commendable – or if you'd like, you could come out with me.'

'I could . . .' And then we found the pause. 'I could do that.' Met each other inside it. 'Yes, I could.'

'You're sure you want to?'

'I am sure.' Another, nicely chafing silence and then I heard myself repeat, 'Yes. I am sure.'

'Okay, then.'

'That was easy.'

'Sometimes it is.'

Which was a lie – it never is.

And, true to form, when we met up in Union Street, we went wrong. For a start, he didn't look the same, I couldn't tell you why: there was simply a type of ugliness in him that I hadn't seen before. For his part, he glanced at me edgily with the kind of concern you'd reserve for an unstable building, or bottled specimens of rare deformities. (I am many things, but not deformed.) We walked behind the back of the cathedral in helpless silence: now and again jarring arms together lightly the way people do when they are unable to reach each other's step.

He stopped, a seagull kiting down the sky ahead of us and then folding to drop, and I wondered if Robert had some fondness for – or phobia of – seagulls. That wouldn't be a good sign, either way. But then the gull wagged off and Robert sighed, 'Look, I'm not being interesting. And this is . . . either we can keep walking and it won't get any better, or you can come for a drive with me and I'll . . . there's somewhere you'd enjoy. I think.'

'You're going to drive off with me.'

'I promise not to kill you.' Again the nervous laugh.

'Well, that's all right, then.'

'Not even injure you.'

'I've studied self-defence.' This was another lie, I had always *intended* to study self-defence, but had never found the time. 'I wouldn't let you injure me.'

'Good . . . tell you what, if we nip back through the shopping mall, we'll be filmed on their CCTV – that way, I'll be caught almost immediately and arrested when they discover your torso abandoned in a drain.'

'A loch, please. Not a drain.'

'Of course – only the best for Hannah. A loch. A nice, romantic loch.'

He could remember *my* name. 'Say that again.'

'A nice, romantic loch.'

'The *first* bit.'

'Of course – only the best for Hannah.'

And no one had ever suggested anything close to that. So I went with Robert Gardener and I got into his car and he drove me clear across the country, to the Shawfield Greyhound Track.

Which is quite unforgivable.

Although, by the time we got here, he was forgiven. I allowed him to be redeemed, because of the tapes. Almost as soon as the car was in motion, Robert was scrabbling riskily in the glove compartment among a dozen or so cassettes, the road ahead careering towards us, shivering beneath and then streaming away, as if he had very little to do with our progress – which was the case.

'Ah, I see . . . you're not going to kill *me*, you're going to kill us *both*. My murder-suicide pact was meant to be *next* week.'

'It's fine . . . it's . . . okay.' He slapped in a tape, then finally patted his free hand down on the wheel again and paid attention to the windscreen. I prepared myself for the usual talk about how Nancy Griffith is really sexy and genuinely talented and bright, or how Neil Young is really sexy and genuinely talented and bright – depending on the hopelessness of the speaker's middle age – or else the speech intended to convey that *I am still young/hip/sexy/genuinely talented and bright enough to thoroughly understand garage/progressive jazz/Radiohead/Christ knows what kind of Mongolian throat music* . . . because ninety-nine in every hundred men never, ever can *just listen* to music.

And then a noise shook through his speakers which made him the one in the hundred: that opening, ghastly chord, clattering down emphatically and sustaining: *tra-daaaa*. It was Jimmy Shand: Jimmy Shand and his band: the Auchtermuchty Sound.

'Oh, my God.' What else could I say? – being suddenly plunged back into a thousand wet afternoons in the gym hall and the smell of rubber soles and Precambrian sweat and thumping through the Canadian Barn Dance, the Lancers, Strip the Willow, the Dashing White Sergeant, the Eightsome Reel, the endless skip-change-of-step and right hand after left and breathe in and breathe out to the stone-steady rhythm of Shand's accordions, their mad and wailing and perversely attractive drone.

'Yes, isn't it.'

'I mean . . . Oh, my God.'

'"The Northern Lights of Old Aberdeen".'

'You *are* insane.'

'But you know you're in safe hands now – no one could ever be murdered in time to Jimmy Shand.'

'*Jesus* . . .' It was becoming shamefully impossible not to tap my feet. '*Christ*. Completely insane.'

'I did hear once that they held soothing country-dance sessions in Carstairs State Hospital.'

'And so the tunes make you homesick.'

'Timesick.' He grinned, 'Aren't you?' seeing that he was right and laughing out loud: a good, hot sound, that fumbled quickly under the opening notes of 'The Bluebell Polka' . . . *Tra-daaa*. 'Mm?'

'If you wore a coloured sash over your shoulder, you were an honorary boy . . . week after week, sash and then no sash. Except for the girl with the incipient moustache – she always had a sash – you know how girls are, unpleasant . . .'

'Well, I had to dance with *real* boys, that's much worse.'

'And in the end they put you all together: co-educational for the full experience: Christmas party, Queen Victoria's birthday, some other notable date: and everything gets embarrassed and nobody has a clue who should be leading and it all goes to hell.'

'Well, everyone knows the accordion is Satan's favourite instrument.'

'And *you* know why Calvinists never have sex standing up.'

'Because people will think they are dancing.'

Which is my favourite joke, its punchline delivered without pause, clean on the beat, Robert simply rattling on after, as if he'd done nothing special, as if no one would ever be tempted to assess compatibility on the strength of seven words set out precisely when they should be.

'I have *Over the Hills and Far Away* too, that's one of his finest albums, we can play it next.' I could feel that his accelerator foot was gently keeping time. 'Ah, yes . . . an extensive body of work.' This Robert beside me, this Robert Gardener, who knew my punchline and was not irritating me, and was not giving rise to any thirst, only a rush, the regular forward pulse of an open rush. And this was his pine-tree air freshener, swinging from the rear-view mirror, and his clean, little footwell carpets and his book of British road maps in the door pocket and this was, as you might say, his distinctly anal-retentive, second-hand Volvo – but, then again, I hate messy interiors, messy cars most of all – and the whole of this was, on every side of me, Robert's – an expression of him – while I was unstoppably thinking

Jimmy bloody Shand – how many generations of us danced to him at school before anything else? – toddlers practically, but already fixed in our timetables, ready at least once a week to be all of a piece and out and jumping to that rhythm, practising the pace of an uneasy heart, the perfect tempo – we'd later learn – for unhurried sex. And how many Scots have made all their love to this one unacknowledged accompaniment, folded somewhere deep in their reptile brain: the back and forth and slip and rise of the Auchtermuchty Sound?

'What are you thinking?' Robert patting the steering wheel: a formal kind of set to his head, the shoulders raised as if he were ducking out from under something and didn't quite expect to make it. 'You can tell me . . . I'm taking all my medication and I'm very stable now. What are you thinking?'

About how I fuck – about how you must, too. 'Oh, ahhm . . . that when Thatcher wrecked our education system, she also really messed up our beat.'

'No need to bring *her* into this – we were having a nice day. Anything else?'

'Watching the ceilidhs on telly with my dad.'

'In the good old days, when we hadn't got a clue and thought we ought to like them.'

'But we *did* like them.'

'Of course.'

My father had a weakness for Shand – the famous band composed, as far as I could see, entirely of dead, old men in extraordinary jackets and the dancers – who were of both sexes but I can only visualise the men – spines bullet-straight, neat in precisely rolled shirtsleeves, darting about with great seriousness and violently short haircuts and potentially – but never, ever actually – reckless kilts.

'My favourite was "Donald, Where's Yer Troosers".' This was my lie, which anticipated his, was hoping for it happily.

'Or there was always the unforgettably moving "Stop Yer Tickling, Jock".'

Lying together is good.

'It's a wonder we're alive.'

But that's not a lie, it's always true: it is a wonder.

'It isn't a wonder, it's a bloody miracle.'

Robert is placing what he claims is a fifty-pence bet with the gaggle of ancient, deaf bookies to one side of the track. I prefer the rather clinical young women at the windows for the Tote: they seem to be judgemental, almost scolding, which pleases me.

Over by the kennels, the next dogs are led out: Hanover Racer leaping and lunging in a way I feel sure should attract inexperienced punters like myself. I am moved to back her but, sadly, have a prior commitment to Clune Tune, a passive, camel-coloured effort, currently urinating copiously.

'Would you like a pie?' Robert returned and standing softly at my shoulder, the breath that carried his question still loitering in the cold and adding to the generally misty silver of the floodlit air. 'Or something . . .'

'Probably something.'

'Come on, then.'

The track's public bar is headachy with cheap tobacco and the tang of cooked fish – which is unnerving because fish is neither cooked nor served within the grounds. Robert is taller than almost everyone – although he is not tall – but he is also visibly softer and moves in the wrong way, has a certain carelessness. His hair has this knack of standing out at the sides of his head, permanently ruffled, which seems rash in our present context.

'What probable something do you want?' And, before I can answer, 'But I've got to drive us back, so I can't join you. Have to be sensible – my licence is currently delicate – points, you know . . . incidents . . .' This news solidifying in my stomach like a tiny, lead handicap weight. I don't want to drink alone.

That is, I don't mind it on principle, but I don't want to do it right now.

Because this is complicated: if I really do want to fuck him, and I really do, then I really do have to be more liquid than I am. In preparation for real physical contact, I have to be freed and insulated and warmed and fortified and these qualities only come to me, or indeed anyone else, when they've had a drink. Because I am experienced in drink, I can judge very accurately how much of it doing things to Robert would require.

But if I drink enough to ease out the actions I might want, then I may not remember what some of those actions were: in fact, it's quite possible I won't remember anything, and this time I would like to. I would like to be there and store every move in safe keeping and know about each one in detail tomorrow morning and thereafter. I would, to be truthful, prefer if this wasn't fucking and was more like something else, something humane.

On the other hand, if I drink and he doesn't then I will have started to travel and he will just stay where he is. I will leave him and be alone, drinking alone. There have even been occasions when this makes me silly and embarrassments take place. He wouldn't like that. Nor would I.

'Hannah?'

'A Scotch and ginger beer.'

'A *what?*'

'Because when it tastes crap I won't have any more. As you can't join me . . .'

'I would like to, but —'

'You can't.' I sound sulky. He pads towards the bar, apparently without having noticed.

I glance along the figures at the counter: a) five foot three and clinically depressive, b) five foot one and with a facial scar, c) Robert, d) perfectly normal and eating a pie while winking at a pair of ladies tucked up in the corner and staring at him, but making no other visible response. In light of the current competition, my companion for the evening looks highly promising.

Actually, Robert's promise, is – even as I study him – cramping between my kidneys and prickling, here and there, with a warm effect which precipitates swallowing and a careful maintenance of stillness, because if I move in this condition I will not be responsible and will want to change things: our angles, temperatures, levels of contentment, states of dress: although there is no chance of my succeeding in any of this, because I am drinking on my own.

I couldn't really take full account of him face on, close to – but, at this remove, he becomes less overwhelming, more accessible and easy to peruse: the aforementioned ruffling over his ears, the life in the movements of his back and that sugges-tion of his hips beneath his jacket (lousy grey jacket), the unloading and reloading of weight from foot to foot, the forces at work in the muscles from ankle to thigh, all closely reflected by his jeans. He should never wear thick jeans, never anything immobile and

There is no point to this – none at all. Why fix on his hands and interrogate and pry – what would be their strength, the fingers' true circumference, how would they fit – making guesses until I taste salt when nothing will come of this?

'Here's your poison.' Robert's hand more three-dimensional than it should be when it sets down my glass full of fizzy, gingered whisky. 'So . . . cheers.' And he waves his own bottle of water in my direction as he sits, as if I needed another reminder of his unalterable state.

'Cheers, yes.' And, by this time, I don't want the drink: I need it, the whole deep lunge of it, rolling down.

'That looks good. You're making me jealous.'

'I don't mean to.' *Not jealous enough.* I haul away the last sip and fold my arms against the lack of anything to hold.

'Shall I get you another?' Nothing accusatory in the question, no more than a fond amusement, which is a good start – fond amusement can be built upon during an evening and grow towards great joint endeavours. If we both take a drink.

There is a mildly communicative silence and I realise Robert is waiting for an answer and for me to face him. I have changed and he is curious, checking to see why. I tilt my head towards him and have only the wrong kind of smile, I can sense it clamping across and mingling self-pity and a heavy effort to look cheerful with a tedious jag of passive-aggressive pique. There isn't a thing I can do to halt it. I try to save my situation by working on my eyes, keeping them warm and amiable. Still, I notice that he has to flinch.

But he makes an effort to keep in touch, to be concerned, 'You okay?'

'I . . . ah, don't know. I think I'm getting a migraine.'

'Shit . . . you think so?'

And, as it happens, I do. My left cheek is already drumming with the usual foreplay: as if a large hand, gloved in chain mail is tapping and tapping at me, the glitter of metal catching in my eye and turning to colours and numbness. Soon that familiar, thin, kaleidoscope twist will be rainbowing in across everywhere I look. And then I'll get the blind spot. And then I'll get the pain. Pretty much the perfect evening, then.

It's stress – I never have this unless I'm stressed. If he was drinking, I wouldn't be stressed. If we were both drinking, I would not be approaching any type of stress. He is such a stupid –

'Anything I can do?'

YES.

I'm trying to make my expression persuasive, something to raise a thirst. 'Oh . . . well, maybe another whisky without the additions – I need to relax. Then it'll go away.'

'You're tense?'

Even though I'm becoming visually impaired, I can see where that's going – all the suggestions that we can both make for removing my various tensions – none of them any use to me tonight.

'A little bit tense, yes.'

'Well, I'm sure we could do something about that.'

'Yes . . .' I may cry. He just has to be this cooperative *now* – it's like watching a lunatic burn your inheritance – you get to see each note, high denominations, all yours, immeasurably useful, and then – a sour flare and a feather of ash and another inviting piece of your future is permanently gone.

He gets me another whisky and then one of its relatives, and then one of its friends and I should be drunk by now, I should be feeling it, I should – in the absence of other pleasures – be in my house with the whole whisky family, all of us curled up tight around our fine, warm, cask-matured, internal fire. But I'm not. I am entirely sober. I can hear owls snatching mice in the park behind us. I can smell the whole of the day before yesterday. I am beginning to have the awareness of bloody angels – were it not for being blind in the one eye and wanting to rip off my skin with my own teeth and hands, because this is unbearable. My skin is unbearable, it is holding me back, holding me in and the shine of his body is hurting it, turning so intense that I ought to be seeing blisters rise and he's so far away across the table and talking about I have no idea what – he's too close to hear, drowned out by the babies crying across the river and long bones knitting in Stirling and people imagining lottery numbers and changing their minds and dreaming, dreaming loud as hand grenades – and why is he so warm when I can't touch him?

It's going to take a long, long drive to bring us home. There is also hardly any room inside the car: most of the space having been appropriated by shame.

We were the best-looking people in there, the prize pair, and we were the ones they asked to leave. I was the one they asked to leave.

Frightening the children.

I wasn't frightening anyone. And if you bring your kids to the dog track, you deserve all they get – the atmosphere of dashed hope and canine hysteria, the passive smoking, the unremitting pitter-pat of all those paws – you should be reported to a social worker for even thinking of taking a young person near that.

I wasn't behaving badly or in a way to cause anyone fright. I had only gone outside the bar for a little air and I was making cheerful remarks. I was restraining myself in every sense. And then if you think someone's stolen your keys from you, you will point that out – I mean, who wouldn't mention that in passing, even if it so happens that you're mistaken. I didn't intend that policemen should be called – I made no such demands.

I can only imagine that we were ejected for our own safety – better to put out the law-abiding couple than empty the whole arena of criminal types. That's what I would suppose.

While we drive away, Robert has wedged in a tape of some Mozarty horn piece, soft enough to talk above, although we are saying nothing.

I am reflecting, not for the first time, that I dislike the kindness of policemen – when they consider you with that weary amusement, as a person not even worthy of arrest.

'Sorry.'

No reply – maybe I didn't speak out loud, or he didn't hear me. 'Sorry.'

'Uh-huh.'

'No, I am.'

'I know you are.'

This is not good. The whole debacle is his fault for not drinking, but I'm going to be blamed.

He won't want to see me again after this.

'I just . . .' *need to be not by myself. Can't tell him that, though. You can never tell anyone that.* 'I mean . . .'

'You have a migraine. It's okay. Let me drive now, take you home.'

I am not aware that I'm going to sleep. Mainly I have that surgical chill in my ribs – the one which indicates an amputation of your hope. Still, I do slide away, the coloured lights that mark out the sides of the motorway streaming past in a regular, soothing swim. I do leave myself.

What wakes me is a lack of motion. We are hours away, returned to our own city, down by the river, and able to enjoy the stretches and clusters of small-town street-lights on the other side, the soft blanks of dark that indicate woods or fields and a solitary push of headlights – another car that's out late, like ours.

Although our engine is off, I realise, and we are no longer shining. Robert's car is parked in the dead stretch of road by the hot-snacks Portakabin – a purveyor of hot snacks has always been here, it seems, overlooking the embankment from various vans and now this. I have never been moved to sample any snacks they have made hot. Not that the place isn't thronged, when open, and no doubt sterling in many ways – I just try to watch what I eat.

Other things by the river have changed. When I was still at school, people could pull up right along here and birdwatch, or fish, or step out and walk – or wait until night and arrive in couples, take it from there – this last, very probably why such access has now been limited by a number of preventative tree plantations and other civic works. During the hours of daylight, my family would often stroll about here, counting seabirds, trying to spot any low-tide seals on the sandbanks: Simon and I pondering the warning notices and grubby life-saving equipment wistfully – we didn't exactly *want* anyone to start drowning, but it would have been fun if somebody *almost* did, if we ourselves could throw the lifebelt and see them catch it, that first grateful clasp.

'Hello.' Two of Robert's fingertips running quietly along my jaw. 'How are you feeling?'

And I'm feeling my mind is still floundering up for the surface while the rest of me, the meat, is striking off in its own direction over-quickly and I'm already holding Robert, even though I've made no conscious effort to reach out. My head winces when I move it too quickly, swims as I'm angled further and further back and his lips are open before mine, determined, coaxing, and he smells of the dog-track bar and of pine-tree air freshener and of his sweat and of himself and his tongue is finding the sourness in my mouth which makes me embarrassed, but it seems Robert doesn't mind.

'Mm-hmm.' He agrees with the kiss and continues it, our noise first amplifying, then mutating until it's like wet flesh dropping, slapping on a floor: there is almost a flavour of that along his teeth, of a butchered something, a wound, and I have expressly imagined holding him and all of the conversation, the testing, the pressure we would make against each other which is so very, very much a fine thing now it's happening, but there is also a slope to it which is unsettling and sly and I feel sick – and he ought to be able to tell this, he is close enough – only no one is stopping anything, we are both going on, and I realise what I'm up to as my head falls forward and his one hand cradles in at the back of my neck: creeps on it, tender and stroking and spending time with my hair while I understand it's just pretending, biding its time until everything is in place – what it really wants to do is hold me and push down.

So then it does.

His heat lifting to my face before I find him and then he's in, a bright taste to him, like metal, and as smooth as inno- cence and this is better; much, much better, and I know that he is beautiful, this much of him is beautiful, although I've seen nothing at all. But now his two hands are over my ears and he smells sweet, confectionary sweet, and he's making this further and faster and blocking my breath and I want to keep from gagging and want the kick in my head to stop and I want to love him and I want to stop this and I want to be able to watch what I eat and I want to use my teeth.

Except that he's caught then, holds his breath, clings on to save his life and gives it up and gives it up and gives it up.

'Sorry.' His voice seems rounder, deeper, altered.

I can't speak yet, the blood is stinging in my scalp. I shouldn't have sat up so quickly. He feels for my wrist and holds it. I can't stop swallowing.

'I said I'm sorry. Taking advantage.'

It isn't him, I don't feel sick because of him. Still, I do wretch in a small way and try to make it sound like a cough. 'It's okay . . . I was . . . joining in.'

'Thank you.'

'No . . . that's . . . Thank *you*.'

I don't drink men often, hardly at all, it isn't a habit. This is the first time I've done it and wanted to. I think I wanted to.

He smoothes my hair, this time without ulterior motives. 'God . . . I shouldn't have done that, it was . . . great, but . . . you never got to . . .'

The car shivers, or my face, my skull: something is shivering. 'No, I never did. It's okay, though. I had fun.' My hands are wet, getting wetter, the fingernails feel loose. 'You have a very nice, ahm . . .'

'Well, it's fond of you, too. Very. Look, I really would like to . . . but I . . . at the moment.'

'I know. We will. Just not now. We can meet up again.' I have to lie down and I have to lie down without him. I have to go home. I believe we will never see each other again and perhaps if we do something more tonight, this morning, we might change that, but I have to go home and lie down. I have to take care of my hands, they seem to be decomposing.

'Where d'you live, darling?' Then the nervous laugh again, because if he's calling me darling, he should already know my address, and because darling seems natural now and won't tomorrow, won't in an hour. 'Where do you live?'

'Go straight on from here. I'll show you.'

While he drives, I keep my fingers tucked under my thighs and I swallow as slowly as I can and think of my throat as numb pipe, all calm.

In the passing lamp flares Robert appears newly washed, younger, someone that I should stay and be kind with, if it weren't for the swirling behind my face and my slack palms and the rest. I'm at fault and he is, too – he didn't drink and so I didn't drink enough, didn't dose things appropriately, and so none of this has happened as it should.

Beyond him, there is the river, pulling away as we climb, every swing of the car magnifying, momentum and inertia straining through me the way that they might in a dream.

And I did dream of the river – over and over, when I was five or six. There I would be, awake in my bed, and then the house would start to sway. The movement was quite gentle, almost as if the building had given a sigh, but immediately I'd be terrified.

I would get up and walk to the window, all my joints gearing oddly because of the fear, and the water would be waiting for me, immeasurably wide and with the dull shine of new lead. Always, there was a full moon, disinterested and obscenely wide, and, straight ahead, there was the rope.

It was huge, thicker than the broadest mooring rope, strand after fat strand woven into it seamlessly. I couldn't see, but I somehow knew that it had been bound clear round the house and fixed inescapably. When I first approached, it was in a lazy sag and still. Then it sprang taut with a low hum, water starting up from it in a long, fine haze of moonlit spray, and my home moved slightly, before the rope settled and eased again.

This process repeated until I was so scared that I imagined I would die soon and leaning so hard against the window that it gave in the way toffee might and bowed out into a bubble around me, let me lean so that I could study the huge knot that had me and my mother and father and brother trapped. I was certain they wouldn't wake, because this was only for me – my fear.

With that knowledge came the final bracing of the rope, its last rise of spindrift, and then my home was sliding, slithering down towards the embankment and the waves, the other buildings in our street and the streets beyond it shrugging out of our way and then returning to their places as if they had never been friends with our house and didn't care. The wave tops and the hawser shone and I began to be able to hear the swell over the sandbanks and it would be soon now – when we either sank at the end of our noose, or were dragged away forever and lost.

I would wake up with that swaying and sliding still at work in my legs, my spine. I sometimes think this is why I am naturally unsteady and I need to be off balance to set myself right.

That time with Robert, I wasn't set right. Another 400 millilitres, maybe less, that would have been the modest help I needed, it would have meant Robert didn't simply drive me to my flat and let me out with a soft, short kiss.

'Thank you.' My voice tiny, transparent.

'Thank you.'

I balanced on the pavement, sucked in the cool dawn.

'Hannah? I'll call you this afternoon to find out how you are.'

'You don't have to.'

'I know that, but I will. Because I want to. And once I've made my mind up – well, you can't shake me. You'll see – I'll be the cross you have to bear.'

Which meant we parted with a lie.

III

But as long as I'm making progress, that's the thing. And, like everyone else, I do – racking up the days, night after morning, I am achieving time. Which is a modest accomplishment, I know, but I don't take it for granted.

Because I was born with the absolute certainty that I would die before leaving thirty. I arrived with ten toes and blue eyes and death firmly in mind. I passed the age when lives should be taken in hand, knowing that no such formalities would be required. For me, there would be no pension, no insurance, no prudent mortgage plan, no fretting over outrages in homes for the elderly, or the ultimate loss of my health and faculties. I was carefree.

And completely wrong, of course.

As of now, I should be six years, eight months and a few days dead. In reality, it looks not unlikely that I'll make forty in due course.

But this is largely good news: for instance, by trusting in what has become a false goal I've still generated an undoubted onward drive and saved myself much useless introspection and unease. I have reached my current position in spite – or even because – of my steadfast denials that I ever could. And my very reasonable unwillingness to bother planning activities beyond my predicted demise has allowed my current lifestyle to excel in improvisation and has encouraged many happy accidents.

I first meet Robert, after all, when I am already years overdue for the grave. Seeing him again, beginning to learn his hands, spending the whole of the following day with the taste of him under my teeth – this also happens totally by chance.

For three weeks after that, of course, he doesn't phone and nor do I, not having his number – or, indeed, the necessary lack of pride to make the call.

And, right now, I'm thinking of Robert and his failings – or possibly mine. I am wondering why it was so easy to be comfortable and friendly when he finally did call, why the two of us decided three weeks could be nothing at all. Meanwhile, I am rolling quickly, irresistibly, close to forty and speeding across the flanks of my present day. I am also standing very still in the doorway of a barn, dizzied with remembered time, the smothering in of my past.

Beyond the lintel's shade, there is the sweetness of grain fields on the breeze, the bland dust of poor soil, baked to a yellowish crust: and salt, too: something of the high-tide line, bladderwrack and rock clefts dank with scrub and gorse: that slightly human, musty fug of heated gorse, the snap of its seeds, the blood drop in the yellow of each flower: which is to say, the smell and taste and everything of my being a child in summer, of running between the blue, narrow shore and the racing depths of barley with my brother until the sun had fallen and the sandy earth was cooled to match the temperature of skin.

I used to be young here. This is where days and days of me were played out harmlessly.

But back to business.

There always will be something to interrupt.

I clear my throat and blink and become what is now expected – an adult selling cardboard to another adult – what a life. 'How many, then?'

'Eh?'

I hate farmers. 'How many do you want?' Especially this farmer.

'Eh?'

No, what I hate are soft-fruit farmers who order a piss-poor handful of 6lb pick-your-own baskets and then lapse into

64

fainting fits and vapours when trails of hapless civilians use, wreck, steal and otherwise outstrip available supplies.

The baskets are for people to put fruit in — so fruit is going to be put in them by people — that's what all your badly spelled, half-arsed, **'Come and Meet the Strawberries and Then Eat Their Children'** *roadside placards are enticing them to do — what did you expect? That they'd bring their own sodding baskets? That they'd hand-plait wicker trugs the night before to save you expense? That they'd fill up their hats and trouser pockets and then go?*

'How many more, Mr Campbell?' We're near the start of the raspberry canes — which are already heaving with mums and dads and kiddies, plucking down enough fruit to keep Dante's inferno endlessly boiling with lakes of crimson jam. 'I mean, you've got what . . . two more weeks like this . . .? the currants . . . blackberries . . . you know how long they'll last . . .'

Farmer Campbell stares at me as if the blackberries are my fault, a distress I have engineered. Then his gaze clatters down to my ankles and twitches about. He frowns and begins to shuffle across the yard towards his house. 'I'll go in and think, like. I'll go in and think.'

He's doing this because I was late, unavoidably delayed on a mission of mercy, but Farmer Campbell doesn't know that: he simply wants to make a point. I delay him and then he delays me. Here I am, offering him uniquely environmental, recyclable, sturdy cardboard baskets — no nasty metal handles, our patented safe and biodegradable webbing instead — and he can't even offer a coffee, never mind a glass of something pleasant, or a firm order. I bet his strawberries are shite, anyway. Every grower I know is producing these weird, new varieties: the fruit keeps well, packs well, freezes well, travels well, shows well — but then you try to eat it and it tastes like wet bicycle tyres, I mean what is the point?

There's a boy shuffling up between the rows of canes — his basket is too heavy for him and he's lunging it forward, then resting it on the ground and picking again, serious, fingers bloody with juice and maybe slightly scratched. When my mother took us to the fields, Simon would be like that: never ate any himself, only solemnly gathered monster amounts of raspberries, because they were his favourite. Mine, too. We used to have a lot in common, even though he could be so stern to his appetites.

Down at the weighing-out scales, I'd be gorged with fruit, almost nauseous, Mother smiling slyly about it – my greed and waste of growing things providing their own punishment. Simon would be grim behind me, struggling with his mounded load, but wanting nobody to help, because this was his business, something he had done. The weigher would wink, or look at him with a nice touch of awe as the scale's needle bounced straight over to some miraculous total for a lad of such tender years and I would try to hate my brother for being someone who was better than me and then I would see the thin lines of blood on his forearms and his fingers, the beaded tracks where the thorns had caught him, and I would be defeated, I would be proud. My little brother being sore and hot and tired, but finishing what he'd started, anyway – if you couldn't be proud of yourself, then you could be proud of Simon.

Still no sign of Campbell.

Five more minutes and I will leave, drive off: the Cardboard Products Group does not need this kind of dilettante custom. CPG's lovely, moulded punnets, self-ventilating single-layer fruit trays and other wholesomely practical containers will no longer be made available to Castlerigg Farm. In fact, Castlerigg Farm can screw itself, along with its owner – he's already using someone else's punnets in any case – nasty plastic ones, I spotted a pile of them in a shed. Farmer Campbell clearly has no concern for the well-being of our planet.

Strictly speaking, CPG may not either. I remain unconvinced by our figures for recycled pulp incorporation and some of our boxes come from Indonesia, for Christ's sake: China. I feel they may not be ethically produced – more like pure, compressed rainforest cut into sheets and then probably put together by limbless tykes in cellars full of rats.

Not that it's any concern of mine, I only sell the stuff.

Although I am basically altruistic and do my bit in other ways – hence my tardy arrival at Castlerigg this afternoon. I was sidetracked by being humanitarian, which takes time.

I'd pulled up in one of those little Fife towns: sternly pictur-esque buildings full of cousins intent on impoverishing their gene pools. I'd found the usual post office-cum-newsagent-cum-bakery (the standard range of products plus peat briquettes, half a dozen dodgy videos for sale on a back shelf, some small and probably stolen electrical goods) and I had bought two flattened ham and salad baps for breakfast, a news-paper and a styrofoam cup of coffee that smelled uncannily like sweat.

There was a small, abused park nearby and I went and sat in it for my meal, admiring the rustic sandstone bridge (spray-painted with charmless expletives, mainly in blue) and the tinkling brook (rich both in weedy nooks and bottles that once contained a cheap, fortified wine). I ignored each unpleasant detail and attempted to be at peace.

Except that over the road an elderly woman was labouring to escape what I could guess was her own garden gate. She had obviously suffered a stroke at some time and had little or no strength on her right side. Her left hand was leaning heavily on a wheelchair, while she tried to push the gate open with her back. The hinges were proving intransigent. There was a deep weariness in the woman's face that seemed to suggest she fought like this every day, took so long about so many things every day that she could no longer afford to acknowl-edge how intolerable this was.

Which is the sort of thing that shouldn't happen: the sort of thing that comes from lack of thought. Some moron in an office somewhere doles out a bloody wheelchair to a fellow human being who hasn't the use of both arms – and how is that human being supposed to get into the chair, out of it, and how are they supposed to push themselves about? Office Moron can't imagine, doesn't want to; as far as Office Moron is concerned a person who can't walk has been issued with a wheelchair, problem solved.

This sort of stupidity makes me angry, how could it not?

Needless to say, I abandoned my snack and nipped across to offer help, hold open the gate while the old dear tottered herself down and into the chair. I smiled what I could feel was a very good smile and, as if she had felt it, she glanced up and gave me a painstaking nod.

By this stage, I could tell that she meant to scoot herself along the pavement backwards, using her good foot – this being, no doubt, her best bet for getting around – what else could she manage unaided? Still, it seemed to be incredibly dangerous and undignified and I wasn't in any hurry to turn up *chez Campbell* and discuss baskets so why not behave as anyone decent would and offer, 'I could push you, if you'd like? I'm just having a break – nothing much to do. Would that be okay?'

I could see that she understood me, but no longer had words to hand. Her body relaxed, though, as soon as she heard my suggestion, slipped back, and I got this half-grin from her – a half being all she could muster.

'Is it this way? The shops? You just point, can you?'

I wasn't going to get a chat, clearly, and I didn't want to blather away as I might to a baby, or a dog – the usual things you meet that can't answer back. Still, there was no call for me to be stand-offish. Having care of a whole other human body like that, noticing every incline and the tiny irregularities in the pavement as they jar up through the handles of the chair – with so much going on in that weird, mechanical-intimate sort of way, you can't just ignore your companion and plod along behind them without trying to break the ice.

'You know I don't have a licence for one of these . . .'

I couldn't tell if that amused her or not. She made what seemed a happy noise inside her throat.

I wouldn't have thought it, but she was actually quite a weight, took a bit of shoving from time to time and I was starting to be rather heated, which wasn't good news for the hair and the business suit – and I favour this suit: chalk-stripe on a grey wool mix, mildly tailored jacket and skirt, matched with a boring, white blouse and librarian's shoes. My reliable ensemble. No need to be troubled about it, though: not when I also had that pleasant, proprietorial warmth growing out around me.

I am a stranger helping a stranger – this can still happen. It's nice. I'm nice.

On the other hand, people were passing us by, here and there, and these were possibly people who knew her. She must be a bit of a character, a landmark, after all: kicking along arse-forwards, day after day: a bit of hazard to watch for, in fact. Most of the town must have recognised her, but me – I was an unknown quantity, perhaps an object of distrust. I was a visiting Samaritan, caring in a way that they would not, but I felt them study me, nonetheless: a tangible, quizzical frisk of interest as each one walked by, no sympathy in it, no fellow feeling.

And I could appreciate their point of view. In a sense, I was abducting this old lady, I was pushing her off without proper introductions. I had no special training, or experience. Good will, I was full of – but who still has any faith in that?

I gentled her down the slope at a kerb and waited, over-cautiously, for every scrap of traffic to move far out of sight. 'Still okay, then? Straight on when we get over?' Her good arm wags to the right. 'Down there? Okey-dokey. Down there it is.'

I never say *okey-dokey*. I don't think anyone else does, either.

We trundled on and the pressure of the town which was, no doubt, staring after, made the hairs lift on my neck. I was beginning to feel undermined. Members of caring professions, they were au fait with wheelchairs and stretchers, trolleys, propelling the vulnerable with efficiency and calm. I didn't know about this, I was guessing, my role was not a comfortable fit.

Onwards, though, onwards. 'Are you visiting a pal, then? Going to a centre? A shop?' The street was narrow: nondescript terraces hemming us in from either side: dirty-white harling and bad windows, closed doors. 'Just out for a wander, are you?' Which was possible, she had the right to go out and ramble, like any pedestrian. Of course, this meant that I could be condemned to pushing her round for the rest of the day.

Or we could have been heading off in a quite incorrect direction. She might have been disorientated, lost. Somebody local might have noticed that I was taking this woman the wrong way. This might have caused them alarm.

I looked behind, but no one was following, there were no visible observers. Still, a definite scrutiny tickled my shoulders, perhaps from someone discreetly in pursuit. I tried to hope I was mistaken and pressed on.

A weak, little sound rose up to me then and I realised the woman in the chair was humming, singing away to herself and looking about and pleased with making no kind of effort as we progressed. So, whoever she was, she had warmed to me, to my smile, and I was letting her have a good start to her day. It didn't matter who was on our trail – we had nothing to hide.

A few paces on and she motioned we should cross the road. The pavement was of the old-fashioned type, elevated, the kerb only descending to the gutter by way of three shallow steps. This meant I would have to multiply the manoeuvre I'd used across previous kerbstones by three, which would be simple but strenuous.

I turned her softly, pitched the chair towards me by a minor angle and then rolled the back wheels over and down the first step without trouble.

I looked at the next steps.

I stopped.

I had to.

Because then I clearly understood what a lovely, put-upon, old lady she was and what a jolly time she was having.

And because then I also clearly understood how terrible it was going to be when I didn't do this properly and dropped her.

I was going to drop her.

I could tell.

I hadn't a clue what I was doing. I had no advice. There was no way things were going to turn out well here.

The lady, she was terribly helpless and fragile and wonderful and no human person like that could be left to rely on somebody like me. I was going to ruin this and harm her when I did. This would be my fault. I wouldn't mean it, but that wouldn't change how sad it was going to be.

My grip was cooling, sliding, on the handles of the chair and the accident was coming, but I couldn't wait for it. I couldn't bear that it wasn't here yet. I was getting upset.

So I did what I had to and opened my hands and the chair kicked forward, bounced, jolted down the second step, while the woman's good hand darted up, trying to ward off the coming sadness, and then there was the quicker roll and thudded landing from the lowest step, her unbalanced trajectory that curved fast across the road, the chair still upright – amazingly upright, and thank God for the lack of traffic – and then she reached the place where the one front wheel collided with the high kerb opposite and tipped the street into the noise of metal and over-turning and her noise and the fall of her body and the way that her pale blue coat would be dirty now.

I ran over to her: I'm not a monster. I ran over and hugged her up and I'm sure she'd only sprained her wrist, and there was otherwise nothing much wrong, apart from this cut on her head, bleeding the way that a head wound does and me with nothing to stop it, not a handkerchief.

She looked at me and wasn't angry, although I'd thought

she would be. Instead, she had this bewildered hurt in her eyes and the start of tears and a horrible, horrible loneliness.

'I'm sorry. I'm so sorry. I'm so sorry. I'll go and get someone. No, I have to. I'm sorry. You need someone to help me.' She held my hand. 'I'm sorry. I need help.'

But I didn't go. I stayed. I'm not a monster.

A minute, or five, or twenty later and a crowd had surrounded me, edged me back, and some housewife, still in slippers, had come out with a blanket, the blood colouring it at once – not too much, not a harmful loss, but definite staining, obvious blood.

I'd thought I would have to explain myself, but actually nobody bothered much with me and, as I knew, the woman I had injured couldn't speak and was confused by the flow of events. She was unable to accuse, or even identify, me. So I allowed myself to be the passer-by who'd found her and then no one in particular, standing for a while and then a stranger who walked away as an ambulance siren echoed in.

I didn't want any of that to happen and I do hope she's all right, I truly hope she is all right. There's no way that I can explain how awful I feel, how guilty. But it was mostly a type of accident and act of God. I'm not a monster. If I'd really meant to harm her, I would be, but I didn't. Sometimes things are unavoidable.

I had to sit and ease in a brandy before I could drive here, to Castlerigg. I used a pub in another town, not that lady's – I won't go back there, couldn't take a drink in it again.

'Is there something the matter, hen?'

Farmer Campbell has soundlessly crossed his courtyard and is holding out a grubby mug of tea. He still seems to be fascinated by my feet and, when I glance down, I can see that my sensible, grey shoes are caked with blood and my tights are spattered. Under my jacket, my blouse is marked with it, I saw that, but I thought I'd washed the rest of it off in the pub toilet.

The stains are thick, glossy, like varnish.

I am not a monster, I only look like one.

'There was.' I take his tea. 'There was this accident I saw. I mean, I was there . . . I touched someone bleeding.'

'I kent there was something.'

'She'll be fine, though. She'll be fine, I'm sure. Sorry.'

Over by the farmhouse door, Mrs Campbell loiters, curious.

'Sorry.'

'No need to be sorry, hen.'

'Sorry.'

I don't know what will happen next.

But, as it turns out, Campbell will offer me the chance of a seat inside and will suggest that I shouldn't be driving. I will shake my head and stand where I am, aware of the burden of my shoes, their new heaviness, and I will swallow down his over-sweetened tea and then we will take his emergency order from my car and put it, clean and cellophane-wrapped, inside the straw-scented darkness of a barn. Campbell will ask me to fill out a form requesting another dozen packs of baskets, which I know is rather more than he really needs or wants to buy.

I am not a monster, but I will profit from my crime.

I will get into my car and follow its steering wheel as it leads me back through the shadowed, turning lanes and under the reddening sun and I will cross the long bridge home as the sky starts burning. My hand will be steady when I reach out to the booth and pay my toll and then I will pull away and take the bends and climbs that bring me to my street, my flat, my bathroom and the shower that I will run until the tank is empty, washing until I am cold, but not quite clean.

'What are you thinking?' Robert is a little smashed, but not as smashed as me.

'*What are you thinking?* – You always fucking say that, what does it *mean*? You're just pretending you already know something. Well, you don't.'

I am glad that we are together these days, together often, but there are times when he's here too much: too large, too loud, too dense. This is one of the times.

A fortnight ago, this bar was unfamiliar to us both, so we have started from scratch in here together, cultivated the ways it can welcome us, and now it is almost our place. So Robert is filling our place, my place, looming into it, blaring, drowning out the pleasant and peaceable atmosphere that comes from the Parson (who isn't a parson) and Sniffer Bobby and Doheny (who I haven't met yet) and Mr Breed with the funny eyes. They are almost our people and, at the moment, they seem more comfortable than him.

Robert stares at me: something behind his expression is in motion, but very slow.

'I said you don't – don't know anything. You.'

He leans on my shoulder, his mouth undecided, but his eyes fighting to focus and grow hard. 'Know everything I need.'

'Fuck you.'

'Fuck *you*.' And he slaps one foot down, beginning to barge past me and strike out for the bar.

I realise it would be weak, clinging, if I tugged him back by the sleeve, but this is what I do in any case. 'No, look, I didn't . . .' My words exhaust themselves while he shrugs himself free.

Then he halts, as if he had intended I should keep my grip. 'What? Didn't what?' The space around him starts to taste of something I don't like – of an absence, a readiness to fight. 'Tell me? Mm?' He frowns, blinks, as if he is unsure of who I am. 'You ask about *my* day? Fucking eight-year-old, bites my thumb – *bites me*. Mother – his mother – does nothing about it. I told her – *showed* her – *sleeve full of blood* – she just laughed. I wasn't even doing anything, whittling at some calculus, hardly anything – little shit bites me. *You want to wait till the hygienist gets you* – I told him – *Think I hurt? She's a fucking nightmare, grown men fucking scream, weep – choke on your own blood, that can happen.*

74

Whispered that before he left the chair. Actually he almost fell out of it, a bit. *Skilled technician.* I am. *I care.* Fixing all these rancid bastards, do they ever say thanks? I don't have to put up with biting. I'm not paid for that.' He pauses and breathes in a mouthful of his Guinness and then forgets that he is angry. His face smoothes like a toddler's, as if he has just woken, tranquil and curious. 'So what about you?' He's beginning to grin. 'Who bit you?' At certain points in the evening, he can shift this way, like the racing of light on a breezy day. He is one man and then gone, as if you've only dreamed him.

Which means that he's not responsible for any previous offence. 'Nobody bit me. Don't be stupid.' Which can be offensive in itself. And I'd like, just now, to keep a hold of my resentment – it will stop me getting tired.

But Robert's working at me, leaning against my arm, making sure I meet at least one solid, lock-picking look, the kind that lets him nudge into my mind and change it. Not that I won't feel better when he does.

Outside, the rain is scraping down in a solid mass, roping and marbling across the coloured glass in the windows and the smallness of the pub seems protective and intended. I would like to stay here. That'll be tricky if I'm still arguing with Robert. And this is just what his expression suggests – that we must be friends and please each other, please ourselves.

He is soothing now, as he means to be. 'What *did* they do to you? Tell Robert what they did and he will go and sort them.'

'Nobody did anything, *I* did . . .' This becomes too complicated to explain and I realise I want to slap him and I want to understand if we're going to be only friends or not – if we're going to meet here, time after time, or if we'll ever leave this tatty box full of elderly men and be somewhere else together again, alone again, the way that we were at the racetrack, in the car. Not that the car was the way I'd have wished, I can recall that it wasn't ideal, but we meant well, we did our best. Anyway, I want us to be alone together and under more suitable circumstances. Or I want to be finally sure that we never will be and able to go away and not think about him. I want him to leave me or help me. I want a clue. 'Fuck you, Robert.'

Of course, this is when he brightens and the colour in his eyes begins to deepen and turn soft. 'Oh, is *that* it?' And I can feel the slip and tumble of the lock.

Together, we raise our arms from our sides just a little to suggest that we would like to hug now, if that's okay with both of us.

Late-evening reflexes stumbling in, our hold rocks and heats and steadies and I don't know if we are both open now and freed for this, or if we've been finally caught by our touch and a mechanism has sprung shut. We may be happy or trapped, but still we blur into each other, that's what I'm sure of, what I like. We balance, unified. I kiss his mouth and miss a little, catch a tart press of fading stout and then his sweet, salt sweat. So I almost forget the way it was this morning when I held the woman on the pavement, held her, and covered myself in her blood.

Robert breathes into my hair, warming the top of my head. His shirt smells of cigarettes and future nakedness. 'Is that it? Fuck me? Fuck you? I mean . . . I mean, the last time . . .' He sounds liquid. So near to last orders, his voice is working towards one smoothed, true sound, it's singing. 'Thought youwere pissed off. After it. When we'd . . . Then. Thoughyou were pissed off withme . . . scared of you . . .'

And I'm almost the same. 'I had to throway a blouse today. My shoes. Chuck 'em.'

'Mm?' Both his hands at the small of my back, resolved and concentrating. We don't fit the bar any more, it hasn't the ambience for this. 'Youblouse . . .'

'Won't wear that suit again.'

'Quiright.' His hip shifting to ease beside the crest of mine. 'You needn't, too . . . not anything you donwant.' He frowns with solicitude and I grow teary, lick his neck. He whispers, forcing the syllables, making them carry his heat. 'So I'll take you home? Go back finish what you started? You'll ruin me, you know that . . . making me want . . . such things.'

'Someone. I threw someone out of a wheelchair today.' Whispering back with Robert's breath so near that we take each other's pace, accommodating every rise and fall. 'Threw an old lady out a wheelchair . . . when theyall came to help her I ran away.' Like this we are invisible and safe, hidden in ourselves. 'I din mean it.'

He twitches against me, then kisses my ear. 'An olady?'

'Yes.'

The twitch digs again, enquiring, 'Little olady?' And his lips tickle my cheek, knowing and playing and stealing me out of my head.

'Yes.'

We both have this tremor now between us, a problem of breath. 'A tiny, little ol . . .' The tremor worsens, jabs. And when I exhale, I discover that we are laughing, both laughing. Very, helplessly and badly and loud. 'A . . . hol lady.'

'Teeny-weeny lady.'

Although we shouldn't be happy, shouldn't even seem happy. 'Wha she do — mug you?'

Although this is awful and hurts our throats and rises up in yelps and coughs and a roaring that sways us, parts us, clatters us in.

'No. But I threw her.'

'Very far?'

And because we are dreadful and have no excuse and because I can't think about it any more, can't have it under my eyelids, or keep the sound she made stuck in my throat, or hear the wee tune she was singing — because I can't put up with it, there is nothing for me — for me and for Robert — but to howl even louder, to shout and squeal.

We are ruined by the time we lean away and see each other, we are wrecked. Robert snuffles and dunts in against my shoulder, eyes wet. 'All this . . . you know? . . . you think you can't believe it . . . sometimes . . . murder and blood and dead babies and God . . . I was telling Doheny, he was here but he's gone . . .' He wipes one cheek with the heel of his hand and sighs unevenly. 'Things like – people eat their children, people do that – God lets them – or what if my father killed my mother? Hmm? I'd be laughing the rest of my life . . .'

'Or *my* father killed *my* mother?'

'Did he? Christ, that's . . . incredibly . . . fuck, I feel nearly sober . . .'

And there is a pause here while we think that we have to go now, leave and make ourselves content. Then we kiss in a small way, this being all that we can bear, while the ache of what we will do next, must do next, hauls us straight out of the pub and across to the car which Robert threads through the shine of the downpour and the running streets until we find my flat.

Beyond that, it's a dash through the sting of rain and letting it make us new, clean, lively, and send us swinging up the stairs, feet unsure of things, but coping well in any case, all the way to my door and the usual business with keys and a shrinking lock and Robert not helping, distracting, but in the end we get inside and start the flail of coats and little arguments with buttons and glimpses of warmth and hints of skin and then both of us are simplified and clear and we do what we should have done weeks before, we do it a lot, we do it until the first birds sing the false dawn, then the real one, until Robert has to scramble out of bed, run to the car with his shirt half fastened, in a rush to be ready for morning surgery.

He accelerates away from the building with a tyre-screech that echoes in the street, earning loud and ironic applause from the flat above mine. Which is fair enough: we may very well have disturbed them – we were undoubtedly noisy enough to have woken anyone and then to have kept them sleepless the whole night. Because that's how we wanted it to be.

IV

Eldest and only children, we're worriers. This is our parents' fault. We are the first time they've done offspring and they have concerns: they suspect we may die or be injured in commonplace, or dreadful, or else quite mysterious ways and so, however happy they may be that we are here, we also prepare in them an undoubted anxiety. We notice this. While we dream in our cots, they prowl round close at hand: partly out of love, or relief that we are quiet, but also because we may simply stop breathing at some preordained, but unknowable, point. Their fears for us weaken the air above our faces and do, in fact, make it tiring to inhale. Surrounded by caution, however affectionate, we grow up suspicious and, whether tentative or reckless, we all know that something awful could overwhelm us at any time.

And then, perhaps, our parents make other, younger children over whom they hardly ever seem to fret. My mother and father – they were thoroughly relaxed around Simon, having tried this parent stuff before without fatalities. So, like a good, eldest child, I worried in their place and kept watch on Simon as if he were kittens, or spun sugar. Whenever I did this I felt contented and in the right, but also aggrieved – not because my parents weren't caring enough towards him, only because it might be that he didn't need their care. As I grew older, I wondered if they saw signs in him that I could not and were therefore sure that Simon wouldn't lead himself to dangers, or be led: that he would be unscathed by nature, while I was not. Needless to say, this worried me.

I now worry most in my mornings, that's why I hate them

– mornings, early evenings, periods spent in bank queues, or near banks, or any part of any Sunday – Sundays are bad. A whole, empty Sunday, lurking on your pillow with the dawn, when you want to stay impenetrable and asleep: you have to avoid that: you have to really concentrate on keeping yourself less than conscious until it's turned Monday again. Or else, you can try my own method of self-defence, which is to work during Sundays and then take your Wednesdays off.

Although this doesn't always help, because a morning is still a morning, even more so when it's taken off. For instance, this Wednesday, the new one I'm staring at – it seems desolate, unsafe, and I am delicate at the moment, due to last night's liquids, and disorientated, too: being currently covered in echoes and ghosts.

Robert left hours ago, but the imprint of him woke me all over again, moving. My skin has shouted up through every dream, playing and replaying him: the shimmer of hands, mouth, stomach, tongue, fingers, his touch as whole as water closing round me, slipping me under, finding everything. And inside, Robert inside, locked, the feel of him rocking, darting, searching, the way he was.

In the vacant daylight, my body has stopped remembering. As soon as I rolled over, stretched, that began to leave me. And my mind can't help me: it knows he was in this bed, nothing more.

So I can smell us having worked here together and that vaguely sugary, caramel scent that he has about himself, but I can't catch a hold of last night – our first proper, improper night – I don't have one fixed detail, except that he fetched me a glass of water.

Lying shoulder to shoulder and the stone weight of his arm across my hip, doubling up our temperature where he touches, until I tell him that I'm thirsty, only for water, just that. And the night is already shading grey outside and we are almost done and I turn with the shift of the mattress and see the shape of him walking from my room – my one room with its walls wedged in against my bed and my table and my sofa and my chair. He goes past the bathroom I've never repainted and on to the kitchen, which I have, and he starts up the clattering search for a glass.

I think of him treating cupboards to the sight of Robert Gardener naked, then closing their doors on some permanent shade of that and stepping back. Finally, I hear him running water, letting it pour until it's raced itself cold in the pipe, until he can slope to my bed, our bed, his hands wet, and offer me the courtesy of water that's almost too chill for my lips, that tastes of him, that tastes of us, us fucking. He shares the glass, then dips his fingers in and lets them drip on to my collar bone.

He tick-tocks me back to the seal of our arms around my memory and then I have the weight of forgetfulness, of losing us.

I would rather remember. I would rather have more.

Then again, I'm surrounded by things that are not as they should be, not what I want. I would like to change the chair that I brought home with me one night and left beside my table to surprise me when I woke – it has a roguish, dog-eared air that I do not enjoy. Likewise, I'd prefer a telephone wholly compatible with British wiring: one which would not generate bills that I have to delay with folded, stapled and purposely illegible cheques. These are not major troubles, but in they rush to pester me, because this is a morning and so I am vulnerable.

They follow me through to the kitchen where I make a small glass of milk with Cointreau, which is both a fruity bracer and light breakfast, as long as you get it down before it curdles. The initial dose is faintly shocking – but you'll trample on a toddler to get the next.

Thereafter, I'm an ounce more bright. Still, this doesn't stop me wondering when Robert might be here again: soon, I would like to hope. Did we arrange that, another visit to my flat? Which is one more thing that I detest, my flat: from the aubergine bathroom suite to the half-finished carpet tiling in the minuscule hall: and its rent is justifiably low, but possibly, in the end, through no fault of my own, I will be beyond paying and turned out on the street and with nowhere else to go, unless I slink off to my parents – my parents who live on the other side of town and who will, doubtless, have heard that I'm back in the dear, old birthplace, back in the gossipy, swollen village that calls itself a city, the greasy, grey-faced hole where no one can ever be truly unobserved.

I *was* going to tell them I'd come home, but first I was busy and then I was nervous and then my delay was embarrassing, a stumbling block in itself, and now it's four months, five, and I worry that I've hurt them and I worry they'll think badly of me and I worry, now that I mention it, whether Robert isn't thinking badly, too – if only because yesterday I threw a woman from a wheelchair to save myself some temporary stress. That isn't a completely normal thing to do.

And, I mean, my life is nowhere near as simple as it may appear. Being me is a job – is labour so time-consuming and expensive that I have to have a second job just to support it. So that I can drink, I have to *get* drink and that isn't something people give away and then there's the drink that I need because I *have* drunk and the other drink I have to keep around because, *sooner or later, I will drink it.* That's a full-time occupation: that's like being a miner, or a nurse. I involve constant work. Robert said he'd be the cross that I would bear, because he didn't under-stand my situation and couldn't know that was a lie. I already have my cross: we've been getting acquainted for years.

The truth of the matter is: yes, you do carry the weight of it, drag it along and heartily wish you were free – especially during mornings, early evenings, periods spent in bank queues, or near banks, or any part of any Sunday. You believe that you should not, and cannot, go on and, naturally, you are right.

84

Because in the end, you will always trade places: this is a physical law: that your cross will change to something merciful, will lift your body up and start the task of bearing you.

I drink myself higher, it's all I need do to ascend. This is my meditation when the worrying gets bad – in conjunction with this lovely truth: that many others long before me have recognised the nature of my calling and left ingenious clues behind them to that effect. Al-khol, ethanol, ethyl alcohol – we christened drink in the magic of distillation, we baptised it with tokens of its heat, the words we give it kindle, burn, shine. They are made out of alchemy, spirits: coloured with Arabic, Latin, Greek: and they hide within their syllables the names for primordial matter and for the ether that soothes between everything, that permeates all substance and all space. C_2H_5OH – generations before its components were discovered, we understood the essence of alcohol, its absolutes: that it is oxygen and hydrogen and carbon – the earth's irreplaceable elements, the water of our life.

I work this all out in my kitchen: how it makes sense and is like a poem, in that it also makes no sense whatsoever, but in any case touches you very much.

When I try to repeat my insights in the bar some few days later, the phrasing does not prosper and I probably lose my thread a little, because I am having to yell – a party of suits has come in and is being disruptive and dragging the volume up. They don't belong here, they are not like the rest of us.

I am yelling at Sniffer Bobby who would be, even in a library, hard of hearing – something to do with explosions and national service. So I have to be loud. I must also be seamless to prevent him from thinking I've finished and then shoving in with an anecdote from the days when he used to sniff. Which is to say, the halcyon time when he rode with removal firms and had as his primary duty the task of sniffing out which boxes and items of furniture and general cubbyholes were being used to hide each household's booze. He loved his work and I am willing to believe that he was extremely good at it, but there is a definite lack of variety in stories which all begin with finding bottles and all end with dropping strangers' ornaments and then passing out in a van.

'Do you see what I mean, though, Bobby? That if there was this kind of a thing in the air, everywhere . . . there isn't, but if there was . . . anyway – we drink it. That's the thing. We look after it. Inside.'

'I looked after thin –'

'It's like being a nun . . . no, like a painter, like that, the man – you know – *tiger, tiger* . . . – him . . . Blake. That's the man. It's like Blake.'

I'm flagging and Bobby can smell it – I can tell he's preparing to wallow off into some saga involving an heirloom dinner service and an unwitting balcony, but I have no more strength to prevent him.

I have spent all evening being cheery and unexpectant and I am exhausted. I am waiting to meet Robert and he is not here. He has been not here for a fortnight, ever since he bolted that morning – maybe running away from me and not towards his surgery – and I have called his number, which I made him write down for me, and I have listened to his answering machine and I have not left a message after his tone, because I don't know what to say. I have called to hear his voice, I have called to try and pick a meaning from it, I have called to guess if he is there and waiting, screening me out.

'. . . oh, he kens everything about the painters – he's an education he is, Doheny, ken? How you're a painter in the first place and no something else. He'll be balancing along the cribby like he's walking to the moon and talking away, an affy boy . . .' Bobby himself will talk away all evening unless someone hits him, swaying up on his toes and then subsiding in a random cycle, as if he has to keep peering over at a far-off cue card just to find his way through his own words.

At one level, I would much rather listen to him than think,

but I don't have the choice – although I can watch his lips, his sounds are dispersing like a softly coloured mist and all I can hear is myself, pacing from wall to wall in my head, exhibiting every sign of cabin fever.

I'm lecturing me about my school uniform. This is super-fluous, because I can remember it perfectly well, but the subtext is clear: I used to wear a blazer with leather patches at the elbows and cared about the Nitrogen Cycle and the Russian and French Revolutions and the difference between *connaître* and *savoir*. I used to know how to swim and proved it on a weekly basis in a regulation bathing costume of startling ugli-ness. I used to be pristine and without swear words or any kind of sexual disgrace. I used not to spend my time trying to sell cardboard, or in pubs full of barmy, old men and screaming suits.

Ah, but I could add that, during my last years at school, I *was* spending my time, in increasingly large amounts, wandering the park after lunch hour in the company of charming and dumpy bottlettes of cider. Before every swimming lesson, I was undressing in a regular state of anxiety caused by crawling skin: not insect-related crawling, only the overall-hatred-of-one's-essential-being type of crawl. That's still a crawl, nonethe-less, and liable to leave a girl feeling unusual, if not unclean. And I could make a big deal about the way I used to picture verb-declension tables, when now I can only picture the ring-pull tops on those bottles of cider (I don't think they make them any more) but *so what*? Everyone is in a state of constant flux, even the dead: they decompose. You change, we change, I change. I can't argue with that, I don't want to. I am not as I was, but no one else is, either – it doesn't mean I'm in decline, it just indicates that time has a habit of passing. Given that years of even average weight will wear down mountains, it's hardly a shock if they've smoothed out parts of me. Take swimming – people say that once you've learned to, you can't forget, but that's a myth, another piece of nonsense: actually the mind is magnificent, given time it can misplace anything. I now have no idea how to conduct myself in water. This is perfectly common and not a reason to get upset.

'Like, he shouldae been lifted, this big sergeant was right there and a panda car and all the lights and that. How he wisnae . . . that's just the boy he is. Doheny, he's . . .'

Bobby's started on the Doheny stories, then – everyone does that here. Whole evenings can disappear in anecdotes about a man I've never met, but already detest, because each of his tales pursues a constant theme: that Doheny gets away with it. He takes the sin without the penance and, no doubt, has never a worry in the world.

Meanwhile, I'm still attempting to chivvy myself into cheerfulness and an improved self-esteem. At least, that's what I'd like to be doing, but it seems that my topic has skipped a beat and – my ego, or id, or whatever and I – we are now making guesses about my heart. There's nothing shaky there, though – my moral well-being is tip-top, I'm very sure. I have a heart of gold.

Then the penny drops, almost tangibly.

My heart.

This is where I was heading, all along.

I've been outmanoeuvred and now I have forced myself far too close to dangerous thoughts of what my heart delights in, of how it has always loved to amuse itself: the things it was made for and the things that it still wants.

I put my hand out to grasp the bar top as the long roll of spotless pleasures I once enjoyed washes in and hits me, makes me sway. The way my mother rubbed the back of my neck when I was tired: her hands impossibly intelligent. I never imagined my own palms and fingers would grow to look like hers: the same shape, but none of the assurance. And, later, when I couldn't please her, when I'd grown into someone incapable of that, I could still bring her close. Creeping through her night house like a stranger, a thief, I could breathe her in:

identify the notes of her usual perfume, privately sensual and light, and, beneath it, a gentleness, a failure of her will, that belonged to me, that was only for me, that we couldn't help.

A person like my mother, they will always forgive you, even while they despise you for every sin which will be the last sin, you promise them faithfully. I didn't intend to disappoint. And I did love to love her and I did love being loved.

The same with my father, whose scent I knew just as perfectly, but as an absence. He occupied a blind spot in my sense of smell, which made it much more wonderful, when I was small, to run up against him and close my eyes and know who he was exactly by the deep, undetectable push of him into my lungs — he was there, but invisible, in the way I was to me, something so near it could never be separate.

And he was good at removing worries, fears. Not that my mother couldn't explain to me beautifully why this or that dire calamity wouldn't give us a second glance. She would draw me off into the kitchen and we would make biscuits and I would forget. Or, if that failed us, she was armed with irresistible statistics and explanations — volcanoes, assassins, foreign troops and other more humdrum afflictions would never have dared approach me while I was under her roof. But I was scared of non-existent horrors, too.

In spite of the highly predictable consequences, I begged and begged to read comics full of vampires which distressed me, or books that I had to leave face down, or trap tight in my shelves, in case their demons might escape and take up residence with me. Werewolves, in particular, were a problem: an evening of Lon Chaney Jr. films, with his sad eyes and hairy feet, could throw me off for weeks — and there are no statistics against werewolves, there is no defence against what can't exist.

Which is where my father came in. He hadn't much to say about my Hammer Horror troubles (or Simon's occasional urges to increase them) but he would listen tirelessly while I recited whatever confection of curses and teeth was obsessing me at the time. Father calmed me by being so clearly a man who was also afraid, an adult who was nervous and needed comfort. (I didn't know then that most adults are like this, but hide it better.) There was, I realised, actually the possibility that my fears were able to frighten him more than me. This seemed so out of proportion that my terrors would shrink and lose credibility and, once I'd exhausted my catalogue of the undead, it would seem only fair to both of us that we should declare them harmless, a hobby, things that no person of my age should fuss about.

Not that the wolf-men didn't tend to stick around – the last to leave, the first to reappear. The lycanthrope's later significance isn't lost on me, of course. How could I not be drawn to such golden-hearted monsters: people who turn amnesiac after dark, whose mornings are groggy and naked and sour-mouthed, whose crimes are always unintended?

Bobby is winking at me. 'Eh, no? Eh?'

I might as well head off home.

'Eh?'

Robert would be here by now, if he was coming. He's not. Again, he's not.

'Eh, no?' Clearly, Bobby's asked me a question and won't let it lie. I could mutter a bland agreement to move things along, but his urgent wink leads me to guess that, despite having spent six or seven decades being truly ugly, Bobby may have drunk himself handsome and could be requesting some kind of erotic insanity on my part. The removal of my central nervous system still wouldn't make this remotely possible and I suspect that my situation may become tricky at any moment, but,

'Thon Doheny, eh? Ye met him, huvye? Meets all the ladies, eh?' He winks again, then begins the massively slow creation of a pantomime frown. 'No offence.'

'No none. Not . . . no. Well, there was offence . . . but not now. I mean, no. Not at all.' I do not wink myself. 'Never met him.'

'Oh.'

'Not an eye have I ever laid on him.'

'Ah, well . . .'

'Couldn't tell him from a greasy, grey-faced hole in the fucking ground.'

'Aye, that . . . happens.'

I'd like to stop doing this and go, 'If he was here, I'd walk right past him.' But I don't seem to be able. 'There was this . . . somebody told me . . . Robert told me.' Bobby drops his head and looks respectful in a way that irritates – I don't know if he's trying to be consoling because I've been dumped, or if he thinks Robert is dead – but, either way, I could do without the sympathy. 'Doesn't matter who told me, point is I've heard about Doheny . . . not unaware . . . I have stories.'

Well, one story: or, rather, a summary impression of the Ideal Alcoholic's infinite resourcefulness. Given that my pronunciation and coherence were not of the best, the hour being late and the atmosphere chokingly smoky, I would summarise my Doheny story as follows:

Although he's supposed to be the Patron Saint of Drinkers, Doheny isn't supernatural. He has his weaker points. It may be that he is so tediously well loved, precisely because he has apparently exposed himself to every inconvenience of the drinking life. Of course, in the stories, he triumphs over each of them with grinding consistency. For example, he has almost never wet a stranger's bed unless this was intended. I find it very hard to believe, but have been told that, away from home, he sports some strange variety of latex underwear – the snug and erotic kind – which encloses both him and his member in a waterproof second skin, a sort of massively overanxious condom. And I'm sure that such items do exist, but I don't wish to picture Doheny – a man who must be in his forties, at least, and who has never been described to me as dashing – slowly working himself down inside a pair. Worse still, the business end of this sheathing is fixed into a length of plastic hose — God knows how this would look — and the hose, in its turn, can be gaffer-taped to any container, window sill, grating, duct or who can imagine what. Doheny, we're meant to accept, arrives equipped and sleeps immobile, like a rock: any unconscious emissions diverted away, just as neatly as he could wish, because Doheny, as everyone says, always thinks things through.

But his thinking is at its most acute when he comes to that final, sad loss of control, the public shame of every underachieving drunk: vomit. With vomit, Doheny excels.

His pockets contain many carrier bags in which he can catch whatever his body decides is superfluous, the whole operation concluded as he stands at a bar, or leads — why not? — a witty conversation, or pleasures some, no doubt rubber-besotted, female. An elegant twist of the bag, a knot, and the warm and supple parcel can be popped down anywhere convenient.

Doheny can also projectile vomit at will and I can see the use of this: when someone is far too annoying, or they have the wrong hair, or when there is no solution and bad history and no love and no more to say and you just want them fucking gone — that would do it, vomit would clear them, they would go.

But he is playful, too — Doheny — and sociable, the unlooked-for-but-sparkling guest at any party. I've been assured that he once treated a number of Finns to a nocturnal skating spree by adding vomit, in not inconsiderable amounts, to the tiled floor of the breakfast room in an unnamed Tallinn hotel. Having explained and then demonstrated the physical principles involved, Doheny then left them to slide about, in great high spirits, until the small hours and the authorities' arrival.

But, to me, the only tale that sounds remotely true is far more personal and has a brand of nasty elegance. When Doheny begins to pass out in any hostile environment, he scrambles for his wallet and throws it deep into whatever pool of half-digested fun he can produce. He then rests unconscious with a quiet mind and all his money safe. Whatever Doheny needs, Doheny keeps — he's like a terrier, that way, like a deadfall trap.

The smoke isn't so bad when I've finished my Doheny

recitation — I can't think why — but I'm suddenly, crashingly tired. My head is drifting back, or to the side, and then nagging till I snap it back into line. The drift and snap are becoming tiring in themselves. I have to get home. People will think that I'm drunk when really I'm exhausted. Anyone would be, spending this much time listening to Bobby, while thinking about Robert, expecting Robert — which is the same name, pretty much, although not the same person, of course. And why is Robert *Robert* and not *Bobby, Robbie, Rab . . .*? Why make this choice and not some other? There must be a meaning in that.

I don't know exactly when, but I sat down during my story and this is proving to be a problem, because I don't seem quite fit to get up again. The chair's arms are slithery leather, highly rounded and possibly waxed, so there's no earthly chance that I'll catch hold of either one. This must contravene health and safety regulations for a public house. I have an average hand, with average strength and I'm a totally normal weight — if *I* can't struggle up out of this then what would a weak person do, a disabled person?

Not that I have any wish to consider a disabled person.

Which is a further disadvantage of this chair — it invites unpleasant recollections.

An armchair in a bar, this kind of bar, this honest, plain and sensible bar. Who would arrange that? It simply isn't practical.

The other complication would be that the bar doesn't have any armchairs, not anywhere.

Not one.

This is a problem.

It never has possessed an armchair. Not as far as I'm aware.

Yes. A problem.

Looking down, here are my hands, my forearms, my thighs and knees in their summertime, tailored, khaki slacks — surprisingly stylish — and that's the edge of my summertime peach short-sleeved blouse and that's definitely a leather armchair underneath me – burgundy sort of thing, good quality, a bit old, and not entirely dissimilar to the armchair

'Hannah?'

there used to be an armchair

'It's three in the morning.'

I can remember an armchair

'Your father went to bed.'

It is perfectly the same as an armchair that's in the living room that's in my parents' house.

'He won't be asleep, but he went to bed. Have you stopped now? Is that what you came here to say?'

The living room which has sneaked in and sprung up around me while I was distracted, talking.

An armchair. Yes.

'Well, I'm going now, too. Do you understand? Hannah?'

This is my mother's voice: no getting away from it.

'You were the best thing in my life.'

If I raise my head now I can look at her: I'm sure she's very close, but I'd rather just listen for a while.

'The best thing.'

Not that listening is good – hearing her make that dry, half-laugh which comes when a person discovers they've been deluded, tricked into believing you're human and they should care. And it's not a surprise that her voice has a pain in it, too, and a weary burn of anger and it sounds small, contracted, which means – not that I didn't know – that she is speaking both to me and about me. This is how I make her sound.

'Your room is there for you. He got it ready. *Do you understand?* Your father got it ready for you.' She's standing now, I can tell, and walking off to my left. 'When I heard you were back, I knew you'd come here in the end. He didn't think so, but I knew.' She breathes with a shallow, troubled, little labour. 'I wish you hadn't. You're killing him.' And I would like it so much if she were only happy, if she had no trouble of any kind.

She breathes some more and then leaves me, once she can see that I do quite understand I'm killing everyone.

I wake at six, unrested, and look at the beautiful room my parents gave me a long time ago: the bookshelves still clinging to Tolkein and Nesbitt and the sharply coloured paperbacks that appeared when I hit my teens, the True Crime and the pseudo-horny thrillers and the textbooks beside the extra text-books my mother bought to help explain them. She wanted me to do well. The poster of the Van Gogh night sky with the twisted pine – I left that behind me when I moved away – and, everywhere else, the drawing-pin holes and the tiny stains of Blu-Tack on the wallpaper with the fawny and grey and cream stripe that I chose with my mother because I thought it looked mature. Actually, it looks like being in prison, but perhaps that is mature.

'I heard you.'

My father leaning against the doorway, as if he is feeling casual, but really he's keeping the wood at his back to steady him – I can see this in his face. And he looks down at me, lying on top of my bed, still fully dressed, and my skin, I would guess, pallid and my lips, I am sure, wine red, as if the drink has made internal injuries.

'Do you want tea? I can make us tea.' As if his doing something shipshape and domestic will change us to straightfor-ward people with a firm relationship. 'Would that be . . . Do you want tea?'

I mean to nod, to please him at least that much, but I can't: my head is too heavy and cautious to be moved. I am fixed here like some terrible carving, my face turned towards him, an object that might remind him of his little girl.

My father is wearing a dressing gown and pyjamas that must be years old. They could almost convince me I'm dreaming a memory, or that I've fallen back inside a year when things were still all right. He's different, though, frailer, pale with time.

I manage the best smile I can and I watch this produce a type of panic, tense him for a hurt that I will cause.

I clear my throat and find I taste unclean. 'Ah, that's . . . I'd . . . I'm sorry.'

'Do you want tea?'

'I'm so sorry.'

One of his hands is tugging at the other and his eyes are wet, which must give him a view of the bedroom very like my own, a spreading blur. Odd how crying can make humdrum objects seem startling, webbed in light.

'No need. No need to be sorry.'

He was right to be fearful, I am hurting him. I don't mean to. And when it's this clear that I'm helpless, can't stop myself doing damage: then I hurt him again.

He opens his mouth and I'm sure that he's going to let loose this dreadful noise, a wail that will bring us both back to our senses, but he only mumbles, 'Oh dear,' and steps forward, blinking intently at the floor. 'That's . . . that's not good.' He crosses to the bedside cabinet and pauses, picks up the tumbler he must have left for me last night beside a plastic bottle of mineral water. I would like to reach and touch him and say thanks, but I do not and he fusses away to the centre of the room and softly kneels. 'That's . . . No wonder, Hannah. No wonder you didn't sleep well.' He stands, still murmuring, walks out into the passage and away.

I cast about for the mineral water and drain the bottle, swallowing the taste of dying and bad responsibility. It takes concentration to sit up, to swing my feet down to the floor, to stand while the blood complains between my stomach and my head.

He's left the tumbler upturned on the carpet, a splinter of light from the window, sparking against it aggressively. And there is a movement underneath, a darkness. Once I've eased myself closer, the motion solidifies into a scuttle of life – the fat body, the wave of legs, the scramble and fall of a spider trapped fast and fighting mechanically at the glass, wearing it down by atoms. It doesn't stop.

Downstairs, I can find no one and it takes me an aching time to search, so I have to climb upstairs again, grimy with chemical sweat, and lie on the bathroom floor for a moment to try and take on its cold. Then I lift myself up, go out and walk past what used to be Simon's room, then what used to be mine and then I fingertip open the final door.

My parents are inside it, on their bed, my mother sitting in her white lace nightdress, her prettiest one, and my father still in his dressing gown, lying curled with his back to the door, his head in her lap. She is resting her palms flat against him, earnest and still, as if she is wishing him stronger, or hoping to draw a poison out.

Only her eyes shift to me when I halt, already trespassing, and we don't speak. It is clear in her face that she hasn't slept, that I mustn't disturb my father any more, that I should go away from their house and leave them be. I think that she will cry soon, but that she doesn't want me here to see.

In one hand, my father is holding an old postcard. If he could, he would have come back to my room, slipped it in under the tumbler and then lifted the spider, taken it outside and let it go alive. He always tries to let things go alive.

V

Filth.

I need filth. That's the only way to swing this, thinking of filth: nothing else is going to get me through.

Because sometimes there *is* nothing else: you have no resources and your personal situation is less than ideal, so what can you do but hope that somewhere low in your imagination there are images and fragments vile enough to simulate at least a gill of Scotch.

Church. Me in a church. What was I thinking? What could I ever have thought would excuse this? I do not go to church.

But here I am.

And my sole support for the rest of the service – forty-five minutes, two days, a week? – if it's longer than half an hour, then it might as well be a week – the only thing scraping me through is the faint, but still repulsive, aftermath left by 200 millilitres of cough medicine.

Cough syrup, it's a curse. Temptation may incline your heart towards it, I realise that: the warmth you know it lights, the way it lingers, that nursery type of numbness it lays down: but the stuff is appalling and does you no good. The flat, slope-shouldered bottles, they're the worst – you can tell they'll be snug in the pocket and hardly any weight and if you're stuck in a certain mindset, the not-drinking-much-these-days mindset, then every brand of cough mixture becomes suddenly, tragically effortless to buy and guzzle down. You want it and then you want more of it and each purchase is a joy, because cough mixture isn't a drink and if you're not drinking a drink, then you can't be drinking.

But don't presume that you'll escape unscathed — these aren't the kind of liquids that will love you: Benilyn, Veno's, Covonia, Buttercup Syrup, or the weird, patent brands with Victorian labels and wicked ingredients, the ones that raise hopes of morphine and laudanum, the ones that you find in those furtively small, independent chemists — well, never mind what the brands are, none of them will even try to make you happy. In fact, many have been emasculated in an untrusting attempt to prevent misuse. Nevertheless, they will all of them give you a 5 a.m. headache that makes you quite certain you hanged yourself overnight, or that you should have.

And they glue the mouth. Waking with your tongue stuck to your teeth and your soft palate, your molars fused together, your gums and cheeks immovable, your lips fixed to your canines and each other — you won't enjoy that. Levering yourself open with your fingers and anticipating blood, trying to decipher your condition while you blink into consciousness — and on one memorably sweaty occasion imagining that your whole mouth has magically ceased to exist — that's no earthly use, not for anyone. That is much less than even you deserve. As are the hours of swilling and scrubbing and retching it will take to get you halfway sluiced and capable of talking.

And talking, that's when you notice — after maybe one day of linctus your speaking voice can drop an octave, more. Try it and you'll see. For a while, you'll bounce back, your vocal cords will shake themselves free, or stretch, or else dilate — I'm unfamiliar with the mechanisms at work, but I know that you'll probably sound like yourself within forty-eight hours. Only, if you keep on with the syrups, the linctuses and mixtures, then eventually you'll end up just like me: singing alto if you're lucky and willing to strain.

Which is exactly what I'm doing now.

'Yet with the woes of sin and strife
The world has suffered long
Beneath the angel str—'

And the rest.

My brother is standing beside me, hitting the same key that I am and chipping a glance across at me, now and then, because I am consequently inaudible. I am breathing correctly and framing up every word, but my growl has disappeared beneath his own. And I am also singing softly, because I'm ashamed of my throat — it is plainly a sign of a badly planned life.

Beside my brother is his wife. My brother has a well-planned life, including hobbies and a marital partner: one with blonde hair to the small of her back and an oblong mouth. My brother is a doctor, he has a career.

And a wife, really a wife. Simon has a wife. How did that happen?

Beside me and to my left is a stylish, young woman worshipper, perfectly soprano, who is shifting, almost shuddering, as I make my best attempt towards 'its ancient splendours fling'. She has decided, I believe, that I am some sort of transvestite, unsuitable for public worship in a Catholic church. When we finally subside on to the pew, she makes very sure that our coats don't brush.

You're uncomfortable? What about me? You think I feel at home here? I'm woozy with Dr Someone's Expectorant Linctus and I haven't been inside a church for decades. I'm not even Catholic, I'm just standing and sitting and kneeling when everyone else does, although — God knows, and I mean that literally — most of us here are tourists, we've come for the carols and are quietly wondering what we'll do if they start to recite something Latin or dole out communion.

Me, I'd go and get that: I've never drunk wine someone's blessed. And in hospitals I always say I'm Catholic in case I want to have the last rites. I do tend to believe that I'll need them and communion would be a start.

Simon wanted me to come here, to the carol service. He

invited me – this was his plan. He'd found out where I work, called up their number, and they'd passed him on to my mobile. Imagine my surprise, braving the fog and the black ice to be about CPG's business and I'm yanked to a perilous halt by his voice, my brother's voice. 'Is that you? This is Simon. *Is* that you?' I pulled up on a dirt track – both hands visibly shaking, who can say why? – and parked the company van beside a hedge. I could pick out every frozen cobweb in the leaves while he was speaking – you wouldn't think a silk so fine could stand to carry a heavy frost, although I've heard it's stronger than you'd guess, I think I read that somewhere.

Simon told me I should come and see him, and that he *wanted* to see me.

The drift from my exhaust like mist across the layers of hills and fields: all frozen to flat grey: everything grey except the white cobwebs, as if they'd been drawn, or scratched clear through to the faultless blank beneath a picture – *Scene from a Selling Life*.

As opposed to *Scene from a Family Life*.

But never mind pictures, it was truly the case that Simon wanted me to come and be with him. I hadn't assumed that, or made it up.

And I couldn't say no when he'd gone to such trouble in searching me out and the best choir for miles would be singing – who can resist a good choir? – and a bit of the festive spirit would do no harm and why hadn't he heard from me? – well, I couldn't completely make that clear – and, hardly surprising, he managed to nudge in a hint that my recent visit to Mother and Father had left its mark.

But Simon's reason for calling, the big one, his great news, the thing he was desperate for me to know? She's pregnant: the wife that I always forget about, she's up the duff. My little brother is going to have a baby. Not sure what the sex is yet, it's too early to say, and they think they'd rather not be told ahead of time: as long as it's healthy, as long as nothing goes amiss, that's what matters most. Here his words got cloudy and there was a fumble of noise and a break while the boy that I used to take care of let himself adjust again to his new and enormous happiness.

So I drove, as directed, to Glasgow, which is where Simon lives, and now I'm sitting in an afterglow of incense in the middle of a church, which is where God lives – right where He can see me, where He can lean in and have a long, hard look.

It's ugly in here where *I* live, inside my skin, I don't pretend it isn't. But what else could it be? There's nothing currently outside me, except a national celebration of being pregnant, the customary, mindless baby-delight: *Laetare, laetare, Virgo parit filium* and the manger and the swaddling and the cherries, the ships, the kings and the fucking star. Nothing but rejoicing, no attempt at balance, no touch of shade to break the endless light for those of us who'd like to rest our eyes. Why is it I've never sung a carol about the slaughtered innocents, the tots Herod put to the sword? I should imagine that there isn't one, or by now I'd have found it and that simply isn't fair.

Just like the fact that our theme for today will be unremitting joy and Mary expecting without sin and I must say that my brother's wife is also quite the lady for keeping things clean – his whole relationship with her is stainless and solid and rich in openly shared moral certainties. They might as well both be virgins: they are inhumanly far from transgression.

Without her, he was different, relaxed.

Not any more, though, not since he's been paired and silted up with ignorance and bliss – the two of them, they have no idea. They never will walk through their days, hemmed in with the scent of a child they haven't got, won't have, can't have. Their lives are not conspiring to keep their son or their daughter permanently out of reach. They don't feel it trot up and rest itself against them when they can't bear to think of it. They don't speak to it under their breath and tell it the things it ought to understand and point out sights of interest and little funny happenings, or explain the peculiar ways some people have of doing this and that. They don't hold it growing and wasting in them like a frozen mist – the impossible baby, the one who would let them be tender. They aren't afraid to name it, because of how sick and meaningless that will make it, will make them.

God can stare down at that for as long as He wants to. A bottle and a half of medicated blackcurrant and menthol and dying childless: that's what I'm full of. He can dip in His finger and taste that at any time, I don't mind. As I was in the beginning, I am now and shall be ever after and I didn't intend me to be this way – He did.

'I'm His fault.'

The woman worshipper startles into turning and seeing my face, the state of it. There's a wriggle of sympathy somewhere in the middle distance of her eyes and bless her for that – why not? – but I sink to my knees with the rest of the congregation before she is moved to make something come of it. My brother nudges me in the shoulder but I ignore him, forehead flattening my hands against the rail: skin wet, eyelids wet, and aiming my disarray tightly down towards the floor, tucking myself out of sight.

If God has to keep His eye on this, then I can't stop Him, but nobody else has to watch.

Sometimes I believe in Hell on Earth, or that Hell *is* Earth, but then I'll remember God: everywhere and endlessly, in each body and in each mind, He has to see everything. God the Only Child, the worrier, the One who frets over details and makes lists. They say Jesus had brothers and sisters – but not God, how could He? He's always all alone with nothing but us.

Not that we're aware of His distress. Or maybe it's been here forever, before the stars and continents, and maybe we'd only notice if it stopped.

Or maybe that's shite.

And, Jesus Christ, it's 'O Little Town of Bethlehem' *next.*

That'll either be up too high, or down too low — I'm not going to manage, wherever they pin the first note. And the incense is stinging my tongue.

I can't resort to a further dash of linctus because my brother will notice and be upset, but I am becoming severely unsteady without it, especially at the thought of climbing back on to my feet. The dome is too far away above me, tensing and stretching against the uprush of faith, and the children in the choir are glistening with goodness and sucking in yards of air, then racing it out, much purer than before, and I am soaking with filthy syrup, although it's not nearly as filthy as I know myself to be.

And that's what I need to save me: filth.

Please, God, grant me filth.

Which leads to guilt, which leads to self-pitying affront and then to more guilt and the tang of hellfire, followed by a burst of undignified whining against the injustice of my lot and then round again and then again until I get too frightened and stop, but at least it creates some kind of energy, enough to rod up through my spine and clamp my knees to pre-empt buckling. And, should I choose to retrieve some specific misdemeanours, I can also enjoy the frisson of sin recalled in a sanctified space, the shiver I was already prone to during school services — although, as a child, I could have split my soul clear open like an apple and found it only minimally unclean, more of an overall creamy colour, an antiqued white instead of the full shine. Today, I can't imagine what it's like: as red as flesh, Jackson Pollocked with indiscretions, worn back to a dirty sliver like old soap. Still it's mine, it's never left me, never tried.

I have no child and no hobbies and no plans in any direction, I can't even sing any more, but I can always rely on my soul, my record of sin. It's my life's work. I lie, blaspheme and covet, I keep Sundays busy and unholy, I quarrel with God and sometimes recourse to violence along with the pettier kinds of theft, I upset my parents and others I know less well,

I've avoided murder – but not for the want of wanting – and I cannot commit adultery, having not married anyone, but I can assist, and as for the many other brands of fornication, well, sampling has taken place.

Fornication. That's the balm to ease my eyes shut and let me hack right through the Little Town of Bethlehem, relying on remote control – after all, I have been singing it since I was six – while I remember watching Robert, myself and Robert: while I study the pulse and stubble at his throat.

No, before that. When I open my front door and he's out in the close, leaning one hand on the institutionally yellow-painted wall. Mr Gardener, live and in person.

I almost swing the whole view shut again and pretend I haven't seen it, because this evening I am practically used to his absence, balanced after so many weeks, and he is the only person who can upset me. But then he smiles.

And this is his true smile, the deep one. This is innocence and apology, this is proof of some irremovable hurt, this is a need that he could die of and the knowledge that I am his cure, this is a nakedness that's just for me, this is how well we know each other and what a terribly fast, raw path that makes for us beyond every defence. This is, I have to admit, why I can do nothing but let him in. 'You took your time.'

The drinker's smile, the key to every lock.

'I was in Canada.'

'For a fucking month?'

'No.' He steps over the threshold gently and blinks at me. 'Only the ordinary type of month. I went out for a pint of milk and when I woke up . . .'

'You were in Canada.'

'Yes.' He says this in a quiet and still mystified way that makes me believe it may be true. 'At first I was . . .'

'Not well?'

'Mm-hmm. And then I didn't have the money to get back. My ticket ended up lost.' His face is thinner and wary.

'Well, I should have words with you, if I were you. Give yourself a good talking-to.'

'Don't worry. I have.'

His jacket is new and seems too big: it's the type of thick, red-and-black-checked lumberjack affair that I suppose you could buy anywhere, but it does look more Canadian than anything else. I can't ask to inspect its label. I consider for an instant that it must be overly hot for the end of September. He smiles again as I frown at it, this time just a tired grin, maybe jet-lagged. 'Bright, isn't it?'

'Slightly. Do you have the matching snowshoes?'

'I didn't think you'd want to see me.'

'Maybe I don't. I just opened the door, I had no idea it was you.'

'I thought you'd recognise my knock.'

'I didn't know you had a knock.'

'The *way* I knock. I thought you'd . . . Is there anyone in the room?' He nods his head to the half-open door, behind which I am keeping no one. I assume we are caught here, standing, because we have lost the power to move.

'No, no. I'm here by myself.'

'I thought there might be someone else.'

'There could have been.'

'I know.'

'But there isn't.'

'I asked in the bar.'

'Oh, did you.'

'They thought there wasn't.'

'They could be wrong.'

'But they're not?' His mouth is uneasy enough when he says this for me to kiss it. He tastes of airline toothpaste, but the rest is familiar: the gift of his weight, his heat, the lean in before he draws me back to him. He's brushed his teeth, but hasn't shaved and this seems fine, the friction of his cheek seems to make him more thoroughly here. There is a flinch in his jaw that I don't understand. His hands smell of meat.

'I wanted you, Mr Gardener.'

'I wanted *you*.'

'You could have phoned.'

'I know . . . but, stuff happened. It was difficult . . . But I know. Could we get out of here? I mean, I'd like to. I want to show you where I work. I want you to see that. I've seen your things. We never got round to mine.'

'Now?'

'Yes.'

'Well . . .'

'Otherwise, there'll be patients . . . I can't show you everything when I have patients. Not the way I would like.'

'What happened while you were gone – to the patients, the surgery?' I try, but not overly hard, to sound unsuspicious.

'Locum . . . Not ideal, though: my disappearing. Not what anyone wants. They were very cross. Everyone was very cross. I did call them. But not you – I am sorry – but I knew you'd be . . . very cross.' He closes his meat hands on either side of my face and a hint of pain thrums in his forearms. 'I'm glad you were at home. Glad you opened the door.' He lets me go. 'I'm on probation now. Lots of probation. With everyone.' And examines my face.

I hadn't felt like the bar that evening, I'd stayed in with a couple of milkshakes and my unlicensed radio – otherwise, he wouldn't have found me, I might have been anywhere.

Instead, I'm fixed in my own hall, waiting while he studies me, until he's searched out whatever he wants, or compared me to a memory, or made sure I'll become one. I lean close until I can taste him in my breath, but I don't touch, because I am being reserved now, still adjusting, and because I am saving him for later. Then I get my jacket and lead him out to the company van.

Robert's voice is small and dry as he directs me and I drive us towards the end of the estuary, to the nice suburbs and then beyond to a little sea town surrounded by caravan parks and stripped grain fields, dark potato rows, almost ready to be torn away.

'This is it.'

It's dark when I pull up outside a dull gleam of whitewash. Sunk into this are a black door and a black-framed window in which stands an animated model of a dentist waving an over-sized toothbrush, up and down, across a set of frighteningly painted teeth. The teeth are large enough to stand level with his chest, crouched like a giant mollusc of some kind, clearly capable of biting him in half. Behind the waving is a back-ground of faded posters about sporting gum shields and pros-thetics and the evils of sweetened drinks for the under-fives.

'Good God.'

'Oh, him. That's Henry — he used to be a cobbler.'

'What?'

'You know — the mechanical cobblers with the wire-rimmed glasses and the white hair and the hammers they batter about near their lasts. They used to be everywhere — like those big, metal boys with the leg braces they'd park outside shops, collecting for something — more paint for metal boys . . . You remember . . .'

'Not really.' I examine the dentist's glasses and wooden rictus — in combination with the white coat and the blankly painted eyes, they strongly suggest a quite different past involving elec-trical torture and South American uniforms.

'We put him in a coat, swapped the hammer for a brush, made up some teeth — that's why his action isn't really what it should be, he's still trying to hammer nails into the gums. Come on.'

Robert unlocks the black door and I follow him up a narrow flight of stairs packed with the smell of heated calcium, mouth-wash and disinfectant and panicked sweat. Behind me the converted cobbler flails endlessly away, trying to subdue the nightmare dentures and possibly wishing for fresh electrodes and rubber gloves.

'Do people *like* that? It doesn't put them off?'

'Everyone's scared of dentists – after him, I seem quite friendly. And I tell the very little nippers that if they don't behave, then the clockwork dentist will come and get them in the night. Never fails to impress – although he actually runs off the mains . . . So. Here we are.' He gently dunts his fist beside an unwilling Yale and then we slip in past the brass plate that proclaims Robert Gardener to be a BDS and an MSc. This seems oddly unlikely, although I'm sure it's true.

The surgery is small and very bright. A glass partition defends the receptionist's desk and alcove, with its predictable picture postcards, bad seaside calendar and merrily orthodontic cartoons. Branching off a central hallway are four doors marked WAITING ROOM, TOILET, X-RAY and MR GARDENER, respectively. The other, intriguingly blank, doors conceal, as Robert shows me, a cramped tea-making nest equipped with a cracked sink and a wooden chair, bearing an unemptied ashtray and many, rather dull shelves of supplies.

'Back in a moment.' He briefly squeezes my arm and then pads away while I consider this last cupboard. If Robert is the man I take him for and if I have gained any benefit from suffering Sniffer Bobby's stories, then it may be that somewhere here, in appropriately devious seclusion, there is at least one alcoholic bottle, tucked up and asleep. I feel, with Bobby's example, that I should be capable of sniffing it out and pouring it awake.

I begin the search.

lignocaine hydrochloride, dexamethasone

I know a man whose work is in these words: in chemicals and how the body lets them touch it.

potassium nitrate, articaine hydrochloride, epinephrine.

I love a man whose work is in

No.

That's not what I wanted to say, that's the word I never think of, in case I'm listening.

polyhexanide, propylene glycol

A slip of the mind, that's what it was. I'm just overreacting because I've missed him and now he's here again. No need for words that I'll regret.

And it's his booze we're after, remember?

As if anyone could forget.

Unruly stacks of boxes full of other, smaller boxes. No drinker's logic in any arrangement that I can see: no trace of subterfuge and hidden tracks, only jars and tiny, svelte containers of strictly dental purpose, everything honest and above board.

zirconium oxide, zinc oxide, epinephrine bitartrate, formaldehyde

But there will be a lie here somewhere: a flagon of disinfectant that isn't, gloves that are not gloves, needles that are not needles, wadding that gives up a chuckle, a cluck of frightened liquid when you shake it.

Yes.

A package of absurdly heavy cotton wadding and, under the top layer, a sheen of glass, the virgin seal around a cap with the scrawly, red signature – *Paddy*. I should have known: it's the lovable-ugly orphan of Irish whiskeys, the one with the big ears that scuffles in the dust at playtimes over by the fence. It's 40 per cent proof, though: who needs a mother and father when you're that.

'I see. You've found me out.' Robert, as quiet as his breath, sets himself behind me, catches my elbows before I can turn, and then rests his chin on the crown of my head. 'But that's for later. This first.'

And gently he explains his substances, rocking until I rock with him, his voice low in his chest, flaring in with his heat to my spine. 'These are the anaesthetics, so I don't hurt anyone. This is a kind you put into the bone – it's very good for awkward cases, for people who can't help feeling too much pain. And this covers wounds and helps to heal them. And this makes everything clean. And this is for preparation, so that I can build a bond. And these are what I build *with*, how I put things right. I have anything I might want for anything. I can be good at what I do, you know? I have been good. Once I've done you can eat and speak and bite and drink and kiss as if you'd never had a problem. People have thanked me. I used to get letters.'

'That's great.'

'It *was* great. It was really great.'

Then Robert lets me move, step out of his reach and round to find him, face him.

'Oh.'

At first it is almost hard to understand that he is naked. Tension putting a fast, shallow rise in his chest and smoothing the skin against his ribs, a fresh bruise large on his hip, the older grazes on both knees, bare feet: I have to take him in piecemeal, because he is so much. Shadows and splinters, that's all I could remember, but here he is whole, the full, pale ache of him. A tick of nerves in one wrist and so he raises his hand to smoothe across his forehead and I follow the motion up until I'm halted by his eyes. He swallows and his blush begins, rimming his ears. Silly, blushing now.

It seems that if I touch him we will cry. 'Robert Gardener. That's you, Robert Gardener.'

We are both very near to sober – he may even be completely sober. And being without clothes is one thing – is a fine thing – but being without clothes and without drinking and about to do what we have to be about to do – that's completely another thing and one that we've never attempted. Like this, I don't know if I can stand how beautiful he is – the rush of that and need and hormones and nothing to smooth it out, nothing to keep me held so I can focus.

I don't want to fall over and I think I might.

Then he gives me that little glance, that small, specific glance you both recognise: the mix of shame and pride and resignation: the way men always have of saying they know you're going to look at their prick next, give it some time.

We've met before, of course – Robert's prick and I – but not like this. We've never been formally introduced.

And there's no room in this for saying anything – not to tell him that he's lovely, that all of him is lovely and couldn't be anything else and not to tell him that I disapprove absolutely of circumcision, but love that he is circumcised, because it lets me be selfish, lets me like to have him always so deeply, clearly stripped for my benefit. Even when he isn't hard he looks closer to it, more ready.

But now he is hard, quite ready enough.

'Robert Gardener.'

He stays as quiet as I do and walks out of the storeroom, waits for me in the hall.

'No. Don't do that. Not at the moment.' Robert gathers my hands together in his before I can reach him. Then, concentrating on his fingers, frowning down, he methodically removes my jacket, my blouse, my bra.

He doesn't pause. 'What we do at the moment is this. And this.'

I hold his head as he bows it and then kisses, suckles the way a son would, then teases, bites, because he is a man and, either way, draws out my heart from me like a thorn. I'm hauled out beyond myself, beneath myself, outside myself, inside his mouth.

I love his tongue. No other word will do it. I love his tongue.

And the sweet scalp underneath his hair and the drive of his breath, the fierce push of his cheek and the howl, our howl, the one we make out of our skin.

Which is all very well, but it isn't filth.

What I was after was filth.
You'd think I could summon something up.

But no.

Not fucking on the padded bench in his waiting room, or on the hallway floor – that's a blood-coloured haze, I can't bring it into focus. I can't even grab at thumping each other down and into the cold vinyl grip of his chair – quite naturally his chair – you're going out with a dentist, you'll have to want to fuck him in his chair, at least talk about doing it – first place you would think of. Although we didn't go there first.

No, we started in the hall, began with unbearable gentleness, with his mouth finding my breasts.

I talked the whole time, babbled, couldn't help it. 'My wee man, my good man, my good lamb, that's . . . that's my man . . . that's shhh, you're my man, it's fine, it's all fine, you're my man, it's fine.'

Which also isn't filth – it's the way you nail yourself to someone else without even thinking: forever and ever, amen.

> 'O holy child of Bethlehem
> Descend to us we pray
> Cast out our sin and enter in
> Be born in us today.'

I scramble for the final line and thump into my seat. Both the woman and my brother stare at me, but I am facing straight ahead and concentrating

I used to roar that out when I was ten or twelve – the last verse would just rake through me and I'd imagine it boiling me clean as it went. I had hopes of moral improvement then and possibly an office job, or something in education, because teachers have the longest holidays.

Two more pages of hymns and a prayer to get through and I'm certain I won't last. I can't govern my breath and I'm sweating. If I don't get some cold, unsanctified air very soon, I will throw up. My leaving early won't please Simon, but my projectile vomiting over co-worshippers would annoy him a lot more.

'Stepping outside.'

He frowns at me, as if I'm a stupid child. 'What?'

I murmur again, 'Stepping outside. Need air.'

'Hannah . . .'

'I'll wait. Outside. I'll wait.' By which point I've already forced the pious soprano to one side and popped a couple of pensioners up out of their seats, disturbing their view of the designated reader, currently intoning something about sheep. I chose to wear the baseball boots this morning, they're comfy for long drives, so each of my footfalls combines an echoing slap with a sharp squeak.

I am a disgrace. I know this. But it's been true for years, there is no reason for it to hurt any more than usual today.

The door growls after me as I try to ease its closing, slowing it with my back.

I sit on the church steps and chug the other 100 millilitres of syrup. This is foolish, because I don't have any more, but it firms me up, lets me enjoy the prickle of frost in my lungs and the fresh, blue day above. Under my skull, I'm as warm as burning toast and close to happy.

This would have been better if Robert had been here, except he didn't want to come.

Although happy retreats as I think of it, suddenly shy and insubstantial.

No. He isn't here, because he didn't know he could be, because I didn't tell him. But I didn't tell him, because I knew he wouldn't want to come. If it hadn't been for Simon, I wouldn't have come.

The cold of the step is soaking through into my legs and there is an oily film of loneliness blurring my teeth.

I'd have lasted the whole of the service with Robert: we'd have kept ourselves straight.

I have never shown Simon any of my partners: even the ones who haven't been a source of shame. Robert, I could take anywhere, he has dignity. But I'm still superstitious: it doesn't do to declare yourself, to identify the joys you'd hate to lose.

Leaching through the stained glass comes the choir, with something complicatedly tuneless and in Latin. They sound, nonetheless, contented and in a while they will patter out, shining, their duty done and the priest will stand somewhere near here and shake parishioners' and strangers' hands and the steam of breath and festivity will be thickened with bursts of fellow feeling and respect, little recollections of childhood, cocoa, early to bed on a Sunday before school.

My own recollections refuse to retreat any further back than Robert's surgery and our final, emptied tiredness. We were cupped close to each other, lying on our sides in the narrow chair, cooling where we didn't touch. I kissed Robert's neck and then eased myself away, went out to the hall, picked up my blouse. I slipped it on while I went and fetched the Paddy's, weaselled it out of its cotton-wool cradle and brought it back to him.

'Here.' I poured out two friendly measures in a pair of his mouthwash cups. 'You awake, love?'

He stirred and rolled on to his back, flickered open his eyes and registered the drink I held towards him with a frown. 'What's this?' Although he knew without asking, sat up and reached out for his measure, examined it, inhaling close above its lip.

'Paddy's.'

'Thought so.'

'You all right?'

'I'm back.' This with his eyes fixed on the whiskey, swinging it slightly in his hand, the tiny swell of the meniscus showing through the thin, white plastic like a shadow between his fingers. 'I'm back.' He opened his mouth and tipped his head, let the Paddy's fall into him.

I sipped mine rather more slowly, but it disappeared just the same in a jolt of heat and I stepped over to be beside him and open a kiss while we were both still burning.

'I'm back.' And he dropped the cup, crossed his arms over his chest, fought in a breath. His eyes closed.

'What is it?'

'Nothing.'

I stroked the skin that I knew now, the touch I'd keep with me, drunk and sober, asleep and awake. 'You can say.' I kissed his eyelids and the start of salt. 'My wee man, you can say.'

'I wasn't going to.' The hard climb of a sob. 'I haven't for three weeks, longer than three weeks.'

The thought that I might have hurt him chilled in. 'What weren't you going to do?'

A cough beat through a sob. 'Drink.'

'What.'

'I was staying off.'

'But that's okay.'

'I was being good.'

'Of course you're good.'

'I was staying off.' And he was still, but crying, the tears rolling back into his hair.

'You only had one. That's nothing – one. Look, we won't have any more. We don't need to. I'll put it away and we'll tidy up and . . . It was just the one . . . Robert, it doesn't matter, there's no harm done. We'll both cut down together, that'll be good – we don't need it. We'll do it together. Okay, love? Okay?'

He rolled on to his side with his back towards me.

And I couldn't let him be that way, not so alone and sad, over so little. 'Robert. Robert, let me . . .' I balanced myself behind him on the chair, lay fitted to his back and hugging this awful, ridiculous pain he had, the one that was flaring into me. 'Come on and we'll forget this. It never happened. You had a wee dream.'

I kissed his ear, his shoulder, I tried to say things that would please him and smoothed my hand down his stomach, then lifted, took him, worked him until he straightened against my palm. He didn't quite want it.

'This isn't –'

'I know. But let it be. Let it go now. That's my man. Let it go. Let it go, my good lamb, my good lamb.'

Until he worked with me, drew and pressed, drove up a new sweat, both of us being savage with him until he couldn't help but come.

The peace of him after that, the surrendered quiet – he was mine, then: so much that I was his.

Which is why I'm reduced to the cough mixture now – I'm not meant to be drinking.

We are both not meant to be drinking – or, at least, not drinking very much. We are doing this together, because we want to. Simon and his wife, they wouldn't understand that kind of sharing. Nor would anyone else in the congregation – I'll guess they'll never have masturbated anyone, for any reason, not even to help them, to make their bad thoughts go away. They'll be unfamiliar with that kind of charity.

They won't understand why I have to be out here, either, holding an empty bottle of blackcurrant linctus. So I might as well head off down the steps, find the CPG van and drive away. I can't explain myself and there's no use trying.

I should never have come here. I don't go to church.

'What do you mean, you don't go to church?'

I knew before I answered that it would be Simon – who else would call my mobile on a Sunday. I hadn't even made it back home before he rang.

'Well, I don't . . . I mean, that doesn't matter. I just felt poorly.'

'Poorly.' Both syllables gritty with sarcasm – my brother never used to sound like this with me.

'Yes.' I realise that the background noise he may be hearing will not aid my case, because I am currently in Stirling and a pub. It's Sunday – things don't open on Sunday. If it's late in the day and you've had no lunch and you want a sandwich, you have to go into a pub. 'Yes, poorly.' I am eating a sandwich.

And drinking a glass of wine.

I have to drink *something*, or else I'll seem rude.

'You couldn't even be bothered to wait for us.'

'I could be bothered, I *was* bothered. But you wouldn't want me there and ill.'

'Gillian had food ready. We were supposed to be celebrating.'

A knot of young guys are suddenly amused by something on the TV and produce the sort of unruly whoop that is only heard in a certain bad class of bar. I know that Simon will have registered this, too.

'But you seem to have your own celebration going on there.'

'No. I'm just having a sandwich.'

'I thought you were poorly.'

'I'm not so bad now. I'm managing a bit of food.'

He doesn't say anything more, just sighs.

'What?'

He doesn't respond and another whoop rises around, I think it's something to do with Australian football.

'Simon, what?'

'C57 mice.'

'What?'

'C57 mice. They're bred to be addicted, to take part in experiments. Give them a choice of alcohol or water and they'll always pick the drink. They can't help it. The way they need alcohol buries every other instinct. They love to kill themselves.'

He stops and I'm left holding silence again. 'What? Is that me? Simon?'

'You know women die quicker, don't you? Always. The winos on park benches – check how many of them are men. The women just die.'

'Is that supposed to be me? You think I'm a wino? You think I'm an *animal*?'

'I think you act like an animal, yes. Goodbye, Hannah.'

'Wha –'

'Goodbye.'

And the reception's so bad on this bloody phone that I can't judge how he said this, not clearly. I'm not sure if he sounded upset, or tired, or sad. And why should I care? – I've just been insulted by my own closest relative. And if I'm an animal, I'd like him to consider that he must be the same – he is my brother. I'd like him to pause for thought. I'd like him to be here now and see me eating my sandwich and drinking a glass of wine and leaving. I can do that.

I *can* do that.

He thinks I'll sit here and get pissed, because that's all a mouse knows how to do.

Well, fuck him.

If he thinks that I have to be drunk all the time, then why not? I'll call his bluff. But I still won't get drunk, I still won't be incapable. I very, very rarely am.

He doesn't know me. I can put the best part of a bottle away and still drive perfectly.

Fuck him.

As it happens, when I lost my job, one of the points in my favour was my spotless driving. I got the van back from Stirling, and from every other professional and private location, perfectly intact. There had been some appointments missed, that's all – having Robert around in a more regular way had upset my sleeping patterns and then I caught this bug after Christmas (I may have been sickening for it at the carol service) and I missed some more appointments and the spring is a crap time to sell anybody cardboard – that's an established fact – but modern business has no flexibility. *We're* supposed to be flexible, the people who do the working, but the businesses, they're allowed to be carved in stone. Big, stupid, unsympathetic stone.

Capitalism – whoever invented that didn't drink – no imagination. They'll just sack the first person they see, no matter what.

'I'm afraid we'll have to –'

'I don't need overtime, the hours. I do extra hours and I don't record them.'

'Miss Luckraft, we will have to le –'

'This time of year, there's no movement. If I had anoth –'

'Hannah, we're letting you go.' Mr Robinson there in his rumpled shirt – he can fire people, screw up their lives with a sentence, but he can't manage ironing shirts. Wife left him. Can't manage keeping a wife who could iron a shirt. Can't manage getting someone else to replace the wife he couldn't keep and who could have ironed his shirts. Although why would she have bothered? – he's just Robinson.

Which is to say, he is a fuck-up. Not even raising his game

123

when he booted me out, no trace of spirit at any point in his delivery. 'I'm sorry, but it's not working out. The end of the month.' Being fired by a mumbling rodent, it just adds insult to your injury.

'But I . . .' I'd been hoping he'd interrupt me again, because I had no more to say, only this general, wordless sense that everything was wrong. But Robinson had no more to say, either. He handed me over some unpleasantly terminal papers and then picked up the phone to avoid further complications. I'm sure he dialled the speaking clock, or his empty house – anything to end the conversation and force me out.

Robinson – one day *he'll* be in trouble and no one will help, they may even hinder instead. I'll never hear about it, but I'll get this soft, bright feeling some afternoon and I'll guess – somewhere Robinson is being done over, really thoroughly kicked about.

Meanwhile, I haven't found another position yet, but when you know cardboard the way that I do, it's only a matter of time, no sense in brooding. I do brood, naturally, but I also understand that I don't need to. I'm more preoccupied with my health at the minute, in any case. Physically, I am not quite what I should be.

The whole thing started with my toe. It was the usual scenario: your left big toe begins to be stiff in the mornings and then uncooperative when you walk and then you notice that it's starting to be reddish and then purple and then one day you're fighting to get on your shoe and you discover this appalling object, smirking at the far end of your foot – something very like a victoria plum, but with a toenail. For a while, you can only limp about with your swelling bundled up in a hill-walking sock and an optional plastic bag for when it's raining.

I prefer not to bother doctors and so I don't have a clue what the trouble was. It passed away after something approaching a fortnight with no permanent harm done. The real difficulties arose thereafter, due to a lack of discipline.

When one half of your body realises it can misbehave and get away with it, then you're in for serious grief. Taking its cue from my foot, the whole of my left side has made just such a decision and I haven't been healthy since.

The next mishap arrived when I was vulnerable and in bed. Robert and I were sitting up together and smoking a ridiculously large cigar, which we had been given earlier in the bar by a man with an American accent who claimed to have worked for the CIA. It was a Cuban cigar and he handed it to us in its silver tube as if this act were as splendidly illegal in our country as it would have been in his. I felt he was a bad example for the CIA to set, but kept my mouth shut in case he knew, or was willing to invent, any interesting stories about spies.

I can't say if there were any stories, that isn't clear now.

But the cigar was irrefutable and we were sucking on it, turn and turn about, until our heads spun: blue, communistic tissues and ropes of smoke gradually crowding up towards my ceiling.

'Hm.'

Robert sighed. 'Hm, I know. I could get used to this. A cigar-smoking dentist. The patients would enjoy that. It would reassure them.'

'Hm.'

'I always was intended for better things.'

'*Hm.*'

I wasn't, in fact, murmuring agreement, or satisfaction – I was making the only noise that I still could.

A dreamy, soupy, horrifying thing was happening. From the tip of my tongue and back, sparkling and spreading, there was this totally authoritative numbness.

I inhaled for what seemed like the course of a day and by the time my lungs were expanded, if not overtaxed, the left side of my tongue was wooden and cold, thicker, foreign. A tingling suffused my cheek, licked up to my eye, kissed my ear and I thought in beautiful, peaceful words, tranquil as cigar smoke,

I'm dying. It's finally starting. This is when I get to die.

I gave up on attracting Robert's attention and monitored the progress of my death: first came the fine wave of tickling ice and then the numbing down the neck, across the chest, along the left arm and pushing clear into the depths of each finger. I imagined peering down and seeing extinction caught for a moment under my nails, a hint of blue light fading.

If I'm having a stroke then it should be in my right side, shouldn't it?

So not a stroke. Unless they're ambidextrous.

Probably not.

Anyway, it doesn't matter.

Not unless I survive.

My deterioration became less straightforward after that: a sleek sense of weakness nibbled down into my leg at the same time as a dunt of nausea staggered me out of bed and off into the bathroom.

'Hannah? Hannah, what's wrong?'

'*Hm.*'

I was moderately sick while Robert stayed in bed and suggested that I shouldn't smoke cigars if I knew I didn't have the head for them.

'*Hm.*'

I returned to him, face doused in water, mouth rinsed, and shifted to find the warmth that my body had left for me in the sheets, even as it ceased to function. I slept then, solidly, for about a day, surfacing to a mildly concerned note on the coverlet.

HANNAH,

CALL ME WHEN / IF YOU WAKE UP. I AM WORRIED.
COME TO THE BAR. I DON'T WANT TO BE WORRIED.
I WILL CALL YOU. YOU WERE TOO FAST ASLEEP.
COME TO THE BAR TONIGHT AND WE WILL MAKE IT
BETTER.

ROBERT, CONCERNED DENTAL PRACTITIONER

I didn't feel particularly off-colour, only dragging. My left foot was lazier than it should have been, likewise my left hand. Good thing it wasn't my right hand, I use that more.

Thinking was possible, but slower in a way that I couldn't precisely identify and the left side of my face was fine, but slightly less alive than it had been. That was the main sense I had – of being less alive than I had been.

'Yes, you don't look great.'

'Thanks a l-lot.' The bar was unruly that night. Something political had happened somewhere and everyone – even the Parson and I'd never heard him raise his voice – had decided to argue about it. I'd discovered that my eyes were delicate and so I was wearing dark glasses which deepened my sensory confusion. 'I don't feel . . . ahm, great.' Squinting up at Robert as he approached our table, yelling tenderly.

'You sure you don't want to see a doctor?'

'Yes. They never tell you anything you haven't already worked out.'

'Not a check-up?'

'I'll be fine.'

'Well, you have this. Do you good.' He popped down a double Scotch that sparked and flirted, even through tinted glass.

'I thought we weren't drinking spirits any more.'

Robert folded himself in beside me on the booth seat. 'Special occasion. I was worried about you.' From behind his back, he magicked another Scotch which he drew at almost nervously. 'No being poorly. No being sad. No letting anything go wrong with you.' I watched the whisky ignite, sharpen his eyes, take him back to the good, high, familiar place that waited for him during all his abstinence. 'Oh, that's . . . that isn't a word of a lie. Yes. Good. Fine flavour.' He took my left hand, mouthed the inside of its wrist. 'Just this one and then we'll get you home, tuck you up.' He tilted in another sip and I watched his throat doing what it was made for, swallowing. I reached over, feeling slightly clumsy, to kiss his Adam's apple and he swallowed again, quick and warm against my mouth. 'Home and tucking very tight.'

'Just this one.'

'Mm-hmm, just one.'

'One's the very thing.'

'But no more than that. One will be just right.'

Three or maybe four hours later, we decided that we ought to go to Dublin.

This is always unwise. Ireland is like a huge, disinterested echo chamber, or a magnifying glass, a distorting mirror, a combination of the three. Whatever unruly tensions you may have in your character, your relationships, your health, your mental equilibrium: every weak and dark and painful place you've got will be screaming and turning elephantine before you've even reached an exit in Dublin airport: before you've collected your bags in that bloody, sepulchral basement where they keep all their baggage conveyors and bad coffee and timetables for buses and gaggles of Dubliners eyeing you and gnawing at fatty baps: letting you see that they know why you've come – you're hoping you'll have fun. They understand about your fun – that it will be *impossible*. No matter where you are. For you, *fun* is a barely legal size of minuscule chocolate bar: your natural ration of all the cheapskate, bonsai snacks and treats and jolly moments that evaporate and leave you feeling swindled and distressed. Fun, real fun, that was never intended for people like you. Because of this, Dubliners laugh inwardly, if not outwardly, as they watch you try to scrabble for your passing case – your case full of clothes to have fun in and uncomfortable underwear.

This welcoming combination alone should tell you how awful things will get and persuade you to turn round and go directly home.

Above all, you should – and never do – remember that Irish people can drink in Ireland: they are Irish, they are used to it.

They can do that whole easygoing, back-to-my-place, pissing-in-the-street-on-occasions-maybe-but-otherwise-in-control and what-a-devil-may-care-scamp-I-am style of drinking. They can pull it off. They are not hoping they'll have fun – they are just drinking. They haven't dragged themselves over the Irish Sea in hopes of bonhomie and entertainments they would never get at home. They do not hit Irish soil and instantly expect to be somebody else – somebody *fun*. They are not plummeting into crevasses of disappointment at each step.

They can, for example, afford to complain about Scots being evil drunks when in Ireland – because the Irish drinkers are at home there, they're mellow, they're not spending a precious holiday ballooning beyond their own reach, watching defects they didn't realise they had stretching up around them like fucking redwoods, with no chance of absolution. They aren't going to get lost in the north of Dublin and see several men with head wounds gently standing against walls in disturbing silence, as if they were waiting for worse, Irish drinkers aren't going to be terrified like that – they aren't going to eat bad soup in Temple Bar and then throw up on the steps of the General Post Office while intending to pay a respectful late-night visit to a place of great historical import. People they love – in fact, dentists they're going out with – will not keep behaving like cretins, like embarrassing New Year uncles, and will not spend every fucking minute dragging about with them, as if they were a pair of fleeing convicts, chained ankle to ankle and hip to hip by a kind of debilitating mutual lust which is *almost* fun but also makes you want to scream. And, beyond that, the left side of any self-respecting Irish drinker will not have decided it should belong to someone else, somebody dead.

Although at the time, believe me, I was much less troubled by my dying sinister half than by my cretinous beloved and that bloody lust.

'Hha!'

Robert had decided to develop a barking laugh. As if he hadn't already ruined himself enough, Dublin was bringing out the dog in him. 'Hha! What have you done? What are you doing?'

Behind him were the orange and brown convolutions of the original seventies, or maybe retro, carpet in the hotel room that he probably couldn't afford to pay for and that I couldn't afford to think about. 'I mean . . . Hha!' He pointed at me and barked again.

By employing numberless, lightning calculations I worked out that he wasn't leaning against the floor, but lying on top of it, which in its turn implied that I was standing over him.

I sat down. 'What do you mean, what have I done?'

'Your head.'

'What about my head?'

'Hho, look at your head. Go on, look. In the bathroon, bath-*room*, look in the mirror there. Go on and look. Oh, I haven't seen anything like that for . . . how long have we been here?'

I wanted to make it very clear that I was aware you should use a mirror when you wanted to see yourself. But I didn't have the energy for explanations. When I stood up again, my neck seemed incredibly weak, like wet paper, distressed cloth. I had to prop myself up with my hands as I walked.

'Oh, you'll laugh when you see it. You will. Oho, you'll laugh . . . How long have we been here?'

The bathroom was furnished with a two-thousand-watt bulb which seemed excessive and dangerous. For safety's sake, I used only one eye to peer at myself.

'Fuck.'

My closed eye was sitting, perfectly normal, in my usual face, the one I had come to expect of me.

'Fuck.'

'Hahn! Told you.' I could hear Robert drumming his heels on the floor and beginning to hoot.

My open eye was squinting out from a bloated mass of greenish white. I had no cheek, no ear, no lips, only this puffy surface with an eyebrow perched across it like the kind of jokey finishing touch you'd slap on to a snowman. I looked like half a snowman. 'Fuck!'

And this is precisely the kind of thing to send you shouting and packing and shouting some more on your way out of the room and so you do this – fighting into your coat while your companion is turning sensible, patting you softly, sympathetically, but still laughing. So you shout yourself clear out of the hotel and into the street and then you bellow for a cab. You do not let anyone else in to travel with you.

Back at the dreadful airport, you mutter your way through requesting a ticket change, your cheek beginning to limit your jaw, everything seizing. You pay the surcharge with £8.73 to spare. Dubliners smirk as they pass you, liking your disappointment and staring until it crests into despair.

You wait for one standby, miss it, wait for another and finally shamble aboard, strangers now helplessly fascinated by your dreadful face.

During your journey, lack of air pressure, or increased solar radiation, or whogivesafuckwhat causes you to swell still further, to solidify, and to suck down four brandy miniatures between your gritting teeth.

In the end, you have to go and see a doctor.

And I do have one: we just don't know each other well.

'So . . . Dear me. What have you been up to?'

'Uh cnt upn m mth.'

'No, I can see that.'

He isn't a great GP, isn't someone I could like, but he doesn't require you to make appointments – all you need do is to show up feeling appalling and then queue. He demands no forethought whatsoever – that always seems to outweigh any shortcomings he might have, medically speaking.

'GgNNph . . .'

'Yes, yes . . . but I am going to have to look down your throat, you know.'

He dibbles in his desk drawer and then stands up, brandishing a tongue depressor and a tiny torch. I don't, as I've said, really know him, but he still seems different today – either more or less real, I can't say. I can't say anything.

'Ull ths ht?'

'It might hurt a bit.' The pallor of his hands is almost blinding and I have to close my good eye as they come too close. He squints at me, appraising. 'You do seem very stiff . . . That's . . .' He tries my jaw, less than gently. 'Now . . . I'm sorry, but I do have to.' I have the impression that he's adjusting for better grip. 'Just try to relax.'

I suspect that I am dribbling, slavering like a hound and then –

'FfffAA.'

A boiling jab lances down the left side of my neck as he cranks my jaws apart, levering at me with his spatula and his torch.

'Uuun.'

I am waiting for him to say, 'Open wide,' before I kick him.

His own mouth seems extraordinarily wide, his chin almost slapping down against his chest. 'Soon be done . . .'

I can hear his jaw whistle as it swings through one dangerous curve after another. And his consonants are peculiar – they sting me, perhaps in my limbic area, although I don't know what that is, but when I imagine it, I feel wounded.

'No, don't close up again . . . don't.'

I haven't intended to move at all, but my face is rejecting his intrusion and has decided to take charge. 'Surru.' My molars snuggle in towards each other unstoppably.

'All well and good being sorry, but I think your throat is closing, swelling shut – you know? Not something we'd want.' If he'd only stop talking, I'd feel less at bay. 'Which means I will need a better peer round than that. So hold still. I do know that it hurts.'

He doesn't. He couldn't begin to guess.

His clammy fingers prod about — I can feel them on those portions of myself which still notice sensations. He is trying to get a purchase. There is an odd smell to him, a dying, leaf-mould scent and his breath lands in a way that seems infectious and the spatula and torch are lunging at me, larger than they should be, which may be an effect of perspective, but usually perspective doesn't confuse me. 'Ah. Here we go. That's it . . . Now.'

There is a pop or crack from somewhere important inside me and then a red-coloured blank and then I realise I am staring at my doctor's ankles. 'Fckr. Fckr. Bstd. Fckn bstd. Fck.' I am on the floor and tightening like someone else's noose.

'Sorry about that . . . Not so good, eh? Had to be done, though.' His foot taps softly in front of my nose, perhaps a little embarrassed. 'Tell you what, just stay there and have a rest. Catch your breath. I'll see another patient in Room Two, nip back in and check on you in a while. Hmm?'

'Bstd.'

I hate him very much, but also I wonder if he is a mirage, a hallucination. And I suspect that a good, real doctor might want to commit me now, because I suspect that he may not be a good, or even slightly real doctor. He may not be a real doctor. He may just be a figment of my puffy, green brain. But he may want to commit me, all the same. I'm not sure.

His toecap withdraws, unmistakably bashful. 'I had students yesterday. Shame they missed this. You're something unusual, you know. That's cheerful, isn't it? Something to be glad of? I mean, I've never exactly seen this before.'

'FFfff.'

Time passes rather slowly once he's gone — either out of my mind, or into Room Two — and the whining in my ears quietens. I hear various feet, far away, going in various directions.

Eventually, I locate the legs of my chair and edge towards it, then work myself up to sit. When my doctor bustles in again, he looks happy to see me hunched in front of his desk. I try to seem as threatening, but sane, as I can.

'Good. Feeling more yourself. You were perfectly safe there, of course – in the recovery position. Now I want you to take this note down to the hospital.' He gives me a tangible note, in a genuine envelope, which crumples when I grip too tight. 'They'll examine you there, perhaps do some tests, and you may have to be kept in at least overnight. Because of your throat. Once that's closed, you're in trouble. You understand?'

Of course I understand. It's only my mouth I can't operate – I don't think with that – not always.

'Sss. Udustd.' I pocket the envelope.

'Fine. And let me know how you get on.' I think he wants to wave as I leave, but then reconsiders, while I lurch up into a standing position and back away from his shining, his hissing, his sweeping teeth. He makes do with nodding his head. 'Great. Take care now. Off you go. Quick as you can, I'd say. Quick as you can. Great . . .'

You may have to be kept in at least overnight.

I do understand that I am unwell and may not recover without help. I am even afraid about this. The mass and the ache of my head set me slewing across the pavement and it is difficult to walk, but some of this is also caused by simple anxiety.

A hospital, though. In overnight. You can't do anything in hospital – it's like joining the army: all waking at dawn and hats and by-laws and statutory shouting.

And in a hospital, you can't drink.

I slew towards a bin and throw away my doctor's letter. This makes me feel very lonely as soon as I do it, turns my bones slightly more frail, but I am also relieved. I don't thrive under imposed restrictions and a hospital is nothing but.

Anyway, you go in with one thing wrong and come out with four or five others. I'll be safer at home. I just need to get there and I'll be sorted, I'll have a nice lie down.

'Simon.'

'Hello. Who is this?'

'Is Simon there?'

His wife sets down the receiver with a theatrical sigh. I can make out the sound of her calling, 'I think it's your sister,' with a barb of irritation. I close my eyes, because that aches less and wait for Simon. He'll do something about this. He'll get me better. He's a doctor. He's my brother. He'll pay no attention if she complains. He shouldn't be with her, anyway – he should be with me.

'Yes.'

'It's Hannah.'

'What's the matter? I can hardly hear you. Look, we're having dinner . . .'

'I'm not well. There's something the matter with me. I'm . . .' And I cry because by now I am very scared and because I want to be with him this evening, the two of us together, eating toasted cheese and wearing our pyjamas and being glad that we're indoors – outside it's raining – and maybe our father will come in, his hair sparking with raindrops after a run across the garden from the greenhouse and he'll stand in the doorway quietly and watch us, as if we might have slipped away while he was out, or changed – but here we are, ourselves and not lost, turning in time to see his face and know that he loves us to the point of pain.

'Hannah? Hannah, have you been drinking?'

'Simon. I'm not well. Please. I don't know . . .'

'Where are you?'

'I'm, I'm at home.'

'Then stay there.'

'No, I. . . please, I need –'

'Stay there and I'll come and get you . . . All right? I'm coming to get you.'

'Simon, I –'

'Just shut up and stay there. It'll take me . . . I don't know two, three hours. Will you be okay by yourself for that long?'

'Yes, I, I think th –'

'Fine.' He mumbles something back to his wife, I don't catch it. 'I'll be there as soon as I can. What's the address?'

I tell him and I try to keep him talking a while longer, but he is determined now – once he makes his mind up, that's that with Simon. So I try to thank him and he won't let me and then I have to say goodbye.

But he will be here – two, three hours and he will be with me.

So I'm going to be all right. I can stand this until he gets here, because I know he's on his way, and when he arrives I'll do whatever he tells me, I'll listen to what he says. He was a good boy and now he's a good man. As long as he's coming to get me, I'll be fine.

And I'm so grateful that I start to cry again, which is difficult, it makes me strain at muscles I can no longer move. I hold my jaws. I moan. I stop.

Simon, he's always there for me, truly. Whatever happens, he cares.

Except that now I'm sure he does care and that he's driving and missing his dinner for my sake and I won't be on my own with this much longer – that's when the drinking voice starts, the one that's seen my soul. It understands me.

Fooled him.

Anything to get him here – that's it, isn't it? Any emotion you can fake.

Well, isn't it?

You fooled him and you weren't found out. Your own brother. Anything to get your way.

Why couldn't you have saved him all this trouble? Why couldn't you have died?

VI

'This smells like a primary school.'

'Well, let's find out if it tastes like one. Open up.'

I don't open up, being unsure what this means, but a hot press of something gluey does indeed make me part my lips and suddenly I am eating without my consent. 'Ffm?'

'Just swallow it, will you, I really don't have time for this.' I'm eating and hearing my brother's voice. My good, kind, beautiful brother who makes me feel guilty by being here, by being good and kind and beautiful.

'You're the one who brought her home.' This in my brother's wife's voice – the lovely Gillian, a woman who renders any guilt ridiculous. It is impossible to think of her badly enough. 'Look, if you don't want to do it, let me. There's no point getting angry.'

'I'm not angry.'

I'm not angry, either – but I don't say. This is between the two of them.

'*Fine.*' And here the sound of the lovely Gillian's lovely feet clacking out into the passageway, unhappy. A door closes emphatically.

And then another spoonful of whatever it is accosts me.

'Why can't you bloody feed yourself? . . . Jesus, Hannah . . .'

'I *can* –' I pause, because I sound so unfeminine and slow. Try again, 'I *can* feed myself.' Not much better – not really good enough for Simon.

Although he seems unsurprised, now that I can see him.

I have come into focus while propped up in a bed and staring past my brother to a chest of drawers, on top of which are two motionless but living cats. I recognise them: they're Gillian's: glassy-eyed little monsters and hideously fat. They look like a pair of fur duffel bags with cats' heads sticking out.

'What are you laughing at?'

'Am I? . . .' I've forgotten how I would tell. 'Nothing.' I'm checking around in the crook of my head for any signs of aching, illness, queasy turns, but there are none. I am only billowy and light-hearted and without especially noticeable pains. If Simon weren't frowning at me, I would guess I was dreaming, or dead.

'Yes, that wouldn't surprise me.' Simon shifts his weight where he's sitting on my bed. The motion makes me rapidly uneasy, which I didn't expect, and when I have caught my breath, I flinch up to see him staring into a bowl of what is clearly porridge. I recognise it now – the sight of it, taste, smell, all the clues provided.

I haven't eaten porridge since we used to have breakfasts together at home. He's made it thick with a little milk added and a touch of dark sugar on top, melting – the way I used to like it then.

And the thought of him taking this care for me rushes a violent shade of some intensity up inside my chest. 'Oh.' It turns me weightless for a moment, but then I sink again.

'What?' Simon stares at me as if I'm an unnecessary accident. '*What?*'

Something about the way that his face changes makes me guess that he's watching me cry – which means that I must be crying. I'm not aware of being sad or, indeed, happy – but I can tell that I'm forcing him to hate me for being not as I was. I am not his sister, or not the sister he remembers, or not the sister that he wants.

'Hannah . . . *fuck.*'

'Sorry.' I put out my hand to him, because I have made him swear, but he stands and steps back, still holding the bowl. I think he's no longer aware of it.

'No.' He pushes at his temple with the heel of his free hand, as if this is a habit, although I have never seen it before. 'No, you're not sorry, you never are.' I really don't know him the way that I used to.

And I find it hard to talk, because of my crying. 'But I —'

'Hannah, just shut up. And sleep. I really think that you should sleep. Go back to sleep. Please. If you wake up and it's dark, check the time before you come through and bother us . . . Try not to break anything.' He gives me his back and walks towards the door.

At least my jaw feels easier, more free. That can't be bad. 'Thank you.' This pauses his progress. I try to work out a meaning in the angle at which he is frozen and simultaneously realise that I now have working nerves in the whole of my face. So I'm starting to be a going concern again — and the billowiness that fills me keeps gentle and soothes. 'Simon? Thank you.'

'No. You don't do that either.' And Simon is almost going to leave, has his hand on the doorknob, but then he turns and is freshly bewildered by the sight of me. 'You don't even remember the doctor being here, do you? Does it interest you that you're going to be okay?' He winces into a smile, a cold one, the kind that no brother of mine should have learned. 'I mean, that you won't die this time — I don't mean that *you'll be okay*. You *can't* be okay.' As he opens the door, 'Of course, she can't be okay. What was I thinking.' He steps off into the dark of the passage. 'She'll never be okay, she doesn't want to.'

The cats flick their attention back to me, settle themselves on their stomachs, fold their paws close under their chests and blink, malevolent.

*Well, what else did he expect? Coming to help me — did he think I wouldn't guess the way he'd help? I was there when he learned to walk — I know everything he'll do. He is always just **obvious**.*

So, of course, he was going to come, as he'd promised, and rescue me. But what was he going to do before we left, while he still had access to my flat? Search the bags, the cupboards, the shoes, the storage jars, the drawers, the toilet cistern, test every possible suspicion, until he'd found my bottles and then he'd open each of them and empty it away. It would have been a compulsion – one he couldn't resist. But I would have been wrong to allow it – not waste on such a scale: it wouldn't have been ecological. Or moral – more like breaking and entering, or some similar crime, and if you love him, you can't let your brother commit a crime.

Which meant that I had to drink all of it first, before he got there. He made me.

It wasn't easy, either. I put things aside for safe keeping and emergencies and sometimes I forget that I still have them and sometimes I over-cater, because I'm in need of comfort – who isn't in need of that? – and sometimes there are other reasons and as a result I had a large and mournful volume to get through before he arrived. My Cointreau, my bison-grass vodka, my absinthe, my little ceramic leprechaun full of whiskey: I mean, each of my friends and acquaintances, the ones that should welcome me home, my special treats and interior outings to see me through troublesome times, or to just *be there* in a guaranteed way *for me*: I had to swallow every ounce of every part of them. Face solidified and my teeth creaking and far too much stress in my system as it was, but I still had to sit on my kitchen floor and rush down the whole of my stock without having the time for a proper goodbye. That's what my brother drove me to.

So when I go back to the flat, there will be nothing inside it to greet me. I'll bet he searched, anyway: Simon – I was foggy by the time he reached me, but I'm sure he laid into the place, gave it the third degree in my relative absence.

I sit up, which goes quite well, and I appear to be fine, although possibly my crying persists. I'm in a pyjama jacket, not my own. It's big enough to almost be a nightshirt on me, so it must be Simon's – his pyjama jacket. Other than this, I am naked. Did he undress me? Did his wife? Did I?

Of course, my clothes and shoes have been hidden somewhere else, to stop me leaving. Which is *very, very predictable.*

They always do this: your mother, your father, your brother, your worried partner: whoever it is doesn't matter, in the end they'll all develop the same symptoms. They will talk about you in the third person while you are there, as if you were an idiot, or a dog. They will eliminate your booze, as if you have no discipline. They will put you somewhere clean and unfamiliar, as if you have been living in a cave. They will take away your clothes and your belongings, as if you were a criminal, and they will lock you in. As if you were a werewolf, a monster, they will lock you in.

Oh, but it's not so awful. After the first time it happens, you realise – they can't keep it up forever, they have other concerns, they lose patience. Not one of them can wish you to be different as long and as hard as you can wish to stay the same. And, in the meantime, you can even see their point, reach common ground – they want you to get healthy, you agree: they think you need to rest now, you agree: they believe that in a few weeks everything will seem more clear and you agree most heartily.

Anyway, it'll be nice to stay with Simon. The awkwardness will go: it must do, we're brother and sister. We'll find each other again and be comfy and we'll talk. I could do with a nice, long talk. Not about anything serious, I don't want to be serious, only to chat. For instance, I'd like to ask him about the man who used to stand down at the corner of our street. On the way back from school, we'd walk past him, or later in the evening when it was summer, he'd be leaning there: an old guy with a pipe, his back propped against a high garden wall and his face to the sun.

I mentioned him to Mother one afternoon. 'Why does he smoke his pipe outside?'

'Maybe his wife doesn't like it in the house.'

'But he isn't there very often.'

'Oh, you mean Mr Russell.'

'I don't know.' I'd never thought that he might have a name. 'Maybe.'

'He isn't there to smoke his pipe.'

'But that's what he does.' It was difficult to imagine he might be smoking against his will. 'Doesn't he like it?'

'He smokes the pipe so he'll look occupied. What he's really doing is looking at the sun and being happy. He's just being happy. For no reason.' She smoothed at the side of her face and I had the odd impression she was thinking of my father and becoming slightly sad, sad in a way that she quite liked.

'But he isn't smiling.'

'He doesn't need to. Go up and get changed – your dinner will be ready soon.' And she slipped past me and out across the garden, knocked on the side of my father's greenhouse and was allowed in. I couldn't see what they did then, because of the condensation and the spread of leaves.

And I wasn't concerned with them, in any case: I was held by the idea that adults might settle themselves behind a habit, some mild camouflage, and then simply be happy, privately and without cause. Gold panners and teachers and circus clowns and archaeologists – all of the people whose professions had caught my eye up to that point – maybe they were only pretending, passing the time with their work, then drifting away to be happy where no one could see. I wanted to grow older into that. I thought such things were possible.

Even more so, when I next passed Mr Russell and – as a sly experiment – grinned at him while he smoked. He peered down at me in surprise, but then developed the most luminous, unblemished, sincere smile I've ever seen. I could wonder today if Russell was a drinker, but I don't believe so – his expression had no edge, no meaning, no request, it anticipated no result: it was simply a release of monumental joy. After proof like that, I had to assume the passing years would haul me up and out to happiness, no doubt about it. Otherwise, why bother?

Otherwise, why bother?

There are people who can make that question helpful, kind – my father, for example. Mother had been right to think of him, go to him in his greenhouse, where he practised concealing his life, because he did bother, he bothered a lot. Busy doing nothing under glass, dabbling in the kitchen, dusting and cleaning each new day while she was at work as if this was a game he'd never played before, something amusingly quixotic and arcane. He had decided this would be the best disguise to guard his happiness. For all I could tell, it may even have worked.

And it wasn't that he lacked other options, qualifications – this was definitely a choice: to be a tea-boiler, house-husband, homemaker and not anything else more manly, or lucrative.

'He was a lawyer. That's how we met.'

We only had this conversation once, my mother and I. It occupied space in a part of the last ceasefire before I left home – nineteen and with very few qualifications of any kind.

'He was a *lawyer*?'

'Don't sound so surprised – he could be anything he wanted.' She said this as if it were nothing remarkable, a fact with hourly confirmations. 'He picked law. Got a scholarship, *two* scholarships. He didn't have a background that made it easy.' Leaning closer, letting me ponder the nourishing background that I'd wasted, she looked at me, at the changeling I'd become. 'You didn't ever notice, did you? How clever he is.'

'I . . .' It was true, I hadn't noticed. But who *does* think their parents are clever, or attractive, or own any of the qualities of strangers? Your parents aren't people to you until they're dead, or at least until it's too late and the harm's been done – that's something everyone understands. 'I didn't think he was stupid . . . I just didn't –'

'I know.'

'But I don't remember –'

'Criminal law. He was very talented, everyone said so. It just didn't suit him. It didn't suit his heart. Afterwards, there was compensation. A pension. We'd never manage with only my wage. Didn't think of that, either, did you? He still supports us.'

I couldn't tell from the way she said this if the compensation *was* the pension, or if something had happened to my father, if the law had hurt him and then had to make amends.

'You shouldn't upset him. No one should upset him. No one should be able to.' She angled for a clear view into my eyes while she said this and so I lowered my head – a proper look at me would only have upset her. And probably this was the time when I decided that I should get out of her way and everyone else's. I can't be certain, but I'd say it seemed much more necessary to leave home after that.

And then Simon must have left, I don't know when, exactly, and here I am in the place that he's made for himself without our parents and without me.

I lie back into one of his soft pillows. I suppose it's Gillian's pillow, too. And these are their fresh sheets and well-aired duvet with matching little blue-and-white stripes, in keeping with the smoothness and the cleanliness of the room – scrubbed pine and dove-coloured walls. They've taken time with this, made it inviting for a guest. No doubt, they have another bedroom they're getting ready for the baby: mobiles and tentative colours and a start on buying toys. Preparation and attention to detail, that's what you need to break a house into a home. I'm aware of the theory. The thought of this being what finally makes me sleep – with home in my head I can't bear to be awake.

Although I do snap up again, I'd presume about five minutes later, dying for a cigarette. This is unusual, because I don't particularly smoke. If somebody gives me one, I'll take it, I won't say no, because that's antisocial, but I'm not what I would call a smoker. There are too many other, better things a person can do with their mouth.

But here I am, wanting a fag in a household where even pronouncing *tobacco* would probably trigger a silent alarm and summon up the drugs squad. And I dreamed for a moment about being younger and not having a night light – is that what kicked off the craving, a bad pun? – or was it memories of Russell's happy pipe? – for whatever reason, I'm unsettled, because in reality, I *didn't* have a night light and this was unjust, this was *wrong*.

My mother, usually my mother, because she was brave, would pad through in the small hours if I was scared, or restless, and she would talk to me and calm me and then she would say, 'Don't worry. I'll just leave the door a bit open as I go. Night-night.'

Which is supposed to be reassuring, but actually it's horrendous, it's a small kind of child abuse. If the door is left open, then bad things can come in and get you. Being shut in a pitch-black room with something dreadful isn't nice, but if the dreadful thing stays quiet and doesn't kill you, then you can get used to it being there and possibly doze off. With an open door, the number of terrors is unlimited. Not only that, but you realise that you will *see them* when they come: glimpse them as they're sneaking, feel their shadows on your forehead, catch the flicker of their eyes before they leap. Because the door is open, you will lie awake all night, too terrified to even call your parents for their help. They will think you are quiet, because you are sleeping. In fact, you are dumbstruck and fear for your life.

Not relevant to me at this age. Except that the bedroom door is partly open, light from the hallway spilling wickedly in and the house restless in a breeze, swarming with tiny noises that I can't identify. Laughable to be nervy this way. I almost can't imagine why I should be.

The alarm clock with the extremely red numbers is stabbing out 01:52, which is later than I expected and rather awkward – hours to wait before I can pop through and ask Simon when I stopped being scared of the dark.

'Hello. Hello?'
    'Fffm . . . *A-ah?*'
'Is that you? Robert?'

'I don't know, what time is it?' His voice childish with sleep, but otherwise comforting and clear.

'Why, are there times of day when you're somebody else?'

'Yes. You're very quiet, what's the matter? And where are you? Are you in your flat?' Robert choosing to stay childish as he wakes, picking the tone that will make me soft. As if I wouldn't be, anyway. 'I tried your flat and I thought you weren't there. Were you hiding? Just because . . . You left me in Dublin by myself. What did you do that for?'

It's so pleasant to hear him that I'm not really listening – the dark hall around me turning cold, but the nastiness of the thicker shadows now receding. I pull the duvet I've carted downstairs with me more effectively round my shoulders and crouch on the floor, back to the wall.

'Well? Now what?' No more of the boy left in him, so he's turning defensive. 'You've woken me up to not speak to me? Hannah, I didn't do anything.'

'I didn't say you did.'

'Yes, but I've played this game in another life, many other lives – you don't have to say, I'm supposed to guess. And then I get it wrong and by the time we've finished fighting we can't remember what was right and, in any case, we don't give a fuck.'

For some reason it never seems likely that Robert has dated other women, that he could have played games with them and disliked it. I mean, he would have been – still is – attractive and has all kinds of additional, positive things about him and women must have noticed this at times and made their moves, but neither of us have spoken about former partners and so they have remained semi-mythical. Which is what I prefer.

'Hannah? Don't do this. Or I'll have to hang up. And I don't want to. Where are you?'

I remember to speak. 'I'm at my brother's. That's why I'm whispering. That's what I called to say.'

'Why whispering? . . . You have a brother?'

'Yes. Don't you?' We don't really speak about anyone else when we're with ourselves – relatives included.

'No. I'm an only child.' His irritation sliding. 'Why are you at your brother's? Have you left me? I mean . . .' Until this last emerges in a panicked mumble.

'I can't leave you. I don't live with you.' Trying to joke him out of it.

But it doesn't work. 'Did you want to? Should I have –'

'Robert, will you hush.'

'*Well, tell me what it is then? What's wrong?*'

And, God forgive me, I am very glad that he's upset, because he has no reason, so there's no risk, I can simply enjoy his concern. 'It's that I'm ill, that's all. Not well.' Before I sort out our misunderstanding thoroughly, easily. 'Remember my head?' This is not a disaster in any sense. 'How it was?' I don't want him sad, but it's lovely to know that he can be on my account. 'The swelling?'

'Yes, of course . . . You were huge . . . Greenish-looking. I was going to say you should see a doctor, but it was just quite funny at first. I mean, I was shocked as well. But it was funny.'

'I'm sure. It's getting better now – thanks for asking.'

'I was going to ask.' The panic flagging higher again.

So I return to being soft and what I hope is maternal. 'But my doctor's no use and my brother . . . he's good, I'm proud of him being good – only he can't treat me, because he's my brother, but he got someone else to and then some antibiotics and . . . I'm not fantastically healthy, but I'm a more reasonable shape.' I'm guessing this, because I haven't seen a mirror in a while, but it seems plausible.

'Your brother's a doctor?'

'Yes.'

'I see.' He's starting to sound gloomy, perhaps slightly sour.

'What's that supposed to mean?'

'Oh . . . I just had . . . you weren't around and I didn't know where you'd gone and – it's been a week since I've seen you, you know.' I hear him wandering about while he says this, a flutter and chink of background noise and a sigh as he sits. I would like to be seeing him sit. He sleeps naked, gets out of bed naked, sees few subsequent reasons to cover up.

'Really?'

'Practically a week, four days since I flew back and then apologies and loathing at the surgery again and this woman turns up – new patient, just moved from some overpriced London practice with piped music and miniature cameras so you can watch your own teeth – once the cable's reamed its way up from your arse – and then you get handjobs to take your mind off the first anaesthetic they give you to ease off the possible pain of the second fucking anaesthetic, I mean –'

I know that I have to stop him when he sets off on dental rants – they depress him and he ends up collapsing into sighs and swearing and then I'm completely unsure if he's finished his story or not, which means my reactions are too early or too late and this spins his depression down and out to blight everything, because my uncertain responses indicate the way that no one can truly identify with dentists. 'You've lost me, love. Was there something bad about the woman?'

'The woman . . .? *Yes*. She had a poncey, bloody filling in an incisor, a front tooth. "*Oh, you might not be able to find it, it was so perfectly coloured to match.*" Yes, I'm only the window cleaner – I can't tell a filling from a tooth . . . I'm just here by mistake until somebody qualified turns up.' His growl fades into a breath large enough to sustain at least the opening of one more tirade and so I nip swiftly in.

'But the woman . . .?'

'Oh, the filling was loose, because it was crap – only six months old and it's swinging like . . . like the sign outside a fucking coaching inn, it's creaking when she breathes . . . So I removed it and put in another. Only there wasn't much tooth left – big filling; tiny, lateral incisor – and I was wondering about you and what you were doing and my hands were a bit uneven, distracted − first thing in the morning, what can you expect . . .'

His breath is magnified by what I can tell is a glass. He swallows and I swallow, too. Of course. My throat narrows, dries with lack. 'What are you drinking?'

'Mm?'

'What are you drinking?'

'Mother's ruin. If you were here it could ruin you, too . . .' The growl sinking to a purr.

'I'd like that.' The oily, cheap-perfume sting of his gin is almost with me, I can smell it in the meat of my mind, hot. 'I'd like that a lot.' And gin would be the way his mouth tastes, the memory of juniper under his tongue and the spirit's bright-ness, its good hurt.

'I know you would.' He swallows again. 'I'd like it, too.'

'Jesus, though, Robert. Don't do that now − not when I'm . . . What happened with the woman?'

Of course, I don't remotely care about her and, of course, he takes another sip before beginning and, of course, I'm aware of precisely the pace it will gather as it kisses down his throat and between his shoulders, as it slips beside his heart. 'Her?' He exhales in a way that shivers my neck. 'I filled the tooth and sent her packing, but she came back, didn't she? This morning. Her tooth didn't seem right, she said. Very whiny about it. But I had a look and . . . I'd drilled too deep. Anyone could have done the same, there wasn't much margin for error − should have told her she needed a crown in the first place, but I was trying to save her the cost and the inconvenience. I was doing my best for the poisonous cow. But I'd gone too deep, exposed the nerve and so it had got . . . it was in a bad way and she's in the chair − you remember my chair − she's in my chair − which I also remember, distractingly − and she's scared and I have to clean the whole tooth out, remove the nerve, do a root canal and she's jumpy and − okay, it isn't delightful as a procedure, but that's no reason for her to get *operatic.* And I'll have to see her again, at least once, more root-canal stuff . . . and she's already bleating about the bill and saying it's all because of me and she doesn't have the time . . . I should have just smiled and sent her away, I should have pretended the thing was just dandy and let her enjoy the abscess at her leisure. See how she'd thrive with a face full of pus.' An aggrieved swallow here. 'The point is – I hate removing nerves. I hate the *thought* of removing nerves. They don't regrow: that's it, once you've finished – they're *gone.* That's practically part of the brain you've dragged out. I mean, you've touched something *nobody should touch.* The patients, they get shaky – partly it's the adrenalin we have in the anaesthetic, makes their reflexes assume they should be scared. But mainly? I know what it is – the body has lost something and understands that it will never be replaced. That's a little piece of death right there, and I've had to touch it, bring it in . . . Hang on . . . more gin.' The sound of movement again, a plodding walk.

'But it's your job, though, darling.'

'Which is why I hate my job.'

'Look, look . . .' I'm not in firm enough form to stand being melancholy and there's nobody sadder than a gin drunk, no point talking to them at all, so I have to keep Robert back from complete immersion. 'How about if we think of . . .' my skull is beginning to weigh a great deal, 'distracting things.'

We all need distractions, they make us laugh. And your options in life distil down to no more than this: laugh or cry, cry or laugh. Quickly, or slowly, it doesn't matter which – you will discover the dreadful and unfunny joke that you are, that we all are. And this condition is insoluble, incurably permanent, no one has ever been able to do a thing about it, but you still have to stay here and occupy your time. So either you can seek out distractions, or else you can worry until you're too senile to understand why: laugh or cry.

'Radio Four.'

'Hm?' Dapper and quick, another dose of gin is filling Robert's glass, too far away. 'Radio Four is shite.'

'Not the Shipping Forecast. Not all that "North Utsire, South Utsire, variable three or four, *good*". And when you hear *good* you're sure it *is* really, totally good – that's built into the voice.'

In this I do truly believe – the restorative powers of the Shipping Forecast. It's late and you're scared and out of luck and everything could be terrible, but it's not, because responsible people are keeping watch over your coast and there is order far beyond you in this marvellous, lapping ring and there is still 'rain in West later' and still *Malin* and still *Hebrides* and still *Dogger, Fisher, German Bight.* 'Go on, you know it's nice.'

'They've changed it – the place names are all different. I don't see how, I mean it's still the same island. They do that kind of thing – change it all till it's shit and they don't even ask.'

'Well, then the way it was: the way you remember. Or . . . or there's . . .' I am not currently filled with handy signposts to the bright side, but I'm making my best attempt. 'Steve Martin juggling . . . that's . . . he never looks as if he can, you know? His hands seem too slow and his feet seem too big and you think that he's going to fall over, come apart somehow, that he's too young to be doing something so complicated, but then he's fine, absolutely fine – in fact, he's *fucking flying*. There's nothing about him clumsy, and he's *not* young, not any more – only something's untouched in him, the way you hope could be possible for you – and he looks like a total idiot, but he isn't that either, in no sense, so you can feel optimistic, because you look a total idiot yourself . . . I mean . . . in fact, anyone funny, anyone who takes away the pain, you've got to be happy they're there, that they exist.' A beat during which he breathes dully, no reaction. 'Haven't you?'

'What about the comedians that aren't funny?'

'If they're not funny, then they're not comedians. Don't be confusing. I mean the proper ones, the ones who stop you wanting to kill yourself. Robert . . . I mean . . . why not think of the good funny people . . .?'

'I suppose.'

'They're a good distraction. I mean the North Utsire, South Utsire type of *good*.'

'I suppose.'

'Then you try to think of another – I'm fucking exhausted.'

And I listen to him smile now, finally, the definite sound of a smile. 'All right.' An easier sigh. 'John Mills. Yeah . . . him. Everything about him. Every thoroughbred, fucking inch. That's a film star – John Mills.'

And, obviously, this is true – and I know what he's going to say next, so I get there first, to keep him company. 'Of course, John Mills – John Mills *and the lager*.'

'*Ice Cold in Alex* and the way he drinks that lager.'

'Oh, yes.'

'Sand in his shoes and filthy and not quite believing in the bar – maybe he's only thinking it very successfully so that it's there – but right in front of him is that smooth, tall, icy, sexy, gorgeous, fucking lager.'

'Carlsberg, I believe.'

'Carlsberg in Alexandria. Oh, the wonders of modern life. Even then. Even with a war on.'

'And you know he'd have walked for it twice as far, walked himself blind and just kept on, crossed any desert you gave him: you know that he has the true want, that it could take him anywhere. He shows you all of that. Which is proper acting.'

'Genius.'

'Genius.'

'God bless him all his days.'

I have never heard Robert bless anyone before.

And we pause and, in two different cities, picture Mills and the black-and-white bar room with the shaded quiet and the ceiling fans and the barman who is courteous and attentive and understands gently and deeply exactly the things that you need. Together, we see the moment when Mills meets his lager, the tender pause before he strokes one finger through its sweat. We sympathise with his lips as they make their first touch.

'Genius.' Robert's voice sounding much closer than before.

'Yes.'

'Your turn.'

'Oh . . . a three-minute egg when someone else has cooked it.'

'If you insist.' He doesn't sound too impressed. 'Do you do something interesting with the egg?'

'I'll show you – the next time we're both in the same room with an egg.' I'm trying to think of more people I like who'd be reasons for keeping chipper, but the only ones I can come up with are James Mason and Humphrey Bogart and Alastair Sim and a number of others, all strangers I've seen in films and long dead.

This might mean that I have no friends. Except I can't believe that. It doesn't seem likely.

'There's something else that's good, that's great.'

'What?' I ask this although the nice solemnity in his pause makes it plain where we're heading. I nudge him on, as I'm supposed to. 'What's good?'

It isn't solely sex with Robert – *he's* my friend. When I consider this seriously, the billowy feeling comes back behind my face and tickles. He makes me warmer, always.

And at the moment he's also sipping gin, delaying his reply. 'What's good is being both in the same room. Being with you. Being with the hard skin on your heels and the place where your lower incisors are uneven and the mole at your hip, near the bone, and the way you don't have any earlobes and –'

'I should work in a carnival sideshow. Thanks.'

'No.' The word slightly bewildered and sweet. 'No. That's the stuff I like, stuff I remember when you're not here. Why are you not here?'

'I told you.'

'What did you tell me?'

'I'm not well.'

'Yes, but you sound better. You could come home now.'

'I haven't got my clothes.'

'So you could come home now.'

'If we talk about this any more I'm going to get into trouble.'

'So I shouldn't tell you that I want to suck your nipples and that the left one is a little bit more cute than the right, but I could be very affectionate to both of them, right now. I could be kissing your tits and then tuning them both into Radio Moscow, right now. There's no end to the –'

'Robert. Please.' The side of my head twitching and the image of being discovered half undressed and having phone sex in a downstairs corridor by my brother, or – how much more delightful – my brother's wife, is not inviting, but at the moment it isn't quite not inviting enough. 'I'm only ill – I'm not dead. If we start doing this, we'll have to finish doing this.'

'Then come over here and finish with me.' His little boy voice back with me again, the naked one, the one that calls you in your bones.

'If I didn't feel like shit and I could get my clothes and out of the house . . . I don't have my car with me . . . it's – Look, I will be there soon. And we can still rehearse, as a stopgap . . . since it happens we're both awake.'

'Nope.'

'What?'

'No rehearsing, if you're not here.'

'*Robert.*'

'Extra incentive – so you'll get better quick. And I'll need to go to sleep soon – I have to be up in . . . four hours. Not that I'm not up now.'

'And I could help you with that.'

'No, no. I'm going to ring off in a minute and go and have a wank. I could really do with one – a long, hard, detailed

wank. Think about you and torment myself until I come . . .
but you won't want to listen to that, because you're poorly
and you're too far away. So you sleep well, all right?'

'You fucker.'

'Mm-hmm. But not tonight. You sleep tight, love. See you
soon.'

'Robert?'

'Mm?'

And a breath dashing in, unwieldy, before I can say, 'I love
you.'

'I love you, too. But I'm still hanging up. You get very well
for me. Please. Night-night.'

There is something smug and puritanical in the small din
from the line once he's disconnected.

Having no alternatives, I scramble to my feet and shuffle
through to Simon's kitchen – where, it turns out, they don't
keep any booze. They also don't keep it in the dining room,
or the bathroom, or in what seems to be their mutual study.
(How charming: even when they're working-from-home, they
can't claw themselves apart.) The cold has sunk into me thoroughly by this time and I've started to tremble badly, which
is distressing my eyes, but I manage to find the living room
and – my angels are generous – dawdling there in the corner
is the drinks cabinet I spent so much time with when I was
young. My parents must have passed it on to their virtually
teetotal son: perhaps as a wedding present, perhaps to save it
wear and tear, to spare it from ever devolving down to me.

Simple oak, nicely understated and with a cheery sheen
which would be visible if I could risk turning on a lamp: a
little cupboard underneath for coasters and paper umbrellas,
napkins, olives, nuts, the time-wasting inconveniences that
amateur drinkers need; above this, an area for pouring, or for
setting down a tray; above this, heaven, which is to say the
pull-down door that opens in front of your face and releases
the sharp, dark, intelligent reek of cloistered alcohol. The hinges

creak in stereo, loud as a drawbridge, the way they always did, and the sound sets something leaping in me, up through the blood it flies – joy. Not the shy joy Mr Russell tended, or the kind that I thought I'd grow up for, but mine, *my joy*: adjusting the world and defining the brain, instantaneous and available by the glass.

Except there's nothing here.

Fuck.

No. Nothing.

I can smell where it's been. I could lean in and lick the wood – but I wouldn't catch more than a sherry stain, if that. This was all that I needed and they've stolen it.

I'm tired and cold and shaking and, as soon as it knows I can find no drink, the fear in the house funnels into the room around me, scuttling inside sounds I can't decipher and racing the dark up, tense against my back. It moves under my ribs, climbing and falling, climbing and falling, like a spider against glass. And louder than anything there is the threat of being dry, trapped dry, alone with no one here but the incomplete me.

'Hannah?'

It is partly a relief to have a group of noises creep in close and then congeal into Gillian – the restrained and feminine disturbance of her arrival as she reaches the room, throws on the light and then walks up to deal with me. She does something in the social services, so dealing with people like me keeps her in work. Not that I expect her to be grateful.

'Looking for something, were we?'

The ominous first-person plural. And that fabulously knowing, sing-song delivery, I wonder if she intends to be quite so dangerously irritating. 'Found it, did you? Oh dear, you can't have. Because *the cupboard is bare.*'

I pity her clients: combating such an Olympian intellect must depress them at every turn. Massive depression and frothing rage must, indeed, dominate their lives. And here she stands like a cartoon matron in her chin-to-ankle nightgown, and wanting me to think she hid the bottles when I know it was Simon. Most likely, he's thrown out the coffee, as well – too stimulating. I might down a whole jar with a Brasso chaser and then run amok.

'What's the matter, *Hannah*? No witty, little comments to make?'

If I did have any comments, I'd much rather waste them on her cats. 'No. Going to bed now.'

'Oh, are you?' She breathes only from her shoulders up, I notice, everything very shallow and frenetic: carrying on like that must eventually damage your health. 'Going to bed. Is that right?' This may be an attempt at sarcasm, it's impossible to tell, and I'm well past caring.

'Have to . . . go to bed. Night.' Because she can say what she likes about me – I don't have be here while she does and I want to be lying down and I want to be unconscious and if I close my eyes when it's this late and I'm this tired – instantly this tired – the effort of listening to her making my skin itch – then surely I will sleep. I would strongly prefer to be asleep. Caught flat underneath the night, alone and alert and with no defences, I don't deserve that. Sleeping is my one way out of here.

I drag myself past her, duvet trailing on the polished hard-wood floor through no trace of visible dust. I wonder if she's gladdened by my demonstration of her domestic proficiency and it may be she says something further to that effect, but I genuinely, physically can no longer hear a word.

I can't do this.

No sleep, not practically any kind of rest, your night full of crawling, the presence of crawling, and dirty rags of something, the taste of rags, of death, and first the morning pouncing down alight and now leering through the windows of the car and coming in to get you, only a pinch of glass to keep it back, and so much of it in your surroundings because Simon is driving you, taking you out to the airport, no matter what you think.

I don't want to go.

And he's repeating about the money – the cost you didn't ask them all to pay – and the reasons why they can't afford it, the coming baby and its needs, the toll of the communal sacrifice. You didn't want it, didn't know about it, would have told them not to, but there it is, past recalling, such a monstrous sum spent and with nothing to show, because they have laid down a kind of bet on you, something unwieldy for you to carry with you on your trip to this clinic, this hospital, this spa, this holding tank you cannot visualise no matter what name it has. They think it might help you to go there and they have this love for you: this hard, immovable, weight of love they are levering down on to your breathing – Simon and Mrs Simon and your parents and the child unborn – the five of them sending you off to win their bet and recover yourself, grow respectable and better until everyone can pretend that's the way you were made.

So I won't go then. I can decide.

But the countryside is rushing ahead of the car, faster than the windscreen, reckless, and sucking you on until you feel very sick and all the while you're plunging downwards to the point where your family's wishes are going to make you disappear.

Please.

To the place with the aeroplane smell – jet fuel and vomit, diseases and sweat and travelling too fast to keep your soul. The scent of all those souls abandoned, tearing, you kick it up when you walk. Simon checks you in like your luggage – you can't think where your luggage came from – and there are men with guns here and surely that could lead to bad mistakes and you should go home now, it's time for that, but your brother tells the desk woman that you won't smoke and will sit near the aisle and that you are carrying no explosives and here is your ticket and boarding pass and here is your passport in order, although it contains the picture of someone who is not truly you and, judging yourself against your papers, it's terribly easy to spot the forgery. The cheap, dull fake.

But Robert knows me – he knows that I'm real and like this and correct.

No Robert with you here, though, only Simon who keeps you drinking coffees, drenches you with them so much that your small bones have started to trill and he's got you reined in where he can watch you, gauge you, until the last possible call when you have to be freed, allowed to go off and be somewhere you'll disappoint him, suspend all bets and disgrace yourself and drink.

He doesn't meet your eye as you spin and wave to him, because he can already see you failing. You are good money going after bad.

At the metal detectors you leave your keys in your pocket – so used to being locked in, you forgot that you had them – and the uniform people pat at you and search you and pass you through with frowns and you ask where the crowds are, the travellers, but no one says and you are very loud here, this corner being full of nods and whispers, which is strange. You are strange, but this is stranger and maybe, along with everything else, you are going deaf.

For their own reasons, individuals bump into you very often, even though they are so few and there is so much space. Not that it matters, because now you are walking, your path is fixed through the things you can buy: ways to tell time and smell not like a monster and ways to smoke and calm the hands and hide the eyes and ways to spend money to make yourself happy and ways to feel filthy because of it, as if you were thumbing through porn, as if people were fucking you here with your own cash.

No.

Fuck them. Fuck that.

That isn't happy. That's sad. And it isn't important, because you don't want anything: you're only looking for a friend. Robert would be one if he was here and you will phone him soon, but you can see your other friends now, your darlings, your sweet dreams.

Although there are so many you can't choose, and the shelves begin to loom, which is a cause of nervous tension.

Never mind, though, you find something, grab at something, and hold on to it like a lifebelt until you can pay.

£11.75.

Which is momentarily – you seem – it is mislaid – but about you, very close – you can assure.

£11.75.

They gave your clothes back, not your money. But you can assure. You look again. There must be something.

Simon, you prick.

The announcement announces your flight. Wallet. You have that. Card – no cash machine, no time – but you may have money on the card, in it, in the card, may have £11.75. You have to try, in any case. Time draining out as the girl at the cash desk, a child in fact, tinkers with your plastic, has to type

its number out, and then the line is down, or broken, decomposing, and then another slow attempt and mechanical noises
follow and, throughout this, she holds fast on to your bottle,
as if it might not be completely yours, when she is absolutely
much too young to drink and cannot understand a single part
of anything about the depth of adult and liquid relationships.

£11.75.

You wait for the paper to curl up and out, the signable
receipt that will confirm the possibility of purchase. You
concentrate on making your signature seem like your own.
You smile with your fullest integrity and charm.

£11.75.

YES.

So God is with you – and, in that case, who is not?

You suit each other, you and God, you're both alone.

In the concourse there's murmuring, faces not in focus,
time-delayed, and newspapers in their hands and they're staring
like cows, like standing flesh.

The toilet is more civilised and smaller, no one here, and
that cool, true friend is yours now and you can see much more,
hear much more, even before it's open and too soon and also,
to be truthful, not fast enough, there's the beauty of swallowing,
the loveliness, the sharp breath from the bottle's neck and the
handsomeness of that first taste, it shouts out, shudders the walls.

Then you can ring him – Robert. You can try the card
again, persuade it to bear a phone call. You're more than equal
to doing that.

'Canada, going to Canada –' telling it to his machine, not
to Robert, Robert isn't there – 'Sorry. Canada –' his answering
machine, which doesn't answer, just repeats the words he left
it months ago. 'Canada, that's . . . Four weeks. I mean, I don't
know. I can come back straight away.'

But you'll be better soon. If they've spent so much money
to make themselves happy, to make you happy, then soon it
must come true and you'll be cured.

You will give yourself up. You will be helped. You are a habit that you can't afford.

That makes sense, that's quite believable.

Although not as real as the press of that bet, the drag of expectations impeding you as you run towards the gate.

But you're weightless by take-off, no further burden to anyone – your limbs hollowed out with rushing and your heart thinned to pure motion, a soft knot of blood that evaporates, burns into joy. And more joy in the quiet, whiskey rattle at your feet, the living, stirring 40 per cent proof of perfection. Add it to yourself and make 100, without fail.

Man behind's kicking your seat. Multiple twitching and flickers from every tiny movie screen and up to the toilet with your proof in its nice bag and back and food you don't need and your eyelids closing harsh against your eyes and swallowing slow and this child in the gangway and she's staring clear inside you and up to the toilet with your proof in its nice bag and back and over you climbs your neighbour who smells of moss and more proof from the attendant and man behind's kicking your seat and a kind of sleep and safety in the blank grind of engines and the half-light and up to the toilet with your proof in its nice bag, but leave it now because it's dead, it's empty, and this makes you sorry and then sit in your seat and watch the attendant take your nice bag from the toilet and look at it and laugh and man behind's kicking your seat and

'*What?*'

You want to know why he hates you, why he is doing this – sitting and reading the paper and doing this to you. But then the headline on his lap distracts you. You want to ask about it.

'What?'

There are military pictures, which you didn't expect.

'What . . .'

He's laughing, smirking, undistracted and wiping his hands

on his sleeves — some sort of oozing there — and then there's
a jolt through the airframe and

You see the headlines again.

'Ah, because, when did this . . .'

Asking your neighbour now — man behind hates you and
is no use — so you call towards your neighbour.

'*We're at **war**?*'

And you can't think how something so large could have
occurred so unawares, a whole war without your knowledge,
and your neighbour hands over her paper, looks at you as if
you are dead and empty and you can't see the print or the
pictures, because they move and make you colour-blind, stone-
blind, and everything in the cabin has no proof now and smells
of bombs and you are sliding into a restless dark where you
float, where you are naked, stripped to your sin, and under
you there is nothing but hot, wet earth, no sign of a human
past remaining beyond this slaughterhouse stench that catches
you, sinks you, drags you above it until you touch, until you
are slithering over the thick, red cling of mud and, here and
there, it jolts beneath you and this has a meaning you understand — that the dead are kicking up, that they remember you
and hear you and can taste that you are there. They want you
down. They want you buried down with them.

It's like being in love – inhale while you're looking at no one: exhale and they're someone, they're more of yourself, an essential extension, your life support. The whole change happens in half a breath. With being tired, truly very tired, it's the same thing.

Blood moves in you, nails grow, your brain ticks by, and you plan and then you execute, hold your agenda, keep your grip, your steering, take account of contingencies and carry them ahead, you are – as far as you are capable – in charge. And then not. Your contingencies evaporate and have no meaning, events are no longer any of your business. You breathe quietly, think nothing, halt.

This must be the way that angels are – how else could they stand it?

During my first day in the clinic – they call it a clinic – I wasn't at peace. I woke up on a carpet in a blurred room I didn't know and I was twisted up in sheets, in white cotton, the hint of a bed far to my left. I had the usual no idea of how I'd got there and this disgusting pain when I tried to roll over and guess my bearings.

I sat up anyway and the sense of bad injury peaked before I could properly work out that I'd just torn away congealed blood from a split in my lip and a number of grazes and a cut above my eye – which had been dressed, but I'd also dislodged the tapes during my period of disarray – and now I was leaning above a sketchy impression of my face, picked out in brown on a virgin bedsheet and – wounds being temperamental – I had already added the odd new touch in crimson. And my mouth had begun to bleed again in earnest.

I flailed the bed back to a kind of order and dabbed where I hurt with my sleeve, a white sleeve – they'd dressed me in some kind of pseudo-surgical gown, thin and shapeless and apparently very prone to creasing. It also showed up fresh blood extremely clearly and I pondered the smears and drops that seemed to be spreading without my doing anything and I breathed in and was troubled, distressed. Then I breathed out and my tiredness took me. I was senseless and silent and past recalling before I could reach the coverlet.

Alcoholics are those excessive drinkers whose dependence on alcohol has attained such a degree that they show a noticeable mental disturbance or an interference with their mental and bodily health, their interpersonal relations and their smooth social and economic functioning; or who show the prodromal signs of such developments. They therefore require treatment.
World Health Organization,
Expert Committee on Mental Health
Alcohol Subcommittee Second Report,
1952

Possibly I'm being oversensitive, but that does sound like a threat. 'They therefore require treatment.' – There's a lack of detachment and subtlety in that – it's interfering. Plus, it appears to be plastered on the back of every door we've got here: no bathroom, bedroom, lounge or, very probably, fuse box is free from the Alcohol Subcommittee's influence. What if I *did* have a mental disturbance of the noticeable kind? Repeated insinuations about my lack of smooth social functioning could nag me right over my edge.

Not that I'm anything other than mellow at the minute. This is undoubtedly a calming place to stay. Sensible, if overly hearty eating, lots of bland liquids and sleep, few responsibilities beyond making my own bed: the Clear Spring Clinic's regimen is exhaustingly healthy. The world may be going to Hell beyond us, but we're fine and know nothing about it – are forbidden to guess.

So my fettle is fine. I didn't realise it was possible to eat this much fruit – all of that peeling and roughage, it seemed very time-consuming when I had other matters in hand. But here I'm gobbling down enough of the stuff to fuel an orang-utan.

This is a sign of my being cooperative, which I am. My compliance is absolute. I came here for treatment freely. I volunteered.

The trouble is, treatment hasn't been forthcoming.

Take today – because I have to, it's my only way through to tomorrow. This morning, we're sitting in a circle again – this means we're doing something to make us better, the kind of something that we get instead of treatment. Apparently it's a known fact that no one has ever recuperated from any unfortunate state without being slapped down into a grisly ring of pink Naugahyde armchairs and made to discuss their personal lives with a dozen emotional vampires listening.

There's a plaintive bastard unburdening himself for us, even now: 'What got me . . . the thing with my daughter . . . I knew where she kept her savings and I just took them. For myself.' This is Sam: he is wearing a badge to that effect and has no other distinguishing features beyond his adenoidal whine and his fifth-degree dandruff, filthy clots of it stuck on the inside of his glasses. 'My own daughter. I took it all.'

Which seems fair enough to me – where would a daughter get money from in the first place, if not her parents? And what could she possibly need it for that would actually be important?

Sam pushes his hand back through his hair every thirty seconds: regular as the clock over the door, but infinitely less tidy. I must end up inhaling at least an ounce of dead, khaki skin from him each session. I've had five days of this already and neither of us seems to be any better – in fact, he seems worse.

He'll cry soon – a compulsive weeper, Sam – which is great. The circle is delighted when anyone cries and usually we get a break then, possibly with biscuits, because the nurses are also delighted by even a dewy eye, never mind a remorseful tear.

Our group has two nurses. Nurse Ogilvie (we can call him Frank) is a broad slab of scrubbed and trimmed exterior with tiny dark eyes and a small, deep mouth marooned in his massive face, nothing to do there but seem overly mobile and too moist. Nurse Forbes (we can call him Nurse Forbes) is taller and stringy with a hint of wiry, nasty strength. Sometimes – today, for example – we get the pair of them at once.

They'll know what prodromal means. I don't. Sounds like a seda-tive. 'Let Prodromal wash your cares away. Larger doses produce euphoria, smooth social and economic functioning and the sensation of being caught in a state of permanent fucking grace.'

That's the kind of prescription to get your respect.

'There was blood everywhere. I didn't know whose it was . . . that is, while I was in the blackout, I could have –'

Yes, yes, you could have done anything: we all could have done anything, we've all had blood everywhere – I'm not impressed. Life is unpredictable: blood's bound to be involved eventually.

It's not that I'm unwilling to participate. I do try. I have a genuine desire to be a different, more comfortable, person when I leave. Matters came to a head and required a firm adjustment which will mean that I have to cut down on my misbehaviours. I can see that change is necessary and I'm aware that I will have to apply myself. In my initial assessment – which they ran through when I was still delicate, had a headache that hurt in the soles of my feet – even then I made sure to be very much aware and in favour of both change and application.

Still, I'm just not satisfied with this. I spent my first three days penned in my room with the wet heaves and the dry heaves and the sweat and the cracked lips and the stiff hair that smells of vomit and disturbs you when you're having a go at sleep. Although that's to be expected – likewise, the dreams full of somebody drowning you and the rattling while you're awake – the whole rigmarole. Been there before. But not in a clinic, not in a caring environment, not where I might have believed I would get trained support. Nurses, they can give you Valium, they can let you ease down gently, they can prove that they **are** bloody nurses, and not a collection of unskilled sadists in pastel uniforms, by doing a tiny bit more than coming in every couple of hours with clean basins and orange squash.

Oh, and showers — the lady nurses help you shower. As if you'd want to, as if tons of leaping water and a resultant lack of air and echoes that would deafen a corpse are what you long for as you lie on your bed in the half-dark and tremble and watch the ceiling creep.

The problem with doing it this way, coming off without chemical aid, is that your head goes all over the place. You can't think. Or you think far too much. Or in far too many dimensions.

Like why didn't I have any grandparents? I'd have enjoyed them, called them Nan-Nan, or Pop-Pop, or some other daft name I thought up when I was two. They would have been stabilising for me.

You wake before dawn and, eyes still shut, you're already going full tilt at remembering a sandwich you ate in school with the best friend you haven't seen for twenty years and you immediately miss her to the point of weeping and then progress to worrying that she's dead.

My mother's parents are dead — house fire before I was born. Nobody ever mentioned my father's, though — as if they'd never been. That's not normal. In a well-balanced family, I would have been informed: the presences and absences would have been accounted for, saved up in a lovely, old shoebox my mother would keep in her dressing-table drawer. We could have looked through it on rainy Sundays — 'That's your birth certificate — 2.15 in the morning, what an early bird. That's your Nan-Nan Luckraft beside her scooter. Pop-Pop was taking the picture: look, you can see part of his thumb. And there's Grandpa McGovern in his sapper's uniform. He was at Dunkirk. A great fan of Jimmy Jewel: you would have liked him.'

There are so many stories I don't have. And who will tell me to anyone when I've gone — Simon? Simon's child? I'll be a diplomatic silence. Or maybe I won't come to mind in the end — as if I'd never been.

Sam is snuffling quietly in his chair, a box of tissues passed along to him with dreadful efficiency, the whole group attempting to seem moved by his grief. Yesterday we were told alcoholics are selfish, so we have worked out that showing concern for our fellow patients – although we have nothing in common – will probably aid our final diagnosis. Alcoholic: who'd want to see *that* in their file? And anyway, there's no point being normal, if you can't get it to show.

These chairs are the colour of testicles, exactly the right shade: that dusky-browny-rose. Is this intentional and, if so, is it meant to make us more or less relaxed?

Oddly, we're not allowed a break – perhaps because Sam cries too easily and represents no particular achievement. We always confess in strict order of clockwise rotation, so a tiny flutter of tension springs up round the room while we realise that Gregory is next. We all have our cinematic low points and our scars, but Gregory is special.

'I can'd shink of anyshing dhuday. No' yealy . . .' His face is perfect, clear as milk, almost painfully young – his trouble lies under his chin where the knife went in: the knife he was holding. We got our chance to decipher the whole story on my first session with the group: clumping my twitchy hands together to prevent embarrassment, and picking out one dulled consonant after another as Gregory was forced into stumbling out the tale of the Montreal evening, the bar, the minor squabble, the girlfriend who started flirting with the ugly businessman and then the yank forward through no one can tell how much time until Gregory is running across the Place Dupuis and falling unluckily and waking up in a hospital with a ragged hole through the floor of his mouth and a very much shorter tongue. It disturbed him that he must have swallowed the missing tip.

Although Gregory is determined to have nothing more for us today. As his silence threatens to solidify, Nurse Forbes chisels in. No soul's going to pass unbared while he's around. 'We can wait. Perhaps you want to talk about how you're finding the clinic.' Gregory's a new arrival, like me. 'Where do you feel you fit into the group? Gregory?'

Obviously, no one sane would even attempt to answer that, but Gregory has to, because those are the rules and giving no reply is the worst of many negative and revealing possibilities.

Roll on lunch. More fruit.

Then, in the afternoon, if we don't have a one-to-one consultation, we're allowed out into the sulphur-scented air. There really is a thermal spring at Clear Spring, channelled off and grimly collected in a green-tiled concrete tank where those of us with permission and no history of suicide can slip into sepia-stained gowns and submerge ourselves in the fizzing, stinking water until the heat makes our eyes ache and our skins turn silky and develop a permanent, mineral reek. At least nobody asks you questions in the tank.

And, from whichever underwater bench you've picked, you can sit and squint up at the valley's slope and the late, shallow snow still shining, because we are high here and in the shade of even higher, cooler mountains. The silvered wood of the central villa hangs in the sunlight like smoke and reminds you of how much this place is costing every hour and of the rules which say that you must go and be with other dried-out drinkers there and conceal what might be misinterpreted as psychopathic traits as you mingle in a social setting. No TV to ease the tension: there's no signal.

Dispersed around the villa on the cosy incline are self-consciously winding paths, various mature trees, some of them budding, and the six clapboard Houses where each of the six groups lives and cooks its evening meals and bickers about cleaning rotas and screams in the night. I live in Thoreau House, which is beside Milton.

'Ish dihicult. I'm no' shuw . . . dhere sho many peopdhe here an I don know dhem.' Gregory talking to the floor, his lowered eyelids faintly blue, as if some tiny hurt is bruising them, and his lashes thick, feminine. 'I shupposhe isholadhed, ash hoe I feedh.'

If they wanted to name our Houses after writers, why not pick people we could like? Hemmingway, Fitzgerald, Thomas, Behan, Parker, Reese — the kind we could take to, good examples. Or Shakespeare: killed himself with a final, birthday bender: the man had style.

Behind Seneca House, there's a thin path of layered bark; I wandered on to it yesterday. It led into a further, closer fold of the valley floor where there are aspens, bark pale and clean as flesh, and at their heart a narrow lake. When I drew near it, a line of ducks clattered over the surface and up, necks craning into thin air, wings flickering. The border of the water was soft, leeching into mud, and so I stayed back from it, from the cream and blue reflections and the silk light. I started to make a circuit of the margin, here and there, a grind of wet snow underfoot.

And then the swan came. Labouring out of a thicket on the far side of the pool, there he was: and I realised I'd never seen one before, not live, not stamping out over an uneven thaw, throat flexed like a snake, grinding straight for me with a wallowing, rolling pivot from hip to hip that might have been comic if it wasn't so intent. Because he was fixed on me now: bowing and launching down into the dark, letting his wings peak and threaten above his back, pushing forward in long, hard kicks to crumple the water at his breast, head switching, side to side, as each black eye got its look at me and the feathers bristled, swelled on the tight lash of his neck.

'He doesn't know you, that's all.'

I'd been too surprised by the bird to notice a grey man, worrying through the trees. Tweed cap and coat, good trousers and zip-up galoshes: he might have been a banker, an executive, out for a break in the park. 'I'm Hitt.'

'What?'

Blurry voice, barely calling ahead of him as he walked up to face me. 'I'm Mr Hitt. I come here often.'

'Okay. Saves me asking.'

'Asking what?'

'If you come here often.'

He wasn't listening, scanning washed-out glances beyond me to the swan. There was also a lightness about him, a clarity in his expression that suggested his attention was too delicate to divide.

'I'm Hannah. Hannah Luckraft.'

'Oh, I'm Mr Hitt.' His head switched round to me, quick as the swan's, and he reached for my hand, shook it once before letting it drop. He was wearing knitted gloves, red, the wool too soft to be anything other than cashmere. 'I had an accident.'

'I'm sorry.'

'No, it's all right.' He was watching the swan again – it had stalled at the bank closest to us and was patrolling back and forth, sipping at the water occasionally and then glaring at me with a bubbling cough. 'The accident I had was a long time ago . . . He doesn't know you and so he's afraid and you seem very tall to him. A tall swan would be dangerous. That's how he understands us – as swans.'

'I see.'

'You should come back and be introduced. I'm here every day at this time. We all are.' Hitt drifted away then, plodding gently into the mud, crouching down to a squat and ignoring me completely, smiling out at the swan.

Drink – it really can do damage. Poor sod's probably rolling in it, but he ends up here. With a swan.

'Hannah.'

And I end up here with Nurse Ogilvie and Nurse Forbes.

I'm staring at the Session Room's cerise walls, trying to find irregularities in the plaster.

Funny feeling you get from a swan – from that swan. You want him to like you, purely because you know he won't.

'Hannah. Do you mean to avoid speaking?' Nurse Ogilvie

asking me this and I know that I should answer, but I'm running a touch slow this morning, I can't quite climb out of the daydream and into the day.

There are no human beings in Clear Spring I could give a toss about. And they won't let me call Robert. They won't let me call anyone.

Nurse Forbes taking charge. 'Hannah, you're checking the clock again. Does that mean you were bored by what others have shared? Do you think they'll be bored by you?'

Beside me, Debbie is glowering at my upper arm, as if I have just sat beside her while she has bravely and honestly and far too fucking quickly poured out the required fluid ounces of heart and I haven't heard a syllable, not a word since Gregory mumbled into life. And this is, in fact, the case.

'I . . . ah . . . I was thinking about the swan.'

Why should feeling as if I'm in primary school be an aid to sobriety?

'What swan?' This from Forbes in the minorly turned-on voice he only uses when something Freudian may be slithering into view.

'There's one on the little lake.'

'No, there's a pair of swans, Hannah.'

'I only saw one.'

'The male?'

'I don't know . . . I thought so.' *I know where you're going with this.* 'Somebody said . . . It was a nice swan. I was going to go —'

'You assumed it was male.'

'I suppose so.'

'Why did you do that?'

And I laugh, because that will prove I'm relaxed and that I have no intention of talking about my sex life, or promiscuity, breaking up couples, relating better to males than females, being occasionally perverse — things that every woman does, or thinks of, and that don't do any harm.

What the fuck does this have to do with drinking, anyway?

'Why are you laughing?' Ogilvie peering at me as if I've hurt myself, his whole face this suffocating wedge of pity.

'Why is that, Hannah? . . .' Forbes at me again. 'And why are you wearing your name badge upside down? Don't you want us to know who you are? Or do you think that we're a joke?'

Fuck you. I see what you're up to. Think I couldn't do your job? I could fucking do it in my sleep.

Still, if in doubt, apologise.

'I'm sorry.'

'What are you sorry about, Hannah?'

'I don't know.'

'Yes, you do, Hannah.'

Fuckyouallofyoufuckinglookingatmewhenyouknowfuckall

Fuck you

'I don't know.'

And the clock on the wall is sliding gently, stretching when I blink and Gregory tipping his head, watching me, tender as something I've misplaced and the air is twisting and thickening in my mouth.

'I don't know.'

'Hannah.'

'I don't know.'

Everything, irretrievably salt.

Fuckyou

And it is plain, even to me, that the group has what it wants now — today I'm the one — head in hands and sucking breath and reduced to childhood noises and crying and crying and crying until I have never been.

Or almost.

Fuckyou

Under the tongue, where I keep myself, there's still something left — because no one gets away that easily. And while the group looks forward to its biscuits and the nurses smile wisely at a job well done and the tissue box is banged against my hand, I am utterly sure in my blood and bone that I let them do this, they haven't won. I haven't broken. I haven't changed. I've simply seen how they're trying to fuck me and I'm going to fuck them back.

VII

We're allowed this – a real wood fire in the Main Lounge before lights out. Closed in with peace and comforts, we can't say that we're suffering, not exactly. Apart from the daytime prying, the insinuations, the relentless search for dirt, and this resultant tension: our sense of the faults that are waiting beyond the door, of postponed but still inevitable hurt.

And there are other ills out there: hungry threats that are larger than us and our personal harms. Things are not quite well with us, we can't deny it – but they are very much worse in the world. We can almost remember how but do not say.

Instead, we delight in the safety any prison will provide: the absence of choices or disorder and our new selves clarified, fixed by confinement. We are already verifiably different from our bad old selves, although perhaps not powerfully altered, not yet.

And we have our inviting hearth, lit to sustain us. It serves multiple high purposes and therefore conforms to the Ultra-Puritan ethic of Clear Spring – 'Get all the blood that you can from this stone and then throw it at two of these edible birds before building it into a wall.' Patients who are practical and over-energetic are led outside to hew and fell themselves into a coma. Supplying us with fuel is intentionally labour-intensive, because no one has ever been trusted with a chainsaw – I did ask – so every bit of the hacking and sawing is done by hand. We currently seem an apathetic lot, but some of us are occasionally persuaded to split logs and experience the thrill of being trusted with an obviously deadly, although low-tech, weapon. The fire itself is the main thing, though – at a loss in company, we can stare at it and not seem introspective. It gives us a ghost of privacy and makes our silences less awkward.

'Decongestant inhalers.'

Not that we're being silent this evening: myself and Tom and Eddie hogging the fireside sofa and Gregory reading in a chair, but still with us, still listening, I can tell. And I am aware that I'm in male company again, but I didn't seek it out. I might just as easily be bonding with other women. I have no sexual agenda, despite what Nurses Ogilvie and Forbes may say.

'What about inhalers?' We're going through things we've heard of, but never tried. Inhalers are a new one on me.

'You eat them, yeah – what else? Eat the sponge part with the chemical in – makes you *fucking insane*.' This is Eddie – a man I understand to have been grotesquely insane in his time. None of us actually knows him, of course, we've only heard him recite his life, just as he's heard us recite ours. Obviously, we expect everyone to be lying as they reminisce – whether a nurse is taking notes or not – but lies are never less than revealing and Eddie's mark him out to be a total lunatic. So he's a stranger, but an intimate one, the way we all are to each other – no hope of returning to small talk when we're being hauled, en masse, through a daily, public Third Degree. I have what may be a good grip on Eddie's major crimes, his styles of infidelity, his childhood fears, but his second wife sounds very unconvincing and I couldn't come up with his surname if you paid me.

Tom mumbles a contribution, trying to impress. 'Whipped cream.' Tom who smells of talcum powder, who has admitted no startling crimes.

'For what – a cholesterol high?' I'm not making fun of him, but he is trying to tell us something old and unremarkable.

'No, the gas –'

Eddie is also unimpressed. 'Yeah, the fucking gas, the propellant for the cream-in-a-can. I know that. But how much could you ever inhale before you were just pushing whipped cream into your fucking brains . . . I fucking hate cream. It's bullshit.' He's been asked to restrain his foul language in the sessions, but he doesn't bother elsewhere – it makes his sweating worse. Rings tattooed on three fingers, a Maori effort on his arm, always in T-shirts, always visibly damp. I made sure he sat furthest from me, so now he's soaking into Tom.

'Well, I have the best one.' This is true, I do. 'I'm not sure how it works, but it's the best.'

'So? Give it up.'

'Foam.'

'Foam? What fucking foam?'

'Foam – foam-rubber foam – like you get in seats. The gas that makes the bubbles in the foam – it makes you high.'

'So you chew on the foam?'

'So you chew on the foam.'

'That's the sickest fucking thing I ever heard. Who the fuck would even think of it?'

Gregory is smiling at his book. He hasn't turned a page in hours. We haven't talked much, for obvious reasons, but he listens with a sort of fury – you can feel the clasp of it. Then the almond eyes sliding a look at you, a brush of contact before he sinks himself away.

'Foam. I'm telling you. You get completely ripped, apparently. And think about how easy it would be – if you wanted to go on a bender, you could just eat your furniture – you'd never need to leave the house. Or, I suppose, in the end, you'd run out, but then all you'd have to do is go to some upholstery place and order more.'

'Need sm more a' them scatter cushions, dude . . .' Eddie lapses into a fake slur. 'Ah'm throwing a *par-dee* . . .' We can do this now, call up our old voices and laugh at them, make cartoons of our former selves, as if they won't be back.

I join in, playing the witless drunk. 'Isss my birthday, so I thought I'd make a chair.' The happy bumbler – the act that

I always did use, not because I was really sober: but because I never was that kind of drunk. I wasn't lovable, or harmless – I just knew what other people want to see. 'No . . . make it *two* chairs . . . never know when you'll have folk popping in. Need to be on the safe side . . . 'void disappointment. And now, my good man, show me your range of adhesives, juss while I'm here. D'you have any raspberry flavour . . .?'

To be tolerated, that's what you aim for. Lurches of apology and concern, pre-emptive laughter, calculated minor clumsiness to cover the mishaps you can't help: the big, soft hands you've grown by the end of the evening paddling out ahead of you to prevent offence.

And I do see this is how a man drinks and, therefore, inappropriate for me. I should have been at home behind my curtains with the methylated gin, the Tia Maria and Blue Nun. I should have been an early-morning shame at the off-licence: make-up uneven, hands trembling into my bag for the greasy purse and then flitting over the counter to snatch up a genteel quarter-bottle, requested with a quiet excuse, even slight surprise, and back to sneak it down mixed with my tea – in the cup, not the pot – nobody there to see me, but female drinking is a sin and should be made invisible. Further downhill, I could have been a regular call to the local minicabs, asking them to fetch my bottles for me, so I could avoid the challenge of a walk, pay the premium to keep in hiding.

That's how you really do go insane. That's how you die alone.

So I stay with the men, because then I'm not alone and because they do their best to be happy. This is the only sensible choice. No pegging out with my face in the three-bar fire and being food for the obligatory poodle, or Pekinese. No tarting around in miniskirts and squealing, sucking up bubble gum-flavoured vodka and flashing my tits at cars. A modicum of dignity, that's not too much to ask.

And how else would I have met Robert? I've got to be with the boys. How else would I meet anyone?

The fire has sunk to a bed of embers, a kind of breathing fluid full of dark and cherry lights, scuttling heat. No point pitching on another log: we have to be snug in our respective Houses by ten sharp. And there's a urine test in Thoreau tonight. What larks.

I leave my boys gently, tell them *goodnight*. The usual drunk's vocabulary of affection: arm-tapping, hair-ruffling, back-punching, hand-squeezing, the swollen kiss: it's withered away, out of bounds. We've discovered we can't control it any more – it makes cartoons of us, full-blown Looney Tunes. Emotions overshadow and then crush us like falling Acme safes, chasms open, cliffs slide by and dynamite fizzes in every rabbit hole and apple pie the nurses can locate. At every contact our big, round, animal feet will bicycle pointlessly in place on the slick curve of our brain pans, while the world opens trapdoors too vicious and too arousing to be borne and bulldogs and coyotes chase us and our defences go astray and we end up grinning, sickly, at one horror or another, while something bad keeps screeling in our skin. This chaos is rarely visible, naturally.

A woman – Belinda? – penned me into a hug when I cried in the group this morning. I stood against her, almost disabled by the catastrophes she was creating behind my eyes, the torments for my animated inner self: the certainty that bastards like her are drawn to suffering, the simultaneous oily wash of her possible kindness, the sudden thought of my mother and claustrophobia and fear and the need to hold Robert, to be held, the want of that solid scale you measure yourself against when you touch a man and only a man.

In the end I had to push her off and then apologise and then say it once more with feeling for the benefit of everyone. As if the whole situation hadn't been her fault. Belinda – that *was* her name. She won't stay sober. Hysterics like that, they can't manage the real world.

Me, I can do this, I've got the hang of sobriety. I've been here eight days without a drop of anything. That's the longest

I haven't drunk since I was at school. If I can do eight days, I can do forever. Ambling back to Thoreau through the lamplight and patchy snowshine, I have to admit the whole process has not been as hard as I'd have thought. Other inmates have told me about luxury drying-out facilities with soothing artificial waterfalls, room service, hair care, and I could be annoyed with my brother when I consider where I've ended up: when I sit down in the communal clamour of another massive, ranch-style meal, or rummage in the laundry basket of abandoned airport paperbacks which is our library, or suffer inside Thoreau's canary paintwork, but I can accept that the Spartan approach may have benefits. I feel clean here, for example: bleached-in-the-blood-of-the-lamb, you-could-eat-off-me clean. There's something going on inside my soul, a sense – at still moments – that it's shining, thriving in the mountain air.

I'm even having different dreams. None of your Salvador Dali subtexts and talking dogs, not any more: not even the average Naked in the General Assembly of the Church of Scotland anxiety trips – I spend every night wide open to the same, repeating parable: no diplomacy, no metaphors, just a Terminal Stage Warning, a great, big nocturnal shout – *Hannah, don't ever do this stuff again.*

The scene is monochrome, grainy to look at with the odd scratch curled in the air and then disappearing like an insect ghost. I am in a film – really *inside* the celluloid – and the flatness of this scares me, the gouging race of the projector's sprocket wheels to either side, the certainty that I can never leave. At my back is a full saloon, wallowing in drifts of charnel-house dust, but still conducting its predictable business: the rigged poker games, the show of blousy whores, the hats and spurs and bandoliers and the pianist punching a keyboard wrist-deep in sand. He produces no sound beyond his fighting breath, but there is an attempt at music fairly audible from the shadows: the sad wavers of a blue-grass fiddle, but mainly a military drum, keeping time with a fat *tap-tap.*

I am leaning at the bar, one boot on the rail, and dressed in the body and clothes of a powder-dry cowboy. Like everyone else here, I am playing my part. I set my Stetson on the counter, lick the salt caked round my lips and, as soon as I do these things, I'm aware that the whole saloon has been waiting for me, that I have set a process into motion and something horrific is on its way.

The bartender, as I expected, sets up a shot glass of the perfect alcohol. It slips in smooth and sweet as milk and sparkles in my breath. It's the warmth of my own true home and a welcome indoors, then the heat of an animal, last-hope, 3 a.m. fuck and then it stings with the tranquil, acid cool of death. And the taste is every good taste I remember and beyond them, more, skirting the undiluted flavour of paradise and into every cell and thought and wish it places the ideal degree of drunkenness.

Even as I sip another, I know this drink is impossible, that nothing the waking world offers me can be as fine as this.

'That's the truth, isn't it? That is the truth.'

Beside me leans the suggestion of a man. When I stare straight at him, he fluctuates, as if he were reflected on molten metal, turbulent oil, but from the corner of my eye I can make out that he's dressed as another cowboy: more dusty cloth, work-hardened palms, a dark hat shading his face. His fingers drum on the bar top in time to the music, producing a fat, *tap-tap*.

'Where did you bury her?' He has an accent I can't place, but I almost recognise his voice. 'Where's the body? You can tell me.'

And this is the terrible news that I'd forgotten, the finale the bar was brought here to receive. He's quite right – I have killed someone. I have committed that last, unforgivable evil and am hollowed out by it, no more than a grinning skin stretched over the start of Hell. There is only enough of me left to be appalled.

'Where's the body?' I'm not sure if he's speaking, or making me hear what he thinks. 'You can't hide it forever, you know that.'

The bartender slides me one more shot and I pour it down, fast as I get it, in a single fist that reams my throat. Perhaps that will be the last drop, too, because we're close to the end here: walls cracking beside me, dissolution gusting and clattering everywhere.

Tap-tap.

'Where is it?'

Tap-tap.

A beating in my neck, like evidence of a malign, new organ.

Tap-tap.

'You do know.'

And the whores are laughing at some secret that I've told them and the pianist is gone and I wipe my face to be free of this suddenly monstrous heat and pick up a fresh glass in hands that are alight with blood.

Tap-tap.

My sleeves are crusted with it, heavy and stiff, my shirt front blossoming with tiny stains that swell, that coalesce, halt at my belt and my dirty jeans that seem quite usual until I finally have to search, the way that everyone knew I'd have to, until I finally lower my eyes for the source of that sound.

Tap-tap.

And watch my blood drip from my trouser cuffs down on to my boots, my red, red boots and the pool around them, the deep, bright waste of my life.

'All you have to do is tell me. Just tell me where the body is.'

It's a wonder I get any rest with that sort of show running, night after night. I sit up at random points in the darkness, dripping with nerves and needy, stiffened with lack. And somewhere in my subconscious, I must truly believe I'm too stupid to grasp the risks of drinking without having them painted in adrenalin on the back wall of my skull.

I blame Thoreau.
Lovely Thoreau.

In through the squeaky door – kept that way to make irregular entries plain to everyone and especially the nurse on duty – and here's the first of many corridors, festooned with mindless placards and slogans –

THINK, THINK, THINK.

HOW IMPORTANT IS IT?

WE ARE ALL GOD'S CHILDREN.

No wonder I have jags of nausea, now and then – not to mention this mental infection in my nights – simplistic drivel is contagious, that's an established fact. That's why I don't vote.

TO SEE OURSELVES AS OTHERS SEE US.

THE WORLD IS AS I AM.

DRUNKENNESS INCREASETH THE RAGE OF A FOOL TILL HE OFFEND: IT DIMINISHETH STRENGTH AND MAKETH WOUNDS.

MIND YOUR HEAD, IT'S OUT TO GET YOU.

Although that last one is plainly true. Your head waits until you're unconscious, then moves in and gives you a kicking you can't duck – revenge for the years of hangovers you've brought it.

Up the wooden stairs and I pass IF YOU SPOT IT, YOU'VE GOT IT, before I can face Room Five which is where I stop.

THIS IS HANNAH'S AND ——'S ROOM.

We're not intended to enjoy the peace of single occupancy, but there aren't enough girls to fill the rooms, just now, so I'm by myself. Waxed timber floor and a rag rug, one narrow pine window, over the narrow pine porch, two narrow pine beds, two narrow pine bedside tables, one narrow pine chest of drawers and one narrow pine wardrobe (gosh, what character-forming knife-fights I could have had over sharing those) and one utilitarian bathroom with toilet, sink and shower, none of them narrow, or pine. Opposite the window there is a badly framed picture of a thin man propped up in bed, two healthy men talking to him in a kind way and a spider of light above them, suggesting that something religious is taking place. In between room inspections, I turn it to the wall.

It's looking out at me now, though, as I take the plastic goblet Nurse Chiselden dodges in to offer me. Then I go into the bathroom and try to produce a test sample on demand.

I passed, no pun intended.

This isn't surprising – rumour has it there's no booze of any description for several hundred miles in all directions. We're told they don't even have surgical alcohol, which doesn't say much for their health-care credentials. The nurses also search us with unpleasant efficiency when we first come in and so, as I've never been one for cooking up boot black and those kinds of tricks, it's been easy to keep my bodily fluids pure.

Still, temptation would be resisted if it arose. I can promise that.

'I wouldn't take a drink if you gave me one, if you put it in my hand.' I'm saying this to Mr Hitt, which is almost the same as saying it to no one. Nurse Forbes has explained to me, with admonitory glee, that Hitt suffers from Korsakoff's syndrome – alcohol-induced dementia – so he begins each day as himself, but with many key events and circumstances missing. This failing breeds a peculiar, gullible eagerness to please. He will accept anyone's explanations for why he has turned out as he is.

'I fell from a hot-air balloon.'

This one is Eddie's – I recognise it. He must have slipped in the rough outline over breakfast.

'I was with my fiancée on a jaunt. Her grief at my many injuries turned her hair white in a day.'

We are standing, Hitt and I, beside the pool, feet sunk in a combination of slush and pillowed moss. I watch the swan patrolling, his mate nervous in the shallows at the far bank, and I'm smiling, almost giggling, with the assurance that I am purer now than any test can show. This place, the slow, green air, the cloak of water: I couldn't have borne it if I weren't clean. Now I'm a smoother fit with it each day. I can be comfortable in nature – it approves of me, is glad to have me back. Even the swans are less wary, the male's wings sleeking back eventually, his glances growing curious, contemplative.

'Well, it's lovely that she cares so much, Mr Hitt.' I'm not uneasy about this lying – it puts a dash of romance through his day, and tomorrow it will have disappeared completely. Of course, he gets tormented sometimes: inmates have told him about dead children, motorway tragedies, rapes – it's only human nature. He's in good hands this afternoon, though. I mean him no harm.

'I'm sure she'll come and visit you, maybe on Friday. Isn't that her usual day?'

'Yes . . .' Mr Hitt blushes experimentally towards his shoes and is convinced. 'Yes, I suppose that she might turn up again on Friday. She is very fond of me.'

'Hopelessly in love.'

Hitt pushes for detail, embellishment: which proves that he must like this, 'When I'm better, we can marry?'

'She asks the nurses every week.'

He nods, quickly complacent. 'I know.' And starts us strolling again. 'Naturally, I ask them, too.'

'Naturally.'

What remains of Mr Hitt will never leave here and he will never be able to care. It's almost appealing, his condition – a new past laid out for you each morning, like a fresh suit of clothes: no cause for regrets, or longing, nobody to miss. Not unless someone lends them to you, and even then, they'll only last until you sleep.

'You and I, we come here together each afternoon.'

Sometimes Hitt says things as if he remembers, but he's just guessing.

'Yes, that's right.'

'We are old friends . . . I knew your father.'

'That's right. You worked together, in the university.' He looks as if he'd be at home in an ivy-covered quad, a study, so why not? 'He is continuing your research. It's going well.'

'Really?' Hitt tugs at his lapels, more academic with every step. 'I'm glad to hear it. Although, I thought . . .' And perhaps here there is a murmur of whatever way he did earn his living, a hint of argument. 'Still . . . research . . .' But he isn't dogmatic. Other people have known better for so long that he's content to relax and rely on anyone. 'No, that is good.'

We have reached Hitt's rock. This is where I've been told to crouch behind him and stay still while he scrambles in his good, soft trousers and his hand-sewn overcoat and sits himself down on the lichened stone, crossed-legged on its lap, his face and hands overhanging a low, sharp drop that hides its roots under the water.

Hitt leans forward and makes a coughing grunt in his throat. The swan was on his way, in any case: first in a ruffed and stiffened display and then a slowing glide. They're used to each other, these two, but – either for my benefit, or as a point of honour – the swan has to demonstrate whose pool this is. After which he halts, as smooth and calm as cloth, and cranes up his neck to Hitt, who has drawn out a bag of bread and places the first *Good afternoon* dab of it into the bird's opened beak.

'Now, now . . . we were only talking. I'm sorry I'm late.' The swan siphons water up to wash down its snack and coughs approvingly. Hitt murmurs to me over his shoulder. 'Always bites my thumb, if he's feeling temperamental . . . never a real bite, of course. . . never anything that's impolite. There now . . . there now . . .'

And hand to beak they sway and chuckle and grumble between themselves and the swan eats and his wife slides closer, tremulous, takes morsels from the water and mutters softly.

'Ah, we have good times, don't we? Lettucc tomorrow. Too

much bread wouldn't be the thing, would it? Although it is nice.'

Possibly this is the only new information that he has remembered since he drank himself out of his mind: the trust of birds and how to speak to them.

'The pen is looking broody, don't you think?'

'Mm?'

The male glances at me, neck feathers shifting as he considers my intrusion and then finds it unimportant. I keep myself low to the ground, although the halted blood is aching in my knees.

'The pen. She seems . . . that way inclined.'

And I recall the lists my mother taught me: that larks come in exaltations and owls in parliaments, that little hares are leverets, that asses are jack and jenny, that swans are cob and pen. She wanted me to have that – the unnecessary beauties among words.

And as I uncover his name, the cob is setting his great, black webs down on the silt, levering himself to stand straight, oddly thin and face to face with Hitt, who breaks bread and offers it, breaks and offers it. 'Now, there's no need to rush.' Hitt crouches back slightly, respectful. 'Shhhh.' And the swan is satisfied, sinks to the water's surface again and drinks.

A breeze herringbones the lake and I catch the musty, warm bedlinen scent of the bird. I could like him and he could like me and, in the end, I could come and feed him for myself. It would do me more good than the endless groups, the vivisection. The questions they ask are never to the point: Forbes and Ogilvie, Ogilvie and Forbes: nothing about larks, about my soul.

Tomorrow morning, I'm supposed to go off and have my skull cracked by some consultant, let him fumble around when there's nothing left for anyone to find. I've been professionally groped here for over a week: whatever thrill there was in it has gone. I'll tell him my dream and he'll grill me about masturbation or fetishes and then try to make me feel abnormal. This doesn't suit people like me – or Hitt. We need something gentle.

The cob stands, this time deep in the pool, unfurls himself upwards and stretches his wings, shudders and claps them with a din like sailcloth and a barking cry. The pen eyes him, indulgent, and then they drift until they are together, heads ducking quietly in time, piercing the water and then rising, shaking off drops of light.

Also tomorrow morning, someone called Martha Rocco is going to be put in my room. I will be spending the rest of my time here, sleeping next to a drunk, with no further chance to do anything personal that might help me relax.

Clear Spring doesn't have my best interests at heart.

'Mr Hitt?'

'Ah?' Hitt's free of the rock and standing, brushing his hands for crumbs and mildly dishevelled – the schoolboy who couldn't help playing in his nice, new uniform. 'Yes?' He glances back at the water with the sort of private content that leads me to believe he is thinking of his wonderful, fictitious fiancée.

'There's no hurry about this or anything . . .' My lips have difficulty with the syllables here, they are turning heavy, slippery. 'None at all . . .' and breathing has lost its rhythm. 'But that money you owe me . . . it would be good if you gave it back.'

'Oh, that . . .' The mirage of her tears at parting, their first tryst and who knows what more, has faded and Hitt becomes fully and decently concerned. 'You see, I forget things, I –'

'I know, I do know that, too. It's not a problem.'

'I'm terribly sorry.'

'No, it's fine.' I could almost stop this, not ask again, and leave him be. 'It's perfectly all right.'

'But I'm sure it's not – how could it? You must tell me how much. I only carry a little with me . . .'

I haven't a clue what 'a little' might mean to Hitt and I am unable to tell him a number, a sum: my throat won't let me. But he reaches into his overcoat and pulls out a well-glossed, healthy wallet. From this he plucks a colourful thickness of Canadian notes – I barely understand what they mean and restrain myself from peering.

'Four hundred?' He eyes me, politely quizzical, and for a sick moment I can't tell if he's checking how much I will need, or how far I will go. Am I really about to rob him?

Well, no I'm not. Not in any genuine way that he will notice. This won't cause him a moment's distress.

And he isn't remotely aware of anything untoward, I'm only reading his expression wrongly.

'Five?'

Not that I'm an idiot – I can calculate the moral costs involved. If there were any other path that I could take, I would have picked it. I just need to be gone before they break into my brain and my bedroom and expect me to thrive. I couldn't stand any of that, not without a drink. And that was the point of my coming here – to keep me away from drinking. I have to leave to keep my peace of mind, which is beyond price.

But I will have to mention a figure soon.

I wipe my mouth.

What kind of money will it take?

The first stage, I'll be hitching, have to be – that's free. Bus tickets? Train tickets? Changing the plane ticket – or is it open? Can they be open? I didn't look. Take the small bag, the holdall, only that one, it's all I'll need.

'No, no, of course it wasn't five. So . . .?' Hitt falters, unsteadied by my silence and the blank spot that I've lied into his brain. He doesn't know what to give me. So he simply holds the money out in front of him and allows me to steal just as much as I like without having to say a thing.

Although, I don't like – I categorically do not like. Everything about this is despicable, but what else is there? I have to leave and nobody will let me, will help. Every time I've mentioned anything, they've only joked that I can start off walking whenever I want, because they've been sure that we're so far from everywhere here and that I'm trapped because I don't have any money.

But now I do.

VIII

How it happens is a long story always.

And sometimes your whole, long explanation will drop on you, into you, eager and uninvited, and it will shudder your joints and your concentration and then jerk you to a stop.

That's why I can't walk any more on this pavement which is near Heathrow Terminal Idon'tcare and also not far from dreadful accommodation where the room key arrives with a tag attached that's shaped like a mutant leaf. I am helplessly nailed between two second-rate locations and trying not to find this symptomatic of my moral state. Traffic passes in the road and someone American-looking – pressed slacks and preternaturally white shoes – is dragging a suitcase my way and glancing anxiously about her at the horrible choice of motels slouched behind me. I can be of no assistance, can't even nod as she trundles past in a tiny cloud of worry and stale Anais Anais.

If I could currently speak, I would tell her – *skip the next place on the left across the car park: it's improperly clean and the beds are extremely unpleasant: I was fucking an obnoxious married man in one last night. Don't know what got into me – that is, I'm sure I can guess, but I don't want to.*

Yes, indeedy, fucking and sucking (I like my degradations to rhyme) with a white-bellied, spineless, wispy-haired freak – that being the sort of lifestyle choice it seems I was born to make. I can't wait to try a new blackout and unleash my luck, in the sure and certain hope it will deliver the most humiliating, Technicolor shames: dense Edgar Allen Poe scenarios which make coming back to consciousness one long and very much adulterated scream. Oh, the fun I have – it could spread all the way to Dublin and back, it's such a cavalcade of joys.

But, in fact, I can't say this, or anything else to the sad American. I'm too busy filling with more recollection than I can hold, so much that it's bruising: the key to Room 356 and the unused knickers in my holdall and going to Heathrow from Canada, *via Budapest* and trying not to kiss the (who could have thought it) married Mr Wispy – who may have been called Mr Stott – those oddly resilient lips, and the smell of him which I still have – or the taste: something, anyway, that I can't be rid of – and the memory of being there and not drunk enough to completely erase him, to ignore the desperate lurching of his tepid, little groin and settle my stomach and *just come* – at least come – and then there's the full English breakfast I haven't eaten and the bill I haven't paid and the money I haven't a right to – Hitt's money – asleep in my wallet along with the credit card of an M. H.Virginas.

This is a total disaster, isn't it?

Plus, I am yawning. This would probably not be visible to the untrained eye, but I am slowly and viciously yawning from my ankles up, the warmth of it undulating in my veins, and I know this yawn will have its nasty way and become absolutely the roaring, unnatural, almost-orgasmic, total-body-spasm, which indicates that, early yesterday, I must have taken some variety of benzodiazepine. Which was very bad of me – after twenty-four hours that stuff is guaranteed to cause me disabling, persistent, drooling yawns. It's problems like this which mean that, unless I can't help myself, I don't ever meddle with drugs.

Nevertheless, they are not my primary concern as hundred-weights of smirking and intimate facts keep falling in at me like the *Potempkin's* anchor chain: link after link after link. They're bullying through now with my farewell to the clinic: the gold and blue British Columbia dawn, gentle and dim, when a tourist couple's SUV first slowed and then waited while I trotted up to reach out for their door and opened it into the usual, dreadful freedoms. Before that, was the trudge from the fence around Clear Spring in the mountain cold and being sure to whistle cheerily and make noises, reassure the night-time bears, my holdall swung over my shoulder to take the weight, but nothing too bad about this situation: mainly the lift and thrill of having grubbed under the rusty chicken wire and broken *outside*, being on my way, stepping home into my filthy, old skin. Before that, I was soft-shoeing harmlessly over the muffled lawns, sliding along between watchful squares and dabs of light and removing myself from therapeutic care, stretching and finally breaking the tracks that led back to Thoreau House and the porch roof I climbed down from and the window I left open and the room I had abandoned with its narrow pine bed.

Where I left Gregory, half awake.

I didn't mean him.

I didn't mean Mr Wispy, either, but I was drunk, so he didn't count. He was like catching flu: he could have happened to anyone.

With Gregory, I was sober. For three nights.

But only because I love Robert.

Only because I *missed* Robert and my tendons and sinews were growing healthy and being communicative again. The detox was working, my body bouncing up quick from the dead and feeling dapper, sensitive, in need – but nobody was there to need me.

Except Gregory with the shine under his skin and his boy's kisses, laughing kisses, that opened and drew you on to the nub of his tongue. And the way that he angled his head down when he lay to hide the grafts and ruin that his knife had left behind. It gave him a double chin, but I didn't mind that.

Poor Gregory.

And poor me – that first, blasting yawn is building up from the small of my back and another take-off hauls along the morning and I shut my eyes and think of Robert and see Gregory bright beneath me in my shadowed room, the pair of us smooth from so much soaking in thermal water and we're slipping, sweating, trembling in the tiny space we've made under the lights-out silence: we can feel it strapped around us, binding us raw against each other, rubbing until the blood growls in our ears and we abandon breathing and finish with a jerking, melancholy burn. The result of life returning, the way it must.

His face then: there'd be an ache of fear in it, along with the soft dark of his look and then the private half-smile: a little for himself and some for me – each time, each night the same. All of him gentleness and calm until we started, until we were moving and moved by the size of him.

But he reminded me of Robert.

I wouldn't have done it, otherwise.

Anyway, letting me have a whole room to myself: what was the clinic trying to do? It was utterly irresponsible. Even a child could have climbed up to that window and there were no proper controls, no effective security measures to prevent inmates slamming each other through every terror in the night until the pair of them came out mindless, bitter with heated sulphur and tranquil and sore.

Oh, God, this is a complete disaster.

And I am, too.

Again.

And this is when Heathrow shrugs around me and the yawn flowers up and my mouth is moving and then the rest of me as well, while my brain's in this state of surrender which leaves me unprepared for the moment when I am very, very sick. Twitching like a puppet and sick to my soul. Although I do manage to miss my own feet.

This isn't too bad, though: it even feels purging and I could do with a purge. I cough a few times, spit discreetly – there are few things more graceless than women who spit – and then I step over the mess as if it has nothing whatever to do with me. Of course, from this moment onward, it *does* have nothing whatever to do with me.

Then it takes a ridiculous period of wandering about – interrupted by yawning and a brief, but hugely expensive, cab ride – to set my body on the path to any measure of permanent recovery.

'And a box of matches, please.'

I find a corner shop of the proper type, stocked with the average, last-minute, urban requirements: newspapers, Domestos, Rizlas, bin liners, cat food, sweets. Cooried into one side are the shelves of wine and the chiller cabinet which gleams quietly to itself and holds, among other items, three cans of lager. I buy these.

'And a box of matches, please.'

I have to buy the box of matches, because purchasing three cans of larger before lunchtime could seem, at a certain level, dysfunctional. It could look as if I have an overbearing need for alcohol. I don't. I'm fresh out of a clinic and I've cleaned up very well and have largely benefited from past mistakes, so the last thing I'm going to need is alcohol – and I don't like lager. Unfortunately, drinking three lagers is the only way to even myself out until the benzos have worn off. So I buy the magic matches and make this respectable.

Three morning cans of lager = embarrassment.

Three morning cans of lager with an added box of matches = shopping.

The elderly assistant regards me with wisdom and kindness and we nod to each other before I leave and take up a relaxed position beside a litter bin in order to empty the lagers, one-two-three: popping them – watching that tiny smoke which will breathe up from any can when it's first opened – and then draining them and dumping them and, of course, yawning throughout.

Above me, the sun is established for the day, sweetly warm, and an amount of spontaneous healing is taking place in many of my systems. I will be steady soon. Exhaust fumes and toxins are birling about and might eventually take their toll on my lungs and so forth, but I'm going to avoid any damage by swinging across the road and taking a dive into the Underground, burrowing along until I come up at King's Cross and can buy a ticket North.

There will be no more drink for me today – I won't require it. This is as true as gravity, as the weight of hydrogen. I am going to take a pleasant and orderly train trip and follow it with a bus ride to my flat. Nothing random or untoward will befall me en route. Enough is, after all, occasionally enough.

I'll have a bath when I arrive and a bit of a spruce up, here and there, before I take a good, deep nap. Then I'll be ready to tell everybody that I'm better and I'm back.

There are few things finer, I think, than being refreshed and ready and strolling into your favourite bar, your local. The way the purr of conversation widens as you pull back on the door and then the convivial wash of pubsmell hugs you in. Pubsmell is heightened at night by extra spillages and smoke, but it's purest in the calm of a still afternoon – and this *is* a still afternoon – when it's much more plainly something to do with the presence of men over time and with disinfectant and enjoyment and homely, comforting staleness and rest for the wicked and likeable dirt. It is a complicated phenomenon, but it's possible to miss it terribly and I would know it anywhere.

It welcomes you into the place that will never change: the booths and stools and the pictures of dead golfers – and, inexplicably, a horse – and the easy, happy curve of the bar that courteously lifts your eye to the mirror and the optics. I know people build miniature gantries in their houses, but this shouldn't be allowed: it's a terrible insult to everyone concerned. The tall gleam of charged glass, the winking ranks of spirits, the delicious confusion of lights and shades and labels, they're only perfected in a pub, a bar, on licensed premises. You wouldn't rig up an altar in your front room, so why imagine you could try it with a gantry?

But every millilitre is ideally sited here and I'm gliding in to greet each one of them, rested by twelve hours of sleep and unscathed by a wholly sober journey. Both halves of me are working as they should do and I have no particular urge to yawn. I am the prodigal returned and washed and perfumed and my hairspray is keeping a grip and, under my casual jeans and feminine sweater, I am wearing pink socks, a fresh bra, brand new knickers and I even took the time to comb my pubic hair. I've never done this before, but it was strangely satisfying and I'm not altogether unlikely to do it again. Mild make-up, but my mascara is tremendously impressive – all of my lashes perfectly aligned, when they usually don't quite manage that, somehow.

I order a simple orange juice: because I can make a non-alcoholic choice, it doesn't put me under any pressure, provoke any lack: and I turn to my right, where I know the familiar faces are already watching me. I haven't wanted to deal with them directly until now, I had an entrance to make, but this is when I ease the head round and check who's here.

Robert.

He should be at work, unless this is a weekend. I ought to have found out what day it is, what date – maybe April the fifth? – it feels like an April the fifth. Yes, because I have an idea that yesterday was the fourth. In other times I would have bought a paper for orientation, but I can't read the papers any more. They hurt.

So I'm not prepared for this, for Robert – I didn't think he'd turn up until later. The others, I anticipated, but at this point they're hazy, muted: I seem unable to take them in with any urgency.

Robert.

He's being especially in focus and three-dimensional, leaning at the back of the booth and giving a packet of crisps undue attention. And he's already set the spring of interest in my stomach: nerves, fondness, exposure, guilt: I didn't want to cope with this in company.

'Hello.'

Bobby, the Parson, Maurice and the man with tattooed hands: they chorus me an answering hello with additional enquiries and remarks – *don't I seem great, very well turned out, that break must have done the trick.*

Robert says nothing. He eats a crisp with quiet malevolence. The boys incline themselves towards him, making a space so that he can chip in and then, when he doesn't, we have to stare in his direction while he still keeps himself belligerently to himself, raising a sip of yellow wine to moisten his fragment of snack. While his head is up, he meets me with a tiny, unreadable glance and then returns to studying his hands.

I paper over the subsequent silence with 'Hello, Robert.'

He manages a dull 'Hello, Hannah' towards the window, as if he's reciting a line he doesn't want. I mime drinking a touch of my orange juice, which I find, like everything else, to be highly unsatisfactory.

He has no right to be upset. He doesn't know a single thing that could upset him.

I stay on my feet and the boys stand to join me. There's no room for another stool at the table and, in any case, they need to shake my hands and, of course, the Parson will try to kiss me, Bobby too, and I will have to duck aside, but pat their arms nicely after, in consolation. Robert is the last to rise and keeps quiet as he brushes past me, grimly heading for the Gents. The contact is unnecessary, deliberate, and gives me the scent of his skin, unbalancing. He would like me to remember and to need him, to be powerless. He's got his wish.

Maurice hisses intently across me at the Parson, 'There are twelve.'

'There are fourteen. Do you want me to name them? With a meditation that's appropriate for each? If it's an argument you're after, Maurice, then you'll need something to argue *about*. At the moment, you're just *wrong*.'

With the Parson safe in a former conversation, I only have

to duck Bobby's advances while the crowd of us drifts up to lodge along the bar.

'There are twelve. It's not something I'm going to forget – *Hail Mary, full of grace, Chieftain o' the pudding race*: repeat until you're thirteen – I *can't* forget.'

'Well, if you're not going to take it seriously.'

'Why should I – it never took me seriously. There are twelve . . . there's *Jesus meets his blessed mother* and there's St Veronica and . . . the three falls, two submissions and a partridge up a pear tree . . . I mean, I don't care, but there are twelve.'

'Fourteen.'

Nobody seems interested in where I've been. Bobby's snuggled into a whisky, the man with the tattooed hands has wandered off and Maurice is doggedly asking for trouble. No one ever discusses religion with the Parson: that's why we call him the Parson. And Robert is still in the Gents. Not that he couldn't have sneaked out and gone by me while I was distracted, but I do believe I would have noticed. Somebody would have noticed. And why would he want to sneak out, in the first place? Why would he be so determined to avoid me?

From here I'll be able to see when the door opens, any movement will catch my eye. Although he should have joined us already.

He's just making me wait.

When I've thought of him constantly and been faithful, kept my love faithful in all of the ways that could matter to anyone.

For fuck's sake, I talked to Gregory about him every night. I spent as much time doing that as I did with the other things. I wanted Gregory to know, to understand I was in love.

And I told him the truth. I am in love.

Robert emerges, looking as if he has washed his face a number of times – neat and flustered, both at once. There is a pause as he sways on one heel and might be moving towards the door, leaving, but then he rubs at his ear and comes forward, mildly awkward. He keeps Maurice and the Parson between us, won't acknowledge anyone, as he slides both elbows on to the bar top and orders a pint of stout. He never drinks beer unless he's stressed.

The Parson is also stressed. 'How are you getting twelve? You just take him up to Calvary and leave him? Anyone can *die* — it's what happens next that counts.'

The bickering is getting a bit much. 'Hey, listen — I've got jet lag. I've been away for a long time. I wanted to be with my friends and have a cheery, peaceful afternoon and for the evening? — I wanted to spend it with people that I like. People I care about.' I am, naturally, only saying this for the benefit of one of those people present — the one who is cutting me dead. 'And so far I've had a shite welcome and you two are just yelling numbers at each other.'

The Parson gathers up his Sabbath voice. 'Stations. We're yelling Stations. And we're not yelling.'

'I don't care! Just stop! It's not as if you actually *are* a parson, is it? We just call you that. Because we're polite.'

The Parson sets down his glass and tries to force a particularly wounded expression on me, which I pre-empt by looking at Maurice instead. This doesn't help, though, because Maurice seems equally upset, perhaps more so.

'He was a priest.'

'What?'

Maurice murmurs at me again, 'He was a priest.' Suddenly acting as if the Parson is the biggest pal he's ever had, when they do nothing but snipe at each other, then go into huffs.

'He was a *priest*?'

Their shoulders are almost touching in a display of distressed affection. It wouldn't surprise me, if they started to hold hands, or weep. Men — always showing off their feelings.

'You were really a . . .? that whole . . .?'

They're being best pals at me, buddies: all faked nobility and comradeship under fire. With me cast as the bitch who's firing.

'You're not pissing about? You mean you really were . . .?'

The pair of them dripping with pained silence and giving theatrical flinches.

'Well, that's . . . your own business . . . Good for you, though. Sorry I didn't know before. Not that it would have altered . . . Good for you.'

Robert is smirking above his pint.

And that's annoying. It's more annoying than the certainty that I'll have to give in: make the first move and go and speak to him, or else he'll just keep on, clinging there like a niggling whelk. Anyway, I can't stay where I am, because everyone here's getting much too highly strung 'You . . . you carry on with your discussion, okay then? Didn't mean to interrupt.'

I manage a casual stroll and attempt another mouthful of the orange, but realise it smells of bile.

'Robert.'

'Hannah.'

'You're very quiet.'

'So are you.'

In the far background the parson has started in again and Old Margaret is asking someone for a light, prior to asking them for a cigarette, and Thomas the surly barman does surly barman things with his disreputable cleaning cloth and every part of this is not important. Buildings exploding in other countries are not important: this season's colour of car and moral dilemmas and new diseases and strip cartoons and children dying and flavours of pasta sauces and the rule of law – they are not important. We are what counts. We are the most that I can think about.

'I'm back.'

'I see that.' He nibbles at his beer. 'Yes. There you are.'

'It wasn't my fault.'

'Yes. There you are.'

We stare straight ahead, study Thomas as if he were a map and murmur to the blank air like rendezvousing spies.

'They just sent me away, Robert, packed me off – I couldn't stop them. I was ill.'

Pointing out that Robert himself went off to Canada and gave me no warning beforehand and left me in limbo for weeks – well, I can't do that, because it's true and will therefore cause offence and may lead on to further truths and very few of them won't hurt us.

'Robert?'

I risk pressing my arm against his and he doesn't withdraw, doesn't do anything beyond feeling the way I know which, for a slow breath, means I have to close my eyes.

'Robert.'

He puts down his glass. 'Did I say you could go?'

'That isn't –'

'Did I say you could go?'

I have no idea what he wants this to mean. 'No. You didn't say I could go.' Beer and wine, the less-committed drinks, you can never be sure how they'll take a person, and they're clearly making Robert upset.

'So?'

'Robert, I –'

'So what do you have to tell me?'

'I don't fucking know. *What?*'

This almost makes him turn to me, connect, and he flushes at the lapse. 'What do you have to tell me?'

I can't think he has any meaningful suspicions, so a confession can't be what he wants. The message I left said I'd be in a clinic, in treatment, under medical supervision – nothing to suggest I might fuck strangers.

One stranger.

Only one that qualifies.

But Mr Robert Gardener does not know anything about that.

But Mr Robert Gardener could guess.

'Robert, what do you want me to say?'

'If you don't know . . .' He stretches, rolls his neck, slaps both his hands on the edge of the bar. 'Look, I really need to get out of here.'

'Well, we could —'

'*By myself.*' Then he coughs, waits, fumbles in his pockets purposelessly, smoothes his hair.

'Robert, I'm sorry.'

'What?' His shoulders beginning the shift to me and his neck following, his frown: an undefined accusation in everything.

'I'm sorry.'

He tilts his head, allows my look to reach his. 'What did you say?' There's no heat in his eyes, only concentration.

'I'm sorry.'

'You're what?' Another tilt.

'*I'm sorry.*'

The solemn mouth ticks, flickers, suggests a softness. 'Once more for luck.'

'I. Am. Sorry.' I reach with my left hand and take his right forefinger, wrap it in my fist, as tight and as Freudian a fit as I can make it. 'And. *You.* Are. A total bastard.'

'Well, what did you expect?'

Which is the trouble with being the way that we are — what we expect. As drinkers, we anticipate the worst, this is our self-defence. We let little fears and disappointments gnaw us in advance; an inoculation against the full-blown griefs we know we'll suffer later. As a result, we wear ourselves down, grow tired and forgetful, which means there'll always be a certain number of incoming disasters which will take us wholly by surprise. And then there are points when we simply relax and trust and are, once again, overwhelmed by events.

I'd become used to spending pleasant times with Robert — I'd come to regard them as guaranteed — which was really an obvious indication that I should expect those times to stop. But I didn't. Because there are other things in my life that I also expect and enjoy and they lower my guard.

Put it this way — I'm a drinker and drinkers are permeable, absorbent. So when I sit next to a man with (for example) a cockney accent, it may well be that I will catch his way of speaking and, as we make ourselves acquainted, he may ask me where I'm from and imagine I'm going to say Stepney, or Brick Lane, or some other Londonish place and then, quite unreasonably, he may get annoyed and disdainful when I say I grew up somewhere not far from Aberdeen. He may act as if I have deceived him, although this has not been my aim, and my behaviour has been unremarkable. It's an essential of our species to be accommodating, part of whatever crowd has been provided: obstreperous in jumble sales, plaintive among policemen, aroused in one specific dentist's chair. And then, once we've gone to the trouble of adjusting, why not keep hold of this or that stylish trait? It's not as if we're stealing – more like multiplying attributes: they stay with the original owner, but we get to play with them as well. Two of my laughs belong to a physics teacher, the way I throw my holdall into cars harks back to a film I saw once, something to do with desert highways. If we're honest, what other reason does anyone have for wasting their money on cinema trips? We go to pick up characteristics, to renovate our personalities with cladding and patches we've filched from the screen.

Nobody is complete – we all need topping up. Alcohol can add a little, but mainly it enlarges what's already there. Environmental factors, traumas, levels of income and training, they can shape me: I can pick and choose what I borrow and what I assimilate. But, for the drinker, there are better possibilities than this. What I wait for are those beautiful, uncommon chances to truly search another human being and be truly searched by them, to shift shapes in each other's company. Accents and laughs are superficial, unsatisfying: they're only where the process starts, as you sink down and grin through the meat of a different life. I've heard it said that drinkers are uncaring, that we don't bond, but nothing could be more untrue. I can be closer to you – more *of you* – in an hour than any teetotaller would be if they kept you drugged and naked in their basement for a month: if they ate your brain.

If you and I were to *be drunk together*, then osmosis would give way to metamorphosis, to more and more permanent change. If you and I were *drunk together often* we might occasionally seem indistinguishable, two liquids blended in one. If, beyond that, we were *in love* − well, you can guess how it would be. Too many days of having your partner swallow down your guilts and like your likes and speak out the heart of your sentences: of understanding without question what you both will do and how and the way you will feel about everything throughout; of losing the line between your skins, your dreams, your heats − this can make you believe you will never be alone, never resubjected to the usual forces and natural laws. You will assume you are free of such things and safe in your own small Eden. You will be wrong, but you will still expect it. You will still hurt when it's gone.

So the very average kiss I exchanged with Robert in the bar that afternoon gave me a headache at once. When our lips touched they were neutral: nothing beyond his sealed presence, not even hostility, only dumb flesh. We tasted of my past being torn away, of denial and theft.

And this wasn't fair. I had inadequate company to cheer me in my glass and I was trying to stay sober and he was dragging me awfully close to being depressed. I'd intended to stay and be happy about my return, blur myself along into a mellow evening and an active, amnesiac night, but now the plans were spoiled. This left me with a single option: to give Robert a kiss even blander than the dab he'd offered me and then head home − to my original home, the one where my parents live.

There were no other choices, not any more. I had that particular sadness which combines a need for family and nostalgia with a knowledge that indulging it will only make matters much worse.

Somewhere under my heart, I knew that much worse would be what I deserved.

My father once took me to the circus. My mother disapproved and, as yet, there was no Simon, so just the two of us went down past the abandoned bandstand to the far corner of the green where a huddle of caravans and straw heaps and what seemed – even to me – quite a small big top all indicated the circus had arrived.

I pretend to remember a small parade before that – one elephant, a nasty clown on stilts, cheaply painted lorries with sour exhausts – but truly I think there was nothing like that, only my need for it. The scenes are unclear: the slide of hooves along our street too disconnected from the thought of zebras.

I did go to the show, though, and I can call up the heavy, sweating air, sagged between the canvas and the cold, odd lights, the fascinating quantity of sawdust – more than I'd ever seen in a butcher's shop – and here were live animals, jolting through their stressed little party pieces before maybe the sawdust claimed them and they turned into meat. But that's as much as I recall.

It was a long time ago and I was extremely young, but that isn't why I have such trouble bringing it to mind. I'm unwilling to see the tired, dull, real circus, because it degrades the much lovelier one I have, perhaps always, kept inside my head.

Everyone goes through a circus phase, of course: the wonderful horror of watching adults behave insanely, the mysterious charge of their costumes, their skin, and all those compounded risks. You can run through the list of charms yourself: the terror of clowns, the unsettling allure of whips and glitter, your identification with those harried and overly willing creatures, the tang of unreasonable display.

They still often televised this perversity when I was a girl and then there was that film with Jimmy Stewart and Charlton Heston – lots of films, in fact, with jealous lovers and wicked ringmasters and anthropomorphic chimps – people *knew* about circuses – they were around. And children were supposed to like them and I was a child. But *my* circus, the one True Circus, I never disclosed: because it had nothing to do with all that.

In my circus, the band plays always: banjos and flat trumpets, out-of-kilter violins, twisted accordions, steam organs and bad, unresonant drums: they grind out in limping waltz time and make the air giddy, gamy with sweat and topple me into the place where there are only circus people, sideshow people, my own people. They have parts that are missing, or parts that are extra in sly and unspeakable ways. They lack propriety, love to exhibit, often practise after-hours. They have marvellous, shocking skills which are not useful anywhere, not anywhere without an audience. Their pasts and their futures are sheened with misfortunes, with an enforced appetite for pain. Their damp and close and everlasting present stiffens with blood on demand. They can read strangers, curse them, work them into helplessness. They are freaks. They are monsters. They are my natural family.

Even so young, I understood that, and hand-holding back to our home with my father I knew that I hadn't seen the True Circus.

'Was that all right, then?'

'Yes.' I leaned against my father's arm and felt him fret. 'But we wouldn't have to go again. It would be the same.'

'And we wouldn't like that.'

'No.'

'Shame your mother didn't come.'

'But she wouldn't like it.'

'No. Too noisy.' He had flinched in his seat at every whip crack and play-explosion.

I had sat very near him to lend support, while I felt guilty for not being frightened and for searching out signs of my other home. 'Noisy. Yes. Can we have milk?' My father's hot milk was the best, he made it as if he was doing magic: by the time it arrived, the taste was almost irrelevant, but very fine.

'Isn't it too warm for milk?'

'Not now.'

'Well, then we'll have milk.' We had come to the end of the green. 'We don't have to say anything about this – just that it was fine. Don't want your mother upset about the animals and noises. Is that all right?'

And it was quite all right and True Circus relaxed its grip on me and allowed us back into our house and Father fussed about his saucepan in the kitchen, adding his cinnamon and vanilla and then poured me half a mug of milk – in case I spilled it – and then didn't drink his own, only settled in his chair and tilted up his chin when my mother came in and stood behind him. This let her stroke his forehead with her hands, over and over and over. When I was finished drinking, I went upstairs to brush my teeth and left them together there: him with his eyes shut and smiling and my mother smoothing back his hair.

In bed after that, I was full of circus music and the hope there'd be a place among the monsters, waiting ready for me.

Of course, it took many more years before I could abandon my domestic family and start looking for the freak show where I'd be a better fit. It was a gradual process. For instance, I don't know when I stopped wanting to think of my parents – that is, when they became too much to bear. By the time I was nineteen or twenty, they were already difficult – changed from the human beings I've known longest to proofs of discomforts and injuries I've inflicted and the predictable lack of mercy I have taught. Now when we meet we are not people:

only unfortunate reminders, bodies of bad evidence. The money they kept on lending me, the money that I took, the falling asleep with my face in the Sunday lunch, the endless trail of lies and breakages and stains and the dirt and the damp and the unnamed disease of myself, at large in their house, more than naked when they saw me, more than obscene, stinking of animal will and sawdust.

And I do feel remorse for every sin. Inside, I am mostly built out of remorse, but no one can manage the weight of that, not constantly. It has to be put away, sent out of mind, because anything else would be stifling, perhaps suicidal. So the idea of my mother and father has to be strictly controlled for the sake of my health. I will cast up little childhood scenes, seek out the clean and early times and dream above them nicely, but beyond that, I'm taking no risks.

Because even one unwary moment might summon up something awful, like the sight of my mother bending down and picking up tiny parts of a smashed lamp and the fine curl in her hair and the way that she wears a cardigan draped around her shoulders sometimes, because she has the poise to look lovely like that, and even her bending is feminine, delicate, and the only reason she has to be doing this is me. I am the one who broke the lamp, I am the one who threw a glass at it, because I was angry, because I was drunk, because I wanted to throw something at her – a tumbler at her – and this made such a falling weakness in me that I aimed for the lamp and hated her more and loved her more and I would cry if she didn't look so tender, if she didn't seem to be exactly the person I should always protect from the scenes of my crimes. I would cry if she wasn't making me a monster.

And no one would want to see that, not ever: most of all not if they knew that it was true.

Although it isn't a question of preference any more – when these things are once woken they stay that way.

So right now I am concentrating on my mother, holding

fast to the way that she is in front of me, at her doorstep, where she is making herself be pleased to see me. I had no reason to suspect that she would do this and I am, therefore, unexpectedly fighting for breath, straining against the pressure of her kindness. She glances a moment too long at the raw line in my eyebrow, the settling scar of my journey to Clear Spring, and then darts me glances and tiny, rushing smiles as she brings me inside and her hand whispers down my arm, desperate and tender. Any more of this and she'll send me entirely cartoon. She ushers me into the living room where a woman sits: somebody I don't know.

'Mrs Anderson, this is my daughter – a surprise visit.' My mother saying this, as if it is the pleasant kind of surprise, even approaching a special occasion: overplaying the whole thing with a ghastly nervousness. She smiles at me again with the silent, huge request that I should be altered for the better and not disgrace her, that I should join her in thinking wishfully till I leave. It cannot be true that less than a fortnight away in dubious treatment can have created a new daughter, a girl she can trust. But this is what she wants. I have no chance to form an expression in reply, because she is already bustling to the kitchen with far too much gaiety.

I need to follow her and tell her out loud that I will, at least, make sure to be a girl here, because I can never be anything else when I am with her. And I do like this, the immediate lifting off of years, there haven't been so many times when I would have changed it.

I can't leave the room, though. I have to sit in my father's armchair – he must be hiding in the greenhouse – and speak to the visitor he's avoiding.

'So . . .' Mrs Anderson hadn't anticipated me. She is shocked in a way that makes me suspect that she may not have known I exist.

'Yes, I just thought I'd pop by. I was away. But I'm not any more . . . You're a . . .'

'I'm not long moved in over the road. Your mother brought me flowers the first day. It was a lovely gesture.'

When I grin now, I actually do mean it. My mother brought flowers, because she does sometimes need to prune them and is proud of their qualities – it had nothing to do with Mrs Anderson. Not that my mother isn't also neighbourly. But her lovely gesture would have invited a mild, distant acquaintance, not the burden of having visitors indoors, disturbing the peace she enjoys here with my father. My mother calls on other people, if she has to – she doesn't want them calling round on her. That's how she is.

I realise I've let the silence open up too far and Mrs Anderson is finding inadequate distraction in her biscuit.

'Sorry, Mrs . . . ahm . . . Anderson, I'm a little sleepy. I was in Canada. And some other places.'

'Really?' She is doing the proper thing – learning about the people attached to someone she considers a future friend. She wants to feel part of things.

'Yes. Business. Slightly. Some money matters: getting money.' I tell her this before I realise that it makes me sound like a drug dealer and that she will now have to ask

'So, what do you do?'

Which I cannot answer with 'Oh, a little theft, monstrosity, credit-card fraud and my hobbies include giving blow jobs to unpleasant men while I'm semi-unconscious. I also drink a lot.'

But my mother returns to save me with 'She used to be in cardboard, but now she has moved on.'

And if 'She used to be in cardboard' is the kind of absurdity that she would only produce under pressure, then 'but now she has moved on' is layered with a savage faith and tenderness and is none of Mrs Anderson's business.

Mother dips low as she sets my teacup on the table at my side and I understand that she is checking my breath for indications of betrayal. When there are none, she glances across with a burst of hope that turns my stomach. I want to admit that I have recently spent days being given tea in half-filled mugs – in case I spilled it – because liquids are troubling when you have the shakes.

She straightens, sets her hand beside my neck and strokes my cheek. I had forgotten she used to do this, I had lost how wonderful it was that she used to do this and the smell of her hands which is the smell of softness and being a woman and her perfume: the sandalwood and fresh grass and safety and comfort of that – the lurch it makes in me back to five years old when we would stand together in the hairdressers, both newly trimmed, and we would look at ourselves in the big mirror, the rest of the world much smaller and less interesting behind us and we would say, as easily as *please* or *happy birthday*, 'We love each other very much.'

For two or three seconds I am afraid that one of us may say this now.

Mrs Anderson compares us as mother and daughter and finds this moving. 'Has she been away a long time?'

'Yes.' The one word loaded, extending invisibly into the sentence I'm meant to hear which is, 'Yes, my daughter was away for a very long time, too long, but she's come back now and I can possibly be free of how she used to be.'

And I do want her to be free. I haven't drunk today, or really yesterday and there were those several other sober days not long ago and this could be positive and something which ought to delight her. But it doesn't *feel* positive. It doesn't *feel* as if drink was the problem – more that *I* was and will be again.

Still, no need to dwell on this. I will borrow my mother's certainty while the room constricts with optimism, although no one has any right to be optimistic about me.

Mother and her guest chat more easily, leaving me to relax and nod whenever nodding seems appropriate. Mrs Anderson would like to ask me some more questions, but she is deftly coaxed aside and eased along into discussing her husband, his death, her moving house and coming here – this has the form of a story she's often told before, but it works in her, all the same – there's something about her allotted role in it which she can't yet believe. I suspect there may be tears soon and then I don't know what we'll do.

I wish for a chiming clock, a dog, a hailstorm – any reasonable distraction. But then my mother begins talking about change and the pair of them calm and I focus on this before my mother says, with no preamble, that she will retire in a month.

Which immediately makes me the one who can't believe.

I know it's due, I understand that, naturally, such eventualities do arise – only not for my mother. Not like this. There's something unacceptable about this. Because nothing unavoidable should come near her, she should always have the opportunity to choose.

The way she is in this living room, this evening, dressed in quiet flowers: the pattern of her blouse, the brooch at her throat: her hands are mildly older, perhaps her face, and her hair, is lighter, but she isn't *old*. Not properly. Not in the way that drives you from your work and steals your health and takes you from yourself. So she shouldn't have mentioned retiring while I'm here. It's going to be her fault if I drop my cup, or sweat, or have to leave with uncompleted explanations.

I wipe my top lip and know that she has noticed. We are both remembering I do that when I'm drunk and, although I am sober, I've started to blush.

Retire – my mother repeats the word and I wait until she will turn to me again: I stop blinking, I hold still to let her search my face and I grin myself honest, grin and grin, because simply *being* honest won't be enough, she won't see it and I want to be the girl that she can trust. I want her to be sure.

Mrs Anderson, the good neighbour, interrupts. 'It'll be a change for you.'

'Change is the thing. Yes.'

'Of course.'

'But we adapt ourselves, don't we? And there are benefits.'

'Yes.' Mrs Anderson the good widow does her best not to sound bereft.

I watch my mother and think that perhaps I have been convincing, because in the middle of speaking, quite out of place, she allows what is really a sigh to break *are* apart from *benefits* and she brushes at her skirt and I am afraid, because she seems happy, and if I can make her happy then I can make her sad again.

And worse, this is the way we used to be: connected. We were beyond drink, before it, born to be completed in each other with no further help. She is the whole of my first thought: a memory of darkness and nothing wrong, only pulling in the sweet night warmth of her and being lost in it, back asleep inside the rightness of everything, loved beyond reason.

Or standing in the bathroom doorway and watching my father shave: that unaccustomed sureness, fluid in his hands: the flick at the end of the stroke and then dipping his razor, shaking it in the basin and up again to clear himself into a deeper innocence, into a huge child with bright lines of soap still left at his sideburns, under his nose and then the rinse and then the towel and then his extraordinary newness.

I watched him often before one morning – I don't know why – I turned round to see my mother leaning against the wall behind me and watching him just as I was, soft and pleased. He smiled because he knew that we were there, but could pretend not to, could forget that he was shy and be handsome for us. And this was love. This was room enough for everyone to love and no harm done.

When Simon was born I loved him, too – all of us, we were each other's and I learned the sound of my mother's voice saying *lovebird*, because that was my name and I cannot remember the word without hearing her in my head: and her other words, the way she would swear without swearing because I was a child – *pig's feet and old curtains* and *oh, Christmas* – the words she still uses today, because she is naturally polite and because they belong to us now and are the way we used to be. She's the only woman I've ever had any time for.

This is why I finish my tea and carefully rebalance the cup on the saucer and watch the sunlight creep across the carpet and I don't make excuses to hide to the bathroom, or any bedroom, because these are places where I drank. And it's why I don't go to the garden and find my father, because this might disturb him and my mother won't have him disturbed. But it's also why I'll have to leave soon.

'You have to go already?' My mother's pain lurching out in the room. Mrs Anderson won't notice, but I see it in my mother's hands, which are like my hands only graceful, and in the light of her eyes, which are like my eyes but not guilty, and in her lips which are like my lips, only clean, all her life clean. 'Do you? Have to go?'

'I'll be back.' I mean this. 'I dropped in on the way to somewhere else.' This is a lie and clatters down like a lie. 'It's that I'm tired. I didn't expect that I'd still be this tired.' If she told me that I could rest here, I would go up to my room and be well, find a pure sleep. I would wake up later and sit on the living-room floor with my head leaned against her knee. 'But I'll be back.' If we were years ago and other people. If God allowed just anything.

'You're sure.'

So now I've managed, I've taken her happiness. And I don't want to act this out while I'm watched by a stranger, but there can't be any other way – alone with her, I'd seem frightening and not better – I'd shake and weep and ruin her, swallow her hope.

It has to be done like this. It has to be carefully levering to my feet and walking to take my mother's hands and having her stand against me and holding her, holding how beautiful she is and made of something which could not stand the way I live and kissing her cheek and her ear and her hair and not crying, buckling that in, and being proud that I can show this to Mrs Anderson who does not know us and who does not understand, but who surely must recognise love when she sees it.

By the time I get home, I genuinely *am* tired, numbingly so, and I stagger through the business of undressing and drop into bed as if I've had a hard, long evening of the more usual type.

When I wake – without hangover, or any specific regret – the curtains are open, as I left them, and the steel shine of a wet dawn is thumping about in the room until I can sit up and organise my senses, establish that the light is silent and the din is coming from my hall.

Either a passing idiot has taken a strong dislike to my front door, or Robert is outside it and wanting to be in. Both possibilities make me unwilling to respond.

'Hannah.' This narrows it down to the second option. 'Hannah, *come on*.' For a while this narrowness offends me. 'Please.'

Then I climb into my jeans and sweater, because a dressing gown won't be appropriate, not if I have to be stern, and I let him inside. He's thick with pubsmell and swinging, heavy with drink, with taking it alone, beyond last orders, when it turns on you and makes you scared of yourself, unwelcome in your own head.

He follows me into the room, kisses my cheek with gin as he jerks past to sit on the bed. 'Sorry.'

I go to my chair and watch him. I've seen the way he is before, I've *been* the way he is before – it's like trying to climb out of a cone, some repulsively geometrical, deep-sided pit made of marble, or metal, or porcelain, or anything else that won't give, that won't warm, that won't let you get a grip. You turn and you slide and you crane up to peer at the things you would like to do, while your moods swoop through you in patterns without sense. In this state, you can disappear under your skin, be lost, do your worst and then instantly forget.

But Robert is mild, for now. 'Really sorry . . . earlier . . . I was an arse.'

'Yes, you were.'

He rubs at his eyes, as if this will clear them. 'Don' say that.'

'You said it first.' I'm hoping he's drunk himself stupid and will stay with that.

'Did, I did. Thass righ'. Did. Sorry.' He stares at the floor, frowning and then brightens, takes off his jacket methodically and makes a painful start on his shirt.

I'm entirely sober, which puts us into separate languages, separate countries. 'What are you doing, Robert?'

'Time for undress.' He beams as if this is a wonderful, original idea, winks and then falters when I don't wink back. Next, he shakes his head like an unhappy toddler, rocking on the bedspread. 'No, doesn't want that, Robert. You're too stinking. I know, I know, I know, I know. Too drunk. I know.' But then he sets back in at his shirt buttons, his concerns evaporated. 'If I have a lie-down.' And he does hinge on to his back, feet still firm on the floor, fingers even clumsier at his chest, confused. 'Oh dear.'

I move to stand above him, to frown at the hair blurred across his forehead and the weight of his hands where they're lifted with each almost-dozing breath and the child that he is again, his helplessness. Under the pubsmell is the flavour of his skin, his full self, the Robert Gardener I have missed for weeks. So I can't shout at him. I can't be sustainably irritated that he's brought me his apologies when he's hidden deep in gin and can't be blamed, or even found. I can only kneel to take his shoes off, his socks.

'Wha' you . . .? Oh. Thass nice. Yeah. Thans.'

I manoeuvre his legs until he is lying out flat on my bed and then watch him roll and curl on to his side with his back towards me. And I hug in behind him and I kiss his hair, which makes him stir a little, and I try to sleep while I hold him and hold the drinking in him, feel it twitch and sparkle as he dreams.

Not that it lets us rest for long.

'Hannah.'

I'm half drifting, imagining I'm close by a high wooden fence, with animals kicking inside it. I need to see what they are.

'Hannah.'

I believe that one of them is talking to me.

'Hannah.'

Robert turns to face me in a scramble of coverlet and loosened clothes. The images of whip cord and slivers of moving life break up, then fade and I open my eyes to him. 'It isn't time to get up yet. Today's Sunday.'

'Want to tell you.' He's drunk now in the soft, bleak way – the one that forces you to talk. It plays interrogator and you say out everything, because otherwise you know that it will eat you, you will disappear for always, never get free. 'Want to tell you something.'

'Okay, okay. What? I'm awake. What?'

'But I can't, though.' And he dives his arms round me, pulls in fast. 'I don't want to.'

I'm becoming slightly claustrophobic, his fear hemming me in. 'It's fine. We're both here, we're both fine. We're together. You can tell me stuff. I won't mind. You know me: in the morning, I won't remember. Neither will you.' At least half of that's true.

'I do love you.' As if this is an injury he'd rather not inflict.

I'm not in the mood for injury. 'And I do love you. So tell me.'

I pat his arms and he loosens a touch, relaxes enough to mouth beside my cheek and then eases down till his head is a live, warm burden across my shoulder, beneath my chin. I've done much the same myself at other times, with other people – they can't get a proper look at you when you're tucked away like that.

'Robert, what's wrong?'

'I can't take you to see my parents.'

'What?'

'I can't take you to see my parents.'

This, in a positive way, is not what I expected. 'That's . . . okay. I don't mind. I hadn't –'

'No, no.' He worries his head in tighter and I stroke my hand from his temple to his neck. I hold his voice. 'I'm an only child.'

'That's right.'

'No, you don't understand.' He breathes, lays his hand over mine and I'm finally sure he will tell me something now that I don't want to know. There's an old pain turning in him, I can almost hear it opening up the space for itself, stretching between soft tissues and harmless thoughts where I can't reach it and lift it away.

'I'm an only child. I haven't seen my father since I was seventeen. I haven't seen my mother since I was seventeen.' His palm is chill, his thumb rubbing my knuckles: back and forth, back and forth. 'I woke up early in the morning. I was worried about my exams, my Highers. I wanted to be a dentist, but my maths wasn't good and that made the chemistry difficult, the physics. But I needed them. I needed maths, too – I needed A passes in everything, because that's what everyone said they would expect and I thought that was important. And this was the summer I'm talking about – I had only about three weeks left to cram it all in and I was up early to study – it's what I was going to do that day, sit with my books. Because I applied myself, I was a good boy, a good pupil, well behaved.

'That morning, it was noisy downstairs, distracting – and not our normal type of noise. People talking softly and walking about, a lot of walking about.'

His thumb keeps moving, back and forth, and I can't stop it, can't try. I lean to kiss his hair, but he doesn't notice.

'And I was wondering why we had visitors and I was working things through in my mind and then I went into the bathroom and I was having a piss and I remember thinking: *No. There's something wrong. It's finally gone wrong.* And then I realised this was the one day that I would not ever forget – this would be the moment that explained me, the moment when I knew I was over – and part of it would always be the memory of standing and having a piss. It had to be like that, didn't it? Otherwise, my life would be a tragedy and not a joke and God wouldn't ever have that – or Luck, or Fate, or the way that I'm fucking made. Doesn't matter who's responsible, I have to be a joke.

'I washed my face for a long time and then I combed my hair and then I went and got dressed. But when I came out of my room again, there was a policewoman there, waiting. She must have been a very quiet person, I hadn't heard her on the stairs. What she said . . . it was some list of words that didn't mean anything and she was far too polite. Nobody is polite to you, not when you're seventeen, not unless there's a room downstairs that you can't go into and your father has been kneeling on the hallway floor beside the front door, but a policeman is helping him up now and studying him, as if he is this . . . something strange, infectious. Then the policeman looks at you and you're infectious, too. When all you've done is wake up in this house and be this son.

'I saw my father's face when he stood, but he wasn't inside it, not anywhere near. Then they took him out. My mother, I didn't see. I never got to see her. They didn't let me. I went to bed the night before and in the morning she was gone.

'Except I knew that wasn't right, wasn't the explanation. I knew what he'd done.'

Then Robert was still and quiet and I almost thought that he was sleeping, but when I shifted against him, stroked his arm, he started again: 'I couldn't tell them much. But he admitted all of it, so they didn't have much use for me. I remember that I was in court, but not why. I have a feeling that I was not significant.

'They weren't sure of what to do with me – not there, or anywhere else after that. No one knew where to put me . . . so I got moved around. But I kept up studying. That was fine. That was just the same. The school said that I needn't, but I took all the exams at the right time. I did very well. I was a good boy, a good pupil. And then I could go away and be a student, study more. So that's what I did. I had a lot of money. Inherited.'

He moved until he was lying with his face pressed into my chest, until I could rock him, close my hands behind his head, wind my legs against his and catch him, keep him from falling.

When he spoke again, he sounded younger and his conso-nants were blurred, 'He wanted me to visit him in prison. I refused. He wrote for a while and I didn't answer and then he stopped. Lack of forgiveness, they said it would hurt me – I didn't say anything, but I thought they could all go and fuck themselves, that's what I thought. Of course, he's out now. But he can't find me. I changed my name – Robert Gardener, that's what I picked.

And I rock him and I tell him, 'That's what I picked, too.' And I hear it sound irrelevant.

'I'm a good boy.'

'That's right.' Both of us mumbling, because we want to be asleep, in a dream where this will come and trouble us, but then move on.

'I have to let you know.'

'That's right.' When we're rested, we'll make love. It will help us get away from this, sometimes that's what it's for. 'That's right.' We'll be together. And he won't talk any more.

'No.' A fidget of movement through him. 'I have to let you know.'

'Let me know what?'

'I have a wife. She lives with my daughter. I have a wife.'

'Is that a problem?'

He is still for a while, but the silence is only reflective, not tense. 'No. It's not a problem.'

'Then that's all right.'

'No, I don't think it's a problem.'

'Fine.'

'But I thought you should know.'

'And now I do. So that's okay.'

And, because it's okay, but we need to leave here very much, have had enough, must start at once – we're going to work ourselves awake, we're going to strip down to distractions, we're going to be hands and tongues and fucking, running ourselves under salt. We're going to bruise and bite until the round wear of him in me, the drag of me caught around him, can erase us, let us seem anonymous.

IX

Getting a job – eventually, it's unavoidable. You have neglected to save savings, your position regarding state benefits is obscure, no secretive great-aunts have left you their Chilean vineyards and estates and so there are no other choices: you have to work.

And fit yourself into the shape of that long, sad stare you first discovered at seventeen, out of school and with a young thirst to support. The stare draws over you, cold and tight, whenever you peer at the small ads in tobacconists' windows and the columns of unwholesome and also entirely unreachable prospects offered in newspapers under *Employment* and the tidy, depressing postcards in the cheapskate agencies and the multiply renamed and euphemised places which I will only ever call labour exchanges, because that speaks of dignity and the Jane Eyre/Ealing Comedy/even Henry James types of position that might lead to adventure and romance, or at least to excitement and occult shocks.

Not that you really believe you might ever get lucky and *find* a job – and as soon as you even consider this, your face changes, you start looking unemployed: unemployable: long-term. Your transformation is completed by the time your eyes have edged across to read the offered rates of pay and then winced back. You add up the stated hours again and think that you don't want to spend forty in a week, or thirty-five in a week, or to-be-arranged-plus-overtime in a week, or actually *any* time in a week doing something that's appalling, but required of you by strangers. You have no applicable skills, but you know what you won't stand for.

And, worse, this bears no relation to those ambitions you once chose, the ones you're still prepared for – it means you'll never be a gold panner, a teacher, or an archaeologist, you'll never clown in the True Circus of your heart. Your future is irretrievable, because the careers you would like involve qualifications, training, a decision on your part to be responsible and adult. The only vacancies you could fill will amount to daily demonstrations of your uselessness.

You are now approaching forty and have already spent far too long washing underwear in a theatre, stacking shelves, cleaning rental power tools – which are, I would mention, often returned in revolting states. You have slotted together grids of doubtful purpose, you have folded free knitting and/or sewing patterns into women's magazines, you have sorted potatoes (for three grotesque hours), you have telephoned telephone owners to tell them about their telephones and you have spent one extremely long weekend in a hotel conference suite, asking people what they found most pleasing about bags of crisps. Every prior experience proves it – there is no point to you.

At least at the end of the crisp job, I got to take some home. But selling cardboard was a godsend: flexible and satisfying in a way that involved no pressure at any stage, because – after all – what sane person could possibly care about who might be buying how many of which kind of box. The job actually managed to be more trivial than me, which seemed to produce this Zen glow across my better days and enabled me to lie my head off in a consistent, promotional manner with hardly a trace of nauseous side effects.

At the moment, though, there's nothing doing: not in cardboard. Nobody wants me any more and yet, for the usual reasons, I continue to want cash. So, on a sodden Tuesday lunchtime, I'm forced to admit I've been driven to make the drinker's most conventional mistake. I've started working in a bar.

'. . . and a peach schnapps . . . and d'you have peanuts?'

'We have dry-roasted, roasted and *beer nuts*. Or cashews.' I know he doesn't have the class to buy cashews.

I also know that we both, my customer and I, have no idea what beer nuts are. We've tasted them, so we're quite sure they contain antiseptic, but we haven't given them much further thought. Not until this week, when I discovered my job involves bearing beer nuts and similar horrors perpetually in mind. I also have to wear this yellow T-shirt and this yelping smile and I also have to be able to say *beer nuts* as if those words are not offensive in every way and I also have to tolerate an order including one watermelon-flavoured Bacardi Breezer, two ginger ales and six whole packets of *beer nuts* and I also have to serve such a piss-poor excuse for a round without first picking up an ashtray and beating it off the proud purchaser's skull for successfully wasting everybody's time.

'Thanks.' He thrusts across the filthy, student type of tenner with his filthy, student type of hand.

'Mm.' I reach into my special jar and give him back some hot, wet change, which he almost drops. He then shuffles his ginger pop and packets away to his lumpy friends who nod and grimace at each other merrily.

I only stop hating them, because I have to give a businessman a double Scotch. There is something about this man's overly boyish goatee and his desperately amusing tie (set against a dark and ailing suit) that strongly suggests he is divorced and initially thought this a good idea, but now spends most of his lunch hours pretending to read in public places and hoping he can pick up girls. I feel him inspect me while I turn to pour his drink, his boneless little glances slithering here and there while I breathe in the scent of his whisky and love it as it deserves.

'Anything else?' I'm careful to say this so that the following unspoken phrase reads *before I punch you in the throat* rather than *you dashing rascal, you — I get off at five o'clock.*

I do, in fact, get off at five o'clock which means that I won't have to suffer him when he scampers in again after work, dreaming he'll meet someone pissed enough to fuck him.

Not that I'm so terribly annoyed with the businessman, per se, or anyone else, for that matter – it's just this bar I despise. It used to be a bank and still has an air of mingled anxiety and gruelling financial prudence – somewhere, the pennies are still being cared for and the pounds are caring smugly for themselves. The furnishings are too modern, the lights are too bright and every glimmer of conviviality disappears at once into the height of the ceiling where it is shredded slowly by unnecessary fans. The punters are cackling, or braying, or showing each other electrical gadgets they've bought, or yelling about lap dancers, or the plans they have to deck their patios. If two or three hand grenades rolled by, I'd joyfully pull their pins, if only to stop the bastards breeding.

Although this isn't completely the problem, either. It's more that a lot of my customers aren't drinking properly, aren't even trying. And, then again, many of them are drinking quite a lot. And meanwhile, because it is good for me and because I promised myself and because I promised other people and because Robert is being supportive, I am, of course, not actually drinking myself. That is, I am taking liquids, but they do not contain alcohol. If I *were* drinking, I would show them how it's done.

But I'm not.

So they don't know me.

I am being underestimated on every side. And I find that grating – anyone would.

'What's wrong?'

I am staring at the top of Robert's arm.

'Hannah? What's wrong?'

This is where men first grow old. Greying doesn't matter, new lines at the eyes – these small changes can be helpful, improving, but there's nothing to be done about the arms. From the shoulder to the elbow, gently, softly, you'll find a delicacy settled in his skin, a minute loosening where it lies above the muscle, a loss of grip. Once this has come it isn't going to leave him.

I didn't intend to notice. 'Nothing's wrong, I'm fine.' And I *am* fine: only I'm thinking of ways he might go, reasons, and most of them don't scare me and I can duck them, I can look the other way – but age and time, they're another prime example of God's slapstick: the body you're just getting fond of when it rots, the loves that you can't keep, the pratfall that always ends you, leaves you blinking up from the dust at your own mortality.

And I've been thinking about mortality more and more lately – another lovely side effect of keeping away from drink. So the last thing I need is to see it clouding Robert.

He stretches – apparently happy and at ease – shakes, rubs his wet hair with his fingers until it furrows and then stands. 'You're not fine. I can tell – I'm a dentist.' These days we take baths together or, more often, we watch each other soak, rub backs, admire the hot, clean infant heat when we step out and on to the tiles the way Robert just has. I swaddle him up in a towel, still playing at bath night, standing behind him and hugging my boy, licking the drops of water from his ear.

I close my eyes and make time leave us be. 'I'm a bit . . . I feel a bit grey. Not for a reason.'

We're in his flat. Before his confession, I'd never seen inside it – I now have a space in the bathroom cabinet and a drawer for my overnight clothes. Robert moved here when he left his wife, or she asked him to leave, and a sense of flight still lingers: the shelves and fitted units are mainly empty – even with my contributions added – there's a gaggle of lonely cans in one kitchen cupboard and a lack of ornaments. Everything tastes of fresh starts and reinvention and vigorous, road-movie freedoms we have yet to explore. This is where we can choose whoever we might want to be, but never pick anyone else, only ourselves together. That must mean we're the best we can imagine. I ought to be comfortable here as a matter of course and I frequently am.

'Well, if you feel grey . . .' He shrugs out of the towel and winks, secure in himself, reassuring, still in mainly good shape, and then eases into a dressing gown which is new enough to have that hotel frisson, an attractive neutrality. 'We could laugh at the television.' We could be anywhere, planning anything.

In fact, we do as he suggests and amble on through to his living room where he keeps the white leather three-piece suite (reduced because of scuffing and small marks) and the oddly large TV set which shines up from the floor when we wake it – Robert keeps forgetting to buy a stand for it and doesn't yet possess a table. At once our channel bleats and yammers into place, keeping us from news and other unwelcome intrusions.

'We've got people like Ah-Mozart there, Ah-Rachmaninov, Ah-Chopin – guide price £120, but bidding up from a pound.' A woman dressed like a minor teen singer is holding CDs in a fan, so that the camera can see them, while another woman, dressed like an older and workmanlike prostitute, waltzes behind her to 'The Blue Danube' while pushing a compli-cated and empty pram. 'Over forty-six hours of classical master-pieces. Look at that – Ah-Schumann, Ah-Beethoven and all starting from a pound, how *can* you beat it?' The pram pros-titute smiles and skips in her too-tight suit, while teensinger's unfettered breasts challenge her T-shirt and we're shown that the pram has functioning brakes and real, revolving wheels, all in an atmosphere of captive hysteria.

This rarely fails to cheer us up – it is selling and suffering and hopeless tat, it is freaks talking gibberish, detaching from their brains, and trying to wheedle the other freaks and the mad and the sad and the long-term unemployed into 75p-per-minute phone calls that may gain them impulse-bought kitchen appliances of no possible earthly use, or very large, remaindered jewellery. It is ugly, insane and shameful and reminds us of life.

'Look at her – mutton dressed as Spam.'

'Would you pay a pound for that?' Robert nudging me, enjoying his favourite question.

'Oh, I'd pay two . . . even two pounds fifty. They've got Ah-Brahms and everything.'

'Forty-six hours . . .'

'Of classical masterpieces.'

'I wonder if they ever get to stop?'

Although, naturally, they show no sign of stopping, 'Pete's in at thirty pounds, Carol's in at thirty-five pounds.' Calling the freaks by their first names to make them feel less alone. 'All you twenty-five-pound bidders, you're on the way out. Forty pounds would get this for you . . . Three times at twenty-eight . . . I'm not bringing the hammer down. . . Thirty pounds, thirty-two . . . I'm closing . . .'

Before a man in a plastic suit tries to explain a tiny, battery-powered chainsaw. Its blade extends just far enough to amputate string, small twigs, perhaps children's fingers. The man's hair, like everyone else's in this purgatory of crap, suggests he has been quite recently burned at the stake.

'And if *you* don't want it, what about your granny, or an auntie, or your mum? . . . for only fifteen pounds. No need to struggle any more, no need for strength in those arms.' Out in the world the freaks are calling up and bidding, perhaps out of love for their grannies and aunties and mums, which is a warming thought.

We lean against each other, warm in any case, and Robert sips a modest glass of red. This doesn't make me uneasy, because he deserves it: having to drill and hook at distressed mouths for most of the day, that'll work up a thirst. Dentist: another job I wouldn't take.

'Still grey?'

'No, not really.' My head is resting at his collarbone and I can hear the wine in him, the way it articulates his heartbeat, makes it sound more bright. I could almost go to sleep beside his soothing shine, if it weren't for the jolt and nag of sober thinking: all the obvious misery of everything. When you catch some flaying headline, or a radio makes you listen to the latest death, the latest dreadful accident, young life blighted, blasphemous pain, when anyone *just has to tell you* anything – drink is supposed to deal with that.

I am delicate and the world is impossibly wrong, is unthinkable and I am not forewarned, forearmed, equipped. I cannot manage. If there was something useful I could do, I would – but there isn't. So I drink.

So I *drank*.

And on all those other evenings, drink has trotted in and softened worries, charmed away internal repetitions of unpleasant facts and lifted my attitude those few vital degrees which prevent everybody from dragging their past behind them like a corpse, while bolting forward through a suicidal haze.

Now I have only my own body's vindictive chemistry to keep myself on track and that isn't enough, so I'm wedged between the TV and Robert, battling to hear anything over the din in my head.

He isn't living with his wife, but he's still married.

What does that mean?

It's good that he talked about it, but the way that he talked about it made the whole thing seem unfinished. It just wasn't clear – was he admitting there was something he hadn't told me and now I know it and that's that, or was he half admitting he hadn't admitted everything and I still don't know the one thing that's important?

Which is what I would have done – the half-admitting. It makes you feel better, makes the other person relax. I'd have tried it.

But with Robert I haven't tried it – I wouldn't.

I haven't admitted anything. Is that the problem? Has he guessed there are things I should say? I haven't told him about anyone, anything. But it's all stuff that isn't important. And I'm not married, never have been.

If it made him leave me.

He wouldn't be here.

If he's married to somebody else, then I can't marry him.

So I don't get to do that.

So I don't have to.

Because I've done the married man stuff before: the serious married man stuff with the calls at odd hours and the lunch-break fucks and him making you meet his wife socially (so that you'll know her, so that you can feel bad, too – except that you don't, because you're not married, that's his problem) and the not going out much in daylight and the wanting to have more of him, the hunger that almost wrecks you when you finally do touch – the whole, huge, locked-in, crucifying, paranoid fantasy. I've done that.

But even while you're choking with your secrecy and need and letting these waves of powerlessness grind at you in the sealed nights and even while you are certain he could complete you, mend you, possibly – why not? – save you – still, there is that small, cold part of you which is glad he won't ask you to compromise, or change, or be at risk – because he's married, that's his problem.

I've even wondered if the married men who have affairs are the sort you would want to keep secret, anyway – partners you'd always prefer to have limited influence. It's never clear with any of them who's really the more second class, despicable, who isn't worth the full commitment. He's the principal betrayer – you have no one to betray. If you measure yourself against him, you're just that fraction more clean.

But if he leaves you for his wife, then she's better than you were, must have qualities you don't possess.

But if *you* leave, then you've found those same qualities else-where.

Or, more often than not, you leave because nothing is better than him – nothing or less than nothing, in my experience. You would rather have no one and peace.

This is all you ever learn – that you are lower than the wife and above the husband, that people always want what they should not.

Robert, though: he isn't what I've done before. He is new, all new.

I stop thinking, burned to a close and realise Robert is watching me, 'Does my having wine bother you?'

'No.'

'Then what does bother you? Hannah? If you don't tell me I'll buy you a chainsaw – then what'll you do?'

And, having decided to tell him nothing and keep the mood sweet, I hear myself be as unhelpful as possible. 'Oh . . . I was thinking there are lots of things that we don't know.'

'About what – the weight of the universe? Are there whales in the afterlife, do they have wings?'

He's stalling for time, having caught my meaning and looks so gentle when he does it, his lips shaping the words in a way that reminds me of how he'll taste, the stubborn little wall his teeth make, the way they like to nip and bluff and then take me in, absolutely in. This is what I want to have in mind, but my drive towards self-destruction seems determined. 'No. There are things we don't know about us.'

He tries another diversion. 'Well, I told you everything about me, everything there is. Except for some stupidities with Doheny, which I don't remember – he remembers, but I'd rather not. Nothing too bad . . . Doheny uses that bar, by the way – that one you work in – eventually you'll meet up. You'll like him.'

'Will I?' I refuse to be diverted. 'You don't know about me.'

He slips his hand inside my dressing gown, takes the slow route from the knee and up and round to cup in at my hip. 'What should I know about you . . .' Of course, this also opens up the towelling, almost to my waist, which is distracting.

'. . . that I don't already know.' There's a trace of impatience in his delivery, which finally makes me regret that I've brought us to this.

I don't look at his face, in case he seems severe. I feel his hand straddle the curve of the bone, letting it part his first and middle fingers.

'Is it when you're drunk? Is it those types of . . .?' He kisses this into my ear. 'When you're drunk, you're not yourself. What you do: it's not yourself.'

'But with you –' My throat has contracted and everything I say sounds reedy. I swallow and try again. 'It's me when I'm with you. When I'm drunk – when I'm *very* drunk – it's still me – when it's with you. And sober. That, too. Then it's me, too. I've never –'

'I know. Me as well.' He kisses again. 'It's okay. We're us. There's nothing to talk about.'

I turn and kiss him back: the rise of bristle, the ghost of lavender soap, the smile – the places I find with my eyes closed, because that way I understand them more.

He unties the cord of my dressing gown. 'Fooled you.'

'Hm?'

'Can't have you being worried and grey.'

'And what stops me from being worried and grey?'

'Having nothing to talk about.'

My stomach feels the soft unfurling of his breath. 'That's right.' And this is better than admitting every sin, this makes far more sense.

Because this is honest, it must be. There's no space here for a lie. When someone is examining you naked, when they are palming your breasts together, so they can lick at both nipples, fast, fast: pause when they know they have you, look up while you ride that first ache 'Nothing to talk about.' – When you are rolling back for him and his fingers so he can draw the whole seam of you, slip and part you, find both the ways you give him and then light them, knuckle-deep, light you right up to the root of your tongue. 'Nothing.' When you lift to him and take him and are slow, slow, murmuring and giggling like children, this must mean you can have no real secrets.

And then you are done and the television chatters about pendants and twelve-carat chains and you have taken the flavour of wine from his mouth until you both taste the same and you sit up, thigh to thigh, enjoying that you're still stripped for each other, the friction in your breath from that.

'How many glasses have you had?'

'Two, three – can't remember . . .' The back of his finger strokes down your breast.

'You leave that alone.' Your thumb brushing the shaft of his cock in return until he lifts your hand away. 'Well, you started it . . . How many glasses?'

'No idea. Why?'

'I'm not complaining – it's nice that you have the wine. I just wondered where you'd got to.'

'Oh . . . sweet drunk. That's all. Sweet drunk.' He settles his arm at the small of my back.

Sweet drunk is lovely, maybe the best of the normal states. It's just as it sounds – warm and biddable and friendly and barely involving alcohol at all. There have been evenings when I have rattled straight past the convivial point and on into serious distress, solely because I've been hoping to get more sweet. Reaching it is like being six again and having ice cream, but if you drink on, it almost always disappears. Robert is stuffed with it, glowing. 'That's a good one, sweet. Looks good on you.'

'Doesn't it just. Although I was thinking of getting chocolate drunk in a bit.'

'Why would you need to?'

'Well, it might be fun . . .' And he picks up his wine and draws a mouthful, eases it down, letting me see the grin behind his eyes.

Chocolate drunk is odd – some drinkers never reach it, some never fail to. Once you're there, if you were chocolate, you'd eat yourself. You are delighted to find you irresistible and no other opinion counts. It leads to complications.

'No, you fancy yourself too much, anyway. What about cat drunk?'

'Don't know that one.' He drags one dressing gown over our laps as we cool.

We've been perfecting our list for months, but haven't run over it lately – not since I've stopped drinking myself. 'Cat drunk – when you do that thing where you look over somebody's shoulder, as if there was a lunatic behind them with an axe. The way cats do.'

'Ah . . . like ghost drunk.'

'Yes, but if you're ghost drunk you could be seeing anything – and you dodge about more.'

'Because of the ghosts.'

'Indeed.'

We've made official definitions for large drunk, small drunk and fire drunk – all of which are obvious, but handy. Then there are the subtle variations of movement – sand drunk: only able to walk as if labouring over sand – locked drunk: only able to rush in spasms from one paralysis to the next – risen drunk: as if you were risen clumsily from the grave – and water drunk, one of Robert's inventions, 'Where the air, without warning, becomes liquid, this causing you to fall, unnaturally slowly, to the ground.'

Deaf drunk, we don't welcome, it makes people belligerent – and is also an instant pain in the arse, if you happen to work in a bar.

'Well, if I can't be chocolate –'

'I told you, you're *already* chocolate.'

'Well then, transparent. I want to be transparent drunk.'

'Do you have enough wine for that? Anyway – *why*?' Not that I've ever met anyone who can will themselves transparent – it always comes to you when you haven't a bad wish in your heart and then leads you astray while you think you're invisible.

'Hm? D'you want to do bad things?' It is proof that alcohol and God have the same sense of humour.

'No. I want to do *very* bad things.' And he gives me the sly boy's grin, the one that is lazy with wine and has a cunning that moves so slowly it becomes a type of candour. 'Some very bad things with you.'

'Will I think they're bad?'

'You don't think anything's bad.'

And I laugh, but partly to occupy the time it takes to wonder what kind of woman I am for him and if there were bad things his wife wouldn't allow.

But if the two of us enjoy what we enjoy, then what's the problem?

He brushes my lower lip with his finger. His hand smells of sex and we understand that we both know this, enjoy it.

He watches me as I kiss his palm. 'I could get Pentecostal drunk.'

'Speaking in tongues? – I could make you do that anyway.'

'Boasting again.'

But what I'd really love is for us to get blessed drunk, child drunk together: to excel ourselves and race into that place of innocence and light where nothing will hurt us and there can be no harm, where we are so powerless and lost that we become holy, that our Maker has to take us in hand.

You see the blessed children all the time, weaving in busy roads which would crush somebody sober, laughing at wounds which would kill – but they're safe entirely. A crew member on the *Titanic*, Joughin was his name – I think that's right – he was the ultimate blessed drunk, blasted out of his mind as the lifeboats filled and the lights went out and the band played the paupers and millionaires to their deaths. But Joughin didn't die. He walked to the stern as no sane man would and rode it clear down to the ocean, then swam away. And he wasn't sucked down along with the wreck, didn't freeze in the pitiless water, even survived a boat's refusal to take anybody so utterly drunk on board. And he was saved and brought to shore alive, of course alive.

The trouble is, you can't ever know this condition personally, because, more deeply that any other drunkenness, it makes you go away. I assume that its bliss comes mainly from this absence of yourself – it burns you up completely and grants you the grace of a temporary death while it curls up and rejoices in your soul. So I couldn't try to share it with Robert – we would neither of us be there.

And I'm not drinking.

Then again, I'm very tired. I've had days and days – over a month – of being tired. These levels of anxiety, my new-found ability to ruin whatever's most precious with suspicions and poisonous memories and fear, the way my head will not shut up, the miseries in my job, the expanding regiments of horrors that charge out in every sleep – I've had enough.

This isn't the way I should be. This isn't the way that anyone should be.

If I still had a doctor, he would have given me medication.

'Robert?'

'Mm?' He threads his fingers in the hair at my temple, combs through. 'Whassit?'

'Do something for me?'

'Course.'

He combs again – it starts a nice tingle at the corners of my eyes. 'Have you finished the bottle?'

'Just. Yes.'

'Go and get another, will you? And bring me a glass.'

'Course.' He kisses my forehead. 'You'll be ready for it now. All set. I knew you could manage stopping.' He kisses each cheek, as lightly as my mother would. 'And I knew you could manage starting again.' He kisses my mouth, lets me take his sweet-drunk tongue between my teeth, flickers and presses, withdraws. 'Welcome back.' He tugs away the dressing gown again.

'I'm not back yet. Go and get the bottle. And my glass.'

X

I'm back in the black house again. It's moving around me, breathing. It always does.

This time, I look at the darkness and understand its shape: the box of walls around me, the peak of the roof that meets above, one slope of the pitch leaning steep against the other – no more to the black house than this. It's as plain as a four-year-old's drawing and nothing inside it but me.

The shake of noise rises, moans, and the unseen, unseeable floor beneath me starts to buckle and then drift. A current drags at it, pulls it from under my feet, before returning, pushing it in, as if I am walking the tide line somewhere, as if I am somehow riding a great sea.

And now the whole house tightens like a sail and seethes with a new motion, something I know is dreadful and heaven-sent, and the seams of the walls begin parting in bright splits and the roof starts to lever away, starts to bleed with narrow glares of white – a Judgement looking for me, breaking through. And I am cold and have been here before and will be here again, will keep on returning until the house is wrecked and takes me with it, until I fall up into the burning absence that I am afraid is the heart of God.

The base of the wall to my left begins to spasm. It gapes.

'Hannah.'

'Mmm?'

God having my name already, God lying in wait, taking an interest I don't want.

'Hannah. Come on. We're nearly there.'

I swallow and lick my lips. 'I'm sorry.'

And I don't taste of the bad end that I'll come to: there's no trace of the black house or the paradise howling outside it, the perpetual roar of light. 'I am. I'm sorry.'

I don't even appear to be dead.

'I am.'

But I recall that I was in a hurry quite recently and then in a cab and now, when I take stock a little, glance about, I see I still *am* in a cab, the same cab. It's daytime, daylight: long, sore ribbons of daylight to either side and sunshine and harried pedestrians with anxious hair and grisly brick buildings that loom over fancy doors and a fenced and gated square containing trees, these huge-leaved trees, trunks smooth and pale and patterned in a way that seems reptilian, too much alive.

Robert, hugging me against him, playfully squeezes my right breast. 'Back with us, are you?' Which might be amusing if every shift of the cab didn't hurt my mind.

'Don't do that.'

The air pushing through the half-opened window is soaking with stress and leaves an aftertaste of shit. Cars grind and slice around us with malicious glee, while our cab executes its own criminal manoeuvres, the driver sipping takeaway coffee as we lurch along and settling to read his paper at red lights.

So we're in London.

Yes, of course, we're in London. I knew that. We're having a break, a long weekend and this is where we chose to have it. I knew that. I knew that we're spending our precious free time in the world's most perversely expensive and unwelcoming capital.

'Did somebody spray something in my eyes?'

'Shhh.' Again he tweaks at me. 'You're just a bit delicate.' He tries to locate the nipple, but it can't be bothered standing up to meet him. 'You're beginning to feel the pace.'

'And you're not, I suppose?'

'Nope.' He passes me a can of fizz and caffeine. 'Had four of these. They contain ox bile. It says so.'

'Terrific.' My voice is furry, soured.

'Take one, it'll perk you up. No point sleeping if we don't have to – we've only got . . . forty-two and a half hours left.'

And this did seem a good plan twenty-nine and a half hours ago – that we'd simply stay awake for the duration. Which we felt would maximise the educational and entertainment value of our trip, but the pills that we bought in the bar on Westbourne Grove – I don't remember when – have begun to make my skin ill-fitting and my eyelids have also become highly abrasive and the muscles in my forearms have been tensed so long that my thumbs have lost all sensation and a good deal of their strength and this is – I can't deny it – keeping me very much awake, but it's also really quite unpleasant.

'What was in those things?'

'What things?' Robert ducking his head unsubtly to indicate our driver and his fiendish capacity to overhear.

'The keeping awake things.' Not that our driver is at all concerned with us – he is crashing over sleeping policemen and meanwhile yelling something about carpets – I hope into a telephone.

Robert whispers, 'I don't know. But they're doing the job, aren't they? They're keeping awake things – and we're keeping awake . . . I think I didn't ask what they were . . . Anyway, he didn't say.'

'I need a drink.'

'We'll have a drink.'

'I need a drink now.'

'We'll have a shower and then we'll go out for a drink.'

'I don't need a shower. I need a drink.'

In our miniature hotel room, I listen to Robert shower and examine the flowers: lampshades with flowers, cushions with

flowers, framed flower prints. The wallpaper heaves with petals
– giant, predatory orchids that lurk above the tulip-covered
fitments and menace the vine-draped curtains and creep
towards the carpet and its slaughterhouse of buds. I couldn't
sleep here even if I wanted to.

Still, I lie on the bed anyway. It's been distressed by some
kind of prior activity, but that's a good thing, because the naked
sheets we've left ourselves are white: just a plain and empty,
godless, ordinary white.

Swaying in a way that is mainly soothing, I begin to get
undressed, because I'm aware that my joints are stiffer than
they should be, that they itch, and that I possibly should find
out why. I notice a gentle rise of dust when I brush my arms,
take down my jeans, a powdery haze against the inside of my
navy blouse. It's there on my underwear, too – my skin is shed-
ding. I'm casting off one whole layer of what is me with maybe
more to follow, who can say.

This revelation makes the itching worse, although I shouldn't
scratch for fear of wearing me away.

But the itch is bad.

So I fingertip softly down my shins, rubbing gently, and
watch another shower of Hannah Luckraft drift off towards
the vegetative writhing on the floor.

'Ho, I thought you wanted a drink.' Robert stands at the
foot of the bed, limbs mildly damp, forefingers tucked in the
waistband of his boxer shorts. 'But we could wait, though.'
One hand makes the predictable, usual dip, tugs out his rigid
cock, and then allows himself a ruminative wank.

Which means whisky – we must have been into the whisky
to get him like that. Hard in a moment, or barely breathing: it
can take him either way – in this case, very hard and very proud
of it. Splay-footed and letting his stomach jut and holding his
favourite thing in all the world: the tallest two-year-old you'll
ever meet. 'Fancy it?' The whisky makes this rhetorical and sets
him on the bed beside me, still wanking, semi-automatically. His

free hand reaches for me, thumbs me open like a book, a little clumsy. 'Or d'you want a drink? A wee drink of Robert before we go? *Afore ye go?*' He giggles and I feel his fingernail as he tries to unlock his way in.

But I'm dry. Never mind the need that's vaguely twitching into place – my tongue and my throat and my skin and my eyeballs and *everywhere*, I'm dry.

'Whatsamatter?' He presses in from another angle, jigs at me with his thumb.

It's the speed, or whatever he's fed me – always leaves me like a fucking iguana on a grill. I might be halfway normal by tomorrow, if then.

He works on his shaft with a little more passion and studies my face as if I am far away and perhaps unfamiliar. 'Hm?'

'It's the pills.'

But Robert's forgotten both the question and the answer and simply kneels up, frowning, flushing. His breathing keeps pace with his fist. And I do want this: the small, pained moment when he comes, when it's warm across my stomach, a light touch against my side, spilling. And I do want his hand, warmer, fingers spread, palming it over my waist and down, smearing my breasts, wiping the last of it under my hair at the back of my neck. And I do want this stain of him on me, tight and silvered, something improper to please my aching skin, and I smile at him as we jar and stammer back into our clothes, recall our thirst, and he also smiles at me, only now I've caught his distance, been infected, so that it seems he's receding from me, the room elongating to keep us beyond our reach.

'Well.' His voice slightly distorted in the elastic air. 'You said you need a drink. Will we go and get one?'

'Yes.'

For some reason I didn't entirely hear myself when I said that, so I try again. 'Yes.' A drink being the very thing to fix us up, have us 100 per cent again and in our correct dimensions. 'Yes.' Tequila, I think. Tequila will sort me.

Or white rum. A single absinthe, if they have some, just for a touch of class. 'We should go and get a drink.' And then I'll settle into something gentle, a mild flow of wine.

What you want for a quality outing is a good sense of composition: when to climb steadily with a Lagavulin, or a Longrow, a Balvenie, when to take on convincing proof, when to level off with, say, a Merlot and when to risk the exotic: a Gammel Dansk, a Karpi, a Rawhide, a questch, an old Coca-Cola bottle full of colourless blindness and joy. It's a knack, building a night.

Robert gives up on his shoelaces and walks over, takes my arm and then coories himself in behind me, rocks his hand at the back of my neck. 'Are you ready? Are you ready to be out with me? I want you out with me. So you can stand by the bar and I'll take my first sip and I'll look at you, I'll look right at you and we'll both know you've my spunk all over you – take that first sip and swallow it and we'll both know. We'll both drink and we'll both know.'

I lean against him, concentrating. 'Okay.' First I feel nothing beyond echoes and a clammy, panicked lack. 'We'll do that.' And then the real thing spikes in me at last, closes my eyes. 'Yes. We will.' Tonight we'll drink the way we always should.

'So you'll remember the good things I do for you. So you'll see. There isn't anything I wouldn't do for you. I'll make you forget every fucker but me.' He checks his watch. 'Forty-one hours and thirteen minutes left.'

Our first sip is round the corner in Marylebone High Street and it kisses our blood, illuminates – just at the good time, before the evening starts, when the sky is folding down to dusk outside and will keep us cosy and here we have space (the right amount of space) and quiet to let the sweet rush of spirits lift us, race our hearts. We stand and face the optics, side by side, no touching, and we could scream our lungs raw, we could break every bottle in here and eat the glass, we could run outside and keep on running and no power created could catch us, we could fuck on the counter naked till the wood burns through and the beauty of us makes the barman mad – we could do anything, but we only turn and see each other, see our love and take the second sip.

Leading to Goodge Street and no bloody room. More tequila. So tight that you have to shout, everyone shouting. Little bastard with a cheap cigar makes a hole in my sleeve. Little bastard. Robert doesn't mind, though. He's red drunk – anyone would say so – crimson drunk, alight. You could read by him. If you had a book. I don't have a book. He doesn't have a book. I kiss his hand because he has great hands and he tastes of cunt and beer. I would wish to kiss his other hand but he won't let me. Little bastard.

Frith Street, Shaftesbury Avenue, back a street, another, the place we were in before, then the other place, Frith Street.

This nice. Really. I think so. Thinso.

We should joina club, then this would be easy, we'd be in our club for duration and drink, because I don'like to walk too much, you know? Bad for you.

The people in here, they are so fucking ugly. Fucking ugly. Fucking ugly. I can say that all night. You can'stopme. Fucking ugly. Fuckinugly. Fuckinugly. You – you're the most fucking ugly. Shit-faced fucker.

Staystreet. Staceystreet. You're fuckinpissed. Can'take your drink. Sad.

Sad

Sad

Sad

Shit-faced inthe gantry mirror. Own mother wouldn'tknow. Sad.

I love my own mother.

Robert. Nice hug with him wouldbegood. Lovely. Sweats like fuck, love that. Salt. Fuckhesgot nice hair. Fantastic hair. Bit grey enough grey right amount tellanyone great hair.

Thisthe house? Issit? Party? Good. Lovely hair. Makesyo wantcry. Great.

'I didn't say, I didn't do anything.'

'You were sucking him off.'

'What?'

'You would have been.'

'What? *Me*? *I* was behaving badly? What the fuck were *you* doing?'

'Playing footsie with him for a fucking hour. Who was he anyway, d'you even know?'

'Was *I* the one who got thrown out?'

'You're just . . . You are just . . .'

'Was the one, was the, was *I* the one who got thrown out?'

'Leave me alone.'

'Was *I* the one who –'

'Fuck off.'

'I wasn't the one.'

'Fuck off!'

Backofachineserestaurant – lane full ofgrease, everything grease and that thick taste, chemical, and I'm trying to piss and not to fall, and not to get dirty and I can't tell what's happening, what's gettng wet. Jeans are a problem.

Somewhere this bastard cunt is singing, same four notes, again and again, same four and aiming at me, wanting to kill me with it, wanting me fucking dead.

Robert supposed to be looking out. But he's not, not looking out, he's pissing, too, against a skip, so he's not looking out and I've started now and so I can't stand, can't hide, anyone could could walk by. Anyone.

'Fucker.'

'You were all over him.'

'You're off your fucking head.'

'Should have just left you to it.'

'Always the same.'
'Yes. You are.'

Sweeping machines going over cobbles, dark smear dragged along behind them and two bands of cleanliness. Gritty light. Bedfordbury. Another day starting, very pushy, when we haven't quite done with the last.

Big, quiet ache, above a rattle of emptying bins, vertigo under your feet. The city peering at you – it gets you in the morning, sees too much, that's why you should stay inside.

We sit on the steps of St Martin's.

We are only tired. We have beds we will go to in a while. The men over there, they don't have beds. They are unfortunate.

We wouldn't take a drink from them if they offered. We don't favour lager and that's all they've got. We are not the same as them. We would like to point out that the way we appear is a complete misunderstanding.

'This is more like it.'
'No, it's not.'

The Natural History Museum swims around me and then halts, jumps into place, sticky with children and throbbing in time to my pulse. This was Robert's suggestion – to have a break, some culture. But the entrance hall alarmed us both, the scream of height inside it and the threatening stairs, the endless, inquisitive din of feet and lips and bickering families. So we've come to hide in here with the stuffed birds, because they are unpopular and quiet.

Still, Robert likes museums, he is keen to show enthusiasm and take part. 'That's . . .' He frowns at a high, wide shrub infested with tiny corpses and trapped behind glass. Christ knows how many artificial eyes fail to blink at him, 'That's . . .' while he searches for a word that could describe them.

'Dead. That's . . . all dead. Everything in here is dead.'

A nasty sleep mugged us back at the hotel and now there

are only twenty one hours and eight minutes – give or take – before we go home.

Robert hisses out a sigh between his teeth and we wander on. Up ahead there is a case of swans – mother, father, children, lumpily preserved – evidence of some dreadful accident. 'Oh God, will you look?' Or just a wholesale slaughter, gleefully displayed.

'*At what?*' Robert's forcing a heat now. '*Well?*' His colour high, mouth tightening round the start of an argument, liking it there.

'The swans.' Which I try to say gently, as if it is just a remark, because I am hung-over in a way that makes me slow and so I have been unable to realise in time that he is hung-over in a way that makes him furious.

'So what's wrong with *them*? Jesus Christ, all I wanted was a little bit of peace. You've done nothing but fucking bitch since we came in.'

'I don't mind being here.'

'Oh, fantastic – thanks for your fucking unreserved support. Again. And last night . . .' He can't remember last night any more than I can,

'I thought we had a nice time last night.' I speak softly, so that he can, too.

But it doesn't work. 'You fucking would.' He is irreversible. 'A nice time . . .' There's nothing in him that I can coax round, even argue with. The best of his head is asleep, or still pissed, and I've been left with this – an angry no one. 'A *nice time.*' Dropping his head and flinching, then constructing his stare, hoping I'll meet it, wanting to hurt himself with that.

'Robert, what the fuck is wrong with you?' And this time I am not speaking softly, because there is no point and he is changing the subject to something which makes no sense.

'You want me to believe it was the pills . . .' He will say whatever strikes him now, whatever will hurt.

'The pills?'

So it is easy for him to step in close beside me and grind out, 'You never had a dry cunt in your life. But now you do with me,' before he ducks back, heads for the next room, feet slightly baffled by each step.

I intend to follow, to yell and make him ashamed, but he has made me ashamed first, he has frightened me with nonsense, made my stomach scared. I have to go back to the entrance, find the toilet and be sick.

When I leave the museum I start to walk north, in no hurry: I don't much want to be in the hotel again, not yet – there's too much Robert there. The breeze is not unkind and follows me, nudging my back, as I head for Hyde Park and its strangely naked green, the flat reach of somewhere which is almost country, which almost smells of spring. I avoid the paths and wish the grass more uneven, feel the lack of scrub and rocks. Down at the lake, swans are begging in huddles, removed from their animal selves, undignified.

Beyond the perimeter, two armoured cars are heading towards Marble Arch. They're painted grey and have PRESS stencilled on them in white and they smell of being far away and death – here, they don't fit. They're part of the wrong war for London: they should be open-topped, khaki, full of young chaps with tin helmets and overcoats, driving too fast and grinning out at arm-in-arm uniformed women, sandbags and comical signs left in chalk to raise morale. They should be from the place that I learned about with Simon: the one that showed how good we were born to be. The one in *The Wooden Horse* and *633 Squadron* and *The Desert Rats* and all of the other dreams where all of the proper humans were busy and forthright and brave and there was maybe a little sadness, but in the end things would be fine, because we were right, we were in the right. We loved that war.

Not that love is my strong point. And I could do without thinking of Simon, or war, or bombs, or shelters, or any fucker not myself.

Myself. No one understands that. No one feels it. I am enough to make me miserable. I am too much to bear. Other people get help, they're supported, they have obvious injuries. Other people don't have to be me.

And sometimes I am unavoidable, so this is when I have to raise my blood sugar, line my stomach and get a grip. Because I have to admit that quite often I don't need sympathy, only a spot of basic maintenance and then chemical intervention.

Swallowed back into the city, I pick out a café and sit, watch a girl make me a stale chicken sandwich and deliver it with an espresso, a half-litre bottle of water and a bill for a three-course meal. The water says it is best before 2027. Ordinarily I don't like to drink things which are intended to last that long.

But I rehydrate with it anyway, and perk myself up with the coffee and gag the chicken down while the apparently drugged waitress lays out tiny medical-looking trays full of dreadful objects intended to be tapas and to give everybody a dash of Hispanic romance. Above the tapas area is a tired neon sign that should read

MAY WE
HELP YOU?

but that actually reads

MAY
HELP

I pay the waitress more money than either of us is worth and get on my way.

How I find the church, I'm not too certain. It's past two and I've been thirsty in Lancaster Gate and then again in Baker Street and someone with Robert's shoulders was in the first pub and somebody with his hair was in the next and men who have some trick of him, a style of walking, a similar shirt: they've tired me now for hours and driven me in here, a narrow-fronted chapel that opens, deep and dim off the crook of the street.

I'd expected calm and these final pews are, indeed, empty and undisturbed, but the altar is a murmuring scramble of school uniforms and musical instruments. Slowly a kind of tune, impossible to identify, limps out from the small musicians while three adult women – I presume teachers – stand among the rest of their child congregation and mime inexplicable actions with exemplary emphasis. Their charges echo them: cradling, plaiting, engraving, stabbing, blowing glass: and all the time mouthing something which barely reaches me, a drifting, dissipating song.

One verse goes badly and is apparently repeated twice while I resist the urge to kneel, to sink and curl myself out of anyone's sight, tent my hands together as if I can still pray.

The children now rearrange themselves, earnest, and take it in turns to deliver small readings from a lectern. The content escapes me beyond the occasional word – *bread, wine, garden, betrayed, forsaken, stripped.*

I did this once. I read. I walked to the front of the school hall and took my place in the little line, stretched my spine until it tickled so I'd be tall enough to hold the holiness I could feel pouring, rolling in. '*Let not your heart be troubled: ye believe in God, believe also in me.*' And my voice floated out, sweet from my throat. '*In my Father's house are many mansions: if it were not so, I would have told you. I go to prepare a place for you. I will come again, and receive you unto myself; that where I am, there ye may be also.*' The complications of it and the melody and the meaning that I couldn't grip, except that it was so fine and shining and a comfort. '*And whither I go ye know, and the way ye know.*'

Simon was watching me, huge-eyed and proud, because I

263

said it for him – the fine, shining comfort – that we're never lost, that our death always calls us, that we know the way.

Between each recitation a few boys and girls rehearse their illustrative mimes. Pilate, whose tie is squint, looks puzzled. Mary is sad. Soldiers point fingers and laugh noiselessly. They tug at the sleeves of Jesus' pullover, pat down a crown of nothing on his head and beat him wildly with thin air. Somebody passes him an invisible weight and he hugs it inaccurately, then drops like a shot detective, like a stuntman taking a punch. So someone else drags the weight along without him, hunching up under its undefined length. Then Jesus is left by himself, awkward, and the other children fidget, because this is near the end, before he leans his arms out against space, balances inside the thought of who he is, and becomes still: for a moment, makes everything still.

They pack themselves up after that: well mannered, promising, no disturbance beyond scuffling and whispers, and they file away past me towards the door.

I don't raise my head to them, don't show them my face, because they wouldn't understand it and I might worry them. I feel one of the teachers pause slightly beside me, perhaps checking to see if I am safe, perhaps setting herself as a shield between her pupils and a dubious stranger: the low, sharp breath of a misguided life. Still, I'll do them no harm, I don't matter: they'll be back here on Good Friday, Easter Sunday, whenever they plan to perform, and they won't even think of me.

Far to the left, across the aisle, something is moving beneath the pews: a dark scuttle, more like a spider than a mouse. When the place has emptied, the fat door breathes back to its frame, sealing me in.

There are six hours, maybe five, of our holiday left when Robert wakes me. The hotel room is jerking with pale television light: a woman in a T-shirt on a perfect beach, saying something about tipping: that the locals don't expect too much.

Robert is burning, wet with a day of drink, thick and heavy with it, hands scalding where they touch.

'Sorry.' The word we learn in so many languages, the only one we absolutely need. 'I am. Sorry. Hannah?'

'Fine. You're sorry.' I'm almost sober, starting to bruise as the alcohol leaves me. 'I'm trying to sleep.'

He stands back from the bed, fights out of his coat and then sits again. 'Donbe like that.' A smooth, clean surface is pushed against my hand. 'See.' I can hear the light swing of liquid inside glass. 'For us.' He kisses my ear. 'For you.'

'What?'

'Vodka.' And he wraps me suddenly against him, holds me inside what feels like a kind of despair. 'I love you.' Closes me in that sweet smell he has, that sweet, sweet skin.

Robert Gardener: the sight of him splintered around me all day: his ghost turning a corner, hailing a cab, drifting across any number of entirely unimportant men.

Robert Gardener with me now, even more when I let my eyes shut, when I feel him smile.

'Hannah? I love you. Sorry.'

'It's okay.' I kiss his ear. 'Where were you?'

'Nowhere.' His arms relax. 'I brought vodka. We can have it now.'

'That's right. We can have it now.'

An untouched bottle and the man who loves me, the man I love.

I am cutting lemon slices: thin half-circles, notched to fit on the lip of a glass. No one likes doing this, because it stings. You think you're intact, not even a paper cut, but the lemon juice will always search out something, sneak in and bite.

When I need to curry favour in the bar, I volunteer for slicing. I usually do need to curry favour, being not necessarily an ideal employee.

'Busy, isn't it?' Robert's in visiting me and on the water tonight. He's also full of fruit and vegetables, he says, to make him well. 'Mm-hmm . . . lot of people in.' I wasn't aware that he'd been ill, but according to him, he's felt out of condition for a while, now every morning this week, he's gobbled down vitamins and a small cup of green liquid that smells of horses and makes him wince. 'Very busy for a Wednesday . . .' The new regime hasn't exactly put a zip in his conversations.

'Give it another hour – then it'll be busy.'

'Don't know how you stand it.'

'Neither do I. Try not to look as if we're talking – the boss is in.'

'All right.' He makes a half-turn and sights down the length of the bar: the leaning, twitching, signalling line of would-be drinkers. 'Another water would be nice.'

'No, it wouldn't.'

'No. It wouldn't. But it would be wet. And you could put a bit of lemon in it.' He seems tired, glum.

'Your wish is my command.'

Abandoning my slicing, I pour him a glass of wet, slap on his lemon and some ice. 'There you go.' And I take his two quid, almost without laughing. Teetotalitarianism, we can't help but punish it: two pounds for a water, two pounds fifty for an orange juice – those fuckers don't stay smug for long with us. 'What about the Atkins Diet? – you could try that.'

He's barely audible. 'No thanks.' Being full of fruit and vegetables can be draining.

'A cow a day, roasted on a bed of cow, stuffed with cow chunks and topped with a single pound of cheese – how could you refuse?'

'No thanks.' I'll fry him some bacon tomorrow – for his own good. And a nice Irish coffee for breakfast.

'Look, I have to do some serving now. But then I'll be down here again for the slicing.' I talk to the side of his head, as if we've never met, are not meeting. 'Whatever we don't need, we dump in the fridge. There are twelve-year-old slices in there – a whole lemon civilisation: art galleries, schools . . .'
His face tries to seem a little amused, but his eyes aren't happy.

'I'd like a word then.'

'Okay. You can have one. When I'm back.' I brush across his fingers with my thumb. We enjoy this because it looks like nothing, a tiny accident, but it means we are together, we are us.

The peak of the evening levels and begins to ease. I barge through a handful of rounds, trying to catch Robert's eye as I move, but he's still tucked in the corner: his back to the wall, his side to the bar top, studying the room, something in his face extremely gentle, soft. Another chance for me to notice how fine he can look.

Then I slide in behind the chopping board again, take up the knife. 'What particular word did you want? Our special tonight is *molybdenum*.'

'Oh, I don't . . .' He folds his arms, nods down his head. 'Maybe this isn't . . .'

The only thing that could make him this upset would be

a bad day at work: an unexpected biter, an under-anaesthetised extraction, somebody else making stupid complaints.

'Come on. You can tell me – I'll even get you started. What's a nice dentist like you doing in a place like this?'

'Leaving.'

'Yeah, it does get a bit much. They'd have to pay me to stay. In fact, they do. But not nearly enough.'

'No, I mean leaving.'

By which he doesn't mean leaving, of course. 'What?'

'I have to go.'

I can't see his eyes. 'Will you be round tonight?'

'Don't make this difficult.'

'Don't – What?' I can't see his eyes.

'I'm going. I have to stop.'

'You can't.' If I could see his eyes, it would make this different.

'That's it, Hannah. I'm sorry.'

'Where?' Questions are good, they make people answer and that means they have to stay. 'Where are you going?'

He rubs his neck, still here.

'Where, Robert?'

'No.' He presses the heels of his hands against his eyelids. 'No. I'm going away. I have . . . the daughter, my daughter. I mean. I don't know.'

'This why you've been on the health kick? Recovering from me?'

'No. No, I just . . .'

'Why did you come here to tell me?' My voice louder than it should be, even with the din around us, the shouting, the fuckmesoon laughs. 'Robert? Didn't I deserve some privacy?'

'You did. You do. I'm sorry. I am.' And now he lets me see his face, when I don't want to, when I am scared of it: the emptiness in it and the scared eyes, the receding light. 'I didn't mean . . .' He reaches forward over the broad top of the bar and grips my wrist, kisses my cheek and withdraws before I can start to touch him back. Then he walks out of the bar, unsteady despite all the water. There's a moment when I lose him in the crush, but he's clear when he reaches the door, I can watch him do that, open it, step through.

When I swing my head, the manager is watching me and I feel myself try to construct a puzzled smile to make her leave me be. And in a while I will drink: drag it in so hard and obviously that it will steal away my job and I will go home and keep on drinking until I destroy whole days of myself, a week, and I will go to his flat at a point I don't remember and find there is a new lock, no curtains, bare floor behind the letter box, everything stripped and no one there and I will drink until the spider comes into my mouth, I will drink until there's no one there, I will drink until I leave me, until I leave myself alone.

But now I am cutting lemon slices: thin half-circles, notched to fit on the lip of a glass. No one likes doing this, because it stings. You think you're intact, not even a paper cut, but the lemon juice will always search out something, sneak in and bite.

The wind is driving sand along the dunes, lifting it like smoke and shadows in a layer that becomes another shoreline flickering over the surface it has scoured to a dun skin.

My head aches with the cold and I'm unsteady and the sea roar has taken every sound. Water-light and perspectives are pummeling round us, racing away until we are all of us unreachable as we waver on in silhouette, curling and leaning against gusts, facing the breakers, or walking along beside them, fighting the length of the beach.

And this is the Hour Long Beach: the one I used to visit when an hour could be endless, when the whip of the air cupped around me, the invincible restlessness, made me run until I fell, made me light-headed, drunk.

I used to imagine this was Our Long Beach, because that's how it felt. But it didn't belong to us, it was just a place we took an hour to walk, somewhere we drove to on family outings: always too chill and blustery for good picnics, even with the windbreak, even in July – always the small shock of sand in what you ate: the rolls, the foil-wrapped chicken legs, the dented strawberry tarts – the signs of parental care, of preparation for my benefit. The love they had for Simon and for me.

No picnic today, though, and my brother isn't with us, because he doesn't believe in me. He thinks I will never get better, only worse. He thinks there is no hope. He is convincing. Still, we came here anyway: my mother and father brought me, showed parental care again, and preparation for my benefit.

They have no idea what to do with me, not any more, and

I can't help them. So they offer me nursery food and cheerful magazines and take me on the jaunts that pleased me thirty years ago. Here, they let me step out a few yards ahead and follow, arm in arm. My mother has a little shopping bag that holds sandwiches we won't eat and a pointless thermos. My father wears a cap I haven't seen before – his free hand flies to it, now and then, to keep it in place. For a while, I turn and walk backwards so I can see them and they can see me and we can seem happy for each other.

But I make them upset. Just by being here and as I am, I do them harm.

So I wouldn't be with them if I could help it, only I haven't been well, really haven't been well. I woke up in a hospital bed one afternoon and found I'd been having trouble with my brain. I had to call and ask a nurse about what I remembered thinking, about being mad – because everything I had believed for the previous week did seem suddenly very mad, clearly changed to nothing, the terror of nothing, idiocy.

The nurse just went back to her station and left me with myself and a ward full of old men staring, flinching at private threats, messing their beds. Still, fairly soon after that, the doctors let me go – once I could prove I was back in my own mind – or fully out of it, not scratching away for days against the inside of my skull.

I was very tired after that and thin – my father said I was looking thin – and so I went home: home to him and my mother and they didn't mind. I hadn't realised before that when you're too sick and exhausted to manipulate or lie and you know you'll get no more from anyone and the people who love you have finally stopped – then all of that seems to provide you with one last chance, precisely when you couldn't care less and are waiting to die. You don't even have to ask, you just stand there and the people who loved you, love you again. They surrender and let you in.

Except Simon.

It's over with him.

But my parents, they haven't given up. They've fed me and let me sleep and now we're at the seaside in gloves and over-coats and it's a bitter May afternoon and will bring us rain and this doesn't matter – I am here and the whip of the air cupped around me, the invincible restlessness, makes me run and I do not fall and I am not drunk, I am only still at my heart for the first time in a month, emptying out into the rage of everything.

I head for the sea's edge across harder and harder sand, over the ribs left by the tide, and I press myself against the slabs and slants of wind until I reach the flat, ambiguous stretch where a thin sheen underfoot turns the sky out flat beneath me. There might be a lake here, low and smooth beyond the last reach of the breakers. And out at this limit, but far ahead, one or two figures tremble, dark against a break of sun. A few others follow behind, it's hard to tell how many – all that's plain is the trick of bright water supporting our feet, the soft blue where we walk on it.

I'm out of breath, I notice: my pulse too lively, butting at me, shuddering my arms. I remember to look for my parents, the doubled shape that could be them, and when I wave as if all is well, the gesture ratchets above my head, jerks out its arc in time to my blood. They wave back and I work on towards the low headland where the shore curves and folds in against itself.

Even with a firmer surface underfoot, I have taken the full hour to reach here – perhaps longer, I don't know when we set out. I'm tired, too: not strong yet, my efforts still smoth-ered by something that I can't identify. And I'm alone now, no one else has come this far.

This is where the sand changes, hardens to a crust that breaks around your foot more and more often until you sink in to your ankle at each step. But you labour up the final rise and find, with one more push, the still place: the sea in a small, round bay, lapping like a summer pool, the scent of seaweed, the air dreaming at your face, motionless, filled with the metal gleam of liquid. You crouch by the water's edge and want to touch it, do touch it, watch your hand reaching into something real and feel it there.

You lift your head and see, a few yards off, a seal: the gleam of it, the face peering over the wavelets at you, inquisitive. And you are not sure if this is true, or if this is a thought of yours, a way of frightening yourself, so you stand up quick and you dry your fingers on your coat and when you search again, there is no seal, there is no sign of anything.

XI

It's raining: nothing too heavy, only a grey dust edging down and putting a shine on to the pavement. A mother helps her daughter from their car, shuts the door softly, and they both begin to walk, comfortably readied for the weather with long, plastic macs – red for the mother, yellow for the girl who swings her arms, tugs at the brim of her matching sou'wester. Even watching them from behind, it's easy to tell they are fond of each other and enjoying the fun their own company makes. Perhaps they are also heading for some treat, but themselves in their macs and the rain are already enough.

From around the corner comes a thin man in a cheap blue blazer, cream shirt, old tan slacks, bad shoes, unshined. At first it seems that he must know the woman and the girl, because when he sees them, he flings up his hands – one of them holding a small umbrella – and he laughs. Stalking across the pavement, light-footed but intentionally slow, he swings from side to side, and the umbrella tugs and burrows in the breeze and his grey hair – already unruly – is getting wet, his blazer, too. He smiles enormously at the girl and manages something approaching a pirouette. As he draws closer, it soon becomes clear he is almost singing – he doesn't have words any listener could decipher, but his hopes are in that direction and, quite plainly, he feels he is producing something fine and musical. This being the case, his peculiar zigzags and darts, the bouncing umbrella, can all be read as pure performance, as proof he believes that he can dance. He is caught in his wish to be *singing and dancing in the rain*, his thoughts towering round him, building the happy prison that will hide his day.

He passes by the couple with a scampering rush, and they turn as he barges on, they giggle. They don't take him as a threat: only wink at each other, because, in providing a contrast, he has made them more special, more sensible, more safe.

By the time he reaches us, my father and I have halted and the man shuffle-stumble-steps across in front of us, veers to the kerb and then plunges across the road without ever acknowledging we are here. He reaches the far side and walks in the gutter for a while, before my father takes my hand and squeezes it, steals my attention.

'We'll just get some bread. Maybe see what fruit they have in. It's never very good this time of year. The fruit.' He's started wearing suede shoes: they give him a flat, defenceless stride.

I don't have that excuse. 'No. I suppose not.' Balancing next to him on ground that I can't trust, taking it slow because anything else stretches my nerves.

We don't mention the man, the drink in him, the shame of it, of me.

'We can go by the river for a while, if you would like.' My father lets my hand go, but with a gentleness, reluctance.

If he touched me again, I would disappear. 'We don't need to.'

'Or we could have a coffee.'

'It's all right.'

'There are places to have coffee. In the bookshop, it's quiet.'

So he sees it in me, then – that I finally need the quiet as much as he does.

'No, it's all right.'

'But I might like to.' His face turned to a shop window, voice colourless.

'Then we will.'

'Not if *you* don't want to.'

'I *do* want to. Please take me for coffee with you.'

Which means that we have to sit upstairs in the dry light of the bookshop and annoy ourselves with oily coffee, lean on the counter and stare at the strangers below, idling and fumbling about the shelves, the whole scene absurdly peaceful and contained. Some faces draw me for the second look – because in so many years I've met them somewhere, because they've come into my pubs, because, after so many years of this place before I left, I must have seen everyone possible, because it is so small here, small as my heart, because in the end I didn't get away, it dragged me back. And always in doorways, in the scatter of crowds, at the brink, there's the chance of Robert, the glimpses of imitations and mistakes, the waste of my waiting for him.

Directly below us are the children's books, my father studying them with a purpose I'd like to ignore. He's arranging a credible start for his next sentence. But I already know what he wants to tell me: I've guessed.

'Well . . . we'll be buying a lot more of *those* now.'

'What, books?' I don't want to help him.

'*Children's* books.'

'Why? Are they good?'

'No . . .' He loses himself for a moment, gives in to his contentment, the great news I haven't brought him. 'At least, I don't know any more what they're like. But I will.'

'Why?'

'Because of Simon.'

'Because of Simon.' It's not that I don't wish them well – my father, my mother and Simon and even Simon's fruitful, far worse half – there's just so very little good luck to be had these days and whatever there is, I need all for myself.

My father rubs my forearm, smoothes across my back. 'They had a boy.'

'Mh-hmm.'

'They had a boy, Hannah. Seven pounds something and healthy and . . . no name yet. They had a boy. I mean . . . I'm a grandfather.' Saying this as if he's discovered a new nationality, a magnificent, undreamed-of country.

'He won't let me visit them, will he? Or *she* won't.' They've had a boy – so he will look like Simon – the way Simon did when we were both unscathed.

'In the end, I'm su—'

'But at the moment, I'm not allowed – I can't see the baby.' Not that I could truthfully stand to. 'I won't be able to see my nephew.' It would ruin me.

'Not right now. But event—'

'It's okay, I'd have done the same.'

'But in—'

'I'd have done the same.'

God, my personal God – you can have whatever kind you want, but this is mine – sometimes He tilts up His hat and sips crimson smoke from His tight, non-tobacco cigar – which is an affectation, He doesn't like cigars, only wishes to underline for you the miracle of His breath – and He feels in the pockets of His old, linen suit for something He has misplaced and then He pauses, gives a milk and azure sigh, and considers all Creation, directing – just for a moment – one mountainous thought towards you, before He wanders on, still searching in His pockets, and you are left with a proof of His interest heading your way: His appalling love.

You will recognise it when it comes because, of course, you know his style.

And so do I.

Which means that, as I leave the bookshop, I can identify the first rush of His gift. It begins as a fresh heat, close at the back of my throat, and there's a shiver of Him in the stronger colours, a palpable interference across the fabric of the street, as His intention forms, grows manifest.

I keep myself busy while it solidifies, walking beside my father as he talks and running through my personal arithmetic.

Hannah Luckraft =

(Due to the enforced absence of alcohol.) No more drinking.

(Due to the enforced absence of Robert.) No more fucking.
And vice versa.
Therefore.
No drinking, no fucking, no loving, no Robert, no joy.
Therefore.
No everything.
Plus.
(Due to the enforced absence of everything.) No children.
No child.
Therefore.
Hannah Luckraft =
Nothing.
And it's bad enough carrying this in my head, without
knowing that my brother has just provided one more reminder
of my utter inadequacy and that my hands shake when the
phone rings and that I cry at the end of quiz shows – because
somebody, somewhere has won – and that I don't earn any
money and *I am living with my mum and dad.*

At which point, I make a left turn with my father into a
grubby street where half a block is thick with scaffolding and
debris and damp plaster reek and cement blooms on the pavement in bucket rings and patches and there's a temporary fence
of plywood panels, nailed to posts. And this is not a lucky place
and I can actually taste God now, I can feel Him lean His thumb
down on my neck, so whatever is coming, will come soon, but
I press on, as if I am normal and all is well. I plod myself through
the grey mud and bits of litter and over the panel that someone
has torn from the fence to lie here, across my way.

I should know better, but I don't.

So I get to feel the odd, slowed sink of my foot as the nail
slides clear through the rubber sole of my baseball boot and
– in a way that is almost interesting – climbs, as my foot
descends on it, to spike in through my skin.

And I could do something about this – fall so that my weight
lifts, stamp on to my other foot, relieve the damaging pressure

in any number of effective, if embarrassing, ways – but I don't. I keep very quiet and finish my step, force it absolutely flat, and then, rather more slowly than usual, I raise my foot back up again, drag it off the cling of metal until it's free.

This is when the pain arrives. A huge and outraged stab of hurt.

I say nothing to my father and fight to preserve my normal gait.

But I do still have options: even if it seemed a little peculiar, I could announce my injury, draw attention to it retrospectively: two, three, five paces after the event.

But, by this point, probably not – not when the panel has gone and also the street and we have turned another corner and it's busy here – a good many people to possibly barge me, or tread on my wound – and my discomfort is becoming quite extreme and my sock feels wet, actually sliding and clinging in a sickening way, and possibly behind me there's a dot, a patch, of blood leaking out into every footprint as I go, which my father may notice.

And that nail won't have been clean. In fact, it must have been filthy – a hotbed of infections, driven up into my instep, right to the tip of the classic, deep, thin type of wound that brings on tetanus in seconds.

By this evening I could be dead.

And here, after so many minutes have gone by, there isn't a chance that I can tell my father.

And here, after so many minutes, is the dark, stiff delight of learning – yet again – that wanting to die and thinking it's suddenly probable I will, are two absolutely different affairs.

And here, after so many, is another sign: my rusty indication of God's intimate concern and – reamed up through my sole – the kind of pun that's unforgivable.

'Hannah? What's the matter?'

'Hm?'

'You're smiling. What's the matter?'

'Nothing.'

'You're sure?'

'Mm-hmm. Could we get the bus home?'

'Now?'

'Yes, I think so. Yes, now.'

In my parents' house, I strip off my shoes, throw both my socks away, then sneak out into their garden in bare feet; eccentricity is something that I've led them to expect. The damp grass aches beneath me, tender, cool. It opens the wound again, gets the blood to flow. So then I come back in, able to limp, and say I've just stepped on something sharp.

My mother drives me to the hospital, impatient about dinner, and waits while a large nurse cleans up my wound and dresses it, thumps an inoculation into my unrelaxed thigh – my other thigh – so that, when I emerge, I am limping on both sides. A further reminder that no one can ever be confident when they say they have had enough.

As we drove away, my mother couldn't understand why I was laughing.

We repeated ourselves after that – my adolescence all over again – they took care of me, made me strong with feeding, kept me clean with polite observation and then had to let me go.

'You'll need help to tidy your flat.' My mother being sensible, imagining the wreck of bottles and temptation, the disarray.

But I couldn't let her see it. 'It's all right.'

'You'll call me.'

'I'll call you when I get in and then when I've finished.'

'Or before that.'

'Or before, if it takes a long time.' Stealing her hope away with me into the taxi for which she has given me money, along with the other money that she gave me the night before, because if I am going to fall from grace, if I am going to buy wicked things, then it should at least disgust me: the notes should blister my fingers, as I misuse them.

My father watches from the bedroom window, waves once when I begin to leave him.

And then I'm back to myself alone. Which is never fantastic, but does, at least, provide a touch more room than I've been used to lately.

The flat, as I open it, is bad. Red bills in the hallway and a weird smell and then, when I nudge back the doors, not a trace of me. There are no empties, no unhappy clothing, no stains, no awfulness in the kitchen: the bed is repulsive, because it stinks of grief, but has no other problems – it's impeccably made with a coverlet that I don't recognise. Someone has been in here and tidied up.

Robert. He's the only one who has a key. Robert. He came back.

And I run round again – living room, kitchen, bathroom, hall – and, yes, there isn't even any dust – when I've always had dust – there's only this terrible, fake lemon/pine-tree atmosphere and cleanness everywhere.

Which was a lovely thing to do for me. He must have guessed I would be very tired. A sweet apology.

My mother gave me two carrier bags – one full of cleaning materials that I won't need today and one heavy with new food: Tupperware boxes of stew and ready-made stuff and potatoes, milk, bread. But the fridge, when I check inside, is surgically clean and already outfitted nicely with margarine, eggs and cheese and a note. Robert would have known the safest place for it would be inside the fridge – where I'd be bound to have a little search about, for more or less innocent reasons. I notice he hasn't put booze in here. He must have heard.

Dear Hannah,

Don't tell anybody I did this. I'll deny it if you do. Mother said you were coming home and you deserved better than the way you were bound to have left it.

Sorry for copying your key. I thought in the end I would need it. To come and find you at the end.

Don't make me.

They'll have told you we have a son now. I'm very happy. Let me stay that way.

He won't have let the practice secretary type it – I'm a private shame. He'll have done it himself. That's why it's so short.

Simon, the fucker. My brother, the fuck.

So, my fresh and sober life unrolls about me, revealing a nice, clean, lunar emptiness. My new reality. Its sole purpose is to make me feel like shit, just when my only support has been amputated, cauterised. Other people manage this, undiluted existence: they are happy and, even when they wake with it howling at them, drooling on their chest, they do not care, they like it, they can't wait for each morning to claw back in again.

But other people aren't like me – they are born anaesthetised. Simon's son will be the same. His father will watch him fit into himself, grow his particular personality, and when that first arrives, fresh and tender and warm from the hands of God, it will come as an intoxication. It will be the best drunk of his life – at least twelve months of staggering and pointing, delight that's as wide and as high as your roof and then asphyxiating rage. He'll revel in the flux of his own substances, his fluids. He'll batter and scream, even will in his teeth so that he can bite, he'll grab at his mother's breasts and then guffaw like a gouty colonel, he'll sway and stumble through any household on illogical missions that put himself at risk.

He'll be the perfect drinker: thrice blessed, thrice protected: drunk, out of his mind and a child. I've seen it before with Simon. I could smell the angels with him, taking care. And when it was over, when he'd taken in his dose, he was a perfectly normal, balanced child. He's never really needed any more.

Me, I'm made differently, I have to drag my little angels

down by force, which is why I'm adding to my inventory of joys by sending myself to the dentist. One particular dentist. I know where he works.

I shouldn't just turn up there: I'm aware of that – it will be wrong and awkward and I shouldn't, I should not. But I will, because wrong and awkward is better than dead from the ankles up – and because my current horizon is a full, flat revolution of lead-coloured dust: 360 degrees of fuck-all, relieved by the heart-warming prospects of begging for a job, buying day-old bread and being unable to masturbate because my skin is still expecting someone else.

I've read the pamphlets, I've been given the stern-but-fair talks by professional people, and I agree with what they've said: I crave mood alteration: this is my trouble, I will accept: my natural mood is of the has-to-be-altered type.

And I have nothing left to alter it.

With no other solutions available: wrong and awkward, here I come.

Out into the filthy car which, miraculously, starts first time and straight across country to the street with the whitewashed wall and the black door and the black-framed window where Henry the war-crime dentist is still threatening with his brush, which I find optimistic – if Henry is at home . . .

'I have a . . . I was just driving past and I have a . . . mystery pain. Is that okay? Are you taking new patients?' I have been naked in this hallway, on this cheap, wood laminate floor. 'I don't know . . . it's at the back, a molar . . . I was driving. And it's a distraction. Not safe.' The air has Robert's heat. 'That's . . . I can – yes, I can fill these in and . . . in thirty minutes? Great.'

I'm awake. It's been a long time since I was so awake.

I take the forms into the waiting room and pick through them, a mild sweat putting dents into the paper at my fingertips. I give myself a false name and a true age and an incorrect address and an allergy to shellfish – I've always wanted one of them.

Robert and I did things in here, too. I didn't expect to remember them so clearly – one moment springing into focus like a slap – over on that bench, when he slowed and sucked my nipple, licked off his spunk.

'Thanks.' I give the receptionist back her little harvest of fake facts. 'So . . . check-up today and then other stuff later?'

She nods at me, as if this is required of her by demons, and then halts her head in the lowered position, apparently studying the appointment book with supernatural force.

'Ahm . . . this'll be with Gardener?'

'Adams.' Glowering over the columns of dates. 'Martin Adams. We haven't changed the plates on the door yet. They let us down.'

'What?'

'The plate people. They let us down.'

'They'll do that. Yes.' Each of the words like chalk under my tongue.

Of course, I can't just walk out, because that would look odd. And so I consent to be tilted back in the chair, our chair, and Martin Adams (who smells of corn flakes) rummages in my mouth as if it's a cutlery drawer and tells me that I need four fillings and one extraction. He isn't surprised that I have been suffering mystery pains and I suppose that I haven't lied to him, I generally have toothache – I would assume most people do – my point is that I didn't come here about teeth. They don't concern me. If they did, I would have had them seen to the first time I came here. I would have kept my clothes on. Or maybe not.

So where the fuck is he?

'Are you okay? Is the pain bad?'

'No . . . Yes.' The nurse, or assistant, or dental hostess, or whatever, is looming above me in her pink hygienic smock, concerned. Martin Adams has nipped away for another form of some kind, plainly overjoyed that I'm going to be so expensive.

'You sure.' She's apparently twelve years old, but I suppose it's more likely she's in her late teens. 'He could give you a prescription for antibiotics – he's mean with them, though. You'll have to ask.' She seems kind.

And if she *is* kind, 'Yes. I mean, I'm fine,' I might as well risk it, since I'm here. Why bother being a sad, old bitch, if nobody can tell. 'Look, actually . . . the dentist that used to be here.' My lips feel overstretched.

'Yes.' She smiles the kind of smile reserved for hopeless animals and sad monsters like me.

'Did you work with him?'

'Bobby G?' The dashing nickname is ironic, some kind of private joke. 'Everybody knew *him*. He still owes them money in the Duke of Buccleugh.'

I am both offended on his behalf and glad that she didn't like him, that he couldn't have liked her. 'Do you know where he's gone?' My hands are wet against the chair.

She's puzzled, wonders what he's done, if he owes *me* money. 'Where he's gone?'

'Yes . . . Yes.' That isn't enough, isn't impressing her. 'It's all right, I don't want anything from him.' My tone making this obviously untrue. 'I mean I do.' And she is worried now, frowning, standing further away. 'It's nothing bad. If I know where he's gone . . . I won't . . .'

I can't see her any more because she's eased behind the chair and it's too late to sit up and turn for her, because feet are approaching the surgery door and I am losing this, have lost it. 'I love him.' Trying to let this sound like proof of the man she didn't know, the things she didn't guess, or understand about him. 'I love him.' But saying it soft, so I don't have to hear it and she may not either, as the wrong dentist bustles in and gives me the chance to write down some more lies.

And my mother's money is, as she might have expected, uncomfortable in my hand as I pay it over for a check-up and an estimate of treatment I'll never get, arranged for a woman called Heather who can't eat shrimps.

'Excuse me. Miss . . . Winter.' My hand dragging open the door as the little assistant trots up. 'You forgot this.' And she hands me an envelope, while studying my face as if I am incomprehensible, ill.

'But I didn't —'

'You did.' She spins and scampers back up the hall. 'Good luck.' Sounding slightly muffled and insincere.

I wait until I'm in the car before I open the envelope, so that I can be in private when I'm disappointed, so that I can let my hands shake and not care. Inside, there's a slip of paper headed RG's Home Address. I'm not sure if she meant this as a punishment or a gift.

Robert's daughter looks a handful. I know it's her, because she has his eyes, which is unfortunate: they're too striking to be feminine, too heavy and dark. I also know it's her because she comes and goes out of 14 Millbank Lane and that is RG's Home Address. The skirt of her school uniform is overly short, the ones she wears at weekends, even shorter. Her walk is surly in the teenage way: lithe and fit and truculent and only accidentally sexy.

I sit here in my car sometimes, watching, and count the things she has from him. So far it's a fast turn of her head, an angle in her shoulders, a way she stands. Of all his ghosts, she is the most convincing.

I am, naturally, not here all the time, not even every day. I have another job now, the result of shameless begging to Thomas in my old bar, my local, probably the only place that would take me on. The gang cheered at the start of my first evening and then, in the course of that evening, discovered I wouldn't give credit, wouldn't cash cheques, wouldn't sell on cheap whisky with bad labels, wouldn't sneak in extra measures, wouldn't give drink for jewellery or the promise of electrical goods, wouldn't fall for the lifetime of tricks that I might once have tried on fresh bartenders myself. They still wheedle, here and there, but they know I'm a Judas — they can't even get me drunk.

The money keeps me ticking over and buys the petrol to get me out here. Where I can hunch in my back seat while Mrs Gardener cleans her windows, puts out the rubbish, goes shopping, comes back. She seems to favour Marks & Spencer's, that expensive ready-made stuff – you might as well order a takeaway, at least that turns up hot.

I try, I do make an effort, to see if we are like each other. But if Robert had a pattern in mind when he picked us, I can't find it. She's taller than me, neater hair with a touch of red in it, fuller hips. For practical things, she dresses like a tomboy, seems much younger and assured. For shopping and perhaps work, perhaps meeting friends of hers, she is rather elegant, even chic.

Maybe I was simply a change for him. As good as a rest. Maybe I was an accident. Maybe I shouldn't expect this to make sense.

I do not ever imagine them having sex.

And I do not ever catch sight of Robert here. He does not stand near windows, he does not leave or arrive, he does not drive off with his daughter to school in the morning, his wife does not call out his name when she unlocks the door.

He didn't leave me for them. He just left.

I tuck my feet along the back seat and lean my head against the window. I stare at the tarmac, the tiny camber of the road. There's a strong smell of coffee and obsession.

Then I am upside down.

'What are you doing here?'

I don't know what I am doing here. I am upside down.

'I said, what are you doing here?' This is a cold voice, disgusted and enjoying its disgust. 'I asked you a question.'

My hands are in the gutter with bad things and my back is strained and I am attempting to sit up. 'I'm . . . I . . .' But then I'll have my back to her again and she may hit me. 'I . . .' I know who this is.

'Get out of the car.'

Robert's wife, so happy that I'm crumpled and rubbing I

don't know what from my fingers on to my jeans and scrambling to be upright, to still be shorter than her, to still be a joke. 'I'm sorry.' I don't like her. I wouldn't under any circumstances.

'Gail said there was somebody watching the house, but I didn't believe her. Then I started to notice you myself. What the fuck are you doing here?'

'I just . . .' A chill turns in my head and *I* should be angry, *I* should be outraged – not her. 'You hurt me.' I slam the car door, but it does no good – only startles me.

Very quiet, dignified. '*I* hurt *you.*'

And I sound like a child now, 'I was trying . . .' as if she has some grown-up authority over me and we're not equals.

'He's not here. I presume he was with you for a while. He mentioned something. Do you know how often he's disappeared? Do you know how much we care, any more? We don't. But you will not watch this house.'

'No, I . . .'

'You will not come near me, or my daughter.'

'I –'

'Or I will call the police. If you weren't so obviously . . . I would already have called them.'

So obviously what?

'I'm sorry.'

'Just go away.'

She hasn't the right to call me anything. 'I'm sorry.' She hasn't the right to stand there until I break, move away.

'If you want to know where he is, try Doheny.' As if this is very funny.

'I don't know Doheny.'

'Or Canada. He was full of that the last time he called us. "Such a wonderful way to get better" – all he had to do was borrow enough to get to Canada. If it wasn't for –'

And she stops herself, because I am not worth telling, I should not know anything more about her life. I should only have the stinging friction of her wishing me gone as I get into the driver's seat and start up, bumble out of the parking space just as stupidly as she knew I was going to. When I check my mirror, she's still there, pressing me along the road with her contempt.

On the way home, I drive as she intends me to, like a slovenly adulteress. I brake late and change lanes as if I want to die, I almost kill a cyclist turning right. Anyone who saw me would know I was bound to wreck something in the end.

Arrogant cow. I should have said something. I should have shown her who I am.

I did show her who I am.

Eventually, I turn down to the river and pull over. It's high tide and the water is a dull, chipped blue beneath the curve of the railway bridge. I concentrate on how cool it would be, how thick. The furious knock of my heart slackens and muffles. A light wind bounces against the car.

Cow.

I wind down the window for a touch of salt and to hear the regular, liquid breath of the estuary.

Fucking cow.

I don't quite know how long has passed since I left Millbank Lane – maybe half an hour, maybe longer. So it takes me half an hour, maybe longer, to recognise the start of an old, good feeling. First a lightness, a sense of disappearing griefs, and then an almost pre-bottle thrum of warmth.

The fucking cow said Canada.

Travel and you leave yourself, escape your soul, fasten your skin against that great, numb blur of motion that puts everything to sleep.

Canada.

Travel and build yourself again with no mistakes.

Canada and I know where.

There's only the matter of how you start.

XII

I'm not drunk, I'm just out of control – there is a difference.
'The Dutch stuff –'

'Beg pardon?'

'I hate it. I mean the *real* Dutch stuff, not the British Dutch
stuff, or the American Dutch stuff – the stuff that *says* it's
Dutch – *Going Dutch, Coming Dutch, Dutch Uncles on the Job,
If the Dutch Cap Fits*, whatever hilarious titles they pick for
the *fake* European stuff. *Not* that. I hate that, too, but it's not
what I'm talking about – I'm talking about the *real* Dutch
stuff, with *real* Dutch people: happy and toned and incredibly
attractive Dutch people having athletic and joyful, consensual
sex in delightful surroundings – *that* stuff – *that's* what I hate.'

I don't want to be talking about this.

'Not that I've seen much. One film . . . bit of another . . .
They might not all . . . A bit of two films . . . We were in this
guy's flat in Amsterdam.'

Any possible subject would be better. This one is for some
other time, and especially some other place.

'You don't want to see that kind of thing. You don't want
to be half in the mood, a bit mad, and then here are these
shiny and sculpted and highly contented people enjoying each
other, the same as you're certain they would if the camera
wasn't watching – I mean, you really believe that – you believe
they're not being exploited one bit – because they're all so
fucking happy – so it looks more like a *sport*, like a demonstration, a *healthy hobby* – and it's supposed to be *stimulating*,
but it can't be, because you're *not* shiny and highly contented,
you couldn't keep up with them if you tried. It's all wrong.

Forcing you to feel that way. It's . . . there's something immoral about it.'

Although I've never doubted, never even much assessed, my performance before, it seems I'm compelled to today. It seems, in fact, that I can't stop dissecting my sexual anxieties in public, when I only came in here because I'm cold and I have jet lag. I would rather be lying down in my hotel, but the whole of my room there was whining and had this peculiar air, abrasive in your throat, and a wearing quality about the lights, a nasty glare, and the woman at the desk didn't like me because it was clear that I couldn't afford to stay anywhere else and I wasn't speaking French and she didn't believe there was a dreadful, really penetrating, whine up in my room and so I had to walk outside into the grey, long barrel of the street and this bit of Montreal is nothing but porn shops and Seaman's Missions and Army Surplus Stores and is generally a big mistake, so I turned up the hill, against the rain, and walked into what seemed to be an acceptable refuge, a decent pub – I'm not good at judging when I'm tired – only it's plainly a terrible dive now that I'm inside and can assess things properly and I'm hours out of joint and yammering on about Dutch pornography – I have no idea why – because of those previous porn shops, I suppose, or because there is drink, unexpected drink, gleaming and radiating on all sides like a poisonous metal, bottled snakes, and this is putting me on edge, and because the place is strange, unpleasant, and because I am, in some way, afraid that I'll be assaulted, and so I am loudly inviting this in as a double bluff.

'They shouldn't make pornography depressing. It defeats the point.'

If I was drinking, playing with the snakes, I would be fine: modulated perfectly, alert but fundamentally secure. Sober, I haven't got a clue. My spine is actually creaking with unease while I also hear myself. 'It's disgusting. Right now, I wouldn't watch one if you paid me.' Yes, I actually do hear myself establish the jovial notion that I can be paid to watch Dutch people having sex.

The man beside me at the bar picks up his beer and tucks the last of it down swiftly. He looks at me and I hold together what I trust is a stern and non-participative face.

He frowns. 'Ya. Okay then. Ya.' There is a mild shake in his head as he swings off his stool and stalks to the door, pushes outside.

The tendons in the backs of my legs relax and I draw a brief mouthful of orange juice up through my straw. (I like to take soft drinks with a straw, it makes them seem further away from alcohol. And I am supposed to be further away from alcohol.)

Mercifully, there is no one to hand for more conversation. In fact, there are only three of us here: the barman, who lurks under the optics reading a mangy paperback, a large biker-looking shape, hunched in a seat with its back towards me and a skinny, grubby type who sits in his wheelchair by one of the booths, his energies focused on grimacing at the door: from one greasy trouser leg the end of a urine bag protrudes, amber and fat. I seem to have found my level perfectly.

Still, the travel plan is running: it's breathing and beating out under the scuffed linoleum, it's alight in my brain, acclimatised already, hot and impatient and awake. And since we've come this far together, I can certainly shake off Greenwich Mean Time and follow through. I have obsessive-compulsive leanings – they are something about me that I like, they mean I will draw pleasure from pursuit and anticipation before I ever reach my goal. They make me determined, which is what I need to be.

Because this wasn't easy. I sold my furniture, my fridge, my stove – which wasn't entirely mine to sell – I paid out a month's rent in advance, I spent a whole afternoon in promises and begging with my mother – not lying, not doing an absolute wrong – simply milking her faith and swearing I'll go back to Clear Spring, which I will.

For Robert.

I will go there to find him, because that's undoubtedly where he is. And this, in its turn, will make me completely well. Therefore, I will go to Clear Spring to get completely well, which also is the very best thing for my mother to believe. So I have allowed her to think the very best and I've hit the road with the cash equivalent of everything I own and also the price of her cloisonné vase, the tiny one with the sculpted dragon twined around it, all curlicues and claws, the one I used to love, the one that she kept from the secret time when she was courting and I wasn't born, the one she has recently auctioned off to raise money for me.

This doesn't make me comfortable or proud, but it follows the path of the plan: it has, in that sense, a pure intention.

Quebec is also a part of the plan – not essential, not ideal, but the cheapest Canadian flight I could buy was the one to Montreal. I've made it over the Atlantic, but I still have most of Canada to cross and this will demand strict discipline. It is terribly, terribly easy to lose direction when you already feel abnormal and maybe some further abnormality, some mild chemical nudge, would set you straight and when your funds are truly your funds and precious and limited, but when they are also rendered meaningless by translation into pretty and colourful foreign currency – when it seems you could spend the whole lot in a couple of minutes and not feel a thing.

Time to go.

The evening is fully in place when I push myself on to the street and start breathing and striding, breathing and striding, because this will keep my purpose clarified.

Robert.

I know I'm drawing closer to my usual self when the two beats of his name can raise a bruise, can open up the dark, old tenderness, the lovely hurt. There's no panic in the thought of him any more, no loneliness, because I am going to Clear

Spring and I will find him there and we'll be washed in the mineral water, side by side, and we'll grow strong.

Or not precisely side by side – they're only allowing me back on the promise of further fees (my mother bargained them down, because they actually *owe me* three weeks) and on the strict understanding that I will be segregated from the men and constantly observed. For which they charge extra.

But we'll be in the same place, Robert and I, and we will manage to work things out, because we are resourceful. We *were drunk together* – there's nothing deeper, and since we both have to be dry, we can do that together and make it bearable. Plus, I have to admit that, although this will be appalling, it will mean that we get to live longer and have more responsive nerves and bodies that do what we ask rather more precisely. I've noticed the difference already and this could be good in sympathetic company.

I fix this in mind as I stumble across my hotel room in the dark, for fear of malevolent bulbs, and then lie in an overtired ache, the bed twitching beneath me, as the walls whine all around.

In the morning my travel choices are limited. The bus would be cheap, but slow, and would either mean paying for rooms along the way or not sleeping for three days, four days, however long. I know from stern experience that wouldn't agree with me. The train would be more expensive, just as slow, and might, once again, mean paying for rooms. I could hire a car and sleep in it, but I'm not too sure I could drive off for thousands of miles on the wrong side of the road without a good deal of quite serious liquid support. And, after my last set of troubles, the court took my licence away, which could make hiring problematic. Catching a plane would break me and only get as close as Edmonton, or involve some impossibly costly death-trap floatplane trip, out into nowhere and, even after that, I'd be stuck and have to rely on hitching. Or I could try hitching from the start – just when I'm mortally, soberly aware of every risk an unknown driver might present. The torturers and perverts cruising through the wilderness, they would be bad enough, but they couldn't top the end-stage drinkers and crazed dependants who'd be aiming for the clinic, going precisely my way.

Still, I am not downhearted when I check out and leave the hotel. Past the dead plants and the groaning lift, I carry my faithful holdall and then have it jolting beside me in the alien streets, an anchor to something of home as I start the long walk to the station. I've settled on trying the train.

And after half an hour I'm sure I must be close. The summery day has exhausted me, left me sticky beneath my shirt, and I have toured this block at least a dozen times – this block where the map says the station has to be. I have followed a railway-looking sign into a shopping mall and out again. I have scrutinised offices, tower blocks, shops, a statue and a Catholic residence. I have looked for trains. I have listened for trains. Nothing.

You can't hide a whole railway station.

Why would you try?

Over the road is a hotel tower with arched windows, like so many layers of drooping eyes. It's the type of clean and caring place I could never afford – the sort that makes passing nearby very faintly shaming. In the doorway a man with a ludicrous hat, an ornate lieutenant governor's pith helmet, manhandles luggage and opens doors as if this is absolutely what he wants to do. Apparent job satisfaction, any type of satisfaction, that's attractive, and I'm tired and no building ought to be able to make me ashamed, so I cross to the entrance steps and climb them, because then the helmeted man may smile at me as if he likes me, as if I am an organised, arriving guest.

'*Bon matin.* Good morning. Checking in?'

But I didn't expect to be taken this literally. 'No, I'm, ahm . . . I'm meeting . . . a friend.'

He examines my sweat, my unlikely holdall, and I would almost welcome his suspicion, because it would be less humiliating than what he does give me – the fatherly smile reserved for the unthreatening and sad.

'Okay. The bar is through there on your left, let me get the door.'

This means I can't wait in the foyer, must go to the bar, a dim and leathery, expensive space where I hide behind a lime and soda water to catch my breath. But it's all right that I'm here, because it was somebody else's suggestion and I don't want to have a drink, so I won't have one. I also believe that dropping in at a watering hole or two like this can immunise your heart against temptation. Plus, there is a slight, innocent comfort in knowing that booze is still available, that it's carrying on a full and active life without me.

'If I come talk with you, would you mind?'

The answer to this question always being, 'Yes, I would mind very deeply and, in addition, I have a communicable disease.' But then he reminds me of me – something dreadful peering back at me from underneath the surface of his eyes, some huge deficiency that scares him.

'Would you mind? I could just go . . .' He is dull-voiced and meaty and neat in a wealthy/casual/North American way.

'No, I don't mind. Sit down – I would buy you a drink, but I don't have any money.' This last because my sympathy can only extend so far.

'That's okay. I have a lot . . . of money.' He makes the announcement as if it's the worst news in the world. 'I can pay.' And this has an edge which tells me that someone has recently broken his heart and so rendered his every possession temporarily de trop.

Which is fine by me. 'I'll let you know when I need another soda water.' Of course, I never met anyone like this when I drank – anyone willing to pay. 'What's her name?'

'Oh, Jesus.' He drops at this, landing in the armchair opposite as if I have hit him with a tray. Accompanying his sigh comes the tang of at least two miserable, early-morning whiskies and I heartily wish I'd been able to guess he would be this raw and leave before he made life complicated. It's not as if everyone doesn't get abandoned, isn't mugged by the ghastly products of their own affection – if we all made a fuss, the world would be chaotic, no one would ever get anything done. 'Oh, *God.*'

'I wouldn't bring Him into this, He won't like it.'

The man squints across at me. I might as well be speaking Japanese. 'Dorothy.' His bottom lip shudders. 'That's her name.'

'Okay. That's her name.' I avoid repeating it – he is too muscular to be controllably distraught. 'Would you like to say what she did? – or you can call her names and I'll agree.'

'I don't want to do that.' Of course he doesn't, not yet. Tomorrow he will, but not today. 'She didn't do anything wrong.'

If we'd both been drinking whisky – although it is barely past ten in the morning – then I would give him a comforting hug. 'That's very unlikely, I'm sure.' I would rub his arm and hold his hand and we would be fucking within half an hour. 'Unless you're a bad person.' Afterwards, we would agree it had been exactly what we needed. '. . . murderer, violent, dog molester, criminal type, in which case –'

'I am.'

'What?' I only made the joke, because I thought it *was* a joke. 'You're a bad person?'

'Yes.'

'You don't look that way.'

'I steal.'

'You *steal.*' I try not to sound too relieved. 'Well, that could be worse, though, couldn't it?'

'*No!*' His round, pink fist thumps down on the table top between us and the bar's well-polished silence thickens, observes. He coughs, swallows and again his bottom lip threatens to fail him. 'I mean . . . I'm sorry. I mean, I explained

302

to her what I do, because she knew about it. But she didn't *understand* and we were . . . we were going to –'

'I know.' I barge in fairly roughly to prevent him from imagining the glowing children and monogrammed golf balls and minor urinary infections they were on the brink of sharing for eternity. 'I know . . . you thought you'd be good together.' This seems to jab him underneath the ribs and so I go on, just to draw him from further despair. 'But some things . . .' Then I halt before I end up saying *just aren't meant to be.*

He grabs for my hand in a non-erotic, drowning way. 'It's my job.'

I meet his intense, little eyes and resist asking, 'What's your fucking job – it's your job to *steal*? Great job. Regular income, I bet. No tax. Why don't you order a wife from the Philippines, or somewhere, get fixed up and leave me be.'

'I'm in insurance. I adjust loss.'

Which removes my remaining compassion in a breath. Because, as he now explains at great, self-pitying length, the loss he adjusts is not his customers'. He is in place to defend his company. He denies claims. This saves an immensely wealthy institution from paying out any of the money its policyholders have paid in. When he denies a claim, people lose their farms, their cars, their houses, they go without physiotherapy, they watch ailing relatives suffer constant pain, they die of untreated cancers, industrial illness, progressive disease. He is a fucker.

'What's your name?'

'Um . . . Matt. My name's Matt Duchamps.'

Matt Duchamps is a fucker.

Although I did once receive compensation for a carpet that was damaged by fire when there was no fire and, indeed, no carpet. Then again, I would never have got the minute, almost irrelevant, insurance cheque if I'd had to deal with somebody like him. 'Matt – I'm Hannah, by the way – look, Matt . . .'

He mumbles on, ignoring me and pretending he shares his

303

former fiancée's loathing for his business. He says he was about to retire in any case, that he was ready to move on for moral reasons.

'*Matt.*'

He stops, shows me the toddler-lost-in-woods face that would have made Dorothy utterly sure she was doing the right thing.

'Matt, you weren't meant for each other.'

His lip is back on the verge of collapse.

'With her, it was the money – she liked you because you had money. She bailed out as soon as she knew you were changing jobs. She was a bitch.'

Matt begins sobbing so inconsolably that a concierge comes over to be sure that all is well. So I pat Matt's hand and appear solicitous. The concierge nods, thinks well of me, and glides off, satisfied.

'*Matt?* Matt, it will be awful and very lonely, but you'll have to move on. You can't get fixated this way – people leave. People leave *you*. But there will be others.' Matt whimpers. 'Others who *don't* leave. Ones who love you for yourself.' A racking chain of sighs suggests that he finds this as implausible as I do. 'You'll be fine.'

'Hannah, let me . . .' He crimps in a remarkable pressure around my fingers and I can't help but picture Dorothy, lying back every night while he prodded and mauled across her like a partially tranquillised bear.

'You don't have to do anything.' I point this out with complete sincerity. 'Really. It was my pleasure.'

'No, no . . . you were here. You listened. No one else seemed like they would. And so I have to give you something.'

Well, if you're insisting – money's always good.

'Really, it was nothing.'

Money, I could accept – on behalf of all insurance claimants, every-where. You wouldn't miss it, would you, Matt? Good old Matt.

He struggles the breadth of his free wrist down into his

inside pocket and brings out an uninspiring fold of thin card. 'Here.'

I stare at it with probably open contempt.

'I was going to surprise her. We'd catch . . . see . . .' He snatches back his gift, opens it out and spreads the contents. 'See, we were going . . .' He swallows wetly. 'It was a surprise. For her. We were catching the train this afternoon and going to Toronto. Then we'd take the trans-Canadian to Vancouver – the whole way. I booked a sleeper car. They, they, they encourage couples. There's an observation deck.'

And I kiss Matt.

'Oh, ah . . . you're welcome. We, I, we had accommodation in Vancouver –'

'That's okay.'

'The Pacific Palisades. Because it sounded so good. *Pacific Palisades* . . . You been to Vancouver?'

'No. Well, yes. But I don't remember. Not really. I was on my way to somewhere else.'

'You want the vouchers? For the hotel?' He's trying to squeeze more gratitude out of me, but I have none, because I'm in a hurry now.

'No. No, I don't.' And I leave before he can attempt to befriend me, exchange addresses, extract a promise of post-cards to be sent en route. I also rush away before he can change his mind, or vanish: before the tickets turn into water, dust. Because this is more luck than I get in a decade.

God, thank you.

I mean it.

I can go to Clear Spring.

*I **will** go to Clear Spring.*

I will start going today.

And I'll get better.

And I'll be good.

Now that you've been good.

Now that you've done this.

You didn't have to do this.
Now that you've helped me.
I will be good.

It was underground — Montreal station. Another twenty minutes and I had it nailed, was queuing for a train to Toronto: where the station is, likewise, buried. Then an afternoon that wandered down towards the lakeside and the bracing sun and endearing seabirds and an indication of my smooth and simple life to come, followed by a night spent sharing a Spartan hostel barracks with three hearty backpacking girls, fresh from New Zealand. This I refused to take as an indication of anything.

And it didn't matter. It was only a tiny blank in the progression of the plan which has delivered me sweetly across a silver and rose morning and into the beautiful, grubby limbo of railway-station passageways and waiting rooms and coffee and escalators and the hard spine of the platform and then up the wonderful metal steps of a train that will take me almost all the way to Clear Spring.

I sit in my little cabin, enjoying its nautical touches: mysterious hooks and shelves and flanges for me to get used to, metal fittings and bulkheads in the usual railway-carriage colours: yellowed-over blues and dusty greens. I will be at home here, neatly boxed behind my slightly insubstantial door.

Which shivers, when we've hardly left the station, with a violently cheery rapping. I open it to unveil a self-consciously dapper attendant. 'Now then, *good* morning . . .' He glances round and then seems wrong-footed, if not dismayed. 'Duchamps? Or Burnaby?'

'Ah, yes.' I didn't know whether these tickets were transferable, so I've decided, for the duration and as a minor holiday, to be Burnaby. 'That's me, Burnaby. Dorothy.' I set about generating an air of dignified disappointment.

'No Duchamps?' He waits, balanced between perky servility and a tactful exit.

'Didn't work out. All the more room for me.' I grin a feisty grin.

'Well, yes. I suppose so, eh?'

'Yes.' With a faint note of wistful acceptance. 'All the more room for me.'

'O-*kay* . . . My name is Charles, *any*thing you need, you just ask. *I'll* be the attendant for this car?' Charles has clearly delivered one too many announcements and his inflections have been terminally affected. 'There are *break*fast muffins and whatnot along to the front, coffee and juices, in the *lower* area of the ob-ser-vation *car*. Cooked breakfast *set* back in the dining *car*. It's all there if you want it.'

I feel that Burnaby wouldn't want it, not while she's being bereft, 'Thanks, but no.' And I turn my head to the sun-dusted window as if I am contemplating other breakfasts, ones full of masculine promise.

'Right you *are* then. *Good* morning.' And the door snaps politely shut. Through the partition I hear two little-old-lady voices bickering next door and the small thumps of luggage, repositioned.

And this will be the only problem on the trip – inside my little cell I can be tranquil: I have my own view, my own toilet, my own sink – but outside, there are other people – there's a whole train stuffed with other people. I sit in one of the two chairs provided for Burnaby and Duchamps while their window shows suburbs and malls sliding back into lumber yards and tractor franchises, birch trees, the naked frame of a timber house dark on the brow of a hill, civilisation unravelling, and I think that I mainly dislike other people – the vast majority of them having been no use to me. In fact, being canned in with a trainload of other people for most of three days does not appeal in any way. Even howling drunk, I wouldn't like it.

It's exactly the sort of present you could expect from a loss adjuster. Matt Duchamps – an absolute fucker.

Naturally, they lure you from seclusion with the thought of food – 'Good *after*noon. The last sitting for *lunch* is now being served in the dining *car*. *Please* make your way *to* the dining *car*. Last *sitting. Than*-kyou.' Meals are included in the ticket and I didn't bring even snacks with me.

So out I go – I have to keep my strength up, be in good form for the clinic and for Robert.

I am preceded along the train by a heavily muscled attendant – rolling solidly ahead as I stagger and sway. His broad skull disappears directly into his shoulders and back, the dense block of his uniform filling the corridor with extraordinary precision. He might almost have been grown to fit it. Finally, he lunges to one side, disappearing with a wink into what I assume is his berth and I am left alone to press on into the dining *car*. Lakes and streams and leaves are giddily picturesque around me as I'm bounced from one elbow to the other until both ache. I sustain myself with a hope that the last sitting will be sparsely attended and quiet, as the name might reasonably suggest.

But I am not remotely shocked to discover my hopes are misplaced as I stumble into a stridently pink car, already packed with diners who peer up at me as if I may be an additional hors d'oeuvre. A grinning waiter shows me – with laborious, faintly mocking, deference – into the only remaining available seat, thus filling the table reserved for misfits and solitaries. I join a silent, male pensioner who eats nothing but dry bread, a middle-aged woman with shaking hands and a scrawny, ill-shaven railway enthusiast. 'You're all equal here, eh? On the railway? Doesn't matter who you are once you're here. We're all equal, eh? You can talk to anyone on a train. Anyone at all.'

And apparently anyone at all is supposed to listen without thoroughly losing their appetite, or killing him. Within moments, and completely against my will, I learn that he is called Marty Kershaw, that he used to work for Canadian Pacific, and that he cannot succumb to a fatal heart attack remotely soon enough.

I soothe and restrain myself by studying the foliage that whips past, but I can tell my fellow inmates are eyeing me instead of their windows. I can see them in reflection, sneaking looks: the mother surrounded by moon-eyed teenagers who slices her food into mouse bites and chews with inordinate care and who is as big as an adult manatee; the man with the Quaker-style beard and monstrous eyebrows who keeps on rubbing at his thighs; his lady companion who blithely wears a chunky wooden necklace, from which there dangles an articulated doll. To be frank, there isn't one among them a sensible child wouldn't run away from at first sight. Each of them alone would give train travel a bad name.

But I'll only have to be here for a couple of hours a day and it's not as if I haven't spent my life among the walking wounded and the odd. There's no credible reason for me to prod at my bison sausages and country vegetables and know that I can't eat them, because my throat is wincing shut in spite of me, because I am, in some way, under threat.

Small talk and engine noise are eddying peaceably about, stories of relatives and travels are being exchanged. Cutlery tinks and scrapes, the train growls on, the waiters wait, there is nothing definably out of place. Which makes the sense of danger worse – because if I alone have noticed it, thought it, then it will notice and think of me, it will seek me out.

I begin to wonder if this is the next phase in my sobriety – the onset of aimless fear. Or perhaps I am simply acknowledging the whole lifetime of terrors I've ignored: the broad accumulations of waiting death: nuclear, chemical, wholesale-industrial, for-fun-and-for-profit death: the rotting atmosphere, the disappearing trees, the plaintively burned orang-utans, the avoidable starvation and discontent, the random injustice, deliberate cruelty, the very new and very old diseases, the frank and coy annihilations that nip and nudge and leer at us, seep through and cripple our resistance, take us away.

Reality – there's nothing but horror in that.

Except this is something else. A personal problem. I can feel it stroking the back of my hair.

This is for me.

A plan I didn't make that's just for me.

Which is when it winks at me: gives me a peek, a tiny unveiling of the dark thing organised inside the car. Whenever I glance towards anyone, they turn away, they shield their eyes, break off their conversations – every person – every time – as if they had rehearsed this, were quietly linked. And they seem to know the waiters too well.

Which is insane. A little paranoia is healthy, but this is insane. I have to eat up my fruit salad and get out of here. Skip the coffee, go to sleep. Skip the coffee, turn the unconvincing lock on my cabin door and go to sleep. Skip the coffee, check the cabin, because you can't secure it while you're out, turn the unconvincing lock and go to sleep. Skip the coffee, check the cabin for someone who might be hidden there, somebody harmful, turn the unconvincing lock, undress, get into bed, then stare at the window, go to sleep.

My bed isn't ready yet, isn't pulled down. So I have to ask Charles to pull down my bed – which is good. Safety in numbers. Then the lock and then the staring and then sleep.

And I'll wake refreshed and this will have receded, it will no longer be true.

Sudbury. I'm looking at ugly Sudbury: the huge, gouged waste of it: dust and metalwork and rock, the imprint of uncontrolled need: and it's offensive, it should make me annoyed, but my head's lolling nicely and I'm calmer, unharried, heavy on my pillow, sinking back.

Until the soft hand of nothing reaches up and cups my face, draws me away.

But the little old ladies are stirring next door. First a peripheral murmur, an additional comfort to wash me away. Then a dull impact that nearly brings me back. Then silence again, sweet engine song and the start of dreaming.

Then a brisk, hard clack of metal beside my ear. It yanks me up and has me sitting before I can open my eyes. The noise whacks in a second time – something vicious happening through the partition. A succession of clatters.

According to my watch, I've slept for fifteen minutes, if that.

And I'm about to get dressed, go out and speak somewhat harshly to the little old ladies, whoever they happen to be, when their sounds transform completely. There are giggles, hurrying feet, more giggles – and the elderly should have their fun, of course: they're still filled with delight that the Second World War didn't kill them – but there are limits. Two days of this and I'll toss them both out on the track.

It changes again, though, their noise, splits into a harder growl and a kind of mewing, dense pauses and then the regular, broad shunt of fucking. There is no other sound like it, no other beat. They're fucking. Presumably old lady one with old lady two – banging each other unmercifully in the mid-afternoon. Possibly without drawing down the blind. Certainly inches away from me.

Now I know the lesbian thing happens – can't understand it myself, but each to their own – and the geriatric shagging, that happens, too. I just don't want to be listening while it does. It's as if I'm intruding and also as if they are making fun of me, or at least showing off, which is unseemly in anyone over fifteen.

Into my clothes, then, and I'll try for a jolting stroll to take me somewhere less obscene. Except that, when I open my door, there is somebody standing, listening, next to the old ladies' berth. It's the woman with the wooden necklace, leaning forward, her hands braced between the walls, smirking. She turns her head to me and winks, the little carved doll swinging free – jointed limbs, long white socks painted over the legs up to the thigh, long white gloves, a white bib across the breast and on to the white neck, the white face with black gloss hair, Cupid's bow crimson mouth, brown eyes. Dressed, it would seem, like an affectation, a piece of girlish whimsy. Hanging as it is, the stretches of unpainted wood seem very naked, the whole effect deliberately erotic.

From the closed berth comes a cry: unjoyful, something to do with pain. The woman licks her lips and slowly, purposely, sets her ear flat to the old ladies' door and her doll seems more and more an offer, or an order, a dirty joke she has to make. I push past her, hurry on, ignoring the throaty, theatrical sigh, the shudder she manufactures when our shoulders touch.

It's not what you'd expect.

No, it isn't what you'd expect.

In a nice, clean train on a usual route.

It is not what you'd expect.

I'm heading for the back of the train now, the way I haven't been before. Ahead of the observation car, a dimmer room lies open, its floor just a whisker lower than the passageway. It has an art deco theme: chrome and leather stools, sculptural lighting, a fine pink glow cast down to warm the vaguely loco-motive details of the bar.

'What can I get you?' The bartender – the only employee I've met on this train with a normal intonation. 'Anything you like.' His uniform buttons glimmer, his hair is brushed to a sleek pelt, his look is soft and patient.

'Ah . . . A ginger beer.'

'A ginger beer. Not a coffee? I have some fresh.'

'No, I'm trying to sleep. But thanks.'

'A ginger beer it is, then.'

'Yes.' When I look down, I can't recall his face. Although it is gentle, distinctive, even fine: it also seems impossible to grasp.

'Nothing stronger?' He's wearing black plush gloves – I've never seen that before on a barman. It's elegant, I think, classy. 'Abstaining for your health?' He suggests this kindly, with insight, no one else here – no freaks, no perverts – only the excellent bartender and me.

'Yes. I am abstaining. For my health.' For some reason I

don't understand, the engine seems muffled, our voices low, but completely audible, relaxed and well produced.

'Good health can never be overestimated.' His gloves spider neatly along the bar top and find a glass while he never slips his glance away from me. 'One ginger beer for the lady.' He could work in radio with a warmth and enunciation as fine as that.

'For Hannah.'

But his natural place would be in a bar, safe in this bar. 'Hannah?' He smiles quietly, nods, tongs ice into my glass and pauses. He understands I am about to correct myself and that I will make my lie so obvious that it could never cause offence. 'Is that so.' He understands everything.

'I mean Burnaby. I'm called Burnaby.'

'Burnaby.' Again a nod. 'Now that is a name. That is.' Firing the ginger beer into the glass, adding the lemon deftly, dealing out the coaster. 'You really picked a good one there, Hannah.'

I take the glass from him, the round, iced weight. I nod and smile my best smile, because we will be friends. I've found the one place on this train where I'm at home. I set the rim to my lips.

Then I find that I'm rolling over in my bunk, grazing my forehead against the partition wall.

According to my watch, I've slept right through more than four hours.

No waking up.

No goings-on from old ladies.

No weird bitch in the corridor.

No bar – which does upset me for a while. It had seemed it would be an especially good bar.

By dinner time I am bored out of my mind and hungry. I've already had more than enough of tranquil vistas blossoming through trees: of lakes, of rocks, of the smothering green that's shining in towards me, thick and repellent with life. I'm beginning to understand Sudbury: why you'd have to scour this down to nothing, grind it clean and start again. I have looked at things enough now – I am full. And next door are the old ladies, behaving themselves impeccably and repeating the train's informative announcements, cooing them out as if they were poetry.

'*So. Ladies* and gentlemen. Mes-*dameset* Me ssieurs. To your left – gauche – the tranquil vista *oh*-ver there . . . You'll see there *the* famous Brass Lake.'

'Brass Lake.'

'That's Brass Lake.'

'Yes, Brass Lake.'

'Brass Lake.'

'Vousvoy *ezla*, le Lac du Cui-vre Jaune. C'est un lac très, très tox-*ique*. Plusieurs vo-ya-gers ont été assassinés *par* ce lac. Deux cent, *on* pense, peu tetreplus. And the Brass Lake cemetery, *you* will see right over yonder, sur votre *droit*.'

'That's the cemetery.'

'That's the cemetery.'

'Brass Lake cemetery.'

I am willing myself to be struck with hysterical deafness but this has no effect, beyond making me feel hysterical. The train drags us forward and I try not to imagine that I am trapped in a nightmare cinema: the endless film reeling off sideways, the narration recited by a lunatic, the audience talking and talking and talking. I am actually happy when the call goes out to eat, to complete the last sitting.

And the familiar gang is here, assembled, when I arrive. Even though I raced out of my cell as soon as I heard the signal, even though the earlier sitting must have taken some time to disperse and there must have been a small delay before the fresh diners could sit – tablecloths to change, or brush, spillages, stains – still, everyone has made it in before me. Not only that, but they are nibbling rolls and chatting, sipping preparatory drinks, like people who've been idling at their tables for half an hour or more. The manatee mother is already eyeing her soup. No one but me is out of breath, or flustered, or disturbed.

Although I am cheered, on closer inspection, to note that the misfits table is short of its pensioner. He's later than me. Or he could still be digesting those two ounces of unbuttered bread that he recklessly crammed in for lunch. He did have the look of someone who was only used to eating once a week. He's most likely shut in a toilet somewhere, drinking his own urine, swallowing razor blades because he can. Smug git. Or perhaps he got off and is now walking nude in the woods, birching himself using genuine birches. Whatever he's up to, as the minutes pass and Shaking Hands Woman trembles her napkin laboriously down over her lap, it becomes clear that he won't be arriving for dinner today.

'Yeah, the old iron horse. Fifteen years I worked on her.' Railway Bore is still horribly with us. 'You wouldn't believe the stories. I could tell you something.'

Yes, and I could recite my latest daydream for you − hot, weird, senile action − that'd curl your hair, mate. If you still had any.

Quaker Beard Man drums his table and forks down mashed potatoes while his companion/lover/wife dissects her meat, that sodding doll still on display, bringing a nice little hint of the gibbet to our proceedings. No wonder I dreamed about it − it's bloody weird − like hanging a voodoo model prostitute round your neck.

'Very interesting, isn't it?' This is the first time that Shaking Hands Woman has spoken to me, or anyone else at our table. 'Yes, very interesting.'

I'm not sure whether to answer her, or not. There could be numberless reasons for her shake, but her sad child's voice, her stunned eyes, the kind of softly luminous hurt that surrounds her − they suggest apocalyptic trauma in her past, a life built out of aftershock. It seems any further intrusion might provoke terminal unease. Still, she appears to be inviting contact, creeping shy glances towards me, tiny darts of intensity shading across her face.

I murmur as blandly as I can. 'Interesting?'

'The doll.' There's something of the playground about this: the approach of the clumsy girl nobody likes, the threat of her trying to make a friend of you. 'You were looking at it. The same as lunchtime.' Tonight she wears a white sweatshirt, the collar of a pink blouse showing above, neat jeans and white trainers with a pair of appliquéd cherries bright on each. Someone like her shouldn't even consider that doll.

'I was just staring into space – the doll got in the way.'

'I think it's interesting.'

'It's . . . it's certainly striking.'

'Where are you from?' She rushes this, as if it's a phrase she has learned from a book of conversations.

'Scotland.'

'The Scotland in England?'

'The Scotland next door to England.'

'Oh, I'm sorry.'

Her chin tucks in and she drops her head and I guess that she may be the type to cry easily. 'Sorry.'

'Not at all. I have no idea where I am most of the time. You were close . . . It's fine . . . I'm not offended.'

But she has retreated completely, frowns at her plate and sighs to herself until it is taken away.

Once again, I spend my time risking indigestion, bolting my food so that I can be free to batter back into my cabin for some privacy, lock my door. Although I will simply be locking it for peace – the sense of doom I had this afternoon has dissipated, possibly settling in Shaking Hands Woman, just for a lark. I am rested and well and only two nights from Clear Spring and I have no sense of other, arcane plans afoot. My fellow-travellers are eccentric, improperly adjusted, but they mean no harm.

As I make for my carriage, I pass the little clutches of seats where passengers will be attempting to go to sleep. In one of them, the manatee mother is arranging and rearranging pillows and bags of snacks while her children stare. Beyond her, the curtains across the corridor bunks are swaying, letting out glimmers of white sheet.

Then at home in my cell the tracks rock and grumble beneath me, I turn out the lamp above my bed and tuck myself in under the night. Against the bare window there is a deep, large dark, a smother of something between me and the stars.

'Good morning, lady, bless you.'

I am attempting to butter a croissant while the carriage shakes and my paper plate flexes threateningly.

'Bless you.'

I am standing, because there is nowhere left to sit.

'Bless you, lady.'

There is nowhere left to sit because the whole of the observation car – and fuck knows why they've dumped the things for breakfast here – is full of Christians. Christians with wall eyes, Christians with mental-home haircuts, Christians with one leg shorter than the other, Christians with medieval heads, Christians who smell of heavy medication and of cats and Terylene.

'Bless you.'

Christians who have doubtless left far more disturbing things, hopping and singing psalms in their root cellars. 'God bless you, lady.'

'I'd rather not, thank you.'

'Excuse me?' This one's teeth are splayed and jumbled, three of them peek over his bottom lip when he's distressed. He is currently distressed.

'I'd rather not be blessed.' I take an unnecessarily large bite from my croissant and then fight off the urge to cough as it flakes into hard, dry layers that fill my mouth. I swallow grittily, eyes moist, while the Christian watches. 'Yes, I'd rather not. I don't want Him to know where I am at the moment, okay?'

'Excuse me?' The baleful morning is washing in on every

side, this being the car with the acres of window through which we may observe – more acres upstairs if you want them – and so the Christian's deformities are especially well-defined: the pimples, the slack jowls, those incredible teeth.

'I *do* excuse you – I excuse you completely. But everything is fine with me, so don't you start calling in undue attention. I have a plan. That's all I need. Thank you.' And I retreat without even gathering up my plastic glass of orange juice, or my plastic beaker of dank coffee.

I trot back down the passage with relative ease – our progress being especially slow at the moment – and am quickly level with the dark, quiet doorway to the bar. I hardly noticed it as I passed by earlier.

'Come in.'

I have never *been* in, except when I was dreaming, but still the voice that calls is not unexpected and I am aware that it belongs to the bartender before I step inside and find him sitting alone on one of the stools drawn up beside his counter. The bar also comes as no surprise – it is as I imagined. Exactly as I imagined. 'Ah, was I here yesterday?'

'On the train yesterday?' Unasked, he pours me a coffee from the flask beside him. He had a cup and saucer ready, the twins of his own. 'Or in here yesterday?'

'I was on the train yesterday.'

'But were you in here yesterday?' He doesn't face me, only stares into his cup, as if he is waiting for something to surface.

'Yes. I mean, was I?'

He slides my drink towards me as I sit next to him, lean on his bar. 'Do *you* think you were?'

'I dreamed I was.' The coffee tastes fantastic. 'But the way it looked was . . . the way it looks. The same. Everything. But I've never been here . . .' My sentence dwindles – it's the coffee, it's too distracting, just too wonderful.

'You must have seen a brochure, one of our posters – the bar is frequently depicted.' He drinks. 'D'you like my coffee?'

'Ah . . . yes. It's amazing. The way I imagined it would be when I was a kid – you know, before you try it and it tastes like paint.'

'It probably still does – but now your mouth is used to it. Your mouth can get used to anything.' He drinks in illustration of his point, rather more deliberately than he needs to. 'I don't think you were in here yesterday. I would have remembered you.'

'I *do* remember *you*. That is, when I *see* you . . . otherwise, you're hard to *visualise* . . . But I recognise you.'

'I am frequently depicted.' He smiles to himself and then to me. 'You want another?'

'Hm?' I have indeed emptied my cup. 'Thank you, I'd love one, it's . . . it's great coffee.'

'Thank you.' He gracefully refills: not a waver, not a wasted drop. 'It's nice to be appreciated.'

'Even the way it smells, the aroma. Great . . .'

'And you have quite a thirst. A healthy thirst.' This is a compliment, heartfelt, but discreet.

'Well, yes.' I can't help but seem shy. 'I have a little thirst, now and again.'

'Ah, yes.' He sips. 'And don't we all.' Then gazes at me, takes me in fully, somehow: testing, enquiring – the force of it expanding one, hot moment and then gone. 'You've never been here, Hannah. I called you in so you could rest. And so you could be away from all those along there.' He nudges in, conspiring. 'Always happens once we get nearer the prairies – that sort of religion.'

'Yes, they're . . .' The coffee is incredible, getting better. 'They're . . .' It's approaching the miraculous.

'An inspiration to Satan?' He dabs at his lips with a tissue. 'You get blessed yet?'

'Oh yes.'

'Mm. I've been blessed a great deal, too – lifetimes of blessings . . .' His eyes shine. 'I must be very holy now.' Smoothing at his hair, he straightens slightly where he sits, gives the impression that he has decided something, made a pleasing choice. 'We're closed, of course, at the moment. Until eleven.'

'Oh, I'm sorry. Should I not be here?'

'You should be here – I invited you. You're welcome.' And he says this kindly, but it seems to end our conversation, because he reaches over the counter to fetch up a folded newspaper and spreads it, begins reading. 'Lot of dying going on.' His voice softened, more closed.

'Hm?'

'Out in the world.'

'Oh. I haven't . . . I don't . . . any more.'

'Atrocities, too. There are always atrocities. They can't help it.' He sucks air between his teeth. 'People – they can't help it.'

I finish my coffee and want more. I stand and pause, as if to suggest that I could be halted by the gift of another cup. 'Well, I'll be getting on, if –'

'Okay.' He doesn't look up. 'I'll see you again, later.'

And I feel he is scanning his paper to avoid me, to spare himself having to see this need that I suddenly have, this humiliation, this flare of shame.

'I'll come back then.' Although I've done nothing wrong.

'Yes, I'm sure you will.'

'That's –' This thick disgust bursts up against my teeth and I have to swallow it, swallow again. 'That's right.' I have to go away, to get some space.

He licks at his finger, flips over a page. 'Goodbye, Hannah.'

My feet have turned stupid, unwilling. It takes me a moment to kick one forward, shift myself. Then I remember. 'There is one difference.' I steady myself on the wall. 'There's a difference between here and what I dreamed. In my dream, you were wearing gloves.'

'But maybe today I took them off.' He keeps on reading, smooth-faced and I can smell his kindness as it pushes at me, trying to save me from further embarrassment.

I take his hint and go.

Outside, the corridor is weirdly solid, aching with stillness – we've drawn to a halt. The view in the window keeps jerking, my eyes anticipating motion where there is none. Sioux Lookout is fixed beside the train, its outdoor air calmly rising up the deep steps of the car as I think of sinking down on to the platform. Passengers I don't recognise are dawdling, smoking, staring at the nondescript wooden houses, at the booze shop, taking photographs of nothing much.

And I am Burnaby, Dorothy Burnaby, at large in her undefined possibility. I could run off and start fires, punch someone born again, I could blacken this name – it's not my own. But instead I am cautious and peer out along the carriage to see Charles peering back, waiting on the bottom step, next door along. Something about him suggests that I shouldn't leave the train, that I would be foolish to try. So I only breathe, sample the large, dark air of a continent and then turn, make for my cabin, limping with the slightly unnerved gait of someone grown accustomed to jolts and bounces. I lock myself in.

I stand by the glass, stand close to being outside. And, in a while, the platform clears, the engine shudders up to strength, and we are lost again, blurring, burrowing west.

I don't expect to see him: Robert.

I don't expect to catch the shape of him, the way he'll scurry sometimes, the pale shine of his skin, between squat trees. This bright, short dart of light.

It isn't him, of course. Can't be. Because Robert is already somewhere else.

And tomorrow I'll be there. Tomorrow evening, I'll be able to sit by the fire and know that it's warming him, too. So high in the mountains, they'll still need the fire, its comfort.

He went there without me and then I did the same and it didn't work. We didn't get better. We have to be both there, together – that's what we need to make us well.

Even if they won't allow us, won't let us be with each other for a while, not the way we'd like. In the end – in the end everything will be all right.

Last night, I woke so very near to the taste of him – as if, while I was sleeping, we had kissed.

Farlane, Redditt, Minaki, Ottermere – there are a fuck of a lot of trees around here. The dull, triangular, sprucey brand of trees. Malachi, Copeland's Landing – and the little old ladies' echoes at every stop and still more fucking trees. I have been staring at fucking trees for fucking hours. And only God can make one and they're our green and graceful friends and without them we'd have nothing left to breathe, but they are *fucking boring.*

Plus, I've now passed from not liking my cell, to hating it passionately. While I was having breakfast, Charles – as his duties require – came by and packed away my bed, folded out the pair of chairs he'd tucked beneath it and now they are filling the place with a sense of lack – because I am one person, but I have two chairs for the daytime and could have two bunks for the night, could have fun using and not using my two bunks for the night, if I were not just one person – but I am. Half of the shelves and nooks and ledges have been provided for the companion I don't have. This is accommodation for Burnaby and Duchamps, for a couple – enough room for me and Robert, enough room to let his absence show.

It would be stupid to think he won't be pleased to see me when I get there.

It would be nerves.

I am very near being depressed when, perhaps fresh from the endless forests and the trials of the wilderness, a monster spider chases past inside my window, long-limbed and glistening. It dashes towards me, then under my chair in the time that I take to lurch up and cling to the sink, understandably alarmed. I am sure I see the final bulk of it squeeze up into one of the cracks that outline where my bed is stowed. Which means that it is hiding in my bed. It is treading on my sheets. It is in there waiting.

And this is what I tell Charles when I find him in the passage, posing with his arm around a blonde girl while her, I would suppose, boyfriend snaps their picture.

'Aren't *you* supposed to take photographs of *them*?'

'Oh, *we* did that already. Can I help *you* with something, Miss Burnaby?' He is neat as ever, his cap at the perfectly jaunty angle.

'A spider.'

'A *spy*-der?'

'I have a very large spider – I think it's gone into my bed.' And when I say this it sounds so unlikely. 'Hiding. Away from the light.' So much like a pathetic come-on, or some kind of feminine panic attack. 'It could be poisonous.' That I blush and then blush more, because I'm blushing.

Charles tugs at his waistcoat, manly and businesslike. I can tell he is thinking of calling me *dear* or *missy*, or something equally grotesque. 'Well . . . *well*, Miss. *Well*, I'll just come *and* attend to that?'

I make a point of letting him go in by himself while I stay outside – this is another precious opportunity, after all, to look at trees. And from the corridor, I can see trees on the *left* side of the track – my cell only offers views of the trees to the right. Blonde and I Would Suppose are entranced by the left-hand trees, oohing and ahing and taking, I'm sure, illegible photographs through the grubby windows. I wish I could share their enthusiasm.

No.

No, I don't. I just do not.

From my cabin I hear a clatter and then stamping. I am about to go in and investigate when, very definitely, there's a white shape in the woods. We are moving, but it is moving, too – I believe running – a pale figure on the run and then extinguished by the curtain of harsh green.

But it was there.

Blonde and I Would Suppose don't seem to have noticed. But it was there.

As if my love had come adrift from me, is out in the forest searching, naked, lost.

'That's that *then*. All dealt with?'

I spin round to meet Charles, tall in my doorway, winking. His face is sheathed in sweat. 'There *is* no spider *in* your bed.' On his shoes there is blood.

'Because you've got rid of it . . .'

He smells chemical, stale. 'There *is* no spider *in* your bed.' I would like him to leave, but instead Blonde and I Would Suppose are dawdling along the passage and out of sight. There is a lot of blood on both Charles's shoes.

'So it's gone, do you mean?'

Charles raises his hands between us slowly, as if he is proud of them, displaying. His fingers almost touch my face. '*Nothing*.' His breath smells of almonds. 'In *your* bed.'

I step away before I can stop myself – I would rather decide to be brave and stare him down, but at present it's clear that I can't.

'Want to check?' There is a film over his teeth, a noticeable texture.

'No.'

There is something wrong with him. 'Sure?'

'Yes.'

'Then *you'd* better go *in* for lunch now.'

'I don't want to.' I am already backing along the passage to be further from the dining car and from my cabin and from Charles.

He doesn't follow, apparently feels there is no need, 'They'll miss you.'

'I don't care.'

'That's *not* a very friendly *attitude*, Miss Burnaby.'

'Fuck you.'

'Tu n'aspas une attitude *très* agrèable. Pasdu tout. *Pas-du-tout.'*

I head for the bar.

Where there is no one.

But that's good — no one is good — exactly what I want. With no one around I get a chance to concentrate.

Because I am not going mad. That isn't something I would do.

So the train is mad.

I slip round behind the bar, looking for coffee.

But thinking a whole train is mad — that's mad in itself. A circus train, a freak train — that doesn't happen.

I find the flask, but it's empty.

I have been ill and stressed and I am tired. Things like this can make your thinking cloudy.

No coffee. And I'd been hoping for some. Nothing like coffee to cheer you. I walk back into the body of the room, sit in one of the upholstered booths.

I haven't been sleeping well. You brainwash prisoners by keeping them from sleep — so no wonder I'm not at the peak of my game. This is a form of torture, this is against international laws.

But here I could get my head down. Curl up in this corner and take a nap.

This is a comfortable place. The booth smells of clean, new leather and peace — even when I rest right up against it, snuggle in. This is good.

This is good.

And my sleep is in a blue-black forest. It lopes under cover, rushes, tears to the edge, to the border where everything stops.

'Announcement *for* Mr *Doheny.* That's pour *Monsieur Doheny.* You *are* wanted in the observation *car. Than*-kyou.'

But I know that's not a real announcement, only another rag of thought, a live thread that connects, then burns to nonsense, disappears. My sleep stands at the margin of the trees and it watches the prairie: the boiling horizon surrounding, dragging the land as tight and flat as cloth, the hunger at the end of everything. My sleep is warm, fast breathing: it remembers to sweat after playing in the trees, it remembers another sweat, gives me the feel of my bare feet on pine needles, the heat of Robert's arm as it curls close from behind me, touches my side.

This makes me too wakeful, though, and I can't stop the rock of the train from breaking in, the stiffness in my shoulders, a small, wet noise I can't identify and the sound of the bartender's voice, very gentle.

'Ah, Hannah, you're awake. Good morning. Or good afternoon, rather.'

I roll on to my back and stretch, while I hear him give a kind of laugh.

'D'you know Nuxalk? No, you wouldn't, I suppose. They still speak it in the Bella Coola Valley. Do you know the valley? Anyway, it has great words – a man told me.'

I clear my throat. 'In a bar.'

'Yes, a man in a bar, perhaps. *A man walks into a bar* – languages are so lovely, they can let you say all that – all anything . . . Well, in Nuxalk, they have this one word.' The wet noise is continuing, odd. '*Unqaaxlamc* – it means drunk, always drinking, that kind of drunk.'

'Must come in handy.' I sit up and then don't say anything.

The bartender sits in the next booth with his paper flat across the table, studying. He is wearing black plush gloves. It's illogical that I would register this before anything else, but still I do. That, and the strange headlines, blurred on his pages, unreadable.

I give this my full attention, while the wet noise carries on and then I have to look round, I have to see Charles. His right hand is busy. His right hand is where the wet noise is happening.

Along the top of the bar, the woman with the shaking hands is lying. She is nude. The mottling of cellulite, the fingers clasped across her breasts, the blush, the tremor in her arms, the frightened eyes – these do not make sense, because she is also attempting to smile, giving me a tiny, bashful nod while her knees are spread, riding the counter, feet hanging down to either side, surreally hidden in her white shoes, the appliquéd cherries still bright, the canvas slightly smeared now. She sweats, she winces, she smiles again while Charles takes a sip of coffee and keeps his right hand working, driving up hard to jolt her spine, her teeth and then withdrawing almost to the knuckle, before punching in again, his shirt and jacket sleeves pressed tight to the hair of her cunt.

Although, of course, this is impossible.

'Yes, Nuxalk.' The bartender frowns mildly at a photograph in his paper. 'One of so many fine tongues. A whole world full of them.'

'What are you –'

'Shit, *she's* tight.' Charles rubs his forehead with the back of his free wrist.

The bartender ignores him, 'Do you want a coffee, Hannah? – I have some.'

I discover I am already standing. 'I'm going. I have to go.'

'No – you *need* a coffee.' Bracing his left hand on her stomach, Charles snaps himself free of the woman, making her yelp and then cry quietly, folding her arms. 'Here you go. *Had* it ready for you.' He holds out a mug of coffee, his fingers glistening, streaked with threads of blood. 'You *will* need it before you proceed to the dining *car.*'

And the bartender does nothing, plays no part.

'I . . . I have to go.'

There is no help.

And this is not real, is undoubtedly not real, but I would like there to be help.

'I have to go.'

Just beyond the doorway stands the huge attendant, completely blocking off one side of the corridor and leering in to see the bar. He is wearing black plush gloves.

'You want to come in *and* try her. My arm's tired? She might be able *to* take you now.'

As Charles laughs I go the only way I can, back towards the dining car, past the rows of other cabins, where I don't want to listen and don't want to see – except each is unoccupied, door open, possessions exposed, but nothing more. And the train is halted in the waste of a great plain, the sunset yawning overhead. There is no sound beyond the breeze against the carriage and the click of heated metal settling.

I reach my door, which is closed.

Inside, my bed has been pulled down into place and freshly made. Laid out on the coverlet are a pair of long white stockings and a pair of long white gloves.

In the window, the sunset is swelling and bleeding. It will break above us soon.

I would stay here, I would lock myself away until tomorrow, if it weren't for the gloves and the stockings: they frighten me.

But then there is the murmur of a voice I recognise and I follow it into the passage and then forward.

The next car is full of people – the Christian with the teeth, the blonde, all kinds of other people – all crushed against the windows in the cabins and passageway, swaying, breathing quickly, taking photographs of things outside, of things that smell of petrol and of burning and that scream.

I can also hear what has to be a crowd around the carriage and I run from it and from the bodies that lean and rub against me as I fight through to the curtained bunks, the car full of bunks, where there is only a pink-limbed sighing, a senseless writhe, heavy on either side, and the stink of ammonia, raw sap, but no harm, no actual harm yet, no more than fucking, although I am still running and maybe missing bad details, signs of injury, but what could I do if I saw them, I couldn't do anything and I can hear slapping, a very loud slapping, and a familiar voice I would like to be with and there, there is the dining car, where I don't want to go and – as soon as I think this – I am inside.

The last sitting diners are ready at their tables, only a few

328

new empty seats and, in one motion, they glance at me with a preoccupied contempt and then they turn back to the Doll Woman – her plate the only one filled with dainty, slippery morsels, tricky to cut, the blood thick on her knife. And closer, there's that slapping sound – very near, in fact – but no voice to go with it, no words leading me on.

The Doll Woman's cutlery glitters, almost silent as she slices. Her husband sits opposite her, nodding, trying to pat her arm fondly and, each time, failing. His hands are fixed together, palm to palm with a thin meat skewer, and they are awkward. The spike of the skewer keeps catching on the tablecloth, making him wince. Then he attempts to reach down and press a napkin to his crotch, cover up the bleeding that has soaked both trouser legs, but his injuries make him clumsy and the spike gets in the way, so he sits back, sighs and then giggles. He smiles at his wife and she giggles, too, and then the whole car is moving and is smiling and there are pliers and each group is adjusting clothing and set to proceed with its own business, which I cannot bear, when the Railway Bore yells, 'Everyone's equal on the railway, eh? Gotta stay.'

Doll Woman claps then, once, and there is stillness. 'No. She has to go the kitchen, the galley. She'll enjoy it there – it's what she's looking for. Go on – make your mother and your father proud for once.'

I go where she tells me, because there is nowhere else and because the dining car has filled with the pleasant din of a happy mealtime and I know that I shouldn't turn back to it, can't look, that it will all be terrible.

Through the far door, and I'm in a tiny room lined with cupboards, everything made of stainless steel. This may mean I am lost.

'No. You're not.' It's the bartender – he must have followed me. 'Galley's the next one along.' But he's out of uniform, dressed in an old linen suit, a soft hat, smoking a cigar. 'I just wandered along to be sure you were properly dressed.' The fingers of one hand search his waistcoat pocket idly. 'A special occasion like this . . .' He tilts back his hat and studies me, takes time. 'Yes. I suppose. Why not.' He breathes out milk and azure smoke that touches me, brushes my skin.

This leaves me, somehow, insecure and so I have to peer down at myself. I am wearing black patent leather shoes, long white stockings that reach half the length of my thighs, long white gloves that close over my elbows. Otherwise I am naked.

'Appropriate.' His eyes moist, unreadable. 'Just the thing for Robert.'

'Robert?'

'Who else?'

If he's here, we might be safe, we might be able to escape this and be free, because we always help each other.

'Shame you didn't comb your hair for him. You both enjoy that.'

'I don't have a comb.'

'Well, neither do I.'

And I am pushed into the galley, his touch on my shoulders fleeting, cool, before I am there and the door is shut behind me and, kneeling in the gangway, is what must be the manatee mother. Stripped, she is even larger, almost inhuman. And I am not sure if she is alive until she starts, 'Mm-hmm. Mm-hmm.' This small murmuring, 'Mm-hmm. Mm-hmm.' As if she's agreeing to items on some dull, personal list, just running her mind along the inventory. 'Mm-hmm. Mm-hmm.'

The splayed mound of her arse faces the doorway, reddened, purpled with blows, individual handprints visible where the bruising is less severe and on she goes with her tiny consents, her mindless repetition, 'Mm-hmm. Mm-hmm.'

Robert isn't here.

I am sure that I'm dreaming, very sure, but now I do need Robert here. He could make this a good dream.

I don't mind being like this, not if it's for him.

And I hear the voice again, the one I know, behind me, in

the outer room – Robert's voice, truly his voice, as if he is chatting there with the bartender, sharing a joke with him.

A dream like this, it's disturbing, but you can focus and make it good.

I never did dress up for him, before, not really. We should do that, once we're out of the clinic. We should have fun.

We could start it now.

The galley door swings wide and there is Robert as he should be, in a pullover and corduroys, soft shirt, his hair just slightly disturbed, and I have that kick, that very fine spring of need that I can't find without him. I have what I have missed, the start of every good and sweet that I have missed. I have my love.

'Robert.'

'Hi.'

I don't mind when I see the bartender has sneaked in, too. This is only in my mind, so he can watch, he can know how beautiful we are.

Robert brushes against me: a long, deliberate contact, and then stands above the manatee.

I want to reassure him. 'I know, love, I haven't a clue what she's doing here, either. But someone's been –'

Which is when he slaps her, doesn't acknowledge me, doesn't say anything, simply flails his hand against the right cheek of her arse and then the left and then again, and then again, shuddering her with each blow.

'Robert. What are you doing?'

He continues to beat her, his breath starting to rise.

'Robert.'

Then he sinks to his knees, one hand rubbing at the folds of her, fumbling, the other unzipping his fly, and I can't see and I can't understand, but I still know precisely, know that twitch, remember I love that first moment when he finds his way, but this is not with me, is not with me, this is his cock up some animal stranger, this is him fucking, this is him

331

wanting, this is the harshness in his throat, this is the private
song, this is his hand turned in my stomach, this is mine, this
is all mine, this is him stealing me, raping me.

It takes only a minute before he's made a boy, a darling,
trembling into his come and curled against her back.

'Robert.'

Then he stands, fastens, straightens himself, goes to the sink
and rinses off his hands.

'Please.'

He turns, stares at me, puzzled, and then shrugs, goes back
to the manatee, starts beating her again.

'He doesn't know you.'

'What?'

The bartender is leaning in, he's close, lifting his eyes gradually to mine, reminding me of my useless body, my pointless
nakedness. 'He doesn't know you, does he? You never told us
that.'

I can hear that I am crying and I don't want him to see.

He cups one of my breasts without interest. 'Another word
of Nuxalk you might learn – *tsusumtim* – they were overtaken
by darkness.'

XIII

And the black house is back; has opened like a mouth. I saw it: heaven's breath blossoming in, shredding in, and all of the shelter of darkness burned to a scream. I saw.

So this is the scorch of white now, this is ash clean, this is the weighing, the inspection, this is being swept away.

And I hope for mercy and I hope for mercy and I hope for mercy and whatever there is left of me hopes for mercy beyond words.

And so the brightness shifts and shrugs and folds above me, lifts me, wraps me and I am wound in light.

'That's the way, Hannah. That's the way.'

And I have this horror, this lack of air, because I can feel it, the dreadful tenderness, the way it begins unlocking everything.

'And, if you help, it's even better. That's it.'

The brush against my skin of hands, of fingertips, of liquid gentleness, the strokes so faint that I start to tremble and cannot stop: my shoulders, the small of my back, my thighs.

No more of the train, no stumbling off with my holdall into the milk and azure breeze, no being gathered up and stretchered, no being driven between mountains, aspens rising, shining in among the spruces like green prayers, no more of the journey — only this turning under white, this touch that I know, that is smoothing my face, my neck, my breasts, loving the way to my hips, the inward ache, the shivering.

'We'd better hurry up — she's getting cold.'

'Yes. *Don't worry, honey, nearly done. Just getting you cleaned up here.*'

'You want to be clean, don't you?'

And I do. I do want that.

'Good girl.'

The hands doubling, worrying at me, two pairs here, lifting my arms and wiping, spreading my fingers apart with a damped cloth and being wrong, being unfamiliar, being nobody I love.

'You're doing good.'

And I do want to be clean, but I want Robert more.

'Oh, she's off.'

'Thought she would be.'

But I'm under this alone, laid out and filled with emptiness.

'That's okay, now. That's okay.'

Women's voices, bored little sentences, the sense of them thinned by the glare of white and my own voice in here, too, making chokes of sound, these weeping noises, things you might hear from a child.

Later that day, or the following afternoon, I go out of Hannah Luckraft's room and I walk down the stairs of Thoreau House and find Clear Spring set out around me, patient and perfectly convincing. I might think I had never left, if it weren't for the onset of summer, the sudden rush of growth.

I take the path through the floral borders: azaleas, the blue glow of rhododendrons, deep, broad ferns, honeysuckle trained against a maple, everything live, eating up the sun – my mother would love it here, the beauty of a garden edging into woods, into forest, into mountain: the only scar, the road that brought me here.

I remember my mother. There are other people, details, items of importance that I have misplaced. I'm aware of that. But I can remember Sniffer Bobby and 8.42 and Paddy and blood and strawberries and Kussbachek, Herod, Henry, Eddie and every millilitre and new knickers and dead golfers and Simon and werewolves and filth and Dogger, Fisher, German Bight, zirconium oxide, Amelia and John Mills and my father

336

and the Auchtermuchty Sound and Benilyn and fuck myself, his sweet-drunk tongue, and fuck myself and Rawhide, absinthe, Lagavulin, dead drunk, red drunk, mad drunk, bad drunk, Marylebone High Street bringing the hammer down and fuck myself and don't tell anybody I did this and forty-six hours of classical masterpieces and God and God and God and the scent of caramel and being sorry, being sorry everywhere, escusezmoi, estutmirleid, seengnohmey, anahasfah, sorry, undskoold, animitzta'eret, midispiache, prasteetye, prepachtyeh, sorry, imipahrerau, bochaanaat, I'm sorry, prominyeteh, proshtahvaheyteh, losiento, I am sorry, I am so very sorry.

I am.

And then here's the gleam of water, the tremor of leaves, the thick rise of rushes and irises at the brink. My lake.

I've thought myself right to the lake.

A duck claps up in a stunted climb, its mate herding ducklings across the shallows and out into the grass where they scatter like mice. I take the thin path worn at the lake's edge, walk over the baked imprints of boots in winter mud and aim for the rock. Already, a pale shape is sailing and pressing across the surface, closing to meet me.

I clamber up the rock and find I recall the warmth of it beneath me. The climb is easy, but slightly awkward and I have to be gentle about it, soft. I don't want to offend him. By the time I am perched, leaning over the water, the swan is there, the blaze of his wings arced up above his back, neck swollen with affront.

'Shhh now . . . It's only me.'

I have bread with me and break it, hand it down to him as he smoothes and shakes himself, reaches up, beak gaping, oddly bristled, almost like the throat of some hot flower.

'There you are, then.' He nips at my thumb gently and then shrinks, takes token sips among the wavelets, coughs. 'Yes, back again. Friends again. I know.' The usual scent from him of warm, early-morning sheets, a well-used bed.

'What were you doing, then, while I was gone?'

And, over to my side, there is another glimmer of movement behind the branches, very bright, but I don't turn to look and the swan only eats and watches me with quick, black eyes. There is nothing really there, nothing for me beyond a memory of skin.

'What did you do without me? What did you do?'

He drifts slightly, drinks, then faces me and stands in the water, stretches himself in a broad white reach, the open feathers glimmering, dragging a howl from the air. He balances on his reflection, beats and beats, and I think that I see something: a mixture of dark and pink, like the touch of an ulcer, a long sore in the root of one wing: but then he is down again and folded and sculling away and I could have been mistaken, that might have happened quite easily.

I call to him and have more bread, but he slips into reeds at the far bank, clambers up and makes his heavy-footed way off to the bushes, puts himself out of my sight.

I worry for him.

And in the evening, I tell somebody he's hurt. I'm almost certain I actually do that. Nurse Forbes, or Nurse Ogilvie, I let one of them know, only I have the impression they are preoccupied, discussing a stunning recovery – two weeks from delirium tremens to normal life. They have never seen the like. They say this has happened to a man called Doheny and I am not surprised. I'm also unsure if they'll remember about the swan.

But I don't fuss. I can write them a note, or speak to them tomorrow. So I just head over to Thoreau House and my old room, open-windowed and thick with sunset birdsong: squeaks and chips and chirring from every side and one long, roping melody above them which someone has told me belongs to a cardinal.

You can't have a wrong thought, listening to this. Sitting in the barley with Simon, my head was always orderly and bright

– full of the birds we couldn't name that carved out notes and spaces, that tickled and soared, and poppies more red than a colour, like the marks of somewhere else, some unnatural place, shimmering, and the height of the stalks there to hide us, because we were small. Then I was clean.

Now I am no one, which is not the same thing.

I sit on the floor, head braced against the bed and the shudder starts up in my back again and both my hands are wet.

And Robert should have been here and I should have been able to find him and tonight we should be together and alive. And we should be each other's mercy, each other's gift, each other's love. And I should be Hannah Luckraft and that should be a joy.

XIV

And for a while, maybe a long while, I do not move or see: I only listen to my room and the birdsong that fades to nowhere and leaves only my alarm clock, my heart, a sudden drag of thunder overhead, like the sound of a broad stone, being rolled away.

I press my skull back hard and feel the side of the mattress changing where I touch it, a knitting and unknitting of springs. Delicate beneath me, lifting my legs by a degree, I understand there is a rise and spread of carpet that displaces the polished wood floor. The tiny disturbance of its arrival, an insect noise, ripples out to meet each wall and fits. I keep my eyes closed and listen to the budding of a desk, a chair, two lamps, two Formica bedside tables, a room key with an ugly fob, the slight creaks at the birth of an ashtray, a minibar fridge, a portable TV. And the taste of this room is stale cigarette smoke, air freshener, bleach, sweat and there is no garden alive outside it, not for miles.

Softly, I glance to the window and there is an English night, a scatter of indecipherable beacons, illuminated buildings and a radar dish, spooning round, cupping through shadows. Marked out with little spills of light, the wide, grey belly of an aircraft grinds up across the dark, recedes into a pattern of red and white and green.

I stand, because all this is solid now, possible and fixed, and I see that my holdall is fat and happy and the bed freshly made.

Behind me, in the bathroom, I hear the small metal glide as the shower curtain closes, then a chatter of water, the comfortable jumble of noises when somebody starts to wash.

I smile.

I reach into my holdall and find the full bottle of Bushmill's undisturbed: that marvellous label: the long, slim door that leads to somewhere else. When Robert has finished, when he steps through, pink with scrubbing, wrapped snug in a towel, then we'll lie on the bed together and we'll talk, we'll tell each other everything. I'll ask him to bring through the glasses and then we'll begin.